JEFF
BILLINGTON

CHICKEN DINNER NEWS

Chicken Dinner News

Print Edition
ISBN: 978-3-98832-012-4
Published by Vine Leaves Press 2023

Cover design by Jessica Bell
Interior design by Amie McCracken

PRAISE

"*Chicken Dinner News* is a well-written, enjoyable read that has a lot to say about our world and the society in which we live. Billington offers a mix of humor and deep thoughts to ponder throughout the novel. The story highlights the precious resources we have in small towns and the challenges of journalism in these days when we question the integrity of the truth. A fresh voice that makes me look forward to seeing more books from this author."
KATHRYN JOHNSON, AUTHOR OF *THE GENTLEMAN POET*

"*Chicken Dinner News* provides a thoughtful glimpse into the angst of a dying and often bigoted Middle American town whose only hope for redemption hinges on the possible influx of 'the Mexicans, the hippies, and the gays.' Billington delivers a compelling story through the eyes of a reluctant small-town newspaper journalist."
J.D. PAINTER, AUTHOR OF *THE BLACK MARCH*

"If you have ever wanted to move to a small town and really make a difference, *Chicken Dinner News* is a must read. It's a gripping tale with charming personalities and plenty of intrigue to keep the pages turning."
CHAD STEBBINS, EXECUTIVE DIRECTOR OF
INTERNATIONAL SOCIETY OF WEEKLY NEWSPAPER EDITORS

ABOUT THE AUTHOR

Raised on a small dairy and poultry farm in Missouri's Ozark Mountains, Jeff Billington spent his childhood listening to family stories and hearing about the changes the twentieth century brought to that celebrated rural region. He has since spent two decades working in the nonprofit and political realms, most of it in Washington, DC and currently resides in Rockville, Maryland. His first novel, *Summers' Second,* was published in the fall of 2022.

jeffbillington.com

For my grandparents, Carl and Lorene and Glenn and Wylene,
who always made me feel important.

CHAPTER 1

THE SURROUNDING LANDSCAPE presented as postcard ideal rolling hills covered in thick groves of old growth oak, maple and walnut, with dramatic bedrock outcroppings breaking up forested monotony. Farmsteads nestled between the worn and ancient peaks, working with the natural contours instead of controlling them. An Americana oasis, but also the middle of nowhere, Ryan Shipley reminded himself as he sped by on a diverging modern four-lane highway, mockingly and brutally carved as a straight line through the hills and hollows of the Missouri half of the Ozark Mountains.

His late father once told him that half a century earlier the more rustic corners of the region served as destinations of choice for vacationers from across the country. But as Branson grew bloated on second-tier entertainment, the natural beauty lost favor, leaving small resort towns floundering while swarms of visitors instead came for the kitsch and frayed nostalgia of the live entertainment mecca.

Of course, none of that mattered to Ryan, as he had not come for leisure, but against his own personal judgment. He belonged in Los Angeles, behind his desk at the *Los Angeles Sun-Herald*.

Instead, that morning, he flew halfway across the country on a journey to an obscure hillbilly town to bury his grandfather. To play the part of the primary griever for a man he physically met but twice, and beyond that shared scarcely a dozen phone calls. But, as the only living descendent, obligation forced the trip, while sense of honor played no part. A grudge festered eighteen years inside him, from when his father died. Naïve it may have been, but at age twelve he assumed his grandfather would travel to California for an only child's funeral. But his grandmother arrived alone, her husband staying in Missouri to manage his weekly newspaper.

In the passing of nearly two decades, the disappointment continued, prompting Ryan to consider returning the favor. But his mother would not allow it, booking his flight and reserving his rental car before he could decline. The more he argued, the more she fought back, bringing up his father's own failings in the relationship between the now-deceased father and son.

His phone barked out directions, interrupting the sullen thoughts swirling in his head, and led him from the comfort of a modern highway to the rumble of a two-lane secondary road pockmarked with potholes. Peppering the byway's grassy shoulder he spotted dozens of signs declaring allegiance to Donald Trump for an election some six months away, while open support for Hillary Clinton or Bernie Sanders appeared nonexistent. Quite the opposite of his neighborhood in Los Angeles, and a reinforcement of his notion of the unsophisticated local stereotype.

The asphalt smoothed beneath the car's tires as White Oak City appeared on the side of the highway in the form of a warped and peeling advertisement for the "White Oak Mobile Home Estates." An identifier for a dismal neighborhood of rows of faded aluminum and vinyl trailers divided by unkempt grassy strips; an unimpressive gateway for his grandfather's beloved town.

The phone spouted out more directions, leading him along a business bypass populated by generic restaurants, nondescript single-story commercial buildings, and a big, flat and decidedly unremarkable high school. His vague childhood memories clashed with the undistinguished townscape surrounding him. He expected Rockwellesque, but the last twenty-five years either obliterated that version or it existed only as an invention of his boyhood imagination.

But he assumed too soon, for the heart of the town delivered on his faded recollections, though smaller and shabbier than they seemed to a five-year-old boy clinging to his mother's hand. He slowed the car as he passed blocks of vintage brick and stone storefronts, an old business district laid out around a large, shaded park, a greenway anchored by a weathered bandstand.

On the north side of the park stood a two-story courthouse of gray stone and neoclassical style, with *Decatur County Courthouse* carved below a seized clock set in a central gable. The remaining three sides held dozens of store fronts that varied in style from elaborate Victorian to minimalist mid-century. Not a single false front or chopped up façade existed among them, a place that escaped the urban renewal butchering of the 1960s and 1970s.

Yes, the town from his childhood visits remained. But something felt off. For beside a meager littering of law offices, title and abstract companies and a few other random businesses, most buildings sat vacant. In fact, on the south side of the square he counted signs of active commerce in only two. Even the striking Art Nouveau bank, perched on the corner, no longer served its original intent, instead degraded into the home of a taxidermist.

He felt as if dropped into the middle of a *Twilight Zone* episode where civilization had ceased to exist, and only its concrete achievements of a century earlier remained. Gold lettering fluttering in the wind caught his attention. On a faded and frayed red canvas awning he read *Decatur County Times-Gazette* and, in smaller lettering below, *Published Weekly*. He slowed the car to a crawl while passing the two-story redbrick building. His head craned in an awkward attempt to catch a glimpse inside, but glare blocked the view.

His phone called out another turn, right in 500 feet. He spotted a rusty street sign for Hydrangea Avenue, but his eyes quickly darted past it to the hulking structure looming in front of him. Larger than the courthouse, the two-story building sat as an epitome of early twentieth century educational architecture. From its prominent central tower to an abundance of terracotta embellishments, the old high school emitted grandeur, yet, like so much of the rest of the town, sat vacant and moldering.

He eased the car onto Hydrangea and started up the gentle slope into a neighborhood of well-shaded residences. The houses echoed the history of the downtown, built in prosperity but now faded from poor maintenance, flawed updating and owner apathy. But despite that decline, the warmth of community lingered, with most homes sporting wide front porches and flowerbeds overflowing with an array of blossoms, even if not well tended.

Reaching the top of the hill, he spotted one house that defied the standard threadbare look of the avenue, a chunky Craftsman painted a crisp white and topped with a vivid green shingle roof. It held an instant familiarity for Ryan, for it was his destination. He pulled the car into the driveway, parking behind a late-model Buick.

He stepped out into the sun, arching his back while thrusting his arms upward, twisting his body to work out the stiffness. The warm mid-May air embraced him, while the rustling of leaves and distant tunes of songbirds filled his ears.

The house felt both familiar and disorienting. He remembered it much larger, as if a quarter of a mile deep, instead of forty or so feet. But other than the impression of shifted proportions, it seemed little changed. From the ample front porch to the broad profiles of the second story's gables, it begged to provide him comfort, an emotional graciousness turned back only by his own obstinance.

How to get inside? He had no key. His mother had spoken on the phone with a woman who worked for his grandfather. But did he have the woman's number? If not, he would be forced to call California and ask his mother for it, which promised an uncomfortable conversation, as she would criticize him for coming unprepared. He leaned in through the open car window and pulled out his phone. But his plan to scan through his mother's texts for the number was cut short by the arrival of a blue Toyota.

"I knew that was you," the driver exclaimed, a heavyset woman with short-cropped gray hair. "Welcome to White Oak City, Ryan. I wish it was on better terms."

"Thank you," he replied as he took a few steps toward her car. "Who are you?"

She chuckled as she climbed out of the Toyota. "You've barely arrived, and a strange lady starts talking to you like she knows you," she remarked, followed by another laugh. "I knew you the instant you drove by. Most people driving down Commercial Street don't slow down and stare into the office when they pass."

She extended her right hand toward him. "I'm Connie Donovan."

He shook her hand and felt eased by her smile. "You called my mom to let her know about my grandfather," he replied.

She let go of his hand and stepped near his car, reaching for the handle of the back driver side door. "I did," she confirmed. "Let's get your stuff inside so you can get settled."

An anxious jolt shot through him, prompting him to lean against the door she planned to open. "That's all right; I'm not staying here," he protested. "Is there a hotel or something around here, though?"

She stepped back from the car and gave him a puzzled look. "Why stay at a hotel instead of here?" she asked. "You own this house, now."

—

In a quarter century's absence, Ryan's memories of the kitchen had faded to a few snippets, based on smell and sentiment more than reality. But reentering it, he felt a resurgence of recollection. He glimpsed his boyhood self, sitting at the green and white enamel table and watching his grandmother roll out piecrust.

The memory came easily, as the room itself remained frozen in time. Its furnishings, fixtures, pictures and knickknacks paused in an era of pistachio green cabinets, chrome atomic-age hardware and linoleum flooring patterned in little gray and green squares.

"Follow me," Connie directed as she looked back from a doorway leading into the rest of the house.

A fog of emotions crowded his head. The room itself, or at least the impression of it, for a moment made him forget his company. He glanced around again and inhaled deeply. The remembered aroma of baking bread brushed his nose. "I'm reminded of something," he answered.

"If it's good, I'd wait all day for you," she responded.

A quiet sigh escaped him as he followed her. They passed through a small butler's pantry and into the home's central hallway, a corridor eight-feet wide and crowded with the staircase to the second floor.

"There are four bedrooms, but only one full bathroom, and it's upstairs," Connie explained, before starting up the steps.

With creaks and groans, the risers protested their ascent to the second story, accentuating that, regardless of its well-kept exterior, the home still reflected its age.

"I figure you'll want the big guest bedroom," she remarked as she led him across the well-lit upstairs landing to a room at the front of the house. "Of course, you can stay in any room you want. Your grandfather's room is across from the stairs. Opposite it is another guest room, but it's mainly used for storage, though there is a bed."

Ryan nodded as he followed her into the room she apparently preferred for him. A row of three large windows looked out across the front yard, while the room's pale-yellow walls and white-painted cast iron bed, made up with a brightly colored quilt, provided tranquil charm.

She sat his bag on the bed and ran her hand across the top of the quilt. "Your grandmother made it," she told him. "There are more here in the house that she made, as well as a few by your great-grandmother."

A sudden shudder spread through his body, prompting him to turn away from Connie and look out the windows. "This room is fine," he muttered as he forced his gaze on the leaves of a large oak tree brushing against the porch roof.

"Take a few minutes to relax and I'll meet you back downstairs," she suggested. "I'll even make you a snack before I leave."

He stood stoic as he listened to her footsteps retreating down the hall and then descending the stairs, only turning back to look upon the quilt with tear bleary eyes when he knew he was alone. When his grandmother died, seven years earlier, he had missed her funeral, though not from lack of want, but instead stuck at home recovering from surgery on a broken ankle.

Unlike the strained feelings he held for his grandfather, his grandmother had nurtured a genuine relationship and love. A bond forged by her annual summer trips to California to visit him and his father, though she always came alone. Those visits continued even after his father died, until her physical decline intervened. Phone calls filled in the rest of the year, once a month to check in, and cards and gifts unfailingly arrived on birthdays, holidays and other special occasions. The old man rarely took part, only getting on the phone for Ryan's birthday or a holiday, the conversation always short.

—

Connie glanced up at him through a pair of red-framed reading glasses that rested on the bridge of her nose. "That didn't take long," she remarked as her eyes fell back down on the paper held taut in her hands. "You didn't have to rush." A stack of documents sat on the kitchen table in front of her, while a plate bearing a sandwich and a pile of tortilla chips waited for him opposite her.

His stomach groaned. He had not eaten since breakfast, and then only a bagel from the airport in Los Angeles.

The paperwork rustled as she combed through it, searching for something. "Eat. I'll go through a little of this, unless you're not feeling up to it."

He nodded, the ham sandwich already in his hands.

She paused a moment, her lips silently moving as she read the document clasped in her hands. "Don't worry about funeral arrangements. He took care of that when your grandmother passed away. And he only had one suit, so it was easy picking out what to bury him in. There are five empty spots in the family plot at Maple Grove Methodist Cemetery, so no cost there, other than opening and closing the grave. He'll be buried next to your grandmother, under a shared headstone."

The food calmed his stomach, but discomfort grew in his thoughts as he listened to the details of the funeral, what his grandfather wanted and what Connie had picked out, even the color and type of flowers.

A thick legal document appeared, pulled out of a large blue envelope. "He named me executor, but the bulk goes to you," she revealed.

"Oh," he remarked with a slight gasp. "I hadn't thought about that."

She offered a warm smile and began flipping through the pages. "He left me $15,000, he left Glo Riley $20,000, and he left $15,000 to the Blackjack Bluff Cemetery fund," she began.

"Wait," he interrupted. "Isn't he being buried someplace else?"

Her eyes narrowed as she looked at him, as if assessing his soul. "He is," she replied. "This is for the upkeep of an older cemetery, where the first few generations of your family to settle in this area are buried."

Ryan leaned back in his chair. His father's cremated remains rested in no cemetery, instead scattered in the waves of the Pacific Ocean.

"There hasn't been anyone buried in it for thirty years," she continued. "But there's a trust set up for the care of it, though not much money in it."

More pages turned, both back and forth, as she continued through the document, naming additional bequests to various individuals and charities, all for amounts less than $5,000. Then she folded the document back together and laid it on the table.

"He left you everything else," she informed him. "You get this house and the 224-acre Shipley family farm, which includes an old farmhouse, barn, and several outbuildings. It's on the highway east of town. You assume ownership of the *Decatur County Times-Gazette*; the *Times-Gazette* building at 205 East Commercial Street; and buildings at 207, 203, 111, 107, 105 and 101 East, and 101, 107 and 106 West Commercial Street; all of his personal possessions, furniture, clothing, artwork and collectibles. Also, you get his remaining liquid assets, which, after deducting what he left to other people and organizations, amounts to approximately $420,000."

His knuckles went white as he clutched the edges of the tabletop, the only thing preventing him from tumbling to the floor.

"Are you ok?" she asked, concern in her voice.

"I'm fine," he answered before taking a deep breath to regain his composure. "I'm surprised. I haven't seen him since I was a kid."

She leaned over the table toward him. "You're his only grandchild. He kept an eye on you. He talked to your mother once a month and had all sorts of pictures of you that she sent. Some are as recent as this Christmas."

He knew his mother had sent his grandmother copies of his school pictures and others taken at holidays and special events, but did not know it continued with his grandfather.

"You look like your dad," Connie then remarked.

An unexpected comment, one that spurred a tear in his eye. "You knew my dad?"

She nodded. "I was his high school English teacher. I taught English at the high school for forty years, before retiring last year. I've also been a part-time copy editor for your grandpa for the last fifteen."

The idea of his father as a teenager had an elusive feel to it. They never talked of it during Ryan's childhood, and by the time he'd grown curious, his dad had died. "What was he like in high school?" he asked.

"Excitable and wanting to see the world and not be trapped in some crummy little town," she offered with a broad smile. "I wasn't surprised when he left. But your grandfather always hoped he would return one day and work at the newspaper. Your dad was smart and a good writer, so I'm sure he would have been good at it. He had the same problem a lot of people do: he didn't want to be his parents. Especially as your grandpa was idolized around here."

—

The door to his grandfather's bedroom swung open with only a gentle tap, allowing the light from the hallway to flood its darkened corners. A purposely shadowy space, with curtains drawn and fastened closed with safety pins. The light switch snapped on and two lamps, one beside the bed and another looming above a sagging wingback chair, further brightened the room. Dozens of framed photographs crowded the dresser top and nightstands, most bearing the faces of his father and himself, while the smells of ointment and newsprint permeated the space.

"How appropriate," Ryan snidely muttered to himself as he stepped inside the shabby room. He crossed to the threadbare wingback chair, its seat crowded with a yellowing stack of newspapers, but felt his sarcasm abandon him upon spotting the familiar flag of the *Los Angeles Sun-Herald,* with the top issue only three weeks past.

The armchair creaked as he dropped down into it, his backside settling into a well-worn indentation alongside the hoard of newspapers. A place his grandfather evidently favored, likely while reading the papers stacked beside him. A disturbance of dust tickled Ryan's nose as he unfolded the top issue, still crisp, in his hands.

Anger bubbled up inside him as his eyes met page three. Scrawled with red ink in the margins and between the lines he found a mass of notes and editing marks annotating an article he had written. How dare his yokel grandfather grade his work and criticize his writing, and do it silently from afar!

He tossed the paper on the floor and grabbed the next one from the stack, finding a similar critique for his article in it. Similar discoveries came in the next four issues, leading him to fling them across the room one by one. Overcome with frustration, he pushed the rest of the pile out of the chair and onto the floor, less the oldest and flattest, which clung to ragged fabric. He uttered a profanity and grabbed up the last defiant paper, feeling it crumble in his hand. His frontpage byline bore an especially egregious amount of corrections. The article came from five years earlier and detailed the circumstances around the surprise resignation of a county supervisor. He cursed as he read, but his anger had muted to embarrassment by the time he'd finished the second paragraph, which his grandfather's pen left unscathed. He agreed with the dead man's revisions. His own writing and coverage of the issue was the offensive part, and his own editor either ignorant or apathetic.

He snatched up another paper from the floor and read. Again, his grandfather's notes correctly called out his gaffes. He followed it with another, then another, until a ringing phone broke him from the exercise in self-doubt. The last newspaper slipped from his hands and landed on its brethren, piled on the floor. He wanted to set a match to them and destroy the evidence of his mediocrity. The phone's shrill mechanical ring sounded again, making his muscles tense. He glanced around the room, spotting a white rotary dial phone sitting on a bedside table.

"Hello," he offered in greeting, after having waited until the eighth ring to answer.

Connie's chipper voice greeted him back, followed by an invitation for him to visit the newspaper office. The week's edition sat ready for the printer, and the staff felt it appropriate for him to come and read the article about his late grandfather before it went out the door. He tried to beg off the invitation, asking to not intrude on the staff's moment, but she firmly overrode his objections, assuring him that his grandfather would have wanted him there, as did the staff.

CHAPTER 2

The few businesses that remained in the downtown blocks had closed and darkened by the time Ryan made his way toward his grandfather's business, while the dimming evening light transformed the street's appearance from derelict to near apocalyptic. He shuddered, despite the air's warmth.

Reaching the newspaper office, he feared he had made a mistake, as it appeared as dark as the rest of the aged buildings around it. Then he noticed slivers of light shining out from between the slats of the closed blinds.

He peered in through a gap between the blinds and the window frame, spotting several people gathered at the back of the office, strangers all. It promised to be an uncomfortable situation, but one unavoidable. He took a deep breath and gripped the battered brass door handle, worn shiny where his hand made contact, but a tarnished green in the rest of its entirety. His thumb eased down to release the latch, but it kept firm, locked. A tension spread out from his chest to his arms and legs, freezing him, until the outline of a person emerged on the opposite side of the door's blinded window.

The prim face of an elderly woman, neatly framed by bobbed white hair, glared out at him through the open door. Her eyes took a second to appraise, before she stepped aside and beckoned him in with a smile and a wave of her hand. He broke free of his petrification and launched himself through the doorway, his foot hitting the doorsill and sending him into a slight stumble in the process. Embarrassment colored his cheeks.

The room seemed cavernous, large and open with a ramshackle waist-high railing dividing reception from the newsroom, and bump-outs in three of the corners, enclosing the restroom, editor's office and stairwell leading to the upper level. Water-damaged lime green paint coated the walls and trim, while rows of pressed-tin squares, embossed with an oak leaf wreath design, covered the ceiling.

The woman neared him, tears glistening beneath red and puffy eyes. Then her arms sprang to life and wrapped around him in an unyielding hug as she raved about his grandfather's virtues.

"Ebetta, give Ryan a chance to come inside." He heard Connie's voice plead.

The woman's grip loosened, though without complete release. "I'm sorry," she muttered. A raspy voice revealing both emotion and heavy smoking.

"It's all right," he assured her as he gently twisted himself free of her grasp.

Connie, standing a few feet behind Ebetta, nodded at him, as if applauding a successful passing of a test. She then laid her hand on the other woman's shoulder, introducing her as the part-time receptionist. They stepped past Ebetta and the dividing rail, entering the newsroom, where others waited.

He met the two reporters first. Jerry, working part time following a career at the local agricultural extension office, and Mandy, the uniquely nonnative member of the staff, who met and married a local boy while in college. Then came the three advertising sales representatives, each younger than Ryan's own thirty years, Mark and Casey, both still in high school, and Mary Beth, only five years out, though already a mother of three. They were followed by the twenty-something Barry, who designed both the pages of the newspaper and the website—which Ryan had no idea existed.

One more member of the staff remained, an older man seated behind a battered metal desk, his face obscured behind the pages of a newspaper. Connie put her hand on Ryan's arm and guided him to the seemingly apathetic man, who then moved his paper down to reveal a heavily creased face, which seemed fixed in a perpetual frown.

"Ryan, I'd like you to meet Glo Riley," Connie offered. "Glo and your grandfather knew each other since they were boys, and worked together here the last sixty years."

The man's unique name flashed familiar. Ryan had heard it before. In fact, just that afternoon, for this weathered and discontent-appearing man had received a bequest in his grandfather's will.

The old man's eyes slowly rose to meet Ryan's gaze. "You're Ross's boy," he growled.

A shiver ran up Ryan's spine at the mention of his father's name. "I am," he answered.

An awkward silence followed.

"I knew your father from the day he was born, met your mother a time or two, seemed like a nice gal," Glo continued, his voice gritty and forceful, but hindered by a wavering undertone of age. "You going to move here and run this paper. like your grandfather wanted?"

A sensation of dry sand clogged Ryan's throat. "Is that what he wanted?" he croaked, sensing every eye in the room watching him. "I don't know why. I'm just a reporter."

Glo's hands leaped up in agitation, nearly ripping the newspaper in two. "You have a journalism degree from some big school," he cried out.

Ryan felt his heart rev up. "Yes, but there's a lot more to this," he protested.

His chair let out a loud squeak as Glo swiveled in it to be face-to-face with the younger man. "This staff, together, knows everything needed to run this paper," he snapped. "As a cumulative, everyone here knows the steps, the processes and the schedules for getting it done. All you need to do is watch and learn, and maybe you can become the man your grandfather hoped."

Sweat bubbled up across Ryan's forehead as his hands twitched with anxiety. Why had he come here? "My life's in Los Angeles," he replied. "My friends, my job, my mom, everything is there. I don't know anything about this place. I've never even considered living here, much less owning some little weekly newspaper."

An unhealthy purple hue flooded Glo's face. "Your grandfather was as wrong as fuck about you," he swore through his gritted teeth, a vein in his forehead pulsing angrily. "He used to talk about his grandson, the great journalist, and that one day he would come to town and run this paper like he did. He said you'd come because of duty, both in your career and for your history. He said you'd want a chance to really make a difference, and the best way to do that is at a little paper. Here, you have a direct impact on people's lives. But, if you don't give a damn, that's fine. I'm sure someone else out there does."

A fragile silence followed as the older man got to his feet to stand as unyielding as Medusa's suitors.

Ryan stepped back, wary of a more physical confrontation from the man. But he immediately realized it was unnecessary, for the aubergine coloring of Glo's complexion paled.

"I'm sorry," Ryan replied. "I barely knew my grandfather. If he wanted me to run this place, he should have asked me."

Glo took a deep breath and his shoulders slumped, his countenance no longer one of defiance, but slipped back into age and disappointment. Without saying another word, he collapsed back into his chair and gazed distantly across the room, a tear streaming down his cheek.

Again, Ryan felt Connie's hand guiding him, this time away from the emotionally exhausted man. "Give him some understanding," she whispered. "Your grandfather was his best friend, and he only wants his legacy to survive."

Her words made Ryan feel empathy, but the insinuation of uprooting his own life—to fulfill a dead man's wish—tempered it.

The murmur of chitchat gradually resumed in the room, with tender remembrances and jovial anecdotes. It both touched and uneased Ryan, as he felt out of place in their mourning. They knew his grandfather far beyond his own relationship with a distant figure and guarded voice.

A burst of laughter echoed through the building, and Ryan used it as an opportunity to slip away from the group. He passed by the newsroom desks and paused in the reception area, making note of two mismatched surplus-style metal desks, one with Ebetta's name on it and the other with Connie's. On the opposite side of the room, past two shabby vinyl couches, one strawberry red and the other avocado green, a photographic gallery covered the wall. He stepped toward it, discovering a pictorial history of the town, 100 plus years of gatherings, buildings, and milestones. Each image exhaustingly described with an attached label.

—

Less than eighty square feet in size, with a desk, three chairs and two filing cabinets crammed into it, the editor's office elicited a caution of claustrophobia. A feeling not calmed by Dean Shipley's personal effects—clumsy stacks of papers, penholders jammed to overflowing and a clutter of framed photographs hogging the walls. Though unlike the historical perspective of the photos in the reception area, these exhibited family pride, depicting Ryan, his father, his grandmother, and various others he assumed as relatives, though likely long dead.

"Whenever your mother sent new pictures, he would buy frames and have them on the wall in a day or two," Connie offered as Ryan looked around the room. "You may not have known him, but he thought highly of you. He had flaws, but he really was a good man."

Many of the photos he'd never seen before, including most of those depicting his father as a boy and young man. Emotions simmered inside him, forcing him to avert his gaze from both the pictures and Connie's view. "I should take these when I go home," he declared in a halting voice.

"When are you planning to leave?" she asked.

"In a week," he answered, feeling relieved that the emotional throbbing had waned.

"You have a lot to do if you're only going to be here a week," she responded.

His eyes strayed back to the cluttered walls, though he forced his focus away from his father's face. Even then, after mere seconds, his cracking emotions again drove him to look away, focusing on the small window at the back of the office, peering out into a shabby back alley. "I may be able to stay a little longer," he allowed, finding it difficult to keep a firm voice. "What's upstairs?"

—

His feet plodded heavily up the stairs, each footfall collapsing through the thick layer of dust that coated the long unused treads. At the top, he paused at a battered door, warped in shape but firmly fit into its jamb. The knob turned freely, but his push failed to swing the door open. He tried again, thrusting his shoulder against the upper panel, but still no movement. Frustration darkened his thoughts. Taking a half step back, he took a deep breath, gave the knob a hard twist and swung his entire body against the door. Dry wood cracked as he made contact, and the door swung open, its long-unoiled hinges creaking loudly in protest.

Pungent odors of mold and rot flooded his nose, roiling his throat with an urge to gag. He momentarily leaned against the doorframe, forcing his thoughts away from the cocktail of stale scents, and allowing his stomach to settle. His eyes quickly acclimated to the dim hallway, allowing him to spot a light switch to his right. A loud pop sounded, and overhead two bare bulbs in cracked ceramic sockets powered on, offering a grim illumination of walls gray with age and filth.

At the front of the building, he discovered a large room spanning the structure's width, naturally brightened by five large and dusty windows overlooking Commercial Street. Old furniture and boxes, all frosted with a generation's worth of dust and cobwebs, heightened the room's desolation. Back down the hall that ran alongside the stairs, another door opened to reveal a small galley kitchen with dinged up enamel cabinets, a small, rusty Magic Chef range and an old Frigidaire refrigerator. All tarnished by abandonment.

The next door he came to featured a yellowed sign identifying its room as the *Morgue*, or the newspaper's archives. Inside, sagging gray metal shelving was stacked high with dusty and yellowed back issues and large, leather-bound collections. Outsized books that spanned March 1897 to December 1997, including two sets of books up until 1947, one for the *White Oak City Times* and another for the *Decatur County Gazette*, signifying the year when the two newspapers merged into one.

At the back end of the narrow hall, one last door stood ajar, a sliver of light escaping. With a tap of his fingertips, it creaked open to reveal a bedroom that would do most haunted houses proud, furnished with a heavy empire revival mahogany bedroom set shrouded beneath a powdery gray crust and gossamer thick cobwebs.

Decades had passed since the bed's last use, though it remained neatly made, despite decay, beneath a patchwork quilt faded from the sun and tattered from temperature and insects.

His curiosity sated and emotions unexpectedly drained, Ryan left the room as he found it, with nothing but fresh footprints on a dusty floor to mark his intrusion.

"Who did the bedroom belong to?" he asked Connie as he sat down on the end of the strawberry red vinyl sofa nearest her.

Nostalgia warmed her eyes as she looked up at him from behind her monitor. "That was your great-grandfather's bedroom for the last few years of his life," she explained. "He was your great-grandfather on your grandmother's side. They called him 'Pappy.' After your great-grandmother died, your grandparents set him up in that apartment.

"When did he die?" Ryan continued his questioning, feeling a need to know more about the man who's home he had invaded.

She leaned back in her chair and put her hand to her cheek. "The mid eighties," she answered. "During the summer. I was teaching a GED class at the high school and one of my students worked here as a cleaning lady. She told us they found him in bed one morning, heart attack."

—

Connie marched across the sidewalk and stepped off the curb into the street, with Ryan following along. With a wave of her hand and a proud smile she motioned to the three buildings now in front of them. "You own all these, the *Times-Gazette* building and both its neighbors. We have 207 Commercial on the left, 205 in the middle and 203 on the right. A haberdashery operated in 207 for a long time, then it became a used bookstore, but vacant for the last couple decades. And 203 is the former town pharmacy, with the old soda fountain still inside."

The buildings represented striking relics of the town's former pride. On the left, the two-story, turn-of-the-century tan brick edifice featured four arched windows running across the upper floor, and on the retail level two massive plate glass windows framed a shabby metal slab door—a likely replacement for a long-gone, better-suited original. It effortlessly overshadowed the simpler block building that housed the newspaper. But the structure on the far right outshined both others.

Walls of crimson red brick and an elaborate green-patinaed copper cornice delivered a true Victorian showplace. Its pedigree, mounted in copper numerals on the brick below the cornice, dated it to 1895, with a century's worth of oxidized residue drizzled beneath the numerals. Large display windows and a recessed double door fronted the first floor, while five windows traversed the upper; four large and double hung with double-pane upper and lower sashes, and on the far right a small oval window, divided into quarters by lead muntin bars.

"It's beautiful," Ryan gushed as he tilted back his head for a better view of the cornice.

"We have one of the most complete historic commercial districts in this part of the state," she said. "There's barely been a single building lost to demolition or fire. I imagine it full of antique shops, restaurants and little boutiques, maybe someplace tourists from Branson might like that it lets them escape overt commercialization and see what a real Ozark Mountains town looks like."

The idealism made him smile. "You've thought about it a lot, haven't you?" he asked, followed with a quiet chuckle.

"When you love a place, you want to do everything you can to make it as wonderful for everyone else as it is to you," she answered in a serious tone.

They started down the street together, stopping half a block along beside the former bank. Though it lacked the Victorian flourishes of the old drug store, the two-story gray-granite building held its own as distinguished architecture, with Palladian windows and intricate glass and bronze details of the Art Nouveau style. Its most defining feature faced them from the corner, a massive set of double doors and matching surround that extended up into a bronze frieze depicting a farmer reaping wheat.

But despite its unmistakable grandeur, the town's denizens had long ago ceased utilizing the building for their financial needs. Its windows—hung with the remnant rags of once fine draperies—now framed the motionless faces of a menagerie of animals, from squirrels and deer to house pets.

"Creepy," Ryan mumbled as he stared into the lifeless glass eyes of a German shepherd.

"Mac's one of your best tenants," Connie countered.

"My grandfather owned this building?" he asked, reappraising the structure with greater appreciation.

"He bought it when they built a new bank building out on the bypass," she explained. "This was once considered the most beautiful building in town," she added as they continued walking down the street.

In rapid succession she pointed out more buildings he owned as they passed the park and crossed to the next block, offering a flood of details for each structure. Reaching 107 West Commercial Street, she presented him with an old grocery store building he now owned before turning and starting back the way they had come. They made it about twenty feet before she stopped again, as if suddenly remembering something. Across a narrow green lawn from them sat a distinguished building of redbrick. It was fronted by two white fluted columns that supported a gabled portico roof, which in turn held a sign identifying it as the *City Hall*.

She pointed toward the building's large gray cornerstone, where the name *Mayor Eugene Shipley* and the date *May 21, 1914* were carved in large text. "That was your great-great-grandfather," she explained.

He offered a polite nod, but no response.

They walked back past the town square, the old bank, the newspaper office, and finally reached Hydrangea Street, where he thanked her for the tour and turned to head up the hill to his grandfather's house. But she placed a hand on his arm and led him in the direction of the lumbering old school building.

"That was my classroom for thirty-two years," she said as they neared the school, her finger pointing to a set of windows on the second floor.

Ryan strained his eyes to peer through the darkened glass, but saw only shadows inside. Generations of students filled its halls for much of the last century, with countless life-molding experiences taking place within.

"Your father, grandfather, grandmother and at least two great-grandparents graduated from here," she said. "As did my son and myself." Quivering emotion sounded in her voice.

"I saw the current high school when I drove into town; this one is much more distinguished," he remarked.

"It is," she agreed. "They said it was too old, too hard to maintain, and too out-of-date. They bought land in the newer part of town and built a new school. Now, this one sits empty. It sold recently, but that could mean bulldozers.

"The visitation's tomorrow night, and the funeral and burial the day after, on Friday," Connie remarked as they turned back toward Hydrangea Street. "I know a lot of people want to meet you."

Unease turned his stomach at the thought of forced conversations about a grandfather he never really knew.

"I'll be there the whole time, so you can let me know if it gets overwhelming." She patted him on the shoulder. "The funeral home is up the hill here. Maybe we should walk up to it, so you know where it is?"

—

The white blaze of the *Whitman-Moore Funeral Home* sign anchored a sweeping green lawn that flowed twenty yards back to the steps of a pale-yellow Victorian mansion. A dignified old house adorned with a wrap-around porch and an overabundance of columns, corbels and moldings, while landscaping lamps bathed the exterior in a buttery glow.

Connie stepped off the sidewalk and started along the walkway to the porch.

"Are we going in?" Ryan asked as he trotted after her.

"You should talk to Chad for a few minutes," she answered as she continued walking. "So, he'll recognize you tomorrow."

Though not eager for the introduction, Ryan mumbled an agreement. A flutter of curtains in a second-story window caught his attention, giving him a glimpse of an older woman receding into the dark. "Who's upstairs?" he asked.

Connie glanced up, though the woman had vanished. "Chad's mother, Estacia Whitman Moore," she explained, taking a haughty tone in pronouncing the woman's full name. "They live upstairs. This was her family home before she married, and her husband turned it into a funeral home."

Stepping up onto the porch, it became evident that while the old mansion appeared clean and maintained from the street, up close its peeling paint and sagging carpentry became obvious. Though he could not criticize it too much, as it fared considerably better than most of what he inherited.

Connie pushed the front door open, triggering an electronic chime. The formal foyer held a large central staircase, with arched doorways to the left and right. Connie turned to the left, entering a long chapel. Rows of pews filled the room, all facing the back of the house, where a heavyset man with salt and pepper hair huddled over an oak casket.

"Be right with you," the man yelled as he busied himself inside the box.

Connie swiftly neared him, while Ryan halted halfway down the aisle dividing the rows into two columns.

"It's me, Chad," she announced. "Is that Dean?"

The man's head bobbed up and down in a deep nod. "It is," he answered. "I was having some trouble with his face. He had a gash from when he fell after the heart attack. But I have it now. Just had to go heavy on the wax."

She looked down into the casket and a pleased smile appeared on her face. "You've done a wonderful job," she effused. "But his hair's too neat. He was always a little more disheveled looking when it came to his hair."

"Mother said the exact same thing," Chad admitted with a chortle.

Connie motioned for Ryan to step forward. "Want to see your grandfather?" she asked.

Chad's body jerked up and he snapped around to face Ryan, the slight smile on his face dissolved into a somber expression. "I'm so sorry about your grandfather's passing." He stepped toward Ryan with his hand extended.

CHAPTER 3

A DULL ACHE SIMMERED in Ryan's left side, a symptom of sleeping on it all night. With a soft flop, he rolled onto his back, looking up at the textured swirls in the ceiling's plaster. His mind fretted over the days to come, leaving his eyes to glaze over, awake but lacking motivation to get out of bed. Apathy crept into his mind and he lapsed back to the edge of sleep, at least until the harsh buzz of the doorbell jolted him awake. He paused in getting out of bed, self-conscious of answering it, but knowing no one else could and the responsibilities of the home now fell to him.

He pulled on the jeans and t-shirt he wore the day before, and hustled down the stairs two at a time, while the doorbell's unpleasant screeching sounded a second and a third time. But upon reaching the door, he found a puzzling scene, as its frosted window revealed nothing but the day's light, no silhouette of a morning visitor. They must have grown tired and left, he reasoned as he swung back around toward the stairs, but then the buzzer sounded again. A chill shot through every inch of his flesh, leaving the hair on the back of his neck standing. He pivoted back toward the door, still seeing no one through the glass. The thumping of his heart filled his ears as he approached it and pulled it open.

His surprise sent him jumping back a half step, having discovered his visitor, who's diminutive stature solved the riddle of seeing no one through the glass. Thick glasses magnified the hazel eyes that gazed up at him from a fleshy and matronly face. Her hands clutched a large turquoise casserole dish covered with foil. "Are you D-D-Dean's grandson?" she asked, her face covered in lines both fine and deep.

He wanted to be suspicious, but nothing about this woman justified it. "I am," he answered. "Can I help you?"

She pursed her lips. "I j-j-just wanted to bring something b-b-by for you," she replied, anxiously looking away from him as she spoke. "I know p-people d-don't have a lot of time for cooking at a time like this." She thrust the casserole dish up in the air toward him.

Sweat seeped out onto his brow. "I appreciate it, but I really don't need anything," he told her. "Thank you though." Insult flashed on her face. In town not even a full day, and already he had broken etiquette and hurt a woman's feelings. "What is it though?" he asked, hoping to segue the question into an opportunity to rectify his impropriety.

She pulled the casserole close to her chest, a tinge of embarrassment on her cheeks. "It's a ham and p-p-potato casserole."

"That sounds very good," he now over-enthusiastically responded. "I would appreciate that very much."

Her eyes narrowed with skepticism. "Are you sure? I d-don't want to impose."

He offered the most benign smile he could muster. "I'm sure. It sounds delicious and I'm afraid I'm not much of a cook."

Though less eager this time, she again lifted the casserole up to him and he took it out of her hands. The instant he grasped it, she let go, turned and trotted down the front steps.

"What's your name?" he called after her, stunned by the abrupt exit.

The clicking of her shoes against the paved stone path paused. "I'm sorry," she responded while glancing back. "I'm Emma Woodhouse. I live t-t-two houses d-down." And she sprinted off.

The casserole warmed his hands, likely minutes from being pulled out of the oven. With his foot, he pushed the front door closed and carried the dish to the kitchen, where he set it on the countertop. He pulled back the foil cover, releasing a savory scent that made its way to his nose. A gurgle of anticipation sounded in his stomach. Where were the plates? He scanned the kitchen, so many cabinet doors. The shrill buzz of the doorbell interrupted him.

Two middle-aged women, one tall and thin, the other short and fat, greeted him. And like the anxious Emma Woodhouse, they carried food. A heavily laden plate of fried chicken rested in the hands of the short one, while the tall one cradled a meringue pie with the care reserved for an infant.

"Your granddaddy was a good man," the short woman blurted out without any introduction. "We'd known him for years. He was always willin' to help someone out. My sister and I wanted to bring somethin' here for his kin. You's his grandbaby, right?" She spoke in fast, short bursts, pausing after every sentence, her plump cheeks turning bright red as she talked, and going pale in the pauses.

"Yes, he was my grandfather," he answered in a reserved tone. "I'm Ryan Shipley, what are your names?"

The short woman moved her right foot forward, crossing the threshold. "I'm Vonica, but people call me Vonnie," she announced in another burst. "This is my sister, Bernice. She knew your daddy. She went to school with him."

Bernice smiled widely at the mention of her name, exposing misshapen teeth and a lipstick smear across them.

He smiled back. "Thank you both very much," he replied as he extended his hands out to them. "Let me take these from you."

With a questioning stare, Vonnie pulled the plate she held back against her ample chest. "Don't you worry," she scolded him. "We know where the kitchen is. We'll take it back."

He stepped aside and let them pass, then followed them to the kitchen.

"Emma musta been here," Vonnie announced as she sat the plate of fried chicken on the counter. "I'd know her casserole dish anywhere." She then swung around to look at him, while Bernice watched from behind her. "I've been cleaning this house ever since your granny died," Vonnie remarked. "I don't know if you'll need me to do that for you, but if you do, here's my number." She reached into the pocket of her baggy culottes, pulled out a crumpled piece of paper and handed it to him. "We'll come over tomorrow before the funeral and help set up for the people and to put out the food," she continued. "Afterward, we'll help you clean up."

It sounded like an imposition, though he did not know if for him or them. "You really don't need to do that; I'm sure I'll be fine," he protested.

With a tilt of her head, Vonnie returned a condescending look. "Boy, you don't need to worry about it," she responded in a firm voice. "We ain't chargin' for that. You don't charge when somebody passes. That ain't Christian. See ya tomorra, and let Connie know we stopped by."

—

By the time Connie arrived in the early afternoon, seven more of his grandfather's friends and neighbors had stopped by and added to the growing banquet. The kitchen countertops sat cluttered with offerings, ranging from roast beef with potatoes and carrots to gooseberry pie. Ryan had never eaten gooseberries before, but the hunched-over old man who brought the pie assured him of its deliciousness.

"What's up with all the food?" he asked Connie as she entered the front door.

She responded with a puzzled look. "What do you mean?"

He nodded in the direction of the kitchen and began walking toward it. "All day people've been coming to the door with food. There's a ton of stuff here."

She offered a gentle laugh. "That's what people do around here when someone dies," she explained as she began inspecting the day's deliveries. "Food for death, flowers for sickness."

The buzz of the doorbell again, but she motioned with her hand for him to stay still as she disappeared down the hall. He peered around the corner and down the hall after her but only heard muffled and brief pleasantries before she closed the door and turned back toward him, a large yellow Tupperware bowl in her hands.

"Macaroni salad," she announced as she neared him.

He stood still, allowing her to pass him. Then he followed her back into the kitchen. "Let me see if I understand this. People don't send flowers to the funeral here, they bring food?"

Her eyes showed both patience and amusement. "They still send flowers, but they bring food too. The food is to provide the mourners with a relief from having to cook. But most of it is for tomorrow after the funeral when everyone comes here. Did a woman named Vonnie come by this morning?"

He paused to think, so many had stopped by, but then he remembered the short, fat woman. "Her and her sister. They brought fried chicken and a pie."

With a sudden vigor, Connie grabbed the plate of fried chicken, quickly pulling back the plastic wrap and grabbing a piece. "This chicken is famous around here." She took a bite. "The recipe is from your grandfather's aunt Rosemary."

The scene brought the first smile of the day to Ryan's face. "I also think I upset a woman," he admitted, feeling the smile fade and his cheeks flush. "She was the first one here and I didn't know I should be accepting food. I told her 'no thank you' and she got a little upset. Then I told her it sounded delicious and I took it. She seemed happier then."

"Who was it?" she inquired as she pulled the last strands of meat from the leg bone.

Again, names clouded his memory. "I don't remember, but she brought that." He pointed to the turquoise casserole dish.

"Emma," she answered with a nod. "As sweet as can be, but very timid."

The doorbell buzzed. She offered a questioning look as to whether she should answer it, but he shook his head and headed to the front door.

With a high poof of blackish-blue hair, bright blue eye make-up and vermillion lipstick, the gaudy appearance of the visitor reminded him of a circus clown. "Hello, can I help you?" he asked.

Teeth yellowed by years of coffee and cigarettes appeared as she smiled at him. "Yes honey, I have food out in the car that needs to be brought in," she answered in a raspy voice. "In the back seat; the door's open. Is Connie in the kitchen? I see her car."

He glanced out to the street, where an older tan Cadillac with a long scratch down the passenger side sat in front of the house. "She is," he answered, followed by the woman brushing him aside in her surge forward.

"I'll talk to her and see you in a few minutes," she declared as she gave a wave in the direction of the car.

—

The reek of cigarette smoke greeted Ryan as he opened the car door, triggering a gagging spasm in his throat. He pulled his head out of the car and back into the fresh air, bringing the impulse under control. A shudder went through his body at the thought, but he took a deep breath and ducked back inside.

Beside a blanket filthy with dog hair he found a cardboard box packed with plastic containers, hopefully sealed tightly enough to protect the contents from the overpowering stench of the pack-a-day car. He heaved the box up into his arms, avoiding contact with the trash and other questionable items in the backseat, and with a slight swing of his hips closed the car door.

The loud chatter of the women's voices traveled out into the hall, allowing him to hear their conversation as he approached the kitchen, the box still in his arms. The visitor mentioned his name, prompting him to shift to the softest of steps to quietly sneak up to the doorway.

"He's a good-looking boy, like his father was," the black-haired woman commented. "You think he's going to stay here?"

He sucked in his breath and edged as close to the doorway as possible, while still staying out of view.

"I don't know," Connie answered. "I don't think he knows anything about us here, and if he doesn't know about us, why would he stay? He lives in a big city. There's so much to do there. My Meade says the same thing. He tells me it would be hard for him to adjust to living in a small town again."

Satisfied with Connie's answer, Ryan took it as his cue to make his presence known.

"There he is," the black-haired woman exclaimed as he stepped into the kitchen. She stood and scurried over to him, pulling items out of the box even before he had it on the counter.

"Here's scalloped potatoes." She shoved a plastic container into his now free hands. "These are rolls. I've already baked them, so they just need to be heated up. Here's some green beans and this is squash. Oh, I have fried okra here too."

Ryan glanced to Connie for help, but she only smiled in return. Once the box had emptied, and with all the containers haphazardly balanced in his hands, he grinned at the black-haired woman. Then he turned and dropped everything on the counter by the refrigerator. "Did you make this all yourself?" he asked as he opened the refrigerator door to make room.

The woman's eyes burned deeply into him as she made her examination. "Me and my momma made it," she answered. "Momma's health isn't good, so she couldn't come by today. But she'll be at the funeral tomorrow."

Not until the woman had left did Connie reveal her name as Lenora Bayridge, widow of a former town mayor. "She's the biggest gossip in town. If you tell her anything, I can guarantee everyone will know it within half an hour."

—

Though still fifteen minutes short of the 5:00 p.m. start time, a handful of cars already sat in the funeral home's parking lot. And the presence of the same tan Cadillac from earlier signaled Ryan knew at least one of the early arrivals. He imagined Lenora Bayridge did not miss many public functions in the town, if only for fear of missing out on the latest news.

The soft recorded notes of old hymns met his ears as he stepped inside the door, and a hum of gentle conversation floated out from the main chapel, where mourners gathered in small groups among the pews.

"Be sure to sign the guest book," Connie said as she led him into the chapel. "It's for posterity's sake."

He left his name as the eighth on the register, with the only ones he recognized being Connie and Lenora. For a moment his attention drifted, as his eyes fell out of focus looking down at the list of names. But a nudge from Connie's elbow brought his attention back, and she signaled for him to follow her to the casket.

Surrounded by a forest of plants and flowers, his grandfather's casket loomed at the front of the room. A chill lingered in the air, and the warm lighting and soft music gave the chapel a more somber feel than he recalled from the evening prior. He stepped close to the casket and looked down at the face, which felt familiar only from photographs.

"Chad did a wonderful job," Lenora gushed, her loud voice clashing with the sedate drone of the room. "The only thing that's wrong is the hair. I've never saw it that neat."

Connie smiled. "I said the same to Chad last night."

For several minutes Ryan stared at his grandfather's face, hoping for some sort of internal enlightenment, but instead a growing uneasiness began to churn. With a sigh, he turned away and scanned the room behind him. The attendance now numbered more than twenty, tripling in less than ten minutes. He glanced across their faces, making eye contact with almost everyone, suggesting a pervasive interest in his own presence. A nervous chill disrupted his body, sending him back to his grandfather's staid face, as a dead man offers no judgment.

How long could he keep focused on his grandfather without it seeming strange? He swallowed his doubt and twisted hard on his heels, taking less than five steps before stumbling into a rush of mourners. One by one, they surged forward, shaking his hand and sharing stories and remembrances. They presented a confusing barrage of names and connections, all referring to his grandfather—and in some cases, his father. He made no effort to commit them to memory. After all, he would soon be back in Los Angeles and far removed from the town and its people, so he nodded and shook their hands in turn and gamely received an occasional hug from the ladies.

After a few minutes, the excited rush ebbed, the ready vignettes exhausted. He lowered his head to appear preoccupied and passed from the crowd to take a seat on the far end of an empty pew.

"I knew your grandfather his entire life," a man proclaimed in an aged croak. "I figured I'd be gone long before he was, but the good Lord had other plans. You know, your family has been here as long as White Oak City has existed, even before. He knew that and loved it."

Ryan opened his mouth to respond, but could think of nothing appropriate, so instead closed it again and nodded in understanding.

Bald and slightly hunched, the old man wore a mottling of liver spots across his wrinkled face, scalp and hands. "This town is as much yours as it was his," the man continued. "I hope you feel that it's a part of you, like it was a part of him, like it's a part of me." He paused. "I hear you don't plan on staying around though. I can't imagine what that's like; to not want to be where your family's heritage is."

Despite the condescension, the words did not anger Ryan. For he recognized a tone of frustration and when he looked at the age-embattled face saw the derelict buildings that cradled the town square. He continued his silence and offered another polite nod of understanding, if not agreement, and patted the old man on the shoulder. A moment more lingered, as the man's eyes burned into Ryan, almost in expectation of a confrontation. But finally, the elderly fellow lowered his head, turned away, and shuffled toward the casket.

—

The clock had barely passed 7:00 and a painful tension throbbed in Ryan's neck and back. He wanted to return to his grandfather's house, grab a beer and collapse on the sofa. Connie stood alone at the casket, perhaps an opportunity to seek leniency.

"Another two hours is the time we have, are you still feeling up to it?" she responded before he even asked his question.

The pain in his neck flared, but quickly receded to a spot just above his shoulders. He nodded, resigned to the reality that leaving would create an impression of disrespect.

Around 150 people filled the chapel now, gathered informally through it, talking and reminiscing. In the back, he spotted Glo talking to the disgruntled old man from earlier, alternating their comments, with one talking while the other nodded in agreement, and occasionally both stopping and staring in Ryan's direction.

He stepped back to the pew and sat down, though his backside barely touched the satin cushion when a plump woman of around sixty dropped down beside him and began extolling now familiar praises of his grandfather. But then her voice abruptly halted, paired with a silence across the room. Glancing back in concern, he saw a white-haired woman slowly pushing a walker up the center aisle. Her face deeply lined, and skin so loosely draped it appeared as if slowly melting away.

"That's your great-great-aunt Rosemary," Connie whispered to him as she urged him into a standing position.

"What are you talking about?" He got to his feet. "I thought all my relatives were dead."

She led him to the aisle. "No," she responded. "You have several distant cousins in this area, like third and fourth cousins and such. But she's the closest living relative you have here. She's your grandfather's aunt."

"How old is she?" he queried, surprised by the revelation.

"Turned ninety-seven in October," she answered. "Still lives alone in her own house. Though she has a grandnephew of her husband's that lives here in town and helps take care of her. That's him following her."

Trailing closely behind the old woman, Ryan saw a middle-aged man, walking in a way that gave the impression of being prepared to catch her if she fell.

The walker came to a halt in front of Ryan, the elderly woman looking him over with her bright blue eyes. "Is this him?" she asked Connie in a soft, frail voice.

Connie smiled. "Yes, Mrs. Tagert. This is Ryan, your great-grand-nephew."

Her quaint, out-of-fashion light blue dress emphasized her frail body and the paper-white pallor of her skin. "I'm your aunt Rosemary." Her voice weak and wavering with age. "Please step with me up to the front."

She cautiously pushed the walker aside and clutched onto Ryan's right arm. Then together, at a deliberate pace, they approached the casket. For the first time since hearing of his grandfather's death, he felt himself becoming overwhelmed with sadness. For the raw emotions he saw on his elderly aunt's face seemed to pulse from her body into his.

She slipped her arm out from his and grasped the side of the oak box. Her silent attention rested on the stilled face. After a hushed moment, the quiet gave way to a soft sniffling, that progressed to restrained sobs. Her frame shivered with sorrow as she released her right hand from the casket, steadying herself with her left. From a pocket in the hip of her dress, she pulled out a lace handkerchief, using it to gently dab away the glistening tears gathering beneath her eyes.

The scene sat heavy on his heart as his vision fogged and tears lapped at the edges of his own eyes. He did not cry for the man in the box, whom he hardly knew, but for the fragile, elderly woman whose aged body trembled with each tired sob. How could he comfort her? A feeling of ineptness swelled in him. He slipped his arm back through hers, keeping her wavering stance upright, and she melted back into his strength.

A moment more of shared silence passed before Rosemary slowly turned and together they returned to the front pew and the small group waiting there to pay their respects. With gentle support, he aided her in sitting down. He then took a moment to introduce himself to her late husband's nephew Marvin and his wife, Liddy, before sitting down beside his aunt.

"Your grandfather meant the world to me," Rosemary whispered once Marvin and Liddy had stepped away to the casket to pay their own respects. "He was the only blood relative within two generations I had left here. The rest are gone, most behind the gates of the Methodist cemetery or the ones that have been gone even longer at Blackjack Bluff." She again produced her handkerchief to blot away her tears.

A middle-aged couple paused at the pew and offered their condolences, and then moved on to the casket.

"One would think, with all the funerals I've been to in my life, I would've gotten over the crying part by now," she said. "But, when it's someone you love, it's as difficult as it was the first time. That was my little brother. He was sixteen and I was nineteen. I went to wake him one morning, but he wasn't in his room. I went out to the barn to see if he was there. And he was, hanging from the rafters, a rope around his neck."

The story sent chills through Ryan's body. He could feel the look of shock on his face, so he bit down on the insides of his cheeks to mute the expression. "He ... he killed himself?"

Rosemary sighed and nodded her head. "I don't know why," she muttered. "He was an extremely good-looking boy. He played baseball for the high school and plenty of girls chased him. But there was something he couldn't talk about." She paused and smiled at Ryan. "He looked a lot like you. He was your great-great-uncle after all and it can be surprising how family traits can pass down. He left a note, saying he was sorry and that he felt like he was a bad person who was dirty and full of sin." She turned away and let out a soft sob. "I don't know what kind of sin he thought he had committed, but he was the sweetest, gentlest boy most people around here ever met. The old Methodist church was packed for his funeral and they even retired his baseball number at the high school. In the old building, before they closed it down, there was a picture of him in the trophy case. It hung there for seventy years or more."

Ryan reached over and put his hand on his aunt's, which rested between them on the pew cushion. "I'm sorry," he muttered. "That's heartbreaking."

She sighed again and then smiled. "I believe that just because someone is dead it doesn't mean they're gone," she revealed. "Whenever I'm at your grandfather's house, which is now your house, I can feel my little brother's presence there. As if he's never left and stays there keeping watch over the family."

A shiver tingled his spine. "He died in the house where I'm staying?"

"That's the old family home," Rosemary replied. "My father built that house before I was born. I grew up there, as did my older brother and sisters and my younger brother. The barn isn't there anymore. My older brother, your great-grandfather, subdivided the lot and gave the back, where the barn had been, to one of my older sisters. She never married but had a small house there and lived in it most of her life."

He felt nauseous as he thought of someone who lived in the house committing suicide there, or at least in a barn that once existed behind it.

"In any old house someone has likely died," she offered in a matter-of-fact tone, as if sensing his discomfort. "They've just been around so long people don't remember. My mother also died in that house, so did my other sister, in childbirth—the baby too. My father died in the old Decatur County hospital, but your grandfather died in it, you knew that though."

—

A group of men loitered on the front porch, talking and smoking as Ryan emerged from the funeral home. They glanced in his direction and offered nods, but nothing more. The quiet and darkness eased the stress in his mind as he strode a few yards along the path to the parking lot. The sweet smell of freshly cut grass filled his nose and led him to wade out into the thick swath of lawn. Drops of dew brushed off the green blades and onto his brown dress shoes, leaving a dark spotting. He looked across the deep lawn toward the row of homes that filled the opposite side of the street. They represented a variety of sizes and styles, but held universal as aged vintages, with most painted a crisp white. Inside their windows he caught glimpses of life, as their inhabitants went about their evening routines, with the bluish fluttering of televisions present in most.

"Are you all right?" Connie asked, breaking him from his observations. "I'm sure it's a bit overwhelming—all these people."

Ryan offered a weak smile and glanced back to the glow of the funeral home's open door. "I don't know if I'd say it's overwhelming; I just feel out of place," he answered. "He knew the entire town, didn't he?"

She nodded. "He did. Some better than others and a lot of them were not close friends but are here out of respect for his place in the community."

His shoes squished as he walked, soaked through by the evening dew. "I don't know how anybody could stand to stay in a dead little town like this for so long," he muttered. "It's like the rest of the world kept going, but no one here figured it out."

She offered a soft and understanding laugh. "You're not the first person who's had that thought. But I think you could make an argument for the exact opposite. It's the rest of the world that stopped. I don't mean stopped as in progress and technology. I mean they've stopped knowing what it means to be good neighbors and to be active in their communities."

CHAPTER 4

THE WHITE OAK PRESBYTERIAN CHURCH cast a domineering presence. Its redbrick front façade featured three tall, arched stained-glass windows depicting in order the birth, life, and death of Christ, while to the right, a broad set of steps led up to a similarly arched set of flame red doors. But leaving no doubt of the point of the day, a distinctive dark green hearse sat parked at the base of the steps.

A small group lingered near the doors. But as Ryan and Connie climbed the steps, it dispersed, leaving behind only his aunt and the funeral director.

"Mrs. Tagert, once again, my condolences," Connie offered to the elderly woman while gently patting her hand.

The nonagenarian leaned heavily on a black cane and her pale face seemed almost ghostly. Ryan stepped close and took her free arm into his.

"Thank you," she whispered to him. "I suppose we go in now."

As impressive on the inside as the outside, a golden-hued light filtered in through the stained-glass windows, and in reflecting on the mahogany woodwork gave the sanctuary an almost ethereal atmosphere. Warmth, not only sensual but emotional, filled the sacred space.

Rosemary clung tightly to him as they inched down the center aisle, with hundreds of solemn faces watching.

At the back of the room rested his grandfather's flower-laden casket, laid beneath a delicately carved pulpit. And to its right sat two chairs, gothic in style, the one on the left occupied by a man with the draped face of a hound dog. On the opposite side, a gray-haired woman played the gentle notes of the hymn "Sweet Hour of Prayer" on the keys of a baby grand piano.

Ryan held tight to his aunt as she slowly turned and took her seat in the second pew. Before taking his own seat beside her, he glanced back across the room they had just traversed, seeing both sympathy and curiosity in the eyes he met.

The man with the jowly face stood up from his gothic chair and approached the pulpit, sweeping his graying brown hair out of his eyes in the process. He then pulled a pair of glasses from his pocket and perched them on the end of his nose. "My friends, in the twenty-eight years I've had the privilege of being the pastor of this church, I've known a lot of fine people," he intoned in a drowsy voice. "Today, we say goodbye to one of the most decent and kind-hearted I've ever had the good grace to call a friend."

A mummer of "amens" reverberated through the room.

"This was a good man, not perfect, but none of us are," the preacher continued. "For some, knowing perfection is impossible, they put in the extra effort to be the best husband, father, friend, community leader, and Christian they can."

Again, came murmurs of agreement.

"The first time I met Dean Shipley, I was only twenty-seven and had been sent here right out of the seminary. Dean, who was born into this community and knew it as well as anyone, told me, 'so you're what we get when we're a dying town.'"

Light laughter filled the church.

"He then put his arm around my shoulder and told me not to worry, that you all needed saving worse than any other town in the state," the preacher continued, a broad smile on his face. "That's how I knew he wasn't perfect because as soon as I met his dear wife and all of you, his wonderful neighbors, I knew I was going to be saved as much by you as you have been by me."

The vignette finished, the preacher segued into a more Messianic eulogy, elaborating on Bible verses about the virtues of selflessness and parlaying that into the parable of the Good Samaritan. Then, without offering verbal direction, he looked to the piano and nodded his head. The pianist responded with a nod of her own and began playing "The Old Rugged Cross." And as the preacher's deep bass voice crooned the words, his somber expression remained steady and unexcited.

Once the song finished, though the final note still seemed to hang in the air, others, each in turn, stepped up to the pulpit, gushing of the dead man's contributions to the community and his neighbors. A parade of remembrances took place before no one else came forward, bringing the pastor back to the pulpit. At first, he said nothing, portraying a look of contentment; but then, with a mischievous gleam in his eye, he gestured for Ryan to come forward.

A stinging pain surged through Ryan's body, as if a vise viciously clamped down on his stomach, twisting and turning it in unnatural positions. Was this man of God trying to humiliate him? He sat frozen, until the gentle prodding of his aunt's hand broke past his emotional paralysis. His mind blank, he stepped toward the pulpit, feeling more like a circus performer than a dutiful grandson. The preacher nodded and warmly shook his hand, before stepping back and leaving Ryan alone, with the full attention of a sanctuary overflowing.

No words of regret or humor came to him, only a burning vision of the staid face of the man in the casket. He glanced back to the preacher, sitting in his ornate chair and nodding in an encouraging manner. His vision fell in and out of focus, as all eyes seemed to burn into him. "I never had the opportunity to know my grandfather in the way that so many of you did," he began, his voice catching. "I talked to him and saw him occasionally through the years, but I didn't know him as the small-town champion I've heard you so lovingly describe."

Curiosity flooded the faces before him.

"In the last few days I've heard so many wonderful stories about him," he continued. "These have educated me on a person and a family history I am only now beginning to understand. I don't know what I'm supposed to be doing now that I'm here and learning what I'm learning, but I'm sure I'm here for a reason. I'm sure I've met all of you for a reason."

A chorus of nodding heads answered the last sentence, including his aunt Rosemary, and Connie, whom he spotted sitting in a folding chair on the far right. He gripped the sides of the pulpit as he dug into his mind, searching for what to say next. The heavy scent of the flowers on his grandfather's casket left him slightly light-headed.

"I've never given this town or the people in it the attention it deserved," he resumed. "I've always known it existed. But I've spent so much time focused on myself, I made the mistake of forgetting what life's like for others, even those in my own family. I know each of you has something to teach me about my grandfather and why he loved this town as much as he did. Thank you for sharing this with me and thank you for being here for my grandfather." His mind froze, so without prayer or platitude, he abruptly stopped, nodded his head to those seated before him and rushed back to his aunt's side.

The preacher, understanding though surprised, returned an awkward nod of his own and resumed his position behind the pulpit, launching into yet another melancholy hymn.

The song faded into the back of Ryan's thoughts as he reflected on his own remarks. Until a few moments earlier, he had planned to leave the town as soon as possible, but it appeared that his subconscious mind might be open to other possibilities. And though he had not said he would remain, his vague comments might appear as a hint for it.

—

An azure sky, broken only by the golden glow of the midday sun, welcomed the funeral procession as it wound its way through the gentle green hills of the countryside. And with the air warm, but not overburdened by humidity, the driver left the windows of the green Lincoln down, so Ryan and Rosemary could enjoy fresh air as they escorted his grandfather's body to its grave. Little in the way of conversation passed between them at first, but once the last vestiges of the town vanished from the rear window, leaving a purely bucolic scene, she spoke. "Do you see that old barn and house down the road to the right?"

He craned his head to peer past his aunt and through the open window. Breaking up some open pastureland, he spotted a tire-rutted stretch of overgrown road leading to the hulking shapes of a copula-crowned gray barn and a sensible Victorian farmhouse which, even shuttered and weathered, demanded respect for a past era. "That's a big barn," he replied to acknowledge her question.

A sigh escaped her trembling lips. "I used to play in the hay loft when I was a little girl, when my grandparents lived there," she recalled in a soft tone.

"Your grandparents lived there?" he replied, then paused a moment to think. "My great-great-great-grandparents owned it?"

She nodded. "They did. Now you do."

A tense jolt hit his body. "What do you mean?" he asked, thinking he misheard.

"You own it. Your grandfather inherited it when my cousin Harrison died. It's the old family farm. It's where our ancestors first settled when they arrived here in the 1850s. The old family cemetery is on the edge of it, overlooking the creek, Blackjack Bluff Cemetery."

Silence again settled between them, and the timeworn ancestral structures grew smaller and smaller as the car drove on, finally vanishing from view at a turn in the road. But even out of sight, the image of the paint-bare house with boarded up windows, sagging wrap-around porch, and shiny tin roof remained in his head. The farm Connie had told him about two days earlier—another white elephant left to him.

The Lincoln slowed as they neared a rustic flagstone-clad building standing on the peak of a hill. The reflection of the sun against the structure's orange and yellow native stone blazed in his eyes. Quaint and roughhewn, the old church fronted their destination. The Lincoln pulled into the driveway to face the burying ground.

Tranquil, if not beautiful, the cemetery held personal charm far beyond what was found in most of those in California, where rows of ground flush headstones eliminated personality for the sake of easy upkeep. Here stood a mismatch of monuments of various sizes and styles, all within a weathered white rail fence. The worn and gothic marble markers hugged close to the rock chapel, and a clear progression of years showed obvious as contemporary granite stones dominated the back half of the hallowed place.

The Lincoln came to a stop on the narrow gravel lane that bisected the cemetery, a car length short of the parked hearse. Enough room, Ryan surmised, for extricating his grandfather's casket to carry it to the grave. The driver moved swiftly to Ryan's door, pulling it open and releasing him from its regal yet morose space. He took a few steps forward, giving the cemetery a closer inspection, but the driver interrupted with a subtle indication to proceed to the other side of the car.

Rosemary remained seated in a manner that reflected the familiar practice of a family mourner. Somber and stoic, she waited for the door to open and then proceeded to rise and exit from the vehicle in a slow and cautious manner, with the attending driver displaying a practiced skill in maneuvering her to a standing position. Ryan offered her his arm, and the two of them slowly followed behind the men carrying the casket to its destination.

Beneath a small green tent and beside a row of chairs, the pallbearers placed the casket above the newly opened grave, and then fell into a somber watch at its foot, as Ryan led his aunt to the chair on the opposite end. With a firm, yet gentle grip he aided her as she sat, and then took the place beside her.

For a few moments a restless rustling passed through crowd, but the appearance of the pastor brought the soft echoes of unease to a stop. The holy man, his sagging face decidedly unemotional, made a few brief remarks on the dead man's character, and then, as if a full realization settled in, he looked up with a face heavy from sorrow and asked that they all sing a final song of "Godspeed." "Softly and tenderly, Jesus is calling," he began in his deep voice, most mourners joining in by the third word.

A tried and true hymn Ryan knew in passing from moments in his life, but without the frequency to have learned the words. It signaled even more distance between him and those crowded around, all singing with reverence.

"See, on the portals, he's waiting and watching, watching for you and for me," the group intoned. And though raspy with age and emotion, even his frail aunt sang along to the devotional. "Come home, come home, ye who are weary, come home," she murmured with the memory of a thousand Sundays. "Earnestly, tenderly, Jesus is calling, calling, o sinner, come home."

At last the voices fell silent and the pastor glanced across the group, a subtle smile on his face, seeming to reflect a measure of pride in the fact that the old inspirational remained ingrained. He cleared his throat and offered a brief prayer, before stepping forward and offering his hand to Ryan, coupled with a quiet blessing. Then the preacher, his eyes dampened with emotion, turned to feeble Rosemary and took her right hand into both of his. For a moment they looked at each other, as if sharing both grief and strength, then he leaned down and whispered into her ear. For a moment, the pain on her face eased, and the preacher straightened back up.

—

A comforting aroma of food and soft voices of introspection welcomed Ryan and Rosemary as they stepped inside the door of his grandfather's house. Nods of acknowledgement and kind words greeted them as he guided his aunt to an overstuffed chair in the living room. He lingered by her side, unsure whether to leave her, but with a weak wave of her hand she urged him off. So, under the weight of trepidation, he slowly maneuvered through the increasing crowd, and the handshakes and sympathies it offered.

The dining room acted as the epicenter, crowded with hungry people and bloated with a smorgasbord of food and desserts, at least twice as much as he remembered from the morning. Buzzing in and out were the two quirky sisters, Vonnie and Bernice, well delivering on their promise of preparing the house. The sight of the feast made his stomach ache, as the stress of the day and constant flow of his grandfather's neighbors and friends dampened the appeal of even the most enticing offerings.

He slipped through the door into the butler's pantry and then into the kitchen, finding Connie washing dishes while the two sisters fussed over rolls. "Is there a beer somewhere?" he asked, recognizing the desperation in his own voice.

Looking up from a half-dried platter cradled in her hands, Connie offered a sympathetic smile. "You shouldn't have a beer around these people," she answered with a gentle chuckle. "A lot of them are Baptist."

A robust laugh erupted from Vonnie. "Of course, that doesn't stop them from doing it when no one's around," she added.

Connie's smile broadened. "You need a break from all this, don't you?" she asked him in a knowing tone.

"Desperately," he gasped.

Vonnie let out another appreciative laugh.

"Ok, Vonnie, Bernice, I know you two can handle this." Connie placed the now dry platter on the kitchen table.

"Of course," Vonnie responded with a nod. "You take that boy somewhere to cool down."

With a brisk rubbing, Connie dried her hands on the faded pink gingham pinafore apron she was wearing, then removed it and folded in on the back of a kitchen chair. She pulled open a drawer and fished around for a moment before lifting out a ring of keys. "Come with me." She led him toward the back door. "We need to go this way, so everyone doesn't see you sneaking out."

They crossed the backyard and came to a small gate that led to a grass service alley, which separated the rear adjoining properties. The barn his great-granduncle died in must've stood near.

"Where are we going?" he queried as they ambled down the alley in the direction of the brick back walls of the buildings lining Commercial Street.

She offered no answer, only a smile in response.

The grass alley ended at a gravel one, spanning the backs of the buildings that made up the south side of the old business district. She continued to guide him past the crumbling rear walls of the decayed town core, until coming to a stop at a much-abused steel slab door.

No label identified what the door hid, but by looking up he recognized it as the only three-story building on the square. And though the grimy rear wall did not reflect it, he knew an especially ornate redbrick Victorian building with a prime corner view of the town square represented the other side.

The keys clinked together as she sifted through them. Finally, she found the one she wanted, a brass one blackened by age. She slipped it into the rusty padlock securing the door, and after a bit of jiggling, the clasp popped open. At first, the door showed indifference in being freed. But by offering it a swing of her ample behind, it gave an inch of clearance. She repeated the action, earning just enough opening to give them access.

She reached her hand into the dark room beyond the door, patting along the interior wall. A pleased smile appeared on her face, followed by a loud crack and the dim light of a warming florescent.

The room contained the tattered remains of a small commercial kitchen. A six-burner range dating to the 1970s dominated one wall, while a built-in refrigerator unit sat as a partially disassembled ghost of its former self, and the contents of a row of grease-encrusted cabinets lay emptied on the floor, creating a minefield of pots, pans and broken dishes.

"I'm guessing this is a restaurant," he remarked in sarcasm as he stepped over the piles of abandoned cookware.

"That and a hotel," she answered as she crossed the room toward a faded green door opposite the one they entered.

"The one I inherited?" he asked in clarification as he followed.

She paused as she reached the door. "The one and only," she replied. "Before the railroad shut down passenger service in the 1960s, a good number of people stayed the night here. They might have been making a long trip across the country and needed a break, or sometimes were even here for business. This town hasn't always been as dead as it is now."

The shabby green door led into inky blackness, where she disappeared for a moment before another crack and sizzle of electricity flooded the space with a greenish glow. A crusty layer of dust coated the room and dark stains from water damage and mold marred the light blue wallpaper and bright red carpeting. Tired diner booths with ripped red Naugahyde upholstery and chipped Formica tables lined the walls, while a hoard of tables and chairs sat piled in rusty steampunk fashion in one corner.

"It's seen better days," she reflected.

He furrowed his brow as he gave the filthy, ransacked space a probing glance. "Even cleaned up I think it would look like a dive," he responded.

In a disapproving manner, she cocked her head at him. "You've got to look past the decay a little bit. And the 1970s décor, please look past that, because when you see my kitchen you'll be able comment on the same problem. Look at the ceiling and ignore the florescent lights. See the plasterwork up there? There used to be three small chandeliers in here. Look at the woodwork on the walls, the old wood panels. They've been painted a nasty color but look beyond the cosmetic. This place was once a classy spot, at least for White Oak City."

He took a deep breath and gave the space another look. Indeed, there survived a shadow of the grace and beauty it once possessed. "Why did you bring me here?" he asked, intuiting the choice as deliberate. "Don't I own several condemned buildings you could have taken me to?"

The second question elicited a chuckle. "There is a reason why I brought you here," she confessed. "In the history of this town a lot of wonderful memories were made here. My high school graduation dinner was here; before it was reduced to the cheap diner you see the ruins of now. The old Citizen's Bank was officially established in this room. The railroad announced its plans to discontinue passenger service here. A day that proved both tragic and historic for the town. It was in this room that your grandfather proposed to your grandmother."

A lump built in his throat. He gave the room another look, this time with the mist of nostalgia glazing his eyes. "It's been a special place for a lot of people then," he reflected. "It makes me sad I can't see what it looked like before it became this mess."

A smile emerged on her face. "It is a special place, one of many in this little town. To those of us that love and live in this town, these places are pretty important. Many of us hold out hope for a miracle coming in and reinvigorating our little town square; so, it doesn't become reduced to parking lots and strip malls." Her voice halted, and with a wave of her hand, she motioned for him to follow her deeper into the derelict building.

A large set of partially ajar pocket doors led them into a central hallway, a space that in its prime undoubtedly impressed visitors. And even though the overhead lighting no longer worked, enough glow filtered in from the dining room to allow him a glimpse of the elaborate wainscoting, which reflected a past era of prosperity. At one end of the hall stood the grand staircase, clad in mahogany and finished out with age-tarnished brass handrails. Opposite the stairs sat the main entrance, which though boarded up on the exterior remained largely intact on the inside, a massive set of doors, each with intricate leaded-glass windows, and a fan transom above, all framed into place with mahogany millwork.

She urged along again, through a set of doors opposite the dining room. Despite the dwindling amount of light that managed in from the room across the hall, the defining characteristics of the former hotel lobby shined through, even as remnants of the plaster ceiling, more on the floor than above, crunched beneath his feet.

He pounded his fist on the marble top front desk, which remained sturdy even as the room around it had slipped into ruin.

"This was still a bustling place when I was a child," she remarked as she stepped near an arrangement of two chairs and a sofa, only the shapes visible beneath grimy dust covers. "By the time I came back after college and started teaching, it was only open four months a year, and then but in hope of cashing in on the Ozark Mountains tourist fad created by television shows like *The Beverly Hillbillies.* Branson grew and pulled interest away from these little towns and people stopped coming altogether."

He closed his eyes and imagined it full of people, with well-polished woodwork gleaming under the soft electric glow of the chandeliers. For a moment the image thrived in his mind, but the musty smell of the place quickly muted his imagination. "I think I'm ready to leave," he announced, repressing a faint urge to vomit. "The smell is getting to be a bit much for me."

With a nod of understanding, she turned and led him back through the building, turning off the light switches behind them as they passed through the dining room and kitchen.

Back outside, and thankful for being rid of the smell of damp and decay, he closed his eyes and took a deep breath. But a man's voice, yelling "watch out," pulled him from his mental pause just in time to avoid being hit by a little girl on a bicycle.

The skid of tire on gravel clouded Ryan's ears as the man pulled his own bicycle to a sudden stop a few feet away. "I'm sorry Mrs. Donovan," the man apologized, while motioning with his hand for the little girl to come to him. "We weren't expecting anyone to be back here." Unease tempered the man's smile. He was somewhere in his late twenties and wore a model's face. "Say you're sorry, Annie," he instructed the girl with a firm, though not angry voice.

With big, soulful eyes the child looked over to Ryan and Connie. She whimpered before mumbling, "I'm sorry," with a trembling bottom lip. "I'm sorry, Daddy," she added as she turned toward the man.

A consoling smile emerged on his face as he patted her head. "That's good," he told her.

Despite the man's politeness, Connie glared at him. Though, for the girl, she offered a kind smile. "It's all right, Annie, and thank you for apologizing," she responded in a chipper voice. "How old are you now?"

The girl's face lit up. "I turned six two weeks ago," she announced.

"You're getting old, aren't you?" Connie gleefully answered. "I remember when your daddy was six."

The girl beamed back in response, but did not say anything more.

Connie's smile faded, and her glare returned. "This is Ryan Shipley," she announced in a stern voice. "He's Dean's grandson."

Ryan leaned forward and shook the man's hand.

"I'm Justin Miller," the man replied. "Sorry about your grandpa."

Ryan nodded and glanced back to Connie, who continued to glare at the increasingly nervous man.

"I guess we need to get moving," Justin murmured as he avoided additional eye contact. "It was nice to see you Mrs. Donovan and good to meet you Ryan."

A silence held between them as Ryan and Connie watched the man and child take off on their bicycles down the alley.

"You didn't seem to like him too much," Ryan remarked as they began walking back in the direction of his grandfather's house.

Connie's face displayed a coldness he did not expect of her. "I don't," she growled. "He's the main reason my son moved so far away."

Ryan turned back down the alley to see if he could still spot the man and girl, but he couldn't. "What happened?" he asked, though he knew he was prying.

"It's a long story, but let's say he lied about something," she answered. "I'll give you all the sordid details some other time."

CHAPTER 5

In a period of two hours on the day after his grandfather's funeral, Ryan's calls to nearly a dozen real estate agents provided a bitter education. In tones ranging from condescending to sympathetic, he learned of the disadvantage that came in owning a dozen or so buildings in a largely vacant business district. What he initially saw as a headache of an inheritance now more closely resembled an inoperable tumor. Even the interest he found with a couple of agents for some of his more marketable properties struck him as underwhelming. Such as the $90,000 they estimated as an asking price for his grandfather's house. A low price for such a well-kept home, but then White Oak City held limited opportunities.

A grumbling in his stomach, and a simmering headache, finally brought his phone calls to a pause. He had unintentionally skipped breakfast, and as a result his tone with the real estate agents had grown increasingly unpleasant. The clock on the mantel showed 2:30; but he realized it sat unwound. He checked his phone. Fifteen minutes until noon, an ideal time to break for lunch.

A fair amount of funeral food remained in the refrigerator, but the thought of holing himself up in the house all day depressed him. He needed a break, if only a short one, to interact with people in some way other than on the phone. The diner on the square could provide an escape, if only for a few minutes.

A needed invigoration hit him as he stepped out into the summer air, a subtle breeze brushed against his cheek as he surveyed the day from the front porch. His grandfather's Buick waited in the driveway, ready for use. But on a day this pleasant, using a car to drive a mere three or four blocks seemed ridiculous, so he locked the front door and took off on foot, ready for his first real one-on-one experience with the town.

—

Sandwiched in the middle of the block on the west side of the square, the diner lived in a building landmarked by an electric blue paint scheme and a faded white and red striped aluminum awning. Stepping inside, Ryan came face-to-face with the busy Saturday lunch crowd, a gathering of people that rivaled in size the attendance at his grandfather's funeral. Far from the polished and over-conceptualized design of most chain restaurants, it contained a basic atmosphere of dingy yellow walls and well-worn Formica tabletops.

A waitress, bustling between tables, paused by him for a second and glibly informed him to take a seat where he could find one. He glanced around the room, not a vacant table in sight and only one stool open at the end of the lunch counter beside an obese man wearing excessively soiled overalls. The leftovers in the refrigerator suddenly seemed appealing, but inquiring eyes from across the room rushed him, leaving him to claim the vacant stool, perching himself on the edge opposite the man whose girth intruded upon it.

The waitress buzzed by again, dropping a tattered menu on the counter and offering assurance that she would return in a minute. He let out a sigh of unease and placed his right foot firmly on the ground, helping him balance on the stool.

The menu, sticky to the touch and scented of maple syrup, offered decidedly country selections, each one a comfort food of rural lore. His eyes had fallen on three options, when the tap of a finger on his shoulder intruded, sending an involuntary twitch through his body. He shifted on his right foot, turning just enough to see the face of his offender. A sense of recognition ran through his mind, but with the dozens of introductions in the last few days, he failed to narrow it down. "We've met, right?" he asked.

The young man smiled. "I'm Mark. I work at the newspaper."

Ryan felt his cheeks warm, embarrassed for not remembering the face and name of someone who technically worked for him.

"Join us for lunch," Mark said, pointing toward a table behind him. "We haven't ordered yet."

Past the smiling young man, Ryan spotted Glo's glowering face. The older man did not seem pleased with the situation. "Thanks, but I was just going to grab something to go and head back to my grandfather's house," Ryan stammered out, anxiety building in his gut. "There's a lot of paperwork and pictures to go through before I go back to Los Angeles."

The smile on Mark's face faded into disappointment.

"You know, I've been going through that stuff for the last two days. I need a break," Ryan said in reverse, worried about insulting someone else.

"Come sit with us," Mark again requested, the smile returned to his face. "Glo's my great uncle, so sometimes we have lunch together on Saturdays."

—

"I heard you're trying to sell everything," Glo loudly announced as the waitress cleared their empty lunch plates. "Had two real estate agents I know call and tell me you're trying to put the entire town on the market."

The eyes and ears of the entire restaurant seemed to twitch in their direction.

"Not the whole town," Ryan protested. "Just some of my grandfather's property."

At first, Glo offered no response, sitting and glaring at his new employer. "To a lot of people in this town, it's more than a few old buildings," he finally responded. "You don't appreciate what life is like in a town like this."

Ryan took a deep breath as his face warmed with flush. "It's not my plan to hurt or upset anybody," he replied. "I can't see myself living here. What would I do in a town like this? And if I'm not going to live here, why should I own these buildings, especially buildings sitting empty and falling apart? Someone needs to buy them and open businesses."

Glo's wrinkled face grew pale as he clenched his jaw. "Don't you think we want that too?" he barked. "There are dozens of towns around here that once had downtowns as pretty as this one, but they were empty too, so they tore them down and left empty lots or put up cheap, ugly steel buildings. There's no character left in those towns and there's so much here, and it must be worth something. Your grandfather knew it. That's why he bought them. That's why he put new roofs on them and covered up windows, to keep them from being damaged and broken into. He worked hard to keep this downtown together."

A sharp pain pulsed behind Ryan's right eye. He hated being lectured, especially by someone who did not know him. He wanted to tell Glo to shut up, and that if he cared so much about the buildings he should buy them and stop complaining. But that would not help. It would only push the knife deeper in the wound for this old man, an unhappy person clinging to the past and ignoring the present.

—

Stepping outside, Ryan fought the urge to take off running across the park. Running from Glo and Mark and the unpleasant conversation that soured lunch. But polite manners and a struggling sense of responsibility forbade it, so he stayed close as they walked down the sidewalk and then crossed the intersection by the old hotel. He glanced up at the building and thought of what he had seen inside and again tried to imagine it in its prime, when the downtown filled with shoppers and visitors on Saturday mornings. But looking around the vacant square, how could one recognize it as Saturday from any other day of the week?

Glo and Mark stopped as they reached the *Times-Gazette's* office, with Ryan continuing with a nod of good afternoon.

"Where are you going?" Glo yelled at him.

With a slight jerk, Ryan stopped and turned around to face the two, both waiting on the sidewalk in front of the office. "My grandfather's house, to go through paperwork," he answered.

"Are you?" Glo responded. "You own a newspaper and we've got a lot to get done today."

What did that mean? Ryan thought to himself. Even though he had inherited the newspaper, he did not work at it. "I wouldn't know what to do," he whined, hoping to dissuade the old man. "Back home I only write articles and edit city desk copy."

Glo shook his head, irritation in his eyes. "You can edit," he growled. "That's exactly what we need you to do. We have content. It needs editing."

Ryan's mind raced in search of a stronger excuse, but nothing plausible came. "I can help for a little while," he relented after an intense staring contest between the two. "How long will this take?"

A smile emerged within the heavy folds of Glo's face. "Not more than twelve or thirteen hours," he declared before stepping inside the door.

—

The crackling of a radio tuned to NPR echoed in the room, but beyond that it held a complete absence of voices or workday hum. Is this some sort of joke? Ryan wondered as he followed Glo and Mark to the newsroom. "Where's everyone else?" he asked.

"We don't work every Saturday, and when we do it's usually just me and the boy here; and of course your grandpa was always with us, before he passed," Glo responded before sitting down behind his desk. "Mark, hand him those correspondents' columns to edit."

The teenager picked up a green folder and handed it to Ryan. Sun-faded with age and worn at the fold nearly into two pieces, Ryan cautiously opened it, trying to prevent its frayed spine from tearing.

Inside he found several sheets of paper, most of them typed and printed, but one, on lined yellow notepaper, stood out. The text, scrawled in messy and uneven handwriting, seemed more child than adult. "Why isn't this typed?" he asked as he held the page up for Mark and Glo to see.

"Grace doesn't know how to type," Mark happily replied. "Ebetta will type it into the computer on Monday."

What a backwoods operation, Ryan thought to himself. Labeled across the top, it read "Ramblings from the Crossing," though part of that title evidently remained in the notepad from which the writer had torn the page. And the rest presented as a mangled mess of cursive and print, much of it nearly illegible. A less professional submission likely did not exist.

"Let me know if you have any questions," Mark commented in an unintentionally ironic way.

"Thanks," Ryan grumbled in an annoyed tone. "Where should I do this at?"

Glo peered up, his eyes fiery with disapproval. "Your office," he moaned. "Where else would you do it?"

The door of the shabby office, which for so long belonged to his grandfather, seemed enveloped in gloom. His stomach turned at the thought of spending the next few hours in the room, where the stale smell of decades of dust and coffee permeated the air. "I'd rather do it out here," he replied in an almost pleading tone.

"Suit yourself." Glo groaned while throwing his hands up in exasperation. "Sit at Mary Beth's desk across from Mark."

While most of the desks in the room held clutter in the form of disheveled stacks of papers and even dirty cups and dishes, Mary Beth's appeared clean and tidy by comparison, each drawer neatly labeled of its contents. Ryan dropped the green folder on the desk, feeling for a second a tinge of guilt for sullying her personal space, but consoled himself by promising to leave it as neat as he'd found it. He flipped the folder open, again revealing the yellow sheet of notepaper, and snatched a red pen from a cup on the desk.

The first sentence contained two misspellings and the improper use of a comma. It felt as if some sort of hazing for the new guy. He glanced around the room, hoping for some sort of nonverbal cue for him to throw it away. But Mark offered a goofy, albeit encouraging smile, while Glo consciously ignored the events of a mere ten feet away.

Seeing no reprieve, he let out a defeated sigh and continued editing the column. After the fourth paragraph, he looked back up from the page. It hemorrhaged red with rewrites and edits. "This is horrible," he proclaimed in a loud voice.

"What is?" Mark asked.

"This woman's submission," he answered, feeling his blood pressure rise in frustration. "In the first three paragraphs all she talks about is her and her family going to Branson. The next paragraph is about how one of her neighbors bought a new pick-up truck. I've tried to rewrite it to make it at least sound decent, but who really gives a damn about all this?"

The comments aroused interest from Glo, who looked up from his own work with a creepy smile. "I wouldn't rewrite that if I was you," the old man advised. "Grace won't like that at all. We correct the spelling and grammar errors and make sure people know what she's talking about."

Ryan's brow furrowed in frustration. "Aren't we supposed to care about decent writing?" he protested. "I can't let this run. I'll leave in all the asinine stuff she talks about, but I've got to make it sound better. Why do you run crap like this anyway?"

Mark glanced up, a startled look on his face. "You've got to run it," he whined. "People get mad if it's not there. That's how everyone gets their names in the paper. Your grandpa always called it the chicken dinner news because it's the most basic news of the community. The little things people like to talk about and know."

Ryan turned to Glo for confirmation. "Is that true? We run these things so people can basically gossip and eavesdrop on each other?" he asked, condescension obvious in his tone.

With a scowl on his face, Glo leaned back in his chair and eyed the two younger men. "That's one way of looking at it," he answered with a subtle nod. "But, it's your paper now. Feel free to take them out."

A surprised gasp escaped Mark as he gaped at Glo in disbelief. The older man responded with a reassuring nod.

"I won't take them out, but I'm going to rewrite them so they're at least publishable," Ryan stubbornly announced, feeling the need to assert authority in the matter, despite now doubting his own judgment.

"It's your newspaper," Glo commented with a flourish of his right hand before returning his attention to his computer.

The old man's gesture and tone gave Ryan trepidation, as if he sensed failure. But poor content remained inexcusable, so he continued editing.

—

"All right kids, it's time to go," Glo announced as it neared 4:00 p.m. He then turned toward Ryan and added, "See you both Monday."

Ryan's temples throbbed, his blood pressure spiking in response to the old man's insinuation that he worked at the newspaper. He wanted to scream out in frustration, but Mark's disarming smile from across the desk quelled his anger. "Is there anything to do around here on a Saturday night?" he asked the teenager, feeling disheartened by the prospect of going back to his grandfather's house and sifting through more papers and photographs. "Is there a bar or a club or something?"

Mark's eyes lit up. "You could go to the Old Barn."

"What's that?" Ryan asked, feeling hesitant at the venue's name.

"It's two miles north of town on RR highway," Mark explained. "They have a live band and dancing and food. They even have beer."

With a loud clearing of his throat, Glo shot Mark a look of fatherly concern. "How would you know, have you ever been there?" he questioned the boy.

A pink blush flooded Mark's cheeks. "Of course not," he responded in a tone that made the validity questionable. "I'm not old enough, but my sister told me about it."

Glo winked at the boy and then turned to Ryan. "That's your only option unless you want to drive to Springfield. But, this is technically a dry county, so you have to purchase an annual membership for the Old Barn."

The archaic practice of local prohibition lived on. Ryan had heard it remained stubbornly in place in some rural communities, and Decatur County seemed as good a candidate as any. "Why does an annual membership make alcohol okay?" he asked.

"There's a loophole, alcohol can't be sold here, except for beer in a private club," Glo explained. "Even then, you aren't technically paying for the beer. You're paying a service fee for them to serve it to you."

Such a blatant loophole, but if it meant access to a beer, Ryan would give it a try. "There's a first time for everything," he conceded. "What type of band do they have, pop, country, rock?"

"Bluegrass," Mark responded with a wide-eyed gaze.

CHAPTER 6

"NAME," A PLUMP MIDDLE-AGED WOMAN asked him. Sitting behind a table inside the Old Barn's entrance, she wore an exhausted expression, one that seemed not so much from a long day as a weary life.

"Ryan Shipley," he answered.

The woman lazily thumbed through the pages attached to her clipboard. "Are you a member?" she questioned him, an annoyed frown on her face.

"Not yet. What do I need to do?" he replied, feeling his skin warm with embarrassment.

She shook her head in mild frustration and pulled a second clipboard out from under the table and handed it to him. "It's twenty-five dollars. Fill out this form and bring it, your ID, and money back to me."

The corner of the clipboard jabbed into the palm of his hand as he grabbed it. He felt as a scolded puppy and was inclined to drop the clipboard back on the table and slip out the door. But that held potential for an even more embarrassing scene.

The form asked little: name, age, address, phone and email, in addition to a place for signing his name and leaving the date. His warehouse club membership required more invasive information.

With apathetic motion, the woman crosschecked his ID with the form and then checked off a couple of boxes on a separate sheet. She then pulled out a piece of paper the size of a business card and filled it out before handing it to him. "That's your membership card," she said. "But it's not necessary to bring it with you when you come back. Your name'll be on the membership list for a year after tonight."

The card's thin stock nearly crumpled in his hand. He thanked her and stepped into the main hall, a large open space with lots of tables for sitting, a stage with a band in the process of setting up, and a large rough pine dance floor that spread from the base of the stage out into center of the room. He had expected the patrons decked out in western wear, with boots and denim, cowboy hats and plaid shirts, but most were in ball caps and t-shirts, more than a few of the latter emblazoned with the newly emerged "Make American Great Again" mantra.

Anxiety flooded him. He saw a room full of people, but not a single familiar face. He had made a mistake in coming. He swung back around toward the door, hoping his exit would not be too obvious, but in the process bumped into a woman with vibrant green and pink eye shadow and a poof of over-teased hair. "I'm so sorry," he stammered.

"It's all right sweetie, don't I recognize you?" she remarked in a slow Southern drawl. "Is this your first time here?"

He nervously smiled. "Yes. I didn't figure it'd be so busy this early."

A spirited laugh escaped her coral painted lips. "Oh sweetie, we're always busy on Saturday nights," she answered with a big smile. "What's your name?"

He muttered, more than spoke, the answer.

"You're Dean's grandson," she exclaimed with the extra emphasis of putting her right hand to her ample chest. "I'm so sorry about your granddad. He was a real fine person, always so friendly and willing to lend a helping hand. He knew both my husband and me since we were little. I went to the funeral, but I didn't go to the cemetery or his house afterward, or we would have met sooner."

Another conversation centered on his grandfather, but even this was better than him awkwardly standing in a corner alone. "That's all right," he replied. "There were plenty of people at the house. I think any more and it would have become a block party."

She nodded in thoughtful understanding. "Makes sense." She patted him on the shoulder. "He was one of a kind. I'm Leona, so you let me know if you need anything. My husband and I own this rocking little place."

He thanked her as she stepped away, leaving him alone again, but at least feeling somewhat more confident. He moved deeper into the hall. A few hundred patrons filled it so far, some sitting at tables, others getting food and drinks, and a handful out on the dance floor moving along to the recorded music playing through the sound system.

A beer would at least give him something to do, instead of standing around like a creeper. He walked to the small bar tucked in one corner and ordered a Bud Light, the only alternative being Budweiser.

He took a drink of the beer. It offered his mouth a refreshing cleanse, easing his anxiety as he weaved between the crowd of locals. An empty table for two waited near the stage, a good place from which to people watch.

Loud cheering and the thumping of boots against the floor erupted to welcome the first chords from the band's guitar. With lively blue eyes, a statuesque lead singer stepped to center stage, her free-hanging silver hair swinging in rhythm with the music. And despite an age past its prime, and a willowy and almost fragile frame, from her resonated a soulful and strong voice, not a tremor or waver in it, belting out Johnny Cash's "Ring of Fire."

The enchantment of the moment, sweetened in its mood by the beer in his hand and the murmur of dozens of voices softly singing in unison around him, awakened something spiritual in him. But then a flash of chestnut hair distracted him. For confidently striding across the dance floor came a strikingly beautiful young woman, her hair cascading off her shoulders while vibrant vermillion lipstick contrasted with her fair skin.

Beneath the table, Ryan's knees nervously rattled against each other. He desired her to come near, but also feared it. Her walk showed boldness, while the way her green dress clung to her body, in a flattering though not skimpy manner, aroused him. He turned his head from one side to the other. She continued to draw near, her green eyes focused on him. He pushed his attention back to the band, but her footsteps came to a halt beside him, and he glanced over to see her pulling out the empty chair. "I-I-I'm Ryan," he sputtered while jerking up onto his feet.

"Good evening," she greeted the crowd, which promptly repeated "good evening" back to her. She nodded in gratitude. "I hope everyone is having a wonderful night and we're happy as always to see every one of you. Now, I'd like to dedicate a song to a dear member of our town that we lost this last week. He was really the heart and soul of White Oak City."

The warmth of Olivia's hand bled through Ryan's shirt and eased his tense shoulders. "She's talking about your grandpa," she murmured.

The affection, both in the room and against his skin, deepened his abashment for being dismissive of the town. On the stage, music started and the woman began to croon. Her voice became breathy as she intoned the vision of a dying town, its commerce gone and legacies dead. She asked for its memory to be cherished, even once its importance had vanished.

Tension built in Ryan's chest as he watched Olivia, humming and nodding in beat with the music. "What is this, I've never heard this song before?" he asked, again feeling the outsider.

She turned toward him and smiled. "A song your grandfather liked," she answered.

"It's about a town like this?"

"There are lots of towns like this," she said. "They ebb and flow with time. People move in, people move out."

He lowered his head and listened, pressing his chin against his chest. "It's the musical definition of the term melancholy."

Her green eyes gazed into his, seeming to sense his emotions. "Yes, and nostalgia and sentimentality, but I don't think there's anything wrong with occasionally feeling melancholy or sentimental. I think when we're being sentimental, it might be because we're focusing on the good things in life, special people and unique things that once made us happy. Some people just want money and instant gratification. Look at people who go to casinos all the time or buy lottery tickets. They're hung up on the instant win, so they throw away what they earned or already have."

The singer repeated the song's refrain, touching on the pain of losing people and places you love, while reminding her listeners to hold onto the love they have now. Eyes glistened across the room as heads nodded to the beat. Goodbye, she repeated again and again as she sang the verses, a send-off for a town or a town's human institutions.

The beer, the song, the stress of the last few days, and now a pretty girl sitting across from him, all overwhelmed his emotions. He breathed deeply, feeling moistness along the lower lid of his right eye. He clamped his jaw and took another deep breath. The impulse for tears waned, so he glanced away from her to brush the wetness from his eye. A knowing smile greeted him when he turned back.

"How're you doing?" she asked in a tender tone.

He faked obliviousness, shrugging his shoulders. "I'm fine."

Her eyes held a starry look. "I don't know," she remarked while continuing to gaze at him. "I thought you might have gotten choked up a little by that song and thinking about your grandpa."

With an arch of his eyebrows, he mustered a slightly insulted look. "It's a nice song and everything," he mumbled in protest. "But I wasn't getting choked up about anything."

She smiled and nodded in a way that implied understanding, without belief.

The next few hours took on a leisurely pace, as the two talked as if they alone occupied the room, letting the music and crowd fade into the background. She shared her story; reared in White Oak City but attending the University of Missouri and finishing a doctorate in sociology with an emphasis on cultural demographics. With more than a touch of regret in her voice, she admitted that although she loved White Oak City, it held no place for her. So before long, she too would leave.

CHAPTER 7

SOMEWHERE IN THE DISTANCE sounded a rhythmic buzzing. Bees, Ryan supposed, his mind focusing away from a frivolous parade of slumber's subconscious thoughts. Too controlled and mechanical, he reasoned, despite his consciousness' continued impediment of his own sleep. Again, it came, "buzz, buzz, buzz," followed by a pause, then another "buzz, buzz, buzz." His bottom lip quivered with uncertainty as the stagnant fog in his mind finally began to lift. But even with his slumber behind him, the buzzing remained. A fragment of reality slipped into his dreams, and an alert that a visitor waited at the front door.

With a slow push of his arms, Ryan lifted himself into a sitting position, fully aware of the need to answer the door, but hopeful the caller would grow restless and leave before he completed the act. He glanced down to the floor, expecting to see his pants left in a slothful pile beside the bed. But their absence, combined with another trio of buzzes echoing up from below, inspired queasiness in his gut. A loud belch erupted from him, offering relief from the nausea; and a wiggle of his backside confirmed he still wore the missing pair of pants.

At a sluggish pace, he descended the stairs, grasping the banister firmly for balance and hoping the buzzing would end before he arrived at the door, allowing him to return to the soft, recuperative comfort of the bed. But through the door's window, he spotted Connie's recognizable outline, confirming the futility of his wish for continued slumber.

"I didn't figure you'd be ready for church," she announced as she stepped inside. "That's why I came an hour early."

He offered a puzzled frown in response. "I'm not going to church," he replied. "I never go to church."

She patted his shoulder and shared a motherly smile. "Your aunt Rosemary told me you said you'd come to church and sit with her today," she reminded him. "So, I volunteered to give you a ride. I tried calling earlier this morning, but you didn't answer." She pats his shoulder again, an extra helping of guilt to motivate him.

Like a wounded animal, he limped behind her as she walked toward the kitchen. "I must have left my phone in the car last night. I had it out when I was getting Olivia's number."

Connie opened the pantry door and fished out a can of coffee and a loaf of bread. "You met our Olivia," she remarked with an approving smile.

"I did," he answered, feeling embarrassed for mentioning the girl.

"She's a real nice young lady," Connie responded in a voice both boastful and protective. "I figured you two would hit it off if you met."

—

"Checking out the competition?" Ryan, now showered and dressed, asked as he sat across the kitchen table from Connie. She had the Sunday edition of the daily newspaper out of Springfield spread out on the table in front of her.

"Oh, they're not competition," she responded with a subtle laugh. "Did you know that daily newspapers have struggled much more because of electronic media than the little community ones like ours? People trust something that is truly a part of their neighborhood more than they do what comes from a larger corporate-owned newspaper." She pushed the A section across the table to him.

"Where does your son live?" he queried as he perused the front page.

The wet glint emerged in her eye. "He lives in Chicago," she answered in a voice slightly strained. "He likes it well enough, but I wish he was closer. I also wish he would come down and visit me more often. It's usually me going to see him."

He contemplated the scenario, agreeing that being visited in Chicago easily beat making regular trips to White Oak City. "Chicago's a bit more exciting," he remarked in the son's favor. "But why doesn't he visit here?"

She sighed and then closed the B section. "He got beat up here; that's why he left," she replied, her face lined with angst. "He doesn't like to come back and be reminded about that, or possibly even see the people who did it. At least that's what I suspect."

His body grew tense, eager to learn details, but worried the answers would further taint his opinion of the town. "Why'd he get beat up?" he asked after a pause, his curiosity outweighing his more altruistic side.

"Because he's gay," Connie bluntly stated.

An angry red flash filled his thoughts. "He got beat up 'because he's gay,'" he repeated in a tense voice, enraged by the thought of the bigoted act.

"By his best friend, no less," she continued. "This is a small town with a lot of small-minded people in it. Most of them are very nice, but they can be unenlightened at the same time, which causes headaches."

Silence hung in the room as he reflected on what he just heard. "What a horrible friend," he finally replied. "Beating him up because he's gay. He can't help it that he's gay."

The last statement brought ease to her face. "I'm glad to hear you say that. The best friend who beat him up had also been fooling around with him. But someone else noticed my son looking at his friend in a more than friend's way. So, this third boy told the best friend what he saw, and the best friend decided the only way he could hide was to beat up my son."

He leaned back in his chair, shaking his head. "That's horrible," he grumbled. "Was it seriously more important to protect his image than to protect his best friend? That's deplorable."

She nodded. "He was scared. In towns like this it's hard to be gay, at least openly gay, and it was even harder ten years ago. In fact, the best friend's still in the closet and you've even met him."

"When?" he asked, surprised by the revelation.

"Remember the young man and little girl riding bikes in the alley behind Commercial Street the afternoon of your grandfather's funeral," she revealed.

Ryan smacked his hand against the top of the table, causing its legs to rattle against the linoleum floor. "That was him?" he exclaimed. "No wonder you were giving him the look of death the entire time."

Pleased malice showed on her face. "He's actually in the middle of a divorce right now," she explained through a smile. "His wife left him for another man, and of course everyone around here is feeling sorry for him. But I've heard one of the reasons she left was because their sex life was nonexistent. Which, knowing what I know, is no surprise."

—

The church sanctuary, echoing with a subtle piano instrumental, felt larger for the Sunday morning ritual than days earlier for his grandfather's service. For while it had filled for the funeral, barely a third of its seats now held occupants. Though, to Ryan's benefit, the sparseness made it easy to spot his aunt, in the third pew from the front on the left side of the aisle, her cottony poof of white hair unmistakable.

Marvin and his wife sat on Rosemary's left, while an empty space remained on her right. "I'm glad you were able to make it," she remarked in greeting as he arrived at the pew.

"It's my pleasure," he responded with a smile, and following her gaze sat in the vacant spot.

She patted his hand and let out a pleased sigh. "I heard you met Olivia last night."

"It seems like everyone knows everything in this town," he replied, his forehead warming with embarrassment.

"Just about," she answered. She then took off her glasses and wiped them clean with a lace handkerchief pulled from her purse.

The notes of the pianist's hymn faded as the hangdog face of the pastor appeared at the pulpit. He motioned with his hand for any standing congregants to take their seats, resulting in a brief shuffling as they complied.

In his three decades of life, Ryan had attended only a handful of church services. But even with that limited experience in religious rites, the basic and traditional tone of this one, compared to other encounters, seemed more authentic.

One churchgoing experience, during his college years, included in its regular Sunday morning program, which seemed a more fitting description than to call it a service, a full-scale rock band accented with some mini pyrotechnics. The production left him with a shallow impression of modern faith, worship that relied on sensationalism to fill seats.

But here, the church functioned on a humbler scale, a single clergyman leading both the preaching and the singing; and two women, one tiny and elderly with her gray hair pulled back in a bun and the other heavy-set and middle-aged, playing the piano and organ respectively.

And the preacher's dry wit and earnest theology was unexpectedly compelling. In fact, Ryan's attention became so engaged in the sermon on the life of Esther, that more than half the service passed before he noticed Olivia on the opposite side of the aisle. Her playful wink, in response to his discovery, bloomed a pink flush on his face.

—

"Young Mr. Shipley," a deep, breathy voice intoned as Ryan and his aunt emerged from the front doors of the church. The preacher, standing outside the doors to greet his parishioners as they exited, offered a broad smile. "I'm glad you could join us this morning," he remarked before offering a compassionate nod to Rosemary. "I hope we can expect to see you again next week."

The comment made Ryan uneasy—as if it prefaced a round of vigorous *proselytizing*. Is this when the fanatic lays his hand on the unbeliever's forehead and screams at him to repent? "I'm not really sure how long I'll be around," he replied. "I have a lot of my grandfather's affairs to take care of, but I'm hoping to do it as quickly as possible."

The preacher's eyes remained calm. No religious furor came showering down; instead only a slow nod. "You don't plan on staying with us permanently?" he asked.

Dampness beaded on Ryan's brow. "Um, well, no. I mean, I've got a job and a life back in California," he answered, hoping his vagueness would end the conversation.

"I see," the pastor responded. "I'm sorry to hear that. You see, old towns like this need some fresh blood in them from time to time."

Ryan anxiously glanced to his side, hoping to segue the conversation to his aunt. But she no longer stood near, as looking down the stairs he spotted Marvin helping her into a car. He looked back to the pastor, who nodded again before mercifully proceeding to the next in line.

Rushing down the steps in an awkward manner, Ryan felt sick to his stomach, not only because of the preacher's remarks, but also his weak response. How does one tell an entire town he has no sympathy for its plight and no intention to help?

But those negative thoughts vanished as he met Olivia, who waited near the bottom of the steps. She wore a pale green summer dress as she nonchalantly leaned against a waist-high brick wall.

"How did you feel when you woke up this morning?" she asked him. "I hope you weren't too tired or hungover?"

"Tired yes, hungover no," he answered, only fibbing on the second part.

She nodded, but her eyes seem unconvinced. "Do you want a ride to your aunt Rosemary's house?"

"Why would I be going to her house?" he asked in reply.

"Well, I'm having dinner there," Olivia explained. "And I was told by her that you'll be there as well."

His smile faded a little, though it did not vanish. "I guess I do need that ride then," he responded. "Though, I didn't know I'd been invited for dinner until now."

—

As much as his grandfather's house exemplified Craftsman architecture of the early twentieth century, his aunt Rosemary's home did likewise for the 1960s ranch. The single-story structure's broad, light gray brick façade and dark shingled, low-profile roofline defined upper-middle-class comfort of a half-century past. And though dated in style, it remained impeccably maintained both structurally and through the care provided to its yard, lush with trees, bushes and flowers.

Ryan pressed the glowing doorbell button, embedded in a small brass box to the right of an over-sized set of oak doors, stained the color of Spanish olives. Somewhere inside the house responded the tinkling of a melodic chime. He leaned close to the door, straining to hear an approach on the opposite side. The sounds of garbled speech and footsteps reached him, and then the door to his left opened, with Marvin's genial face peering out.

They walked down a short, tiled entry hall and into a sunken living room that featured a massive gray brick wall, which drastically overpowered its purpose, that of a surround for a relatively modest fireplace. Gray wood-grain paneling covered the room's remaining three walls and floor-to-ceiling windows offered a picturesque view of the lawn. Even the furniture, as pristine as it remained, tied back more to the time of the home's construction than the current day.

"Ryan, is that you?" he heard his aunt's voice call out from a doorway to his right.

"Yes, it is," he replied as he and Olivia followed the sound of her voice to the kitchen.

She buzzed around the room, hands-on in every aspect of the dinner's preparations, despite Liddy's hustling to slow her down.

"It's about ready," his aunt remarked, her voice sounding almost fragile. "You and Olivia can set the table."

—

"Will you be staying here permanently?" Rosemary asked in a polite, though intense tone, once the dinner had been eaten.

A dry lump clogged Ryan's throat, forcing him to swallow hard. "I haven't decided yet what I'm going to do," he answered, hoping it served as the least upsetting response. "I have my entire life back in LA, but now I have all of this."

Across the table, Olivia's eyes narrow. "I thought you told me you were going to sell everything and go back to California," she interjected, an impish smile on her face.

"I ... I haven't made any final decisions on that yet," he protested, feeling betrayed by the younger woman's comment.

"Sell everything?" his aunt echoed, her skin ashen. "What about your house and the farm?"

Ryan nervously glanced around the table, hoping for support from Marvin or Liddy, but only inquisitive stares greeted him. "I haven't made any final decisions," he argued, hoping to subdue the topic. "I might sell some things, like some of the buildings downtown, and keep the rest."

"You probably couldn't give most of those buildings away," Marvin remarked. "Some of them need a lot of work and even the ones that don't, who would you find that would want to open a business there? The commercial district has shifted out to the highway."

Apart from Ryan, everyone nodded in agreement. "There must be something that can be done with them," he countered. "They really are beautiful buildings, like that bank or the old hotel."

The faintest pink reemerged on Rosemary's cheeks. "Maybe you should do it," she commented. "You could take the initiative and save our downtown."

A nervous jitter developed in Ryan's right hand, the result of feeling cornered. He took a deep breath. "How can I do that? I know nothing about economic development or historic preservation."

"You can learn that; you're a smart young man," Rosemary answered. "You just need to try. There are plenty of little towns that have been able to breathe some life into their downtowns. Maybe we could get some antique stores or little specialty shops to come in here. We could be a destination for people to visit, like Eureka Springs."

The potential challenges seemed overwhelming in his mind. "Maybe all I want to do is go back to Los Angeles," he admitted. "Sell everything and go home."

Rosemary straightened her frail body into a stern posture. "This is your home," she retorted. "You might not realize it, but this was your home long before you were born. It'll only cease to be your home when neither of us is here or care any longer."

The declaration left the table in silence. He glanced around at the faces surrounding him, evading the upset eyes of the elderly woman. "Why does it have to be up to me?" he broke the silence by asking.

"Because that's what fate does, it does the choosing, not you," Rosemary replied.

—

"Your aunt means well," Olivia remarked as she and Ryan walked down the side of the street. "She's like so many people in this town. They see you as some sort of low-grade savior. Even if you did little more than keep the newspaper running, that'd be enough. But, I'd be lying if I didn't tell you that some have grander hopes than that."

He glanced back to his aunt's house, where they had left her with Marvin and Liddy in an after-dinner game of pitch. "Why can't they back off just a little?" he barked in a frustrated tone as he kicked at loose gravel. "I never asked for this responsibility they all believe belongs to me. It doesn't belong to me. It belonged to my grandfather. But now they're trying to insist it's mine too."

Olivia paused in her step and brushed her brown hair from her eyes. "All I'm saying is you should look at what you have to gain by staying here," she offered.

With a deep breath, he filed her comment away in the back of his mind for later consideration, and, to his relief, she abandoned the subject. Instead she shared gossipy stories about the people who lived in the houses they passed, revealing a beauty parlor's wealth of information on local love affairs and the teenagers who got in trouble for smoking pot.

Nearly an hour passed before they returned to his aunt's house, finding Marvin and Liddy's car gone and the front door slightly ajar. Ryan knocked loudly and paused to hear a response. From down the hallway, his aunt's voice called for them to come inside.

Seated in an overstuffed blue chair in a well-lit corner of the living room, Rosemary rested with her crochet work in her lap and her thin legs and slipper-clad feet resting on a matching ottoman. She smiled at them. "There you are," she remarked and moved her handiwork to the arm of the chair. "I hope you had a nice walk."

Olivia crouched down beside the chair and took one of Rosemary's frail hands into her own. "Yes, we did," she responded in a soothing voice.

A sentimental smile rose on Rosemary's face and she motioned for Ryan to come near. "Sit on the end of the sofa nearest me. I have some pictures I want to show you."

He sat as directed and watched as his aunt grabbed a tattered shoebox from the small table between them. Old photos, from black and white to vivid Kodachrome, filled the box to the point of overflowing.

She dug into it, quickly scanning through the images. Then, after a pause of recognition, she pulled out a faded image and held it up for him to see. It revealed a family of seven, all in vintage apparel. A suited father in a distinguished Edwardian armchair as his wife stood beside him in a long dark dress, with a baby swaddled in white held snuggly in her right arm. Four more children gathered closely around, ranging in age from about two to early teens, three girls, all in long white dresses with bows in their hair, and a lanky boy, the oldest, standing on the opposite side of the father's chair from the mother. "That's me." She pointed to the cluster of three girls.

"Which one?" he asked as he took the photo from her.

"The middle one," she answered. "I was about four when that photo was taken. It would have been 1928 or so."

He looked closely at the frozen face of the young girl and then back at the elderly woman beside him, her attention returned to the contents of the shoebox. Similarities did exist, pouting lips and lively eyes, but for positive identification he trusted her word. Flipping the photo over, he found a listing of the names of the people in it, along with their ages at the time taken.

"I label all my photos," she proudly announced. "When I inherited my mother's photos, none of them were labeled and it took me years to figure out who everyone was. A couple of them I never did figure out for sure." She reached her trembling right hand out toward him and he returned the photo to her. "The boy who's standing is your great-grandfather and the two adults are my parents, so your great-great-grandparents," she explained and then paused. "I'm the only one still living."

His heart ached as he reexamined the photo, now held with reverence in his aunt's hand. Somewhere in the defined chin and narrow nose of the teenage boy, he glimpsed his own father. "Who was it that committed suicide?" he asked, feeling instantly ashamed for his insensitivity.

"That was George, the baby," she explained, followed by a deep sigh. The photo, still clutched in her hand, sagged down into her lap. "My time is near though," she added, and then placed it in the shoebox.

"What do you mean?" he asked.

An unintentionally patronizing smile appeared on her face. "I can't live forever, and I feel it's going to be sooner, rather than later," she remarked in an accepting voice.

"Why would you think that?" he asked, though recognizing it as likely true.

"I'm ready for it," she answered. "I'm not going to fight it when it comes, and, to be honest, I look forward to it."

The last statement surprised him. Who treated death as a welcome visitor? Who, outside of the clinically depressed or emotionally disturbed, saw the end of their life as a welcome event?

"Young people," she remarked, likely in response to the agape look on his face. "You can't understand how someone could say that. But I've lived my life, with all the good and the bad that comes with it. I've done my part. You haven't done yours yet, have you?"

The idea of doing one's part seemed ambiguous, but he knew he did not welcome death. "I still want to live, if that's what you mean," he replied, feeling it the sincerest answer he could offer.

"It seems so black and white when you're young," she murmured while reaching her hands out toward Ryan on her right and Olivia on her left. "It's not about being alive. It's about doing your part. Maybe your part is here in this town."

CHAPTER 8

THE HARSH STRAINS of an electronic "1812 Overture" jarred Ryan awake. The music, a questionable ringtone choice for his cellphone, left him floundering for a moment as he broke from his sleep. With a blind grasp, he clutched the still-ringing phone and swung it close to his bleary eyes. An unfamiliar number flashed on the screen, though it carried the local area code and the time of 8:45 a.m. He considered sending it to voicemail, but the chance of it being Olivia vetoed that, so he took a deep breath and held it to his ear.

"Where's the editor?" Glo's raspy voice snapped through the receiver.

"What do you mean?" Ryan asked, his head still dull from the night's rest.

"It's your job to get the week started," the old man responded. "Your grandfather was always the first one here on Monday mornings."

Ryan rolled his eyes, relieved Glo could not see his frustrated reaction. "All right, I'll be there in a few minutes," he answered, unwilling to start the day arguing. "But I've got errands to take care of, so I won't be there the whole day."

Glo offered a displeased snort. "You're the boss," he sarcastically declared before hanging up.

—

Forty-five minutes passed between the demanding phone call and Ryan arriving at the newspaper office, where he discovered the entire staff, minus the two high school students, already deep into the week's work. He could offer no complaints to their work ethic, but the fact that all talking ceased as he stepped inside the door left him wary. Throughout his life, he found himself overly sensitive to what others said or thought of him, so to note a sudden hush descending on a room at his entrance reinforced his apprehensions.

"All right," Glo growled, not giving Ryan a chance to get settled. "It's time for our staff meeting. Ebetta, put the phone on hold for a few minutes so you and Connie can join us."

In a practiced cadence, the staff assembled into an awkwardly shaped ring in the middle of the newsroom. Creating a noisy rustling as people and chairs pulled into alignment. Then, silence took hold, and every eye focused on Ryan.

"Is the editor going to start this or not?" Glo demanded, his index finger waving in Ryan's direction.

"You mean me?" Ryan responded, his shrill tone revealing shock toward the older man's insistence.

"That's right," Glo shot back.

A painful pressure bloomed behind Ryan's right eye. He opened his mouth, a poorly planned and overly defensive diatribe ready to pour out, but Connie spoke first. "All right, all right," she interjected. "Glo, you know he doesn't know how we operate here. Can't you lead this meeting?"

Glo shot her a sour look, but obligingly took charge, going down a printed checklist of updates on the details of everything in the works, from articles and advertising to obituaries and photography. The old man freely offered help to those with questions and provided detailed explanations of the processes, which Ryan accepted as being for his benefit.

Once he completed the rundown, Glo, wearing a sly smile, turned to Ryan. "The town council meeting is Wednesday; you're going to cover that," he directed more than asked.

Another responsibility revealed. "What do you mean?" Ryan inquired in a falsely naïve tone. An approach he hoped would lower expectations.

"The town council meeting. Your grandfather always covered it," Glo replied.

The implication from the old grouch seemed to be designating a permanent role. "I can do that," Ryan mumbled, while four chairs away, Connie smiled.

"Ok," Glo quipped, nodding his head in approval. "It'll need to be a write-up on whether they all attend and what the issues are. If something that sounds important happens, it might need a separate article. But ask me to make sure."

Ryan nodded in response, a subconscious smile curving up at the ends of his mouth. He bit down on the insides of his cheeks, trying to suppress it, fearing it made him appear weak. But his restraint instead led to a feeling of guilt for not being genuine because for the first time in a week he did not feel like a complete outsider.

—

As it neared 3:00 p.m., Ryan laid aside his editing and returned his attention to his original plan for the day, calling more real estate agents about his inherited properties. And for the next two hours, he delivered his pitch on the town's potential and how his business and properties sat ripe for a revival. But with uncanny replication, each of the eight agents he reached discounted his assertions and excused themselves from his proposition, claiming the work not worth the reward.

His mind whirled with anxiety as he called a ninth. But finally, a slightly obliging, though far from ecstatic, answer returned, along with arrangements for an in-town visit a week from Saturday. One bite, as uncertain as it might yet turn out, gave him the opportunity to relax. He sunk back deep into his chair and took on a broad smile, which greeted Connie when she stepped into his office at a quarter to five, wearing an even bigger one on her face.

"Guess what," she said.

"I don't know," he responded while shaking his head. "Did someone come in and offer me a $1,000,000 for the entire town?"

The wisecrack failed to impress, as Connie cocked her head slightly to the side and disapprovingly glared at him.

"Yeah, I didn't figure." He rolled his eyes.

"My son is coming to visit," she announced in a voice firm enough to bring his attention back from tongue-in-cheek pronouncements. "It's the first time he'll have been here in five years." An aura of happiness seemed to emanate off her.

"I'm glad to hear that," Ryan offered with a sincere smile. "I know you miss him."

Connie nodded. "I do talk to him nearly every day on the phone, but it's different from being near him," she said, a hint of melancholy in her voice. "Anyway, he'll be here a week from this coming Saturday. You'll get to meet him."

Ryan felt a tinge of offense in the fact that Connie assumed he would still be around, despite knowing his plans with the real estate agent ensured it. "If I'm still here, I'd love to meet him," he replied, feeling a pang of guilt for his insincerity.

"I don't think there's much you can do about that," she countered. "Even if you manage to sell the whole town tomorrow, I don't think you'll be able to get out of here that quickly."

—

The town hall's main corridor held an ominous atmosphere, eerily silent and vacant, despite the fact the town council meeting would start in twenty minutes. Ryan imagined several other ways he'd rather be spending his Wednesday night. But here he lingered, absorbing the scene around him, from dark woodwork and dim glass globe ceiling lights to a shabby arrangement of framed black-and-white photos haphazardly hanging on one of the yellowed and cracked plaster walls.

He stepped close to the wall and peered at the dusty portraits, feeling slightly unsettled by the scowls of the old men who stared back. *Who are they?* he wondered. But looking above, he read in faded hand-lettering "Mayors of White Oak City." A murmur of understanding escaped him, and he returned his attention to the honored images, universally rigid and lacking diversity. One face drew his attention. It held a familiarity that seemed like more than chance. With his thumb, he rubbed the grime off the glass. The name below the photo identified the man as his great-great-grandfather Eugene Shipley. Dates of service, some seventy-five years past, came with it and then an inscription, much like the one on the cornerstone, denoting his role in the town hall's building.

His ancestors appeared inescapable. He took a step back from the pictures and swung around, now facing a battered set of double doors, above which he spotted another hand-lettered sign. Though faded with age and marred by peeling paint, enough remained to identify the doors as the entrance to the town council chamber. He walked up to them and bit down on his lip.

To his relief, beyond the doors he discovered a cheerier space than the connecting hall. A crisp robin egg blue paint coated the walls and natural light from large windows that looked out on Commercial Street flooded in the room. And though surprisingly small for the seat of the town's government, the layout served its purpose. It included a dais for the council at the front and five short rows of benches, with a center aisle dividing them into two columns, enough to fit about fifty spectators.

He sat down in the second row, and for ten minutes sat alone, wondering if he had arrived at the right place. Finally, a handful of others arrived, including mayoral widow Lenora Bayridge, who insisted on smearing lipstick across his cheeks in a clumsy attempt at sophistication. By the scheduled start time, the crowd had reached fifteen, including two officials sitting at a small table to the right of the dais, a middle-aged female town clerk, and an ancient man with a battered placard perched in front of him that identified him as the town attorney.

At five minutes past the scheduled start time, the grating squeak of an unoiled door brought a silence to the room's murmur, and the members of the council emerged onto the dais. Ryan felt a vague familiarity with a few of the faces, leaving him to place them among the army of mourners he had met since his arrival. And he noted an eerie consistency between them and the photographs in the hall, every member being male, white and well past forty, signaling a lingering cultural rigidity. For while the lack of an ethnic minority did not surprise him, as he could not recall seeing a single non-white person since arriving in White Oak City, it felt odd that in the twenty-first century, even here, not a single woman sat on the council.

Without opening formality, the blustery-faced mayor proceeded with the agenda in an apathetic manner. In doing so it confirmed for Ryan that regardless of the size of a city, topics like increasing water fees, rezoning property, and dealing with other municipal housekeeping needs held as the prime responsibilities of elected officials. In fact, based on the mediocrity of the initial topics, he wrote off the council meeting as a source for additional articles. At least he did until the nasally voice of the town clerk began to read out the details of a proposed poultry processing plant.

Grumbling began nearly as the first words left her mouth, and it quickly progressed to a roar. Members of the council and several residents in attendance noisily quipped in protest of the project. And they advanced to sharp and vile shouts as she explained that as it would be built outside the town on unincorporated property, the council held few legal options for opposing its construction. The audible anger in the room boiled, forcing the clerk to pause for a moment so the contempt could quiet enough for her to offer up a toothless official recourse. Namely submitting opinions either for or against it to the county planning commission, a commission she explained that held limited authority of its own as the county had little in the way of zoning restrictions.

Sporting a quivering lower lip, the pudgy mayor glared at the clerk, waiting for her to finish her report. "I'm all for the economic side of it," he fired off, sending a shower of spit out of his mouth with the enunciation of each word. "But I think all of us realize that this type of facility, with more than 750 people showing up out of who knows where, is bound to bring all sorts of wetbacks to our town."

An audible gasp escaped Ryan in response to the mayor's use of the slur. Even in a rural area like this, it seemed a term like that would be an inappropriate choice for an elected official. At its best the mayor's remark showed ignorance, and at its worst racism.

Shiny streaks glistened down the mayor's forehead as his fervent mood drove the sweat out of him. "We have a nice little town here and it's no secret what happens when you have large numbers of those people move into a community," he blustered. "They bring crime, drugs and public drunkenness. We won't even be able to understand what they're saying. Mr. Trump can't become president and build his wall soon enough for me."

Queasiness bubbled in Ryan's gut, as he worried that he alone found the mayor's commentary offensive. Glancing around the room, he spotted several heads nodding in unison with the diatribe. But then, if only minimally restoring his faith, he spotted one woman, two rows behind him, rolling her eyes as the mayor's rant continued.

The mayor's speech continued and digressed from talking about the impact of a Hispanic influx on the community to slanderously offering a general condemnation of the morals of the entire ethnicity. Then, in a seemingly grand pronouncement, with the passion of a preacher on Sunday morning he jumped to his feet behind the dais and proclaimed that Mexicans "don't bathe like us" and always seem to have a "peculiar odor."

If not for his duty as a journalist to stay and report on the situation, Ryan felt the urge to stand and walk out of the meeting in disgust.

As the mayor stood there, red faced and eyes bulging, another council member broke in with a calming, though somewhat condescending admonishment for the city's highest official. "Now Reggie," the man commented while leaning back in his chair and looking up at the still standing man. "Don't you think you're getting a little too worked up about this?"

The mayor rolled his fat red face to one side, facing his colleague. "No, I don't," he answered with a scowl. "As a matter of fact, I don't think you're getting worked up enough. We're facing the potential destruction of our way of life."

The council member, a thin, middle-aged man with a large nose and short white hair, did not become angry or aggressive in retort. Instead, he continued to calmly make his point. "Our way of life was destroyed forty-five years ago when passenger rail service ended here, and then it got worse thirty-five years ago when we allowed zoning to let businesses build cheap little metal structures along the highway and abandon the downtown. Only a handful of businesses are left downtown, which used to be our pride and joy. This plant and these 'people' may be our salvation. Wouldn't it be nice to see people working and shopping here again? Sure, we might have to learn a few phrases of Spanish, or better yet, teach them a few of English, but I wouldn't be opposed to a good Mexican restaurant opening on Commercial Street. Maybe our new, young newspaper editor even has a building they can rent for it." The man winked in Ryan's direction.

Though the mayor's complexion paled during the council member's interlude, it quickly regained its fiery undertones once the white-haired man finished. "These people are going to be illegal; they'll be breaking the law by being here," he exploded in another angry rant. "I can deal with them if they're legal, but they won't be, mark my words. Just look at all these immigration raids they do. It'll be the same here."

Ryan's right hand cramped as he rushed in taking notes of the banter between the two officials. He flexed his hand for a few seconds before continuing his recording of the political parody playing out in front of him. For a moment, he imagined a flash of disapproval from Glo in relation to so publicly airing the mayor's behavior, but Ryan didn't care. This deserved top billing in the week's newspaper, regardless of what anyone in the office might think.

But finally, following a few additional digressions and more bemoaning by the mayor, the heated topic ended. That is, once the white-haired councilman laid out the facts for a third time, explaining the county left it nearly impossible to kill construction of the plant and that outside of submitting comments to that next layer of local government, the council could do nothing legally to prevent it.

Agitated by the intensity of his own assertions, the mayor slammed his fist against the top of the dais and demanded they move on to the next item on the agenda. Then, in an unfazed voice, perhaps trained by similar theatrics in the past, the town clerk progressed down the schedule and read through the specifications of a request for the rezoning of the old high school property to high-density residential and an accompanying request for an all-inclusive construction permit for the lot.

The anger of the previous topic ebbed from the eyes of those in the room. Curiosity turned to a man with thinning hair and a prominent beer gut as he confidently strode up the center aisle and stopped at the podium that faced the dais. His demeanor seemed out of character for the town, as he carried an air of arrogance and aloofness.

The mayor's beady eyes stared down at the man. "Are you Calvin Woodmont?" he asked, squinting to make a better assessment.

"That's me, Mr. Mayor," the man responded in a high-pitched voice that carried an unusually clear and suspect Southern accent.

The mayor paused for a moment while continuing to glare. "What's your plan for the old high school?" he asked as he thumbed through the related paperwork in an unfocused manner.

At first the man said nothing, then he offered a wide smile. "I'm gonna put apartments there," he answered, self-assuredly slapping his hand against the top of the podium.

The cramp in Ryan's own hand throbbed.

"What makes you think we need apartments?" the mayor questioned, a squeak emanating from his chair as he adjusted his girth.

The man shook his head in a feigned disbelief and let out a high-pitched chuckle. "When this chicken plant is built, those people got to live somewhere," he explained. "I figure I'll be ahead of the curve."

A flush of beet red enlivened the mayor's face at the mention of the plant, but it quickly faded to a lighter cherry tone, followed by him nodding his head in an almost solemn understanding. "How many apartments are you planning on putting there?" he asked.

With his eyes squinted nearly shut, Woodmont mused on the question for a moment. "I figure I can fit in eight and still have some parking and yard area."

The mayor's eyes rolled upward in his head as he mentally worked out the number. But his face showed no enlightenment; instead confusion dimmed his eyes. "Eight," he repeated. "That's a big building; it's two stories not including the basement and there's something like twenty classrooms."

For the first time since confidently marching up to the podium, unease appeared on Woodmont's face. "I'm going to tear that building down," he answered in a slow voice, now void of its drawl. Gasps of disbelief sounded in the room, leaving Woodmont to respond with a hesitant smile. "I've got a contract on modular buildings that will be trucked down here and put together as a single-story apartment complex," he explained, gripping the sides of the podium with his hands. "They're all two bedrooms, except two that have three bedrooms."

Horror and insult flared up on the mayor's face, as if watching his own child being ripped apart by wolves. Similar reactions followed on the faces of two of the other council members, though the white-haired member appeared unfazed.

"You're going to tear down the high school," the mayor stammered out, his face the hue of a well-aged merlot.

Woodmont responded with a cocky nod. "My plan is to have the lot cleared in two weeks and I can get the modulars in place within the next month."

Nostalgic tears filled the mayor's eyes, his body shaking with emotion. "You'll not be tearing that building down," he lashed out. "That building is the heart of this town. My father went there. I went there. My son and daughter went there. It will not be torn down."

"I own that building," Woodmont retorted. "I have the right to do with my property as I please. Either you give me the permit, so I can tear it down, or I'll allow it to sit there and rot and become an eyesore like every other building in this town."

Anger throbbed on the mayor's crimson face, his mouth sputtering to make a denouncement. But then, with a slight gesture of his hand, the white-haired councilman signaled to the mayor to hold his tongue. "How did you come to own that property?" the councilman asked in a genial manner. "After the school moved out, I thought the property reverted to the Benson family in Springfield, who originally donated the land for the school a century ago."

Woodmont nodded. "I purchased it from Esther Benson Clyde's heirs last fall, after she passed away. She'd been friends with my aunt. So, I knew about the property."

The fat, quivering lips of the mayor started mouthing again, anxious to unleash another torrent of anger, but the white-haired councilman again silenced him. "Are you sure there's nothing we can say to persuade you to refrain from tearing down the school?" the councilman asked with a forceful though unemotional manner. "Possibly find an alternative buyer or work with you to help renovate the existing structure into apartments."

Any pretense of politeness vanished from Woodmont's composure as he loudly snorted in response to the question. "I appreciate your interest in working with me," he responded. "But, you see, I've already purchased those modular units. The building has to come down."

Unfazed, the councilman nodded in acknowledgement. "Perhaps we can help you find some alternative land to put those on," he suggested. "I know several lots around town that would work."

Woodmont's smarmy smile faded into a deep scowl, which seemed to add an extra ten years to his appearance. "No," he insisted. "They'll be going on my property, right down at the end of this street. That's where I want them to go. Your nostalgia for some rotting old building means nothing to me and if you try to prevent it, I'll sue this town and you know I'm well within my rights to do so."

The white-haired councilman's ambivalent expression remained unchanged as he again politely nodded. "It's true, our zoning laws are not overly strict in these matters. But you should have done your homework. That building is registered by the state as a historic structure. This was done when Esther Clyde regained ownership of it, as she wanted it protected. As such, there's a mandatory four-month review and waiting period before we can approve the demolition of it. So now, are you sure you don't want us to help you in any of the ways I've described?"

Woodmont's complexion turned a shade of red that rivaled even the deep burgundy of the mayor's. "You small-town, ignorant bureaucrats," the flustered developer started. "How dare you try to hold up the only progress your little hole in the ground's seen in years. Either you get the ball moving on my plan tonight, or you'll be hearing from my lawyers."

Without pause, the white-haired councilman leaned back in his chair and smiled. "If you think that's necessary," he replied.

The pages of Ryan's notebook had nearly filled, as he scribbled in large letters at a furious pace to keep up with the exchange unfolding in front of him. In less than an hour, this one meeting shifted from apathetic to heated, while producing two prominent and unexpected articles for the front page.

Other council members weighed in, each of them railing against Woodmont for threatening to destroy their perceived heritage. But finally, after reaching his limit of aggressive questioning, Woodmont, with a loud cough of irritation, turned his back to the dais and stomped out of the chamber, bemoaning his displeasure as he exited. The stomping of his feet remaining audible as the council voted to deny his request.

With the night's excitement having peaked, the energy in the room fizzled as the council dredged through its remaining trivial matters, losing half its attendees as the clock approached 11:00 p.m. Finally, a half hour more past that, the sound of the mayor's gavel brought the meeting to a close, and an exhausted Ryan leapt to his feet, eager for the exit. But that initial rush of freedom betrayed him, as a tap on his shoulder brought him to a halt, only a few feet from his escape.

Turning around, the smiling face of the white-haired councilman greeted him. "I'm Beau LeSalle." The man extended his hand in greeting. "I apologize for not introducing myself at your grandfather's funeral."

Ryan reached out his own hand to meet the pleasantry. "That's all right," he responded as they shook. "I met so many people that day I doubt I'd have remembered you anyway. Tell me, are all the council meetings this exciting?"

Beau smiled and let out a chuckle. "No, chicken plants and tearing down buildings do not show up on our agenda as a regular rule. Or do you just mean Reggie?"

Another name Ryan did not know. "Reggie?" he asked.

"Reggie, the mayor. He's really a nice man. He just gets carried away sometimes. For instance, I don't think he really has anything against Latinos, I think he's afraid to see his hometown change."

Ryan nodded, though he remained offended by the nonchalant way the mayor blurted out stereotypes as undisputed facts. "Looking around, I'd say this town needs some change," he said.

Beau concurred. "It does. I'm working on him. It's just going to take a while. Now, as far as the school goes, our little town may be dead, but we're awfully proud of our old buildings. Did you know that except for a single fire in the mid-1990s, we've managed to preserve every building in our downtown since 1964? Your grandfather's hope was that someday, because of our diligence in preserving our beautiful old buildings, we might be able to cash in on them."

Ryan pulled his notebook back out of his bag and took notes on Beau's narrative, which touched on Ryan's grandfather buying buildings starting in the 1970s to save them from destruction. Beau also shared his stake in the issue, as he owned a hardware store on the eastern side of the square, opposite the café. It was a family business on his wife's side that dated back three generations. They also owned several additional buildings around the square, with the total structures owned by them and Ryan accounting for roughly fifty percent of the buildings in the historic district, though claiming only a thirty-five percent occupancy rate.

"That's one reason why I'm not so opposed to the chicken plant," Beau conceded. "I wouldn't mind renting out some of those store fronts for small businesses."

The intersection of historic preservation and economic benefit seemed a logical one, and one where Ryan saw that Beau's outlook paralleled his own. Perhaps an ally existed in the town. But the arrival of the ruddy-faced mayor interrupted their discussion.

A dried film of sweat crusted Reggie's forehead, though his flesh resumed a healthy pink tone instead of the pulsing red from a half an hour earlier. "I see you've met Dean's grandson," the mayor loudly remarked to Beau.

"Just a moment ago," he answered. "Seems like a nice boy. We were talking about all the old buildings he and I own in this town."

Reggie nodded in the posture of a lopsided bobble-head. "We're thankful your grandfather saved them," the mayor extolled while making a wide sweep of his right arm. "There was a clown back in the '90s who wanted to level the entire western block. He said it would get rid of an eyesore and invite people back into town. Personally, I don't mind a little eyesore when it has leaded glass windows and pressed tin ceilings in it. I may be a fool about a lot of things, but I know you couldn't build a little town like this again. And I hope you're gonna work with us to make it grand again. I know that's what your grandfather hoped."

—

The greenish glow of the streetlamps offered only a dim illumination of the buildings that crowded Commercial Street, mercifully fading out worn features and years of neglect so obvious during the day. For with the scars of time receded into the shadows, the dramatic peaks and ornamentation that crowned them emerged as something more profound, as if a veiled trove of fine art inertly hid here, only accessible once the sun set.

As Ryan strolled through the tattered heart of the town, the humid summer air wrapped itself around him like a damp blanket. And nostalgia for a place still new to him swept through his mind, his eyes darting across elaborate rooflines set against a star-pocked sky.

Absorbed in these affectionate thoughts, he blindly stepped past Olivia as she waited for him on a bench in front of the newspaper office. But with a soft stroke of her hand, she pulled him out of his contemplations. "Howdy stranger," she remarked in greeting. "How was your first town council meeting?"

He paused in an open-mouthed stupor, his mind shifting in introspection from the edifices looming around him to the glowing face in front of him. He smiled and stepped close to her. "It was interesting," he answered, feeling awkward in his latent response. "That mayor is something else. He's racist for one thing, and on top of that he has a very hard time maintaining his composure."

A knowing grin emerged on her face as she cocked her head slightly to the right, her hair swaying back and forth. "That's Reggie all right," she agreed. "He's really a nice man. He just has a hard time looking at the bigger picture and he doesn't like change."

Ryan sighed in resignation at the now repetitive excuse and reached out with his right hand, taking hold of her left.

"Why don't you walk me home?" she suggested as she accepted his gesture. "We can talk more about our dysfunctional mayor on the way."

They strolled through the darkened residential avenues laying north of Commercial Street, with Ryan trusting her lead into the unfamiliar neighborhood. At first, they shared a silence, but after a few moments his thoughts drifted back to the council meeting. He returned to the topic of the mayor, quickly dropping his reserved tone and railing against the man's response and attitude regarding both the poultry plant and the background of the assumed workforce.

She leaned against him, her lilac scent tickling his nose. "I mostly agree with you," she said. "I think it may be the only way left that this town can rebuild itself. But, these people've lived here a long time and their parents and their parents' parents lived here before them. They're afraid, for the most part, that their traditions would be destroyed. Granted, some of them are genuinely racist, but I think most are only scared of seeing the life they're comfortable with change."

He paused in his step as he thought about the comment, which ignited his own raw emotions. "How can they be comfortable?" he protested. "The downtown is dying, or actually, it's already dead. I'd think the comfort had been sucked out when half of the buildings here were boarded up and abandoned."

His mouth slacked open, as he prepared to further press his point of view. Though at this moment it felt pointless, as she held no opposition to his beliefs.

The evening dew hung heavy, beading up on blades, leaves, and petals and soaking into his skin like butter melting into a warm piece of toast. But despite the discomfort the swampy humidity caused, this time of evening became almost magical with the flickering of lightning bugs, a surreal and rose-colored mystique.

"You think the people of this town can realize this is the opportunity they need to save it?" he asked after a few moments, forgetting his decision to end the conversation.

She smiled. "I think it's going to be tough for them to realize this is what needs to happen so this can be a living town again. There needs to be a strong civic leader to get the ball rolling. One with an open mind that'll help guide them, though patiently, in learning how to be an accepting town, a town that wants to survive, even if that means change. I guess that person isn't going to be you though because you need to get back to Los Angeles."

His body jerked as it came to a sudden stop, his hand pulling away from her as she kept moving. He stood still, knowingly now and manipulatively, waiting to see if she too stopped. But she did not, so he jogged forward to catch her. "You know, if I didn't know any better, I'd say this is a guilt trip you're trying to lay on me," he complained.

A mischievous glint appeared in her eye. "But you know better, so that's not what it is," she countered.

CHAPTER 9

"I CAN'T BELIEVE THEY'D LET someone tear down the school," Mandy exclaimed. "So much of our history is in it."

The door had not even shut behind Ryan when the first protest reached his ears. He stepped past the reception area and into the newsroom where a dozen eyes stared into him. He glanced over to the door of his grandfather's office, wishing for the shelter it offered. "It didn't sound to me like the town council wants it torn down," he said. "And they said a historic designation on the building could delay it."

Wearing a stern look of defiance, Ebetta shook her head in a patronizing way. "Ohhhh, I know they'll try," she declared in the honeyed voice of a pre-school teacher. "I know old Reggie'll fight for it. His family's been here almost as long as yours."

Something in the woman's pronouncement, whether tone or verse, gave Ryan unease. "Anyway, I think the big story from last night is the chicken processing plant," he declared.

Ebetta responded with a wet clucking of her tongue. "You are right, yes you are," she proclaimed, her head bobbing up and down in agreement. "We need to keep that out of here. We don't want those people coming into this town and turning it into some sort of a Tijuana."

His stomach twisted in discomfort and he glanced around the room, hoping for protest or concern, but received only blank stares. "Well," he cautiously started. "I think there are a lot of aspects concerning it. It might help the town."

Ebetta's jaw dropped, her eyes bulging. "Help the town?" she scornfully echoed. "Oh sweetie, you don't understand. I know you're used to a big city where everybody ignores each other. But that's not how it is here. Those people would come in and ruin the place."

Again, he eyed the room. This must offend someone, he thought. But no one appeared inclined to push back against the comments. Glo leaned back in his chair, observing the situation while pretending to read the Springfield daily.

Ebetta's judgmental eye seared into him, as though discovering a deep shame in him—liberal leanings.

"It would be wise to use the newspaper to thoroughly examine all the pluses and minuses of the issue," he reasoned in a hesitant manner, his mouth feeling dry as sand. "That's the job of a newspaper after all, to present all the facts."

She stepped close and lightly patted him on the shoulder. "Of course, honey," she responded with condescension. "But there aren't any pluses in this. I think you should stick with saving our schoolhouse. And we can hope Donald Trump will take care of the rest."

A hint of blood soured Ryan's mouth as he bit down on his tongue, a preventative tactic for avoiding a smarmy retort.

Unobservant of his restraint, Ebetta flashed an insincere smile before turning away and trotting off to her desk. He stood frozen, stunned by the discussion, even angry at himself for not stepping toe-to-toe with her.

The sounds of typing and chatter reemerged, offering him the opportunity to escape into the privacy of the editor's office. But, as he walked past Glo's desk, the pensive look on the old man's face brought him to a stop. "What do you think?" Ryan asked in a low tone.

The old man, still pretending to read the newspaper, did not look up, but his eyebrows rose in consideration. "About what?"

Ryan took in a deep breath of air and let out a soft sigh. "About the lead story," he prodded.

A slight ruffling of the newspaper's pages suggested more thought. "You're the editor. That's up to you."

Was the curmudgeon really stonewalling him, or encouraging him to stand on his own feet and decide? "Fine," Ryan barked. "The lead story is the chicken plant and the second story the schoolhouse."

Glo nodded his approval, though so slight Ryan almost missed it. "Maybe a couple stories about the chicken plant," the old man suggested.

"You're right," Ryan agreed. "One on the plant itself, what the economic benefit would be, and one on reactions to it and maybe even one on what's happened in other towns where similar facilities have been built. And, I think, an editorial too."

Again, Glo nodded. "What'll the editorial say?"

Ryan already knew what he wanted it to say. He wanted to scold the town for being distrustful of new people, but he worried about where that might lead. "It'll depend on what the articles uncover," he answered, feeling disingenuous in his reply.

Glo smiled. "No, it won't," he countered. "You already know what it'll say. And it'll be in support of it."

The old man read him like a book. "Why do you assume that?" Ryan asked.

The pages of the newspaper again rustled as Glo moved to a new section. "Because it would be a good thing and because you know it would and so did your grandfather," he replied in a quiet, yet stern voice. "We talked about it a couple months ago, when the company first made the announcement."

Anxiety crept into Ryan's gut. "I don't think they'll agree, the staff or the town," he reasoned.

Glo's eyes lifted off the pages of the newspaper and burned into him. "It doesn't matter if they do," he grumbled. "What matters is that you write it from a strong, educated stance. One they won't be able to rip apart easily. That's what your job is. No one's gonna quit because they disagree with an editorial. They may argue with you about it, in fact I can guarantee Ebetta will. She might even call you a bad name, but you'll live with it."

A feeling of relief began to dampen the anxiety. "Thanks for the advice," Ryan responded with genuine gratitude.

—

His eyes, scouring for the most miniscule of errors, scanned through the printed proof of the front page, while across the room Barry prepared to upload the finished electronic files of the newspaper to the printer in Springfield. The issue could rival that of most major dailies, Ryan thought as he took a deep breath, hoping his first edition as editor would not be the paper's downfall. He nodded to Barry to hit send.

Despite his doubt concerning his place in the town, Ryan felt confident in the work and leadership he contributed. Articles on both the chicken plant and old school building held space on the front page; and inside, two editorials, one on each of those heated topics, and both authored by Ryan, argued for the benefit of both.

Intuition told him that the editorial in favor of the chicken plant would attract significant lightning. And while the notion of goodwill toward newcomers served as a key message in the editorial's argument, its primary focus concerned what the commercial endeavor would mean for the local economy. Once he'd completed writing it, he thoroughly vetted it with Glo and then passed it around to the staff, where it found a few detractors, but surprisingly received support from the majority. Though Ebetta, to no one's surprise, spoke in excessively acidic terms against it.

But even the editorial on the schoolhouse drew mixed reviews. While most of the staff agreed with preserving it if possible, Jerry dissented with the thought of the town having enough other issues to worry about without focusing on saving one empty building. To Ryan's relief, the protest lacked the vitriolic edge that Ebetta unleashed on him for the first editorial, and it likewise proved unsuccessful in swaying him.

Then, as the day, and week, drew to a close, the exhausted staff filtered out of the office early, leaving Ryan alone in the cavernous space. He felt awkward there, despite owning the building, like a child that had wandered someplace his mother warned him not to go. A ridiculous thought he realized, so he brushed it out of his mind, or at least from the forefront. He took the opportunity to better absorb the place, drifting to the clutter of old photos and front pages that, in cheap and dinged frames, weighted down the cracked plaster walls. Staid faces stared back at him from the faded snapshots and yellowed newsprint, offering little visual recognition, but the names attached to each felt increasingly familiar. A meager few he recognized as having met, while most of his familiarity encompassed passing references, such as engraved prestige in the capstones of the town's buildings or monikers carved into the cemetery's headstones.

A tapping on glass broke his attention from the town's pictorial and written history, as encapsulated in this faded vestige of the fourth estate. It felt like an intrusion, but catching sight of Olivia's smiling face through the glass of the front door brought an immediate reversal. His heart sped up and the excitement he felt left the tips of his fingers tingling.

"Howdy stranger," she greeted him with an exaggerated twang as he pulled the door open. "I figured I'd find you here."

His giddiness spilled out in a broad smile. "Well," he responded, feeling his face flush with embarrassment. "I'm glad you came to find me." The casualness of her attire distracted him, a light blue sleeveless top and cut-off jean, her hair pulled back into a neat ponytail.

She offered a playful wink as she stepped past him and into the reception area. "I know you are," she replied.

Feeling a rush of lightheaded excitement, Ryan took hold of her hand and led her to the red sofa, where he motioned for her to sit. She eased her pose up onto one hip, anticipating him sitting beside her, but instead of joining her, he flashed a nervous smile and jaunted off to his office to grab copies of the editorials.

—

"There's irony here," Olivia remarked, after having read the editorials.

Anxious warmth rooted out through Ryan's body, blossoming through his skin as drops of perspiration. "What do you mean?" he asked, his tone uneasy.

But her face betrayed no concern, only a hit of curiosity in the slight arch of her eyebrows. "It reads, on the surface, as a contradictory pair of views," she explained. "On one hand you argue change is good and needed, and on the other you advocate for the preservation of an obsolete building that, as it is, has no practical purpose."

For a second, a slight feeling of offense bubbled up in him in response to her questioning. But it fizzled faster than it frothed as he recognized in her tone the distinct nuance of support.

"Can't you argue for progress and at the same time champion preservation of an important piece of the town's history?" he countered.

She nodded and slipped her right arm around his left. "I agree with everything you've written. But you're not set in your ways about what this town's future is. Many of your readers are. They want it to be like it was in 1950 forever, but it's already not like that. And they need to know there are ways to make it better, even if it can't be like it once was."

The warmth of her arm intertwined with his offered both comfort and excitement. His heart fluttered, and his fingers tingled. Should he respond to her or give into his more romantic nature and kiss her. "I know," he answered, choosing the safer option. "But, when I walk around this town, I see tired, old, decaying buildings. I know that's not what my grandfather wanted."

Olivia's arm tightened against his, pulling his body closer to hers. "You want to have some fun?" she asked him, a broad grin on her face.

A tender, yet softly erotic vision of the delicate curves of her body flickered in his mind. "Sure," he responded giddily, though he knew her thoughts were unlikely to mirror his.

In a spurt of girlish glee, she leaped to her feet and motioned for him to follow her. "Let's go swimming in Dogwood Creek," she demanded more than proposed, an enthusiastic smile on her face.

The sky outside held bright, though the day drew close to evening. "It's almost dark," her retorted, taken off guard by her idea.

A sour glare replaced her smile. "We have at least three hours," she argued. "And you haven't been there yet, have you?"

Ryan shook his head, despite his uncertainty of where she meant he had not been.

"I knew it," she cried. "And the best place to go swimming in the creek is at your farm."

—

Except for the clingy resistance of a dusty pair of tire ruts, the lane leading to the old farmhouse wallowed on the losing side of a battle with nature, with untamed grass and weeds increasingly obscuring its purpose. A few more years of neglect and the path would reach a point of invisibility, for the native flora already announced their presence by loudly bristling against the undercarriage of their car.

Ryan watched as the shuttered farmhouse and weathered barn grew in prestige until they loomed above the car as it passed through the overgrown farmyard, its fences in ruins and outbuildings conceding to collapse. Temptation pleaded with him to fling open the car door and explore the melancholic place. But he feared sharing with Olivia the nostalgic swelling in his chest, instead stifling his emotions as they moved past the buildings and into a field of gently waving alfalfa, where a trampled car path cut across the pasture's crown. From the crest of the field's peak, his eyes traced the matted trail as it descended the other side and blended into a thick tree line, where a cluster of three vehicles sat.

"We'll have some company," Olivia remarked as she steered the car to join the other cars. "You'll know at least one of them."

He gave no verbal response, offering only the confusion shown by a knit brow and agape mouth.

"The red Toyota pick-up is Mark's," Olivia explained.

Recognition of the name floundered for a second, but a quick mental review of his recent acquaintances brought it to him. "Mark, from the newspaper?" he asked.

She nodded. "That's the one." She pulled her car alongside the truck. "He's probably here with his younger brother."

A well-worn footpath cut through the forested hillside, the first hundred yards shrouded in dense woodland. But then the timber thinned to reveal a stirring vista of a dramatic bend in the creek, where golden rays of the dipping western sun trickled through the leaves of old growth trees, yielding glimmering gilt flecks on the water's surface.

A broad, flat red clay ledge stretched out in front of them, jutting up above the flow and offering a commanding view of the creek for miles in both directions. Ryan strode out to the drop-off and peered into the water below him. A dark sapphire pocket churned there, offering a promise of coolness. He stepped to the very edge, half intending to leap from the red clay bank and into the vibrant blue water below. But then a rustling in the trees behind him pulled his mind back from its spontaneous desire, allowing him but a few seconds to step out of the way as Mark dashed across the ledge and leapt into the water.

The rippling of the boisterous splash still in their ears, Olivia offered Ryan a playful smile. "Now get down to your suit so you can give it a go," she teased him.

He gazed out across the water again, his excitement and rush from a moment earlier now tempered with caution. "How deep is it?" he questioned her.

An impatient sigh escaped her. "Only about six feet, so it's best to pull your legs up to your torso when you jump in," she cautioned.

A shiver of uncertainty ran up his spine. "Like a cannonball?"

She offered an apathetic nod. "Exactly."

Nervousness clawed at his gut, but his manhood suddenly felt questioned. He swallowed hard and clumsily pulled off his shirt, which she greeted with a playful whistle. Embarrassed warmth filled his cheeks and forehead. "You like a man with a slim, hairless and pale chest," he responded in self-jest.

But before she could reply in either earnest or jest, a now-drenched Mark came bounding back up onto the clay ledge. "Hiya boss," the boy said. "Thanks for letting us park at your farm so we can go swimming."

Ryan nodded, noticing Mark's exceptionally well-built seventeen-year-old body. He glanced to Olivia, then back to Mark, his self-esteem wilting with every glance.

As if sensing his unease, Olivia strode over to him and draped her arm around him, laying her hand on his bare chest. "Looking good, sexy," she playfully encouraged him.

The warmth of her skin and her frisky affirmation provided enough confidence to push back his insecurities. He slipped out of her embrace and charged toward the rim of the red clay bluff.

His arms pulling his knees tight against his chest, he plunged into the blue depth, the icy water enveloping his body. Extending his legs beneath him, his toes slid across the algae-covered rocks that lined the bed. He pushed his feet down with a hard kick, giving enough force for his head to break back through the surface of the water and into the warm sunlight, where an excited yell escaped his lips.

"You better get over here before Mark lands on you," warned a teenage boy standing on a nearby gravel bank.

Ryan swam toward him for about ten feet, then stood and waded the rest of the way out of the water. A loud splash erupted behind him. He turned back and watched the rippling water for a second, before Olivia's head came bobbing up to the surface. "It's refreshing, isn't it," she proclaimed as she swam toward him.

"It's freezing," Ryan protested with a coy smirk. "I wasn't expecting it to be that cold."

Olivia stood as she neared the shallow edge of the creek and then walked toward him. "That's because of all the springs; cold rushing water from deep underground," she exclaimed. "I see you've met everyone."

He glanced in the direction of the boy who'd yelled at him, and spotted three more teenagers, all intently watching them. He looked back at Olivia and shook his head. With a casual motion of her hand, she pointed and called off their names and connections: her cousin's daughter Tish, Mark's brother Blake, and two of their friends, a boyfriend and girlfriend named Zane and Rebecca.

The next half hour was spent with the seven taking turns jumping off the clay ledge and then horsing around in the frigid pool at its base. But as evening's dimness arrived, with the sun vanishing below the horizon, Olivia suggested ceding the creek back to nature, at least for the night. The group gathered their belongings and hiked back up the trail that cut through the woods.

"Hey boss, can I see the inside of your house?" Mark asked Ryan once they reached their vehicles.

The question felt staged. "Sure," Ryan answered. "You can even have something to eat. People keep bringing me food, even though I've been here for more than a week."

Mark smiled and shook his head. "Not that house, the farmhouse on the hill," he motioned toward the shuttered building with his thumb.

Though now dusk, the house's placement high on the hill kept it well lit, even in the fading light. "Oh, yeah," Ryan responded, feeling awkward in his misunderstanding. "I'd be happy to, but I don't have a key."

Olivia nudged him with her shoulder. "I do," she admitted.

—

A smattering of stubborn flakes of robin egg blue paint clung to the heavy oak door, though the bulk of the surface, denuded by decades of peeling, had faded to a weathered gray. And despite the door's compromised appearance, the sanctity of the house remained intact, with an intimidating, if rusty, padlock keeping it secure.

Ryan thumbed through the dozens of keys on the large stainless-steel loop, hoping one would appear evident, and allow him to avoid the tedious task of trying each one. But a sense of futility began to creep in as he neared the end of the loop, then a subtle bit of providence arrived as he came upon a worn brass key with a ragged tag attached. In a messy scrawl, the tag read "farmhouse." The key slipped into the lock and with little effort he popped the shackle open. He pulled the lock off the door and held it in his hand. Heavy, strong and durable; its weight pulling ever so slightly down, evoking his grandfather's protective nature for nostalgic places.

The doorknob presented no resistance, though the warped door offered some fight. The second time in less than two weeks he faced such a stubborn door. But his experience the week prior prepared him. So, with a hard swing of his right shoulder, just above the doorknob, he nudged it open to a passable degree. Though, in doing so, he caused a cringe-worthy creak of unoiled hinges and released a gust of stagnant air.

With Olivia at his side, he led the group through the door and into a small mudroom, which in turn deposited them into the main hall. Despite the farmhouse's modest exterior, the hall retained a subtle elegance, with a handsome mahogany staircase and an abundance of millwork. From there, the explorers separated and began to wander through and discover the dusty rooms. Rooms far from empty, with furniture and personal remnants scattered throughout, leftovers of the out-of-style and obsolete variety.

Ryan found enchantment in the wistful look in Olivia's eyes. "Maybe, by leaving these pieces here, they've become prized possessions," she philosophized.

The threadbare fabrics and age-crackled varnish left Ryan wincing at the thought of the lingering artifacts as treasures. "What do you mean?" he asked as they started up the stairs.

She pouted her lips. "The pieces that are missing, where are they now?" she asked. "Maybe in your house, mixed with other pieces of different time periods and styles. But this place is a slice of history. Everything reflects its past. Your grandfather's house has pieces of that, but it's not as true as this."

Olivia's unapologetic sentimentality fell counter to his upbringing in the often-detached world of southern California. But the tenderness he heard in her reply stirred something similar inside of him.

The upstairs rooms, now dimming in the waning sun, offered a different feel from those downstairs, where the furniture and other effects sat in a disheveled mess. For here, the belongings of the previous occupants remained frozen in an ethereal time decades past. Four complete bedrooms eerily enduring beneath the protection of dust-caked and yellowed covers.

In the largest, Olivia folded the sheet protecting the dressing table, revealing it as fully stocked with dried-out makeup and other feminine grooming aids, while a 1990 calendar hung on the wall beside the table's mirror. "That must have been about when your grandfather's cousin died," Olivia surmised. "And all of this, still here, exactly as left."

He felt an uneasy tingling in his side, a physical manifestation of his heartache for the home's long dead residents. Dizziness set in and the room became blurry, leading him to grab hold of the nearest piece of furniture, sending its grimy cover plummeting to the floor into a dusty pile. Left revealed was a highboy dresser with a mahogany finish that had a warm glow in the soft evening light. He noticed the bottom drawer stuck stubbornly out, so he reached down and gave it a slight push, but it refused to budge. He pulled it out a few inches more and tried again, with a little more force, though it came to the same stop. Huffing a sigh of frustration, he pulled it completely open, bringing into view a tattered white photo album, which Olivia swiftly grabbed.

She motioned for him to sit beside her, on the edge of the bed, and once he had obeyed, she opened the album's cover and delicately proceeded through its leaves. Its brittle black pages offered a detailed photographic essay of the lives of the man and woman who had made the house their home.

It portrayed them through all life's stages, poignant moments both uplifting and sad, and each progressive page, engraved in the faces, exposed the march of time. From fresh-faced youths mounted on heavy paper cards to midcentury black and white snapshots of middle age and ending with the lined and sagging faces of their advanced years in vibrant Kodachromes. Sandwiched in the middle appeared the cheerful face of a son, gaily represented from birth, through childhood and young adulthood, then tragically exiting via military telegram and yellowed obituary.

An emotional tremor pulsed through Olivia's body as they paused on the page dedicated to a son who died young. Ryan leaned close to her, his own emotions brimming, slipped his arm around her waist and pulled her close. The heat of emotion burned between them, his eyes blearing with tears.

The last few pages concluded the couple's lives, poorly-focused photos of the elderly woman in a nursing home bed, her husband by her side. Then an obituary, longer than normal and featuring Ryan's grandfather's byline, a type of public notice usually reserved for only the most notable of notables. It praised Alice for her commitment to friends, family and neighbors and for the strength she showed after the death of her only child. Only a few more photos remained on a final page, including an image of the widower at a town function with Ryan's grandparents. Then, tucked inside the back cover they found a few greeting cards of the get-well variety, though none specifically making that claim, as if the senders already knew the conclusion. Finally, haphazardly placed among the cards, they found one last obituary. Unlike the notices for the son and wife, it came unsecured, floating unattached as the unstable epilogue to the lives of the three family members.

For a moment, neither spoke, sitting quietly side by side with the closed album resting in Olivia's lap. Then, without a word, Ryan reached over and laid his hand on the album, pausing for but a moment before sliding the book over onto his own lap. "I'm going to take this with me," he murmured. "It feels wrong to leave their entire lives trapped in this tired old house."

A pained smiled showed on Olivia's face as a tear trickled down her cheek. The sight of that emotion left Ryan's chest swelling and his eyes spilling a few drops of their own, as he resisted the urge to turn away, instead exposing his tenderness to her as she did for him. "Shame on you," he affectionately scolded her as he again pulled her tight against him. "You shouldn't make me cry."

The warmth of her body soaked into his, leading him to rest his head on her shoulder and breathe in her scent. An intoxicating euphoria filled him, so he raised his head back up, gazed into her lively green eyes, and kissed her. The softness of her lips welcomed him as he pressed against her, not the intense kiss of passion, but one of gentle yearning and emotional need.

CHAPTER 10

THE CHIMES OF THE COURTHOUSE CLOCK, marking the noon hour, rang in the background as the irate phone calls began. An unwrapped sandwich, no bite yet enjoyed, sat temptingly on the desk in front of Ryan as his phone beckoned. He glanced across the office, spotting Ebetta looking back at him, spite in her eyes.

"Good afternoon, this is—" he started before getting angrily cutoff by a nasally female voice. Discarding even the most basic pleasantry or introduction, she declared him an idiot for thinking "illegals" should be encouraged to move to the town, and then admonished him for so quickly bringing shame to his late grandfather's name. The only response he allowed himself came as a sigh of displeasure and wishing her a good day before hanging up the phone.

It proved the start of an avalanche of similar calls, twenty-two in a few hours' time, with nineteen being expressly negative responses to the chicken plant editorial. Colorful and derogatory language came with most; and several, most notably one from the town's Southern Baptist minister, informed him he "should try living in the town a little longer before trying to change it" and that his "obvious ignorance in the ways of decent god-fearing people should not be appearing on any newspaper's pages." A few calls even verged on threats, with one going so far as to tell him to watch what he puts in the paper if he plans on keeping the paper, or even his house, much longer. Then another suggested the town should "send all the wetbacks" to his house, where they could make him fat "off beans and tortillas."

Once 5 o'clock passed, he felt relief that he could stop taking the calls, at least until Monday morning. But then, as if intuiting his hope for respite, the harsh ring again burned into his ears. Across the office, Ebetta smiled as she picked up the receiver. He strained, while trying not to look like it, to listen in on the office half of the conversation, but heard no more than a faint murmur from Ebetta. Her voice paused, and in a severe tone she yelled at him to pick up the holding call.

The muscles in his back contracted in a painful spasm. "How can I help you?" he greeted the caller in a whimper.

But instead of another coarse and aggressive voice, as he expected, he heard the wavering, gentle tone of an aged woman. "Are you Dean's grandson?" she asked.

He replied in the affirmation.

"Then you're the one I want to talk to," she exclaimed, her voice gaining a sudden vigor. "My name's Grace Browning."

He recognized the name, but having met so many people since arriving, could not recall her individually. "I apologize if we've met, but there've been a lot of people in the last week or so and I'm afraid I'm having trouble remembering exactly who everyone is," he replied.

Grace hummed into her end of the phone. "Well, I'm the one whose article you ruined today."

The realization clicked in his mind, leaving an uneasy lump in his throat. She authored the handwritten column he edited the previous Saturday. "I'm sorry, I didn't mean to ruin anything," he bumbled in reply, feeling his face flush with unease.

"Sweetie, I'm sure you didn't, but that's not my writing," she declared. "Now I must tell everyone I didn't write it, so they don't get confused. They won't know what to think about it when they read it."

Despite feeling embarrassed for being called out for his edits, Ryan was perplexed. He purposely left all of her—what he thought dull—tidbits and anecdotes in the column; only trying to organize it and rewrite it to make it sound more professional. "I thought I was helping," he explained. "I didn't think it would be a problem."

The woman grew quiet, as if sorry for offending him for doing something that offended her. "I'm sure you didn't," she finally answered. "But it is. My friends and family always expect it, and now it's completely different. I don't know what they'll think. Like I said, I'll have to tell them I didn't write it."

His ego urged him to stand his ground and tell her he improved it, but he realized the hardnosed tactics that might work in Los Angeles would likely fail here. And her sweet, aged voice had already wormed its way into his conscious. "How about next week I only edit for spelling and grammar," Ryan offered as a compromise. "And I can put a disclaimer on it saying this week's column was inadvertently and improperly edited."

Through the line came more humming as Grace considered the proposal. "I guess that'll work. After all, it's getting late and it's a Friday. And I know you have a date tonight."

A polite laugh escaped Ryan's lips. "I don't have a date tonight," he confessed.

"No?" Grace responded in surprise.

A wide smile spread across his face as he thought about how people in the town perceived him. "No, not tonight," he confidently assured her.

A grunt of disbelief came back. "That's interesting. I could swear I heard that my niece Olivia was taking you to Springfield tonight."

—

With her feet propped atop the porch railing, Olivia rested in a lazy slouch in the porch glider watching as Ryan strode across the yard toward her.

"How's it going stranger?" she asked once he made it to the porch.

The porch creaked beneath his feet as he neared her. "I'm good, happy today's over," he replied through a weary smile.

Understanding showed in her eyes. "I thought I'd try to brighten your day," she offered. "I did hear it may have been a bit exhausting."

His shoulders and chest sagged, the tension in his body finally easing as the sweet scent of wild roses filled his nose. "You mean the phone calls?"

She replied with a sympathetic nod. "Yes, those. I heard half the town called to complain."

He dropped into the glider beside here. "I wasn't expecting them to be so staunch," he admitted, following the comment with a nervous laugh.

Her feet slid off the railing, and she used them to push the glider into motion. "In White Oak City, they're always staunch," she said.

He nodded. "Even a preacher," he whined. "He told me I hadn't been here long enough to tell people they need to change."

Her smile widened. "The Rev. Hollis P. Pettigrew, as judgmental a Southern Baptist as ever walked this earth," she declared. "He's not a big fan of most people, so don't feel too special for having been talked down by him."

—

The study offered a cool and dry respite from the hot and humid front porch, and its seclusion offered the introvert in Ryan an atmosphere in which to recharge. Olivia sat beside him on the brown chesterfield sofa, but they did not touch. He wanted to pull her close, but insecurity swelled inside him. The kiss from the night before still felt unreal and he feared too direct of an advance now would sour her emotions.

She leaned against him. "I have an idea to help you get your mind off your worries," she offered.

"It's not to go to Springfield for dinner is it?"

Her jaw dropped in surprise. "How do you know that?" she snapped at him.

A hearty laugh erupted from him. "A woman named Grace Browning told me."

Olivia pressed the tips of her fingers to her lips to stifle a laugh. "Of course," she responded. "She's my great aunt. That means Mom talked to Aunt Grace this afternoon."

Ryan felt a tinge of pleasure in discovering that even living here for most of a lifetime did not remove all the town's surprises. "Oh, and I'd love to go," he added.

"I don't know that I still want to take you," she countered. "I don't necessarily want the entire town knowing what I'm doing. Maybe I'll go home and read."

Feeling a burst of confidence, he hooked his arm around her and pulled her close. "I don't think I'm gonna let you leave. Especially if all you're planning to do tonight is go home and read."

—

Olivia bubbled over with stories of trips to Springfield's public square to watch the city's annual Christmas parade, as they strolled across the shabby space with dinner in their bellies. A now defunct department store towered above them, inside of which she had sat on Santa's lap annually for more than a decade's worth of photos. "Now, it's just an empty building," she reflected as she gazed up at the looming structure. "It's not just White Oak City that has empty buildings."

The comment weighed on Ryan's mind, prompting him to scrutinize the square more closely. But despite some obvious age and neglect, this place still held a quiet hum of life, unlike the gloomy buildings that populated the Decatur County square. For here, businesses kept sputtering on in most of the buildings, ramshackle as some may be, and the cars and people, while not thriving in numbers, kept the area from true ghost town status, regardless of the albatross that dominated it.

Off in the distance, he heard strains of live music, which grew louder as Olivia guided them down a quiet street. She then took them down a dark and grimy ally, but they safely emerged onto a street of tattered storefronts, with a large three-story Victorian-era building dominating the center of the block. Restored and well lit, it melodically announced itself as the source of the strains of jazz echoing across the downtown.

An ornate mahogany bar, backed with massive gilt-framed mirrors and oversized and age-crackled paintings of reclining nude women, dominated the room. But this night's true focus emanated from beyond the bar, where at the back of the room a small stage stood and a meager though attentive audience soaked up the sounds of an elegantly dressed quartet.

At first, Ryan only noticed the instrumental aspects of the performance, but then from the shadows to the right of the stage emerged a tall, slender and graceful woman of about seventy, her grayed hair wrapped into a perfectly coifed beehive and a flowing blue-gray gossamer gown swirling around her frame. She seemed an idealized version of the female standards singer. And with a watchful eye on her audience, and an index finger tapping against her microphone in beat with the music, she opened her sensuous red lips.

Her vocals filled the room, enchanting the audience and sending chills up Ryan's spine as he lost himself in her serenade. A passion, perhaps induced by a combination of the divine voice and a lingering wine buzz from dinner, swept over him, driving him in desire toward Olivia. But she unwittingly rejected his zeal, stepping from his grasp as she made her way between tables, motioning for him to follow her to a table for two, just feet from the stage and its captivating warbler.

For the next twenty minutes, as the songstress continued to captivate the room, Ryan found himself both enraptured by the voice and repertoire and mystified by a nagging familiarity. Then, as the woman announced a break in her non-singing voice, it hit him. This elegant singer of the classics of Cole Porter, Johnny Mercer and Hoagy Carmichael was the same downhome bluegrass singer from the night he met Olivia. A boyish feeling of achievement rushed through his mind and he turned to face his date and share his realization, but the scratch of chair legs against the floor shifted his attention to his other side, where the vocalist in question had settled into a seat beside him.

"So, this is Ryan?" the older woman asked Olivia in confirmation, her voice strong, yet feminine.

Olivia nodded and winked at Ryan. "It is. What do you think of him?" she responded with a confident grin.

The older woman eyed him. "He looks like his grandfather," she remarked.

"You think so?" Olivia queried, now also giving him a studious look.

The singer drummed her fingertips on the tabletop. "I know so," she replied. "You forget, I knew his grandfather when he was young and handsome too."

The softness of Olivia's eyes as she admired him sent his heart racing. "Ryan, this is Hazel Loutrou," she explained. "She lives down the street from your aunt."

Hazel's kind smile glowed bright in contrast to her dark red lipstick. "I adore Rosemary," she gushed. "She's always been the sweetest woman. When I was a little girl, she always had something special to eat at her house—cookies, cakes and pies."

"How well did you know my grandfather?" Ryan asked, feeling a deeper story existed there.

A misty glimmer danced in Hazel's eyes as she thought over the question. "I once had the biggest crush on your grandfather, though he was a few years older than me," she answered, tears collecting atop her cheeks. "I hate getting old. Sometimes it feels like all you do is sit back and wait for the people who made up your memories to die away."

Beneath the table, Olivia's hand tightened around his. His throat caught as he tried to respond, so he swallowed and tried again. "Have you always been a singer?" he asked, changing the subject. "I would think that would make you a little uncommon in White Oak."

Hazel let out an amused laugh. "You dear boy," she exclaimed. "Do you think everyone in that town has always been there?"

The answer confused him. "You said you grew up there," he said.

With her warm smile, Hazel patted him on the shoulder. "I did," she responded. "But I wasn't there for all the years in between. When I was seventeen, realizing the man I loved would not be mine, I went to Chicago. I got a job working in some horrible little office and I started singing in some little dives. I was always told I had a nice voice, so I figured I should use it. And there I stayed. I got married, then divorced, then married again, had a daughter, was widowed, and kept singing the whole time."

Someone else who could not be happy in White Oak City, he thought. "Sounds exciting, and busy."

She sighed, and her eyes seemed to look through him. "It was busy; exciting, not so much," she explained with a shrug of her shoulders. "You see, after a while, you just kind of get into the rhythm of things. I never became some big recording artist, but I was happy doing what I was doing. I'm happy doing it now. Hell, it gets me out of White Oak City two nights a week."

The last sentence stuck in his mind. "Why did you come back?"

"Because it's home," she bluntly responded. "It also makes me the eccentric liberal, yet lovable, woman in the town. I have a small amount of local fame and give singing and piano lessons to a handful of children. I keep happy."

Olivia's hand tightened around his under the table, this time paired with a smile.

"I guess that's what matters," he agreed.

"While I wouldn't give up my Chicago experiences for anything, the last couple of years have been wonderful, especially with friends in my life like your grandfather," Hazel added.

His chest warmed at the mention, and he rewarded Hazel with a rare genuine smile in honor of his grandfather's memory, for it seemed the old widower may have enjoyed a late-in-life girlfriend.

—

Olivia pulled her car to a stop beside his grandfather's darkened house. They sat in silence for a moment, though desire urged him to lean over and kiss her. Coward, he thought to himself as his fingers clumsily fidgeted with the seatbelt. Then the car shook, as Olivia opened the driver's door and got out. He did likewise.

They stood across the car from each other, their skin shimmering in the humid night air. Giddiness overtook him, eliciting a dopey smile on his face. She presented no such playfulness, only confidence. "Could you grab the bag in the back seat for me?" she asked, breaking the quiet.

He pulled open the back door and lifted out the blue overnight bag. "This is kind of heavy," he remarked as he hoisted it up into the air.

An embarrassed blush filled her cheeks. "I'm sorry," she answered. "I always pack too much for overnight stays."

CHAPTER 11

Careful not to disturb her sleep, Ryan gently rolled up onto his side and watched as Olivia continued to doze, the morning sun casting a glow along her figure. With each breath, the patchwork quilt covering her rose and fell. And though the night before now seemed more fiction than reality, she rested beside him.

A slight shudder took hold of her body and her eyelids fluttered open. "Why are you looking at me?" she asked, her green eyes drowsy with sleep.

He smiled. "I don't know, I just am," he answered.

A yawn of clinging exhaustion escaped her. "Clever retort," she offered in a groggy voice. "Do you use that on all the girls?"

He shook his head. "First, there aren't many girls. Second, none have been like you."

With a delicate arching of her back, she adjusted to take a better view of him. "Oh," she replied. "Is that good or bad?"

Offering a contented sigh, Ryan reached out and rubbed her bare shoulder. "For you, it's a very good thing," he stated, and then leaned over and kissed her on the forehead.

She nodded in acceptance. "That's good to know," she murmured.

Slipping his arm around her, he pulled her body tight against his, realizing as they touched that they both remained naked. A flicker of excitement sparked, but the harsh buzz of the doorbell interrupted.

"Oh Christ," he exclaimed. "Who the hell is that?"

A girlish giggle escaped Olivia. "You better go find out; it might be important," she teased. "Then again, it could be a door-to-door vacuum salesman."

He huffed loudly. "It better be important."

The smiling face of a light-haired man in his early thirties waited in greeting as Ryan swung the front door open. "Hi," the man chirped while reaching out his right hand. "I'm Paul Mason."

Another name to forget, Ryan thought as he extended his own hand in response. "I'm Ryan."

The man's smile widened. "I figured. May I come in?"

The question seemed presumptuous. "Who are you?" Ryan questioned him.

"Paul Mason from Red Mountain Consolidated Realty," he explained, a look of surprise on his face. "I talked to a woman in your office yesterday about moving up our appointment time and she said 7:30 would be a fine."

The name Ryan now recalled. "A woman in my office?"

Paul nodded. "Yes, her name was." He paused to look in his notebook. "Ebetta, that's it."

Ryan could feel the veins in his forehead pulsing with anger. "Oh, it seems the message wasn't passed on to me. But, you're here, so let's get the ball rolling." He motioned for Paul to follow him to the dining room.

"I think I know someone who might be interested in the newspaper," Paul explained as he followed Ryan. "I've talked with them and I think it's promising."

"That's great," Ryan exclaimed. "I've been waiting for some good news ever since I got here. I came here for a funeral and had the ownership of half of a ghost town dropped in my lap."

Paul offered a polite laugh. "It sounds better to call it a bedroom community when trying to sell it. Ghost town sounds like something you'd find in the old West."

—

Ryan left Paul at the dining room table and slipped into the kitchen to start some coffee, as he felt desperate for something to jolt him out of his morning daze. The coffee would take a few minutes, so he filled a couple of glasses with water and returned to the dining room, where he discovered Olivia sitting across the table from the real estate agent and entertaining him with a brief history of the town.

"I see you've already introduced yourselves," Ryan remarked, feeling his face flush pink with embarrassment. He placed a glass of water in front of each of them.

Paul looked at him with a beaming smile. "Yes, Olivia is helping bring me up to speed," he explained. "It should help when dealing with potential buyers."

A sly smile appeared on her face as she leaned back in her chair and glanced toward Ryan.

"You said you already have some interest in some of the properties," Ryan remarked as he sat beside her.

The real estate agent leafed through a folder sitting in front of him, though he was careful in hiding its contents. "The newspaper anyway, but they don't necessarily want the building," Paul answered. "They own a lot of weekly newspapers in the area and it's not uncommon for them to add new ones to their portfolio. Then, there's a man that might want to purchase a couple of the downtown buildings for storage, but the farm and the bulk of the rest we'd just put on the market."

Ryan nodded. "What type of storage would the buildings be used for?" he asked.

A wrinkle of unease appeared on Paul's forehead as he paused before answering the question. "He owns a feed mill and wants some square footage in the area for local distribution. Like a warehouse."

A tremor of anxiety formed in Ryan's stomach. "Board up the windows and stack it full of grain?" he surmised.

The real estate agent leaned back in his chair and glanced toward the window. "That's the meat of it," he answered, and then looked back in their direction. "I know it's not very romantic for old main street façades. But, for a quick turnaround, it's all I can offer. Maybe once this chicken plant is built there'll be more call for traditional uses of the buildings. Though, at the same time, there are twenty-something empty commercial buildings in this town, which is a hard sell for people who want to open up little boutiques or such."

Ryan drummed his fingers on the tabletop. "How'd you know about the chicken plant?" he asked.

"Your website," Paul answered. "And I saw there's some resistance."

The gleam of the morning sun on the top of the polished table hammered at Ryan's hangover. "Yeah, I'm surprised the phone hasn't been ringing all morning," he replied while shaking his head.

Olivia interrupted with a throaty cough. "That's because I turned off the ringer last night," she noted, inspiring appreciative laughs from both Ryan and Paul.

"That solves that mystery," Ryan offered as a pleased warmth filled his chest. "Personally, I think the chicken plant would be a good thing for the town, but these people are set in their ways and a lot of them are downright prejudiced. Are you sure you don't know of anyone else who might be interested in some of the buildings?"

Paul shook his head. "The newspaper should be a fairly easy sale," he observed in an upbeat tone. "It's a paper in a county seat, so there are always contracts to publish public record notices in it. Nothing attracts buyers more than a steady income."

Ryan's mind drifted for a moment, burdened by the assumed reaction of the town to his potential fire sale of the downtown.

"What if he gave the buildings away or sold them for token amounts?" Olivia said, interrupting Ryan's mental wrangling.

Paul's eyebrow cocked up in interest. "What do you mean?"

"Think about it," she said, her eyes intensely focused on Ryan. "The downtown is really complete. Not a single hole where an old building's been lost. Can't you imagine it as an antique or crafts destination?"

An unconvinced sigh came from Paul. "It's a possibility, but I don't know how practical it would be. Most of those buildings need work, and what's to attract people here to set up those types of businesses?"

Her smile widened. "That's why you give them the buildings for free or offer them a pay the taxes and insurance only kind of lease," she explained. "And, as far as fixing them up goes, I know there are historic tax rebates available for that type of work. We'd just need to get them on the state register or have the city declare that area as blighted to qualify for them."

Paul's smile showed a warming to the idea. "There'd have to be some sort of brokerage fee for my office though. Otherwise, we couldn't do much to help out. And you'd have to find a way to let people know about it to encourage them to open businesses here. Then you'd need some sort of advertising campaign to bring shoppers."

Olivia nodded in agreement with each of Paul's challenges. "I know, there are tons of details to work out," she agreed. "I think first we need to take it to the city council and see if they would support it, maybe even help fund it."

This could not be an entirely new idea, Ryan thought, feeling slightly misled for only now hearing about it. But he could not help but like it. Even if it only ended up being partially successful, it still might help him leave the town without feeling like a villain. "I wouldn't get paid for anything," he interjected, half-joking.

A scowl crossed Olivia's face. "Until a week or so ago, you didn't know you owned any of it. In addition, you'd be helping do what your grandfather wanted, giving the town hope."

—

The perfume of wild roses greeted Ryan as he stepped out onto the front porch. And despite the warming of the morning air by an unobstructed sun ascending over the town, the predawn crispness remained, offering a deep, cool, invigorating breath.

Olivia and the real estate agent followed in step as Ryan led them down the driveway toward the town square. But delay hit them even before they reached the sidewalk in front of the house, a bad omen in the form of the neighbor Emma Woodhouse. With an elderly Pomeranian tucked into her elbow, she stared up at Ryan with dull brown eyes, magnified to the size of tennis balls by her thick glasses.

Olivia neared the woman with a warm smile. "Good morning Mrs. Woodhouse, how are you today?" she offered in greeting.

The woman continued staring at Ryan in an uncomfortable way, glancing to Olivia only momentarily with a shy smile. "I'm good Olivia," she replied. "I-I-It's nice to see you. But not so n-n-nice to see you Mr. Sh-Shipley. I-I-I read your editorial. I-I-I've already written a l-l-letter."

A discomforting chill ran up his spine. Beyond the slight in her language, her tone and seeming aversion to him prematurely amplified the negativity he expected in the letter. "I look forward to reading it," he replied, tight-lipped.

And despite the somewhat dull-minded expression on her face, his condescending response triggered a dirty look and sent her vigorously marching away, her elderly dog struggling in her tense grip.

The exchange on the street in front of his grandfather's house only deepened the disappointment Ryan felt as the deserted town square came into view. For despite seeing it nearly every day for the last few weeks, with the real estate agent now in tow the glut of vacant storefronts and lack of commercial traffic inspired a case of heartburn.

A reasonable person would see no future in this void. Except for a small group of cars parked in front of the diner, only one other vehicle sat on the square, in front of the only other business appearing open this morning—the old hardware store.

Ryan's hands tingled with numbness as he took a deep breath, wishing the scene more closely resembled that of the faded photographs hanging inside the newspaper office, those showing a lively White Oak City on Saturday morning in years past. Memories of better times, when the square bustled with cars lining the streets and sidewalks jammed with people, both town folk and farmers alike, conducting their weekly commerce.

—

Plump and slow from a heavy breakfast, the three emerged from the diner and stepped back into the day's growing swelter. Ryan's hairline glistened with perspiration, equally from anxiety and heavy humidity.

"Let's have a look at what you own," Paul said as he gave the town square an earnest appraisal.

An uneasy smile came to Ryan's face. "I'll try to remember which they all are, but I don't have Connie's list on me to be a hundred percent sure," he answered, feeling inadequately prepared. He then took a deep breath and led them to the front of the newspaper office, from where Connie's tour started and from where he felt most confident in being able to give a complete tour himself. Every inch of paint on the front façade seemed peeling or faded, twisting his stomach into knots.

"I own the *Times-Gazette* building here at 205 and the buildings on each side of it, 207 and 203," he explained, feeling slightly lightheaded. "I know that 203 was the old drug store and still has the original soda fountain in it." He paused for a deep breath, hoping Olivia would correct him if he got any information wrong.

The real estate agent stepped to the window of the old drugstore and peered in through the glass. "The windows are covered up on the inside," he commented with a sour look. "At some point we'll need to have all these assessed. Do you have the keys?"

Ryan nodded. "They're on a key ring back at my grandfather's house. I can grab them if you want."

Paul shook his head as he walked over to 207 and peered into its window as well. "What's upstairs?" he asked.

Ryan's mind went blank as he tried to think back to whether Connie had given him that information. "There's an apartment above the newspaper office and I'm not sure what's above this one," he answered.

Paul's eyes glowered with impatience. "How about above the drug store?" he asked as he returned to the ornate red brick building.

Patches of sweat seeped through the fabric of Ryan's shirt. "I don't remember," he answered, shrugging his shoulders.

The touch of Olivia's hand on his arm calmed him. "It was professional offices," she said. "I remember from when I was little. There was a tax preparation office and I saw a doctor's name on another door, which was empty even then."

Even the pretense of polite small talk vanished between them as they continued down Commercial Street, Paul giving each building they passed a visual inspection, even those not belonging to Ryan—the actions of a man sizing up an entire town, not just individual properties.

The stately design of the former White Oak Citizens Bank brought Ryan a breath of encouragement. "I own this one too," he announced as they crossed the street to stand beside it.

A hint of interest appeared in Paul's eyes. "This is a beauty," he allowed as he ogled the elaborate stone edifice. "If you can get this sold or leased out as some nice boutique or antiques shop, you'll have an anchor." But then the excitement melted from his face. "Whoa, it looks like there's already a tenant. Commercial Street Taxidermy might need to be persuaded to move down the block a bit. Some might be a little reluctant to do their shopping in a building adorned with stuffed raccoons."

Ryan shuffled his feet across the sidewalk's cracked concrete. "I haven't even met this guy," he said. "But he is one of the few paying tenants I have."

The real estate agent stepped back from the bank building and looked up and down Commercial Street, from the old high school in one direction into the indeterminable distance of the other. "You own ten buildings on this main street out of twenty-five or twenty-six," he remarked. "The future of this downtown does hinge on you. If you want money, I can help you sell at least a few of them, maybe more. You won't get a lot for them, but it will be something. The most valuable asset is the newspaper, which, if you want, you could try and require the building be sold with it."

The metallic taste of displeasure bloomed in Ryan's mouth. "What about the four houses and the farm?" he asked, hoping for better prospects.

Paul's eyes narrowed. "Residential properties can always be sold, it just depends on how much you'd take for them," he answered. "If we sold every structure you own in this town, I might get you $400,000, if I can find buyers."

Hundreds of thousands less than Ryan anticipated. "That doesn't sound like much considering how much property there is," he responded.

With a sweeping motion of his hand, Paul brought their attention back to the empty street. "I know, but I'll be lucky if I can get you $10,000 each for these old commercial buildings. Unless there's some sort of local economic stimulus, these buildings will continue to sit and decay. It doesn't help that one of the focal points of the town is that boarded-up old school. It's not a good omen to entrepreneurs."

—

The breeze across the front lawn carried the sweet scent of freshly cut grass to Ryan's nose as he and Olivia rocked back and forth in the glider. "My gut's twisted in knots," he admitted. Paul had left town more than an hour earlier, but the deflated expectations he delivered remained.

Taking hold of his hand, Olivia offered a gentle squeeze and nodded in a silent understanding.

"What can I do?" he whimpered. "I just want to sell it all and get out of here."

She replied with a sour look and disgruntled groan. "You think that's the only answer?"

His shoes dug into the weathered porch decking, bringing the glider to a jerky stop. "What, should I live here and be master over a decayed town?" he countered. "No, I don't think that would be an improvement for me or the town."

"How about my idea?" she asked.

What idea? he wondered, his head, still pulsing from the stress of the day, left his thoughts fractured. "Tell me again."

An irritated glare met his eyes. "Selling or leasing the buildings for low amounts to get people and businesses into the town," she explained.

The idea had seemed near brilliant when first mentioned this morning, but the disappointments of the day eroded it by such a degree it now seemed almost farcical. "Are you serious about that?" he asked.

Her nose edged up into the air as she peered at him in a disapproving manner. "As a matter of fact, I am," she declared. "A couple years ago civil engineering students from Rolla did a profile of the town and what could be done to improve commerce. That was one solution."

The edges of his mouth twitched, tempting him to smile in approval, but he feared doing so would undermine his motivation to get out of Missouri. "There's more of a conspiracy in this town than anyone will admit to me," he replied, his smile involuntarily appearing. "Your idea is an awful lot like Connie's idea. This has been talked about behind my back, hasn't it?"

Her eyes gleefully twinkled. "It's not like there's ever been an official proposal for it," she conceded. "But some folks have tossed around the idea."

He shook his head. "It figures something like this is happening behind my back," he replied. "Everybody must have seen me as some big dupe when I arrived."

The soft touch of her hand eased the tension in his shoulder. "This predates you, sweetheart," she explained. "Your grandfather talked about it for a couple years before he died. He just didn't have the energy to get the plan in motion. Perhaps he hoped you would."

Ryan stamped his foot down against the porch deck, causing the glider to shudder. "You know," he exclaimed. "About ninety percent of the time I want to drop all of this and go back to LA."

Her hand moved down his arm and entwined with his fingers. "What about that other ten percent of the time?"

He leaped up onto his feet and leaned over the porch railing, looking out across the front yard. "That's when I've been looking at your pretty face too long or have had too much to drink and think with a little paint it could look like something from Norman Rockwell. But I think we both know there's no such thing. And this town really needs to get over that dream."

Puzzled thoughts brewed on her face. "There's a town a little bit west of here that had all these old downtown buildings and it really became a popular place as far as antiques were concerned," she said. "I don't know why we couldn't do the same here."

An aching guilt rose in Ryan's gut, a response to his own negativity. He turned around and leaned back against the railing, facing her. "Why would people come here when they have this other little town to go to?" he asked.

She fidgeted with unease. "That town was wiped out by a tornado," she answered while trying to casually look off into the distance.

"What if a tornado came through here?" he chided her.

She grimaced. "These buildings have been here a long time without being wiped out by one," she responded.

"This other town probably thought the same thing," he countered. "Maybe it's just about time for that to happen here. Do I have insurance on those buildings? That'd solve my problem."

A whispery whistle sounded as she breathed through her clenched teeth. "Stop kidding around about that. People die in tornados. It's not something to laugh at or see as an opportunity to be shed of your white elephants."

A burst of laughter escaped him, and he dropped back down into the glider beside her, pushing his foot against the railing to get it rocking. "Even you know they're white elephants," he exclaimed.

A quick fury flashed in her eyes. "Well, better a white ele—" she began to lash out, but the ringing of her own cell phone cut her short. "Hello," she offered in friendly greeting as she answered it. "Oh, hi Connie. What are you up to?" A broad smile emerged on her face. "We'd love too," she answered, followed by another pause. "Actually, I'm with him right now." Pause. "No, we're sitting on the porch talking." The frustration from a moment earlier had completely vanished from her face, replaced by a sunny smile. "I don't know about that, but I've been enjoying myself," she remarked as she gave him a coy glance. "We'll be there in an hour, does that work?" Pause. "Should we bring anything?" Pause. "Tell him I'm looking forward to seeing him too." Pause. "See you soon." She hung up the phone and slipped it into her pocket.

"Looking forward to seeing whom?" he said.

She turned to face him, her mood no longer displeased. "Meade, Connie's son," she replied.

"I thought he was coming next weekend," he replied.

"That's what he told her, but he wanted to surprise her by arriving a week early," she explained. "And it worked. She's excited, and so am I. He was one of my best friends in high school."

Ryan again used his foot to get the glider into motion and slipped his arm around Olivia's waist to pull her close. "Connie told me about what happened to him in high school," he revealed. "That's bullshit. I can't believe they were able to get away with beating him up."

The joy in her eyes faded to melancholy. "All because of Justin," she mused. "Justin turned on him to save his own back. And Meade took it because he loved him. At least as much as you love a high school sweetheart."

They stayed silent the next few moments, leaning against each other and gazing across the yard.

"I met him, by the way," Ryan announced and broke the quiet.

"Met whom?" she asked.

He snuggled closer against her. "This Justin guy. The day of my grandfather's funeral, Connie took me on a walk down the alley behind the old buildings. We ran into him and his daughter. They were riding bikes there."

Olivia's fingers laced with his. "Annie's a little sweetheart."

He nodded. "Connie told me he's getting divorced," he added.

"His wife left him for another man," Olivia explained with a chuckle. "I guess she wasn't getting what she wanted at home, which makes sense based on what we know about him."

—

Connie's house fell outside of the well-aged neighborhoods that clung close to the town square. The redbrick ranch-style house of a plain and practical 1960s design sat on the sparser northern side of the town, near the new high school and a few blocks from his aunt Rosemary. There was little architecturally to distinguish it from the other houses surrounding it, as they all carried matching hallmarks of a single tract home design. But despite the limitations of architectural style, Connie's front yard presented a full blast of personality with a lush wonderland of colorful flora and lawn ornaments. From giant beds of irises and dozens of well-tended rosebushes to tribes of bearded gnomes and several brightly colored gazing balls, an over-the-top mix of formal garden and amusement park.

Connie nearly leaped off her front porch to greet them as they made their way up the walk; before giddily rushing them toward the door, all the while hugging them and chatting about Meade's surprise appearance. Her prattle continued even once inside, until the emergence from the back hallway of a tall young man with dark hair and classic features.

"You have to forgive my mom," Meade explained in a calm tenor voice. "She's been rather impulsive since I arrived."

A glowing smile filled Connie's face as she stepped toward her son and slipped an arm around him. "Why shouldn't I be? It's not every day my baby boy shows up a week early. I typically expect him an hour late."

Meade playfully rolled his eyes in reaction to his mother and then jutted his hand out in Ryan's direction. "Hi, I'm Meade," he offered as they shook, a secure, though not aggressive, handshake.

"I'm Ryan," he replied with a smile. "I've heard a lot about you."

The wide grin on Meade's face displayed a set of, if not perfect, exceptionally white teeth. "I can say the same about you. She's been telling me all about Mr. Shipley's grandson. I'm sorry about your grandfather, by the way. He always treated me well, even when others didn't."

A warm pride swelled in Ryan's chest. "I'm glad to hear it," he replied.

Then, with an agile twist of his feet, Meade shifted his attention to Olivia. "How're you doing gorgeous?" he asked, offering a mischievous wink at the end.

"I wondered when you were going to finish the flirting and get around to me," she playfully chastised him. "You keep getting better and better looking. If only you were straight, I'd drop this one."

Meade offered an appreciative laugh. "I can promise you, if I was into girls, I'd give this one a run for his money," he countered with a nod toward Ryan.

"You two stop it," Connie playfully warned. "Do you think I don't remember the little compliment game you two would play in high school to bug your teachers. I remember it well, and the complaints it generated."

He turned from Olivia and caught his mother up in a tight embrace. "You're gonna have to suffer with it for the next two weeks," he scolded her.

"Two weeks? Really?" Olivia asked in surprise.

Meade nodded. "That I am," he declared.

"This'll be the longest you've been here since graduation," Olivia stated.

Unease showed on Meade's face as he thought about the remark. "I'm scouting out a possible new branch for my office in Springfield," he explained. "So, part of it'll be work, but I knew Mom would want me to stay here, instead of at some hotel."

Her eyes narrowing, Olivia hummed an impish tune. "A new branch? Do you think you might be moving back to the area?" she probed.

"I know this one would love it if I did," Meade commented while nudging his mother with his elbow. "But I wouldn't move to White Oak, possibly Springfield. But even that I'm not promising."

Connie leaned against her son, a hopeful smile on her face. "I think I could live with that compromise." She steered her visitors toward the back of the house, where inside a screened porch waited a picnic table set with lemonade, sandwiches and potato salad.

The creaking and cracking of aged and brittle wicker sounded as Meade and Ryan settled into the chairs on one side of the table.

"Ryan, my mom tells me you're trying to unload all of the old buildings downtown," Meade remarked as he reached across the table to grab a sandwich.

Ryan exhaled a groan of discontent. "I don't know what else to do with them," he responded. "I have a job and a life back in Los Angeles.

And I think it would be hard to manage the newspaper and all of those buildings from there."

Silence followed as Meade took a moment to chew. "I would think so," he finally replied while nodding. "You could always move here."

A throb of frustration pulsed behind Ryan's right eye. "I see your mom's been telling you her hopes for me," he countered. "I can't picture myself here, working my ass off every week in the drone of small-town politics. On top of that, my mom's in Los Angeles, and I'm her only kid."

Across the table, Connie and Olivia traded glances. "When I talked to your mom last night, she said she'd be open to moving here," the older woman said.

A chill ran up Ryan's spine. "You talked to my mom last night?" he asked, feeling betrayed.

"Didn't I tell you?" she replied with a faux sense of surprise. "I've talked to her every other day or so since you arrived."

Agitation sped up Ryan's heart. "Why?" he demanded.

With a shrug of her shoulders, Connie picked up a sandwich and laid it on her plate. "She calls me," she explained. "Maybe she wants an outsider's view of what's going on here."

The throbbing behind his eye quickened to match the accelerated beat of his heart. "That sounds like her," he snapped back as he grabbed a sandwich for himself. "Always nosing in on what I'm doing."

Olivia sighed. "It is her business. You're her boy. You'll always be her business."

A grunt of indignation came as the politest response Ryan could offer. "Thanks for reminding me."

"I'm right there with you," said Meade.

Connie leaned toward her son and poked him in the arm with her finger. "Pipe down. Oh, that reminds me—my overprotective mother part, that is—Ryan met Justin."

Meade's smile hardened into a sneer. "Really?" he replied. "Did he try to pick you up at a truck stop or an adult video store?"

A loud snort erupted from Connie's nose, forcing her to put a hand to her face.

"I met him when your mom was showing me my grandfather's buildings," Ryan explained, feeling uneasy about the new topic. "He was with his little girl."

Olivia and Connie's eyes shifted to Meade, waiting for a reaction.

"I guess he's still getting divorced?" Meade asked in a cold tone.

"He is," Olivia confirmed. "Mariann's already engaged to her new guy."

With a grumble of disgust, Meade shook his head. "No surprise that marriage failed."

Another stint of silence followed while each of them fiddled with their food.

"His little girl is adorable," Olivia finally remarked, an obvious effort to counter the negativity. "She's a sweetheart too."

Another quiet interlude followed.

"I guess I should be glad for that then," Meade murmured.

"Yes, you should," said Connie before her gaze turned to Ryan. "I heard you had a visit from a real estate agent today."

An urge to vomit bubbled in Ryan's throat. Confrontation often led to that feeling for him, but with a couple of deep breaths he quelled it. "How do you know that?" he asked, feeling embarrassed for not warning her.

She offered a motherly smile. "It's a small town, you hear everything," she answered. "Plus, Emma Woodhouse saw a car parked in your driveway with a real estate agent decal on the side and then saw you walking around town with him."

"Emma didn't seem very happy when we saw her," Ryan remarked.

"She voiced some disappointment with Ryan's editorial," Olivia said.

"I read that," Meade exclaimed, his smile returned. "I agree with you. This town needs to be more welcoming, if only to add some new people."

Connie's own smile shifted to a frown of concern as she shook her head. "In this town it'll be an uphill battle."

Ham, Ryan thought as he chewed his sandwich, he would have preferred turkey. "I guess I could always give everything I own away," he theorized. "Let whatever squatters that want it come and take it. That's what Olivia thinks, anyway."

"That's not what I think; I'm not talking about giving it away," she countered, giving his arm a light pinch in retaliation. "It would be low leases that cover your taxes, repairs and insurance. You wouldn't be making any money, but you'd be helping the town and eventually you might make some money."

Ryan shook his head. "You say this like I'll be living here. I won't be. I'll be in Los Angeles."

Olivia rolled her eyes. "You keep saying," she moaned. "But that's no reason to make this town suffer."

Attempting another bite of his sandwich seemed pointless with the comments hanging in the air, so he put it back on his plate. "How will I be making it suffer any more than it already is?" he protested.

"By turning its downtown into a seed and feed warehouse," she argued.

"What do you mean?" Connie asked.

Why did everyone have to know his business? Ryan wondered. "There's a man interested in buying some of the buildings to use as a local warehouse for his livestock feed business," he explained.

For the first time since meeting her, Ryan saw disappointment in Connie's eyes. "That's unfortunate," she murmured.

He said no more, picked his sandwich up and took another bite.

"What are you two up to tonight?" Olivia asked their hosts.

"I'm taking Mom to her first gay bar," Meade answered with a smug smile.

Amused surprise bloomed on Connie's face. "When did we decide this?" she demanded, followed by another snort.

Leaning back in his chair, Meade nodded. "It's been decided for you," he answered. "You're going to get to see some twenty-one-year-old shirtless hard bodies."

Despite her guise of reservation, Connie's eyes betrayed interest. "I don't know about that," she replied.

"I'd be up for it, if you don't mind company," Olivia volunteered. "How about you? You game for something a little different?" she asked Ryan.

—

"I'm almost painfully nostalgic," Meade remarked as the car passed the weathered and sagging "Welcome to White Oak City" sign. "In a different time, I could be happy living here."

Ryan turned the notion over in his mind for a moment before looking out the window and catching sight of an abandoned and rusty trailer park sitting outside the town's main gateway. "Why's that?" he inquired, trying to repress snobbish undertones.

Meade mulled his answer. "There's something comforting about a close-knit community. You know pretty much everybody. You can trust your mechanic not to rip you off. And, if you need help building a shed or cleaning out your gutters, you can always find someone to do it."

A pleased sigh reflected Connie's agreement.

"I thought you loved Chicago," Olivia countered.

"I do, it's a lot of fun," Meade responded. "There's always something to entertain myself with, some show, some event, lots of friends. But I sometimes don't know how much of that is real and how much filler. I could be happy just sitting on the porch and enjoying a nice bottle of wine on a Saturday evening. Savoring life, not being burdened by it."

Ryan glanced up, meeting Meade's inquisitive eyes in the rearview mirror. "That's awfully idealistic, don't you think?" he said.

"Life'll never be easy, but I think there's something noble about living in a small town," Meade explained. "You're not trying to rule the world; you're trying to have a good life. If I thought I wouldn't be shunned or regulated to second class, I'd work in Springfield and live in White Oak. Take a couple of trips a year to Chicago or New York, just to remind myself what the city is like, but keep home in my small town."

His mother turned from watching the countryside to him. "Why are we heading to Springfield then?" she asked.

A crafty smile filled his face. "This, my dear momma, is for your entertainment," he responded.

"My entertainment? Really?"

His deep laugh filled the car. "Maybe a little for mine," he replied, still smiling. "After all, if I move to Springfield, I need to know what my dating life would be like. Ryan, if White Oak was a nice, clean, well-maintained town, would you consider staying there?"

Connie twisted to face the back seat to make sure she did not miss his answer, while Olivia, more subtly, leaned her unturned head toward him.

With three quick, deep and calming breaths, Ryan prepared himself. "Being nice and clean wouldn't make up for the rest of it," he replied. "It's like you said, people here don't like change, they don't like different. I'm sure they'd be fine with the town being fixed up if it meant reopening the five-and-dime and getting a doctor or dentist to set up shop. But they don't want any improvement if they think it'll have them outnumbered, regardless of who it is—the Mexicans, the hippies, the gays. They're adverse to diversity. They'd be happy if everyone in town could be genetically engineered so each successive generation would look identical to the previous one."

Despite her smile, Connie shook her head. "You stereotype the people here too much," she countered. "Try and give them a little more credit and understanding."

Ryan knew he deserved some chastisement, as his generalizations went beyond what he believed. "You know what I mean," he responded. "Sure, people've been nice to me, but until this week I hadn't given them a reason otherwise. Can you imagine the letters to the editor the paper will get on Monday regarding the chicken plant and the people it'll bring?"

Olivia's hand tightened around his. "I know of three you'll be getting," she offered. "One from my father, one from my aunt and one from the neighbor across the street."

Sweat beaded along Ryan's hairline. "This is what I'm talking about," he complained.

CHAPTER 12

A PAINFUL THROB OF REGRET pulsed in Ryan's head, and opening his eyes only antagonized it. The breech of sunlight onto his senses intensified his discomfort like something akin to an ax blade separating his frontal lobes. With a gasping breath of surrender, he lapsed back into a semiconscious rest, hoping to sleep off his self-inflicted condition. But with the vigor of an electrical shock, his reprieve from a night of heavy drinking vanished in the digital chimes of a phone's ring tone.

The lumpy mattress shifted and bulged beneath him as Olivia turned over to answer her cell phone. "Good morning Mom," she offered in a chipper voice. "That sounds like a nice idea." A pause followed. "What time do you want us there?"

Ryan emitted a low grunt, which he hoped signaled both his displeasure at being forced awake and as a warning against any impositions being placed on him.

She hummed as she listened to her mother's instruction. "Yes, 9:30 will be fine," she confirmed. "See you soon."

The bedside clock announced it as 8:45, and though Ryan desperately hoped differently, he feared the newly made plans encroached upon his desire for more sleep.

"Wake up," she ordered him in a tender though firm voice, her warm breath tickling his ear. "We're having breakfast with my parents in forty-five minutes and then we're going to church with them."

He protested with a loud and defiant moan.

"I think you'll need to enunciate a little better than that," she whispered, her lips brushing against his ear.

With a discomforting shift, Ryan flipped over onto his back and looked up at her through painful, dry eyes. "I don't feel good," he mumbled, his mouth cottony.

She sternly nodded. "I see. Could that have something to do with you getting completely wasted at that gay bar last night?"

The throbbing intensified, making it painful to respond with a dirty look.

"I'm lucky you didn't run off with that skinny, curly-haired boy that liked you so much," she chided him. "I've never been jilted for another man before and I don't know how I would handle it."

The aching of his joints left him desperate for a glass of water and aspirin. "To be honest, I don't remember most of what happened after we got to the bar," he remarked in an exhausted voice. "Except, I remember Connie being treated like some sort of royalty after everyone found out she was Meade's mother and it was her first time in a gay bar."

A warm smile filled her face. "Wasn't that sweet? I guess they like to show moms a good time when they go there."

He smiled back at her. "How did we get home? I remember both Meade and Connie drinking quite a bit."

She nodded. "They did, in fact I'd expect Meade is worse off today than you are. I drove us all home. Last night was a lot of fun though. You seemed to enjoy it anyway."

A dull pain filled his head as he pushed himself up into a sitting position. "Yeah, I guess I did," he admitted. "But do I really have to get up to go have breakfast with you and your parents?"

—

The sandstone siding of the two-story house gleamed in the morning sun with the intensity of orange neon. A startling contrast to the shadowy first glimpse Ryan got of it the evening a week earlier when he escorted Olivia home. It inspired in him a sense of sentimental longing, though he recognized it not as a yearning for any aspect of his own past, but a desire for the charm of a revitalized White Oak City.

The forest green door popped open as they treaded up the porch steps, revealing a petite woman with a youthful bob of gray hair. "Hello Ryan," she offered in greeting as he and Olivia stepped inside the home. "I'm Maggie, Olivia's mom. I met you momentarily after your grandpa's funeral, but I also know you met a lot of people that day."

Ryan replied with a broad smile. "Yes, I did," he admitted. "And, to be honest, I don't remember who most of them were."

Maggie offered a motherly smile and polite nod before motioning for him to follow her through a door at the back of the entry hall. "Don't you worry. After a couple months you'll know everyone in town. Now, I know I've been told you plan on leaving, but some of us hope you decide to stick around."

Biting down on his lip, he held back the curt response simmering in his head and followed her through the door and into the kitchen, a room stuck in the 1970s with canary yellow cabinets and worn and chipped green Formica countertops.

A buoyant smile still on her face, Maggie directed him to sit down at the small table in a clumsy sunroom addition. He turned around for guidance from Olivia, but she no longer followed.

"She went to get her daddy," Maggie announced, her country accent now unmistakable. "You sit down, and they'll be right with us."

The unease of his lingering hangover twisted and turned in his stomach, amplified by his apprehension of being left alone with Maggie. He sat and began to nervously tap his fingers across the top of the breakfast table, unsure of what to say to the woman buzzing around the kitchen making breakfast. He took three deep breaths to calm his nerves and then jumped to his feet to offer her aid. But before he could utter a word, the door swung open and in stepped Olivia, followed by a hulking man with salt and pepper hair and a weathered and intimidating face.

Ryan stepped toward them, eager to provide as respectful a greeting as possible.

"Ryan, I want you to meet my dad, Gene," Olivia offered in introduction.

Gene's hand overwhelmed Ryan's in both size and strength as they shook. "Met you momentarily at your granddaddy's service, but didn't getta chance to talk to ya," he stated in a country vernacular even more pronounced than his wife's. "Whyn't you go ahead and have a seat and we can talk now."

Like an obedient puppy, Ryan sat down and waited as Gene took the seat opposite. The sunroom shook as the older man heavily plopped down into his chair. "Your granddaddy was a good man," he started. "Knew him for thirty-five years, ever since I married Maggie and moved here. She knew 'im her entire life, being born here and all."

Ryan offered a timid smile. "Everyone's been so friendly and nice to me since I got here," he replied, unsure of what to say.

The big man nodded. "That's good, though I don't know if they'll stay that way after that piece in the paper," Gene remarked, which he followed with a dissatisfied grunt.

Hearing the comment, Olivia abandoned her mother and marched to the table, clutching her father's shoulder with her hand. "Now Daddy, what'd we talk about," she warned.

Exasperation flushed Gene's face, but he nodded in submission. "Don't ya worry about that li'l girl." He groaned. "I'm not gonna talk about it. He'll see my letter tomorrow and then he'll know how I feel about it. I'm just talking in general here."

Her hand remained on her father's shoulder for a moment longer before she pulled away and returned to her mother's side.

"Regardless," Gene continued in a more deliberate tone. "I think you'll find most folks here are good, decent people."

Ryan nodded. "I've already learned that," he conceded.

—

Though dated by decades of changing styles, Rosemary's snow-white hair swept up into its stoic beehive made her the easiest person to spot in the Methodist church's sanctuary. Seated in what Ryan now accepted as her customary place in the third pew, she projected the image of a prim lady, sitting polite and reserved as the gossipy Lenora Bayridge, excessively accenting her remarks with her hands, spoke to her from the center aisle.

"I should say hi to my aunt," Ryan muttered to Olivia as they followed Maggie and Gene to their regular pew.

She slid her arm into the crook of his and tightly clasped his hand. "I'll come with you."

As they neared his aunt's pew, Lenora took notice and flashed a wide smile, exposing a smear of bright pink lipstick across her front teeth. She then leaned down to the older woman's ear and whispered something before stepping to the opposite side of the aisle and taking her own seat.

"Good morning, Aunt Rosemary," Ryan offered in greeting.

Her pale, age-creased face gazed up at him, a faint smile on her lips. "I was wondering if you were going to make it this morning," she replied. "I've saved places for you and Olivia."

The request triggered a slight panic, as he nervously glanced toward Olivia, unsure if they should take the seats, as they had arrived with her parents.

But with a gentle guiding push, Olivia steered him to the reserved spots. "We'd love to sit with you," she announced while offering him a wink, easing his concern.

The quiet chatter of the sanctuary came to a halt, as, with a worn black Bible clutched in his hand, the droopy-faced preacher sauntered up to the pulpit and glanced out among his thin flock. An inaudible sigh appeared to leave him, though Ryan could not tell if it signaled content or discontent, as the holy man's staid expression offered no other clues.

After a quiet clearing of his throat, the reverend opened his Bible and began his sermon. He started with a reference to the lessons of the Sermon on the Mount, before segueing into a lecture on being welcoming and kind and serving as a beacon of charity and compassion. Ryan could not help but feel his own controversial editorial may have helped inspire it.

Unlike the glossy, high-energy Sunday services of the handful of evangelical churches Ryan previously visited in Los Angeles, White Oak City's Methodist church seemed reliably sedate and traditional in its approach. The simplicity and lack of gimmicks gave the message a deeper sincerity. He had never felt so much as an inkling of holy inspiration at the over-produced productions put on in LA's mega churches, but sitting here, in the third pew between his aunt and Olivia, he felt something either emotional or spiritual stirring in him.

As the service reached its end, the preacher offered a closing prayer and cued the organist and pianist for a habitual refrain of "Joyful, Joyful, We Adore Thee," though the shuffling of feet and murmur of exiting congregants muted the sharpness of the well-worn song. Ryan, following Olivia's lead, rose to his feet and stepped to the aisle, from where he leaned down and presented his arm to aid his aunt in standing. The elderly woman took a slow breath and looked up, offering an appreciative nod before carefully hooking her thin arm into his and, with trying effort, slowly pulling herself up onto her feet.

An embarrassed flush colored Ryan's face as the truth of Rosemary's mortality lingered between them. With each thump of her cane, Rosemary moved a few inches forward, carefully balanced between his arm and her support. In his few short weeks in the town, her health appeared to have significantly deteriorated.

Emerging from the dimness of the church into the glare of the summer sun, he found his eyes briefly overwhelmed, before spotting the preacher perched on the top step, shaking hands and dispensing pleasant platitudes to his parishioners as they passed. When Rosemary's turn came, the reverend's dour expression transformed into a gentle smile, melting ten years from his age. "Hello, you dear, dear woman," he warmly greeted her as he took her left hand into both of his. "I hope you enjoyed today's service."

A sense of appreciation added color to Rosemary's pale cheeks. "Of course," she answered with a contented smile. "And I can't help but think that this young man next to me might have had something to do with the subject matter."

The preacher turned and appraised Ryan, the warm smile transforming into a Cheshire grin. "An artist never names his muse," he responded with faux snobbery.

Rosemary leaned against Ryan for a moment in an acknowledgement of success. "I think the proper term is a magician never reveals his tricks," she replied in a light manner. "But I'll let you keep your pride."

The preacher's own cheeks now blushed pink as he responded with a laugh. "You go on home now and get your rest. I plan to drop by and see you this week and I want you in top sparring form."

—

The aroma of a cooking Sunday dinner greeted them as Rosemary's front door opened. "Who's cooking?" Ryan asked, as he, with Olivia helping on the opposite side, walked his aunt past the threshold.

Pausing for a moment, Rosemary pulled heavily against Ryan's arm as she slid her keys back into her purse. "That's Vonnie," she replied as she zipped her purse shut. "Get my walker, will you dear?" she asked Olivia.

The folded walker leaned was against the entryway's wall, so Olivia unfolded it and positioned it in front of Rosemary.

At first, the older woman did not move, as if judging her own strength. But then, with a deep breath that made her entire body tremble in exhaustion, she began a slow procession across the living room and down the hall to her bedroom. Ryan and Olivia escorted her as far as the hallway, and then watched, ready to come to her aid if the journey proved too difficult.

"The same Vonnie that helped at my house after my grandfather died?" he quietly asked Olivia once his aunt was out of sight.

"I thought you knew," she answered. "Your aunt hires her as a part-time housekeeper. She comes in and cleans and cooks a few times a week, though it's been increasing in frequency lately."

He nodded. "I guess I assumed Aunt Rosemary did all the work, or maybe Marvin or Liddy."

"How're you today, young man?" a cheery voice asked from behind them.

Turning around, he recognized the jovial visage of the plump woman. "I'm well, ma'am," he replied with a friendly smile. "You seem to take care of everyone in this town."

Her answer came with a wide smile, which even on her full face seemed to reach the extremes of both sides. "I like to keep busy," Vonnie explained. "And I've sure been hearing some stories about you."

An embarrassed blush warmed his cheeks. "Good, I hope."

The smile remained on Vonnie's face. "Most," she answered. "Anyway, I needa finish dinner. And it's nice to see you too Olivia."

Olivia's fingers weaved in between Ryan's. "Thank you, you too," she replied to Vonnie, and then looped her arm around his waist once the older woman had disappeared. "For being the guy that riled up an entire town, you have awfully thin skin," she taunted him.

"What do you mean?" he shot back.

She sighed and leaned against him. "Your face went white as a sheet when she mentioned hearing about you from others," she explained.

—

"It means a lot to me, having you here," Rosemary remarked as she reached across the table to pat Ryan's arm. "I wondered what you were like. Your father was a nice young man, like you. He often visited and even after he moved away always sent me birthday and Christmas cards."

In Ryan's mind a memory kindled, and a tear gathered in the corner of his eye, recalling a boyhood conversation with his father about a favorite aunt. "I get more out of this than you do," he assured her, an emotional halting in his voice.

Her age-weakened posture corrected to an almost aristocratic pose. "That makes sense," she observed with a prophetic air. "You're supposed to. You have an entire life ahead of you, and the people you meet and talk with should help you develop morals and intuition. And you're doing a grand job so far."

A tear trickled down his cheek and he smiled. Though he normally felt embarrassed when being lauded, appreciation from his aunt created a feeling of pride.

"I heard you're selling your house," she continued in little more than a whisper.

He opened his mouth to respond, but only a dry wheeze came out. He swallowed hard, one moment praise, the next calling out his shame. "It makes sense, if I sell the newspaper," he hoarsely answered.

She sunk back into her chair, a slight figure against dark mahogany wood and olive velvet upholstery. "I was born in that house," she said. "Ninety-two years ago, this fall."

Pressure gathered in his chest, nearly to the point of suffocation. "I remember you mentioning that," he murmured in response.

Her blue eyes disappeared for a moment behind pale, almost translucent, eyelids. "A lifetime ago," she uttered in a ghostly voice. "So was your grandfather and your great-grandfather. My father, your great-great-grandfather, built it in 1916."

"I had no idea there was so much family history in it. Who lived on the farm?" he asked, hoping to shift topics.

A weak smile emerged on her tired face. "The farm's where my father was born in 1876, and his father before him in 1853," she explained. "My grandfather was the first member of our family born here, six months after his parents arrived from Tennessee. When he was a boy, the Civil War happened. Thus, when I was a girl, he told me stories of the skirmishes that happened around the farm and how bushwhackers came on four different occasions, stealing food and livestock, and even burning down the barn. He had an uncle that was killed by them, after he followed them to get back stolen mules."

The story seemed more like the movies than real events that his ancestors faced on the farm a few miles away. "They lived in the house that's there now?" he asked.

She shook her head. "Oh, no. That house was built in 1890, after the old one collapsed following a big snow storm. My grandmother died when it happened. Everyone else was outside trying to get ice and snow off the roof. She'd been sick and unable to get out of bed, so she laid there, listening to the roof creak under the weight. Finally, the timbers snapped and it all came down on top of her."

"How tragic." Olivia gasped. "You never knew your grandmother?"

With a slow shift, Rosemary turned in her chair to face Olivia. "Not that one," the older woman answered. "But Ryan's house, where he's living, was built to replace one that had belonged to my mother's mother, so she lived with us in it when I was a girl. In fact, I shared a room with her until I was twelve, and she passed away." Rosemary turned back to Ryan. "That old house is like a member of the family. It has witnessed our births, our life's adventures and for several, their deaths. All those who've lived in it have loved it, and don't we all kind of want to be able to die someplace we love. I love that house too, but I also love this one."

Tears streaked down Olivia's cheeks and dripped off her chin to leave damp polka dots on the tablecloth. "I couldn't agree more," she proclaimed. "What an incredible connection that gives you to your house, Ryan."

Such a history also meant much emotional baggage, he thought to himself. But, at the same time, he could not help but feel sentimental. For generations his family lived and experienced all of life's defining moments in those same rooms.

CHAPTER 13

Self-righteousness fogged the air as Ryan arrived at the newspaper office early Monday morning. For despite the contours of Ebetta's mouth being those that typically denote genial affection, the steely gaze of her eyes seemed more akin with arrogance.

She leered at him as he nodded to her in greeting. "Good morning," she addressed him in a cold voice, but only once he passed far enough by for a response to be inconvenient. "This has arrived for you since Friday." On the edge of her desk sat a three-inch pile of opened mail.

The woman obviously found pleasure in his discomfort. With a quick pivot of his feet, he headed back in her direction, coming to a stop at the edge of her desk. An unwelcoming chill ran up his spine.

The stack of letters rested precariously on the edge, a positioning that seemed deliberate. He reached down to scoop them up from underneath, just as her foot gave the underside of the desk a jarring kick. They came tumbling down, but by luck, most of them fell into his hand's ready grasp, only a few slipping past him. The term "Mexican Lover" stared up at him from one of those that landed on the floor.

In defiance of the smugness on Ebetta's face, he calmly straightened back up, all the correspondence now in his hands, and spent an exaggerated moment shuffling the letters while staring her in the eyes. "I'll take these back to my desk," he snarled. "After I get a chance to go through them, I'll bring you the best and you can typeset them into the system."

Her eyes angrily blazed. "I'll wait on that, sugar," she replied. Then the phone on her desk rang. She answered in her most syrupy voice, and then paused to listen. "Why he just came in and I'd love to transfer you to his phone," she replied. "You better go answer that. He wants to talk to you about the editorial," she taunted Ryan as she sent the call to the editor's office.

Taking three deep breaths to calm himself, he walked away from her. "Fine," he snapped as he headed in the direction of the ringing phone. "But no calls on the editorial today. You ask them if that's what they're calling about and if it is, tell them that due to a high volume of interest we are only taking written responses or comments on it at this time."

—

A pulsing stress headache left Ryan's temples aching, making the task of sifting through the stack of letters exceptionally arduous. He leaned back in his chair and closed his eyes, trying to sweep all thoughts from his mind, if only momentarily. With the exhale of a deep breath, he opened his eyes again and gazed out into the newsroom. Most of the staff now sat at their desks, with cheerful morning chatter being shared among them. He wished for enough good humor to join them, but he could only offer a scowl and unease. So instead, he pulled an envelope off the stack and tore it open. The language he read would make a pornographic film seem genteel, and with no signature or return address, he started his first unpublishable pile.

For the next two hours he plodded through the rest of the stack, categorizing them into piles that best defined the content of each. The negative pile held fourteen, the negative with abusive language five, the negative and nearly illiterate three, and the positive pile, a surprising three. Then came twenty-five emails, all negative, that Ebetta forwarded to him from the paper's feedback email address, though he suspected she may have permanently deleted any positive ones before he had the chance to see them. By the time he finished sorting and determining which twenty to pass onto Ebetta for publication, lunchtime had arrived.

His back ached from sitting hunched over in his chair, so he stood up and stretched before stepping out into the newsroom. Hopeful for company for lunch, he felt disappointment in a near empty newsroom, spotting only Ebetta at the front desk and Mary Beth and Mandy at their own. "Where is everybody?" he asked.

The clicking of Mary Beth's typing ceased as she looked up at him. "Jerry and Glo went to lunch at the diner, Connie has a dentist appointment in Springfield, and Mark and Casey are taking a college writing course at MSU this afternoon," she answered, her eyes never leaving her computer monitor.

He briefly loitered near the two women, hoping either Mandy or Mary Beth would inquire about his lunch plans. Though having surrendered an answer to his question, they returned to a more apathetic attitude concerning his presence. That left Ebetta, but he could think of no one he would want to go to lunch with less, so he let out a disappointed sigh and stepped back inside his office to grab the keys to his grandfather's house. But then the dull dinging of the cowbell pulled his attention to the front office, where he saw Meade stepping inside the door.

"Hi sugar," Ebetta offered Meade in greeting, while giving the young man a judgmental eye. "Your momma isn't here right now."

The young man nodded while gesturing to Ryan. "I know. I'm here to see Ryan."

Ebetta went rigid in response before turning her head in Ryan's direction and giving him an inquisitorial look. "I see." She exhaled a breath of air, emulating the hissing of a snake.

A relieved smile came to Ryan's face as he approached Meade, his hand outstretched in greeting. "Hey buddy," he exclaimed as they shook. "I guess you recovered all right from Saturday night?"

Ebetta's eyes grew in wonder.

"I did fine; Mom forced lots of water down me when we got home," he replied, ignoring the receptionist's stare. "She seemed to think I've never had to stem a hangover before."

They laughed, and Ebetta delivered a snort of disapproval, prompting Meade to turn his head just enough so she couldn't see him roll his eyes in annoyance. "Anyway," he continued. "Olivia said she was busy taking her grandmother to the doctor, so I suggested I come by and you and I get some lunch together."

Ryan nodded, thankful for the surprise company. "That's a great idea. I was about to go home and try to make do with what's there, but I'm sure you can think of something better."

—

Ryan closed his eyes as he collapsed into the passenger seat. "That bitch is driving me crazy," he announced once Meade had the car moving in the direction of the old high school. "Did you notice her staring at us the entire time?"

Meade flashed a crafty grin. "Maybe she thinks I'm trying to steal you from Olivia," he quipped.

"I hadn't thought about that," Ryan replied. "Why don't we start making out in front of her when we get back? Maybe it'll give her a heart attack."

In an entertained, though disapproving manner, Meade shook his head. "I'm sure she'd say something like 'I'm praying for you boys' or such," he answered, using a nasally tone to mock her voice. "At least that's what she always tells my mom about me. She's never specific about what she's praying for, but we assume it's the gay thing. Small town sensibilities."

Ryan nodded in agreement with the sarcasm. "And you all want me to stay here," he groaned.

For a moment, Meade offered no response, but then he shrugged his shoulders. "I'd have more than one friend to see when I visit. When I walk in the grocery store here, half of them, those that recognize me, stop talking and stare."

Such narrow mindsets, Ryan thought, but still feeling drained from sifting through the morning hate mail, he said nothing more, wanting to avoid a discussion on the town's bias. Instead, he took in the scenery as Meade drove the car east of town. They passed the farm and the cemetery where his grandfather lay buried, and then turned left off the state highway and onto a small paved road. About two miles along, the pavement ended at a weathered and imposing two-story, wood-frame building. A small dirt parking lot, half filled with cars, stretched across the front of the building, and a faded and peeling sign above the entrance proclaimed it as the best catfish in the county.

Meade pulled the car to a stop in a space near the entrance. "I know what you're thinking, 'where the hell did he bring me?'" he admitted without prompting. "But the Johansson Inn is some of the best food around, even if the ambiance is a little pre-war, no plumbing."

Hesitation kindled in Ryan's mind, but he trusted Meade's judgment. "Looking at the number of cars, it's either good food or an excellent place to stay at on vacation," he half-heartedly offered.

"Stay at on vacation?" Meade asked, confusion showing on his face. "Oh, the inn part of the name. They don't rent rooms here, at least not any more. It's just a restaurant."

—

Though initially glossing over Meade's remark on the primitive style of the place, upon stepping inside Ryan found it not overstated. The roughhewn paneling of the interior walls and the exposed beams of the ceiling, combined with an assortment of rakes, horse harnesses, and other farming implements tacked to the walls in a haphazard display, gave it the unapologetic appearance of the inside of a barn. The dining area itself proved nothing more than long tables butted up against each other in rows across the room, with battered and mismatched metal folding chairs for seating.

A prune-faced old man sitting behind the cash register glanced up at them. "Take a seat anywhere boys. If you want the buffet, help yourselves and Selma'll get you some drinks."

Meade nodded to the man and led Ryan to a table across the room from the entrance, where a short, fat woman with long, oily, brown hair approached them. "What do y'all want to drink?" she asked in the raspy voice of a smoker.

"I'll have a Diet Coke," Meade responded.

"Iced tea for me," Ryan answered.

The woman nodded while giving Meade an intense inspection, as if deciding if she knew him. "You both want the buffet?" she asked.

"Yes," Meade answered.

Ryan let out a soft laugh. "Aren't you the strong, take-charge type, ordering for me and all," he joked, earning a suspicious glare from the waitress.

The line through the buffet moved quickly, with Meade giving Ryan recommendations and what—the catfish—and what not—the salmon—to try. And from the first bite, Ryan felt thankful for Meade's direction in both the restaurant and food choices, for, despite its remote location and lack of refinement, the cooking beat out much of what he knew at even high-end Los Angeles restaurants.

"How does one resist coming here daily? It's much better than the diner," he remarked as he scraped up the last bits of food from of his second pass through the buffet. But Meade, happy and talkative throughout the rest of the meal, now offered no response. Ryan looked up from his plate to see a nervous expression across the table from him. "What's wrong?" he asked.

With a slow blink, Meade's distant, taut gaze vanished, replaced by a panicky scan of the room. "Oh," he responded. "I see someone."

Leaning slightly to his right, Ryan craned his neck around to follow the direction of Meade's eyes, spotting at the restaurant's entrance a group of three men. One had a familiar, though not immediately recognizable face. "I think I've met the guy in the green polo," he said as he turned back around.

Meade shifted erratically in his chair, mimicking Ryan's movements as if trying to hide himself. "You have," he muttered.

Looking back a second time might seem suspicious, so Ryan tried to reimagine the man's face in his mind. "What's his name?" he asked, hoping to jog his memory.

Drops of sweat had bubbled up along Meade's hairline. "Justin Miller," he answered in a low voice, his lips barely moving.

"Wait, the guy you knew in high school? The prick that beat you up?"

Meade said nothing in response as he kept peering past Ryan, while simultaneously trying to hide behind him.

"How about as they get their food, I pay the check and we get out of here?" Ryan suggested as he stood.

With a few pats of his napkin, Meade dried off his sweaty forehead. "That's probably a good idea," he answered as he also got to his feet. "Let's go."

The prune-faced man at the register seemed less concerned about getting the money right than Meade's odd behavior, so Ryan added an extra five dollars to the tip, which seemed to quell any worries.

"Wait," Meade exclaimed, having refocused long enough to realize Ryan had settled the bill. "I was going to cover it."

Ryan offered an understanding smile. "I think you deserve the treat today," he remarked as he pushed the door open for them to leave. The midday sun struck brightly against them, providing an instant of glaring exposure for the patrons inside, from where a man's voice yelled Meade's name.

His face blanching white, Meade charged forward in a dash to the car, with Ryan following in a quick trot. But the man in the green polo rushed as well, reaching the car as Meade struggled to fish the keys out of his pocket.

Panting from his own exertions, Justin's expression reflected unease. "I thought that was you," he said. "I ... I wanted to say hello."

The color remained drained from Meade's face, with his lips only the faintest of pink. "Hello," he responded in a shaky voice.

They avoided eye contact while still watching each other. "I heard you were in town," Justin continued. "I hoped we could have a chance to talk."

The apprehension on Meade's face eased as he gazed off into the woods behind the restaurant. "Have you met Ryan Shipley?" he asked.

A hint of accusation surfaced in Justin's eyes as he glanced at Ryan. "Um, yeah, a few weeks ago," he responded coldly. "It's nice to see you again."

Ryan offered only a nod.

Justin stepped closer to Meade, impeding the opening of the car door. With a discontented sigh, Meade gently pushed the door against Justin's body, urging him a step back.

"Meade, can I please talk to you?" Justin pleaded as he moved back. "It's been a long time. I need to tell you some things."

If anguish emitted an odor, Ryan imagined it as the faint burned smell he noticed as Meade dropped down into the driver's seat, his left hand resting on the open car door, ready to pull it shut. "I can't now," he answered. "I need to get Ryan back to work. If you want, come to dinner at my mom's house on Wednesday night. I'll tell her to expect you."

Justin's jaw dropped. "Your mom's house?" he whimpered. "Can't we meet someplace else?"

Meade sternly shook his head. "That's the only time I have available," he countered.

—

With the 5 o'clock chime of the office's regulator clock still in his ears, Ryan glanced up as the clanking of the cowbell announced a visitor. He feared yet another letter or agitated reader arrived to berate him, but instead a chipper and smiling Olivia had stepped inside. "Good afternoon," she greeted Ebetta.

Ebetta's posture stiffened with a sense of superiority. "Good afternoon to you," she replied with a prim smile. "You here to see Ryan?"

Olivia waved at him. "I missed lunch with him, so I gotta get him for dinner," she replied.

Spite simmered on Ebetta's face as she also looked in his direction. "That's nice. Yes. He had lunch with Connie's son, Meade," Ebetta explained, putting an emphasis on the word lunch.

Olivia's face belied a hint of suspicion, as if she sensed Ebetta's intent. "I know," she happily responded. "I'd asked Meade to come by and take him to Johansson's."

A hesitant, but somewhat approving nod, followed from Ebetta, likely rewarding herself that she did not work for a homosexual.

But Olivia did not wait for additional response, turning away from her and stepping toward the gate that divided the front office from the newsroom. "I'm going to grab him now," she announced as she left the older woman's domain.

Trying not to appear too eager, Ryan waited until she passed two-thirds of the newsroom before he slipped out from behind his desk to greet her. "Don't you look especially good today," he offered in compliment as she neared him.

She paused to think up a retort. "I did take Grandma to the doctor, so I figured I needed to look good if I have any hope of getting one for a husband," she chided him.

Ryan offered a haughty nod. "I see," he replied. "Any luck with that?"

Her eyes sparkled as she sidestepped his extended arms. "Not this time. Though there was an exceptionally flirty, partially-retired doctor that kept trying to look down the front of my top. I guess next time I should wear something lower-cut, so he won't have to strain so hard. I'd hate to give him a heart attack."

The image of a salivating old man leaning over enough to nearly topple himself while trying to glimpse Olivia's breasts flashed in his head, leaving him laughing loudly. "I had no idea you were so giving," he kidded before pivoting on his feet and catching her in his arms.

A schoolgirl giggle escaped her as she accepted his embrace.

"Have you talked to Meade since lunch?" he asked her.

Her slackened body firmed up as she thought. "No, I haven't, but did you have a good lunch? I told him to take you to the catfish restaurant. It's a little seedy, but the food's great."

He nodded. "The food was great," he agreed. "But there was a bit of an uncomfortable situation as we left."

"What happened?"

With a soft rubbing, he massaged her upper arms to relax her. "We ran into Justin Miller."

Again, her body went tense. "Oh my god. Did he say anything?"

Tightening his arms around her, he let out a sigh. "As a matter of fact, he did. He said he wanted to talk to Meade. In fact, he insisted on talking to him."

With a gentle push, she broke away from his hold, leaving only his left hand on her hip. "What did they talk about?" she asked.

He shook his head and then placed his right hand on her shoulder. "They didn't, at least not much. Instead, they made plans for Justin to come to Connie's house for dinner on Wednesday. They'll talk then."

A red flush filled her cheeks. "Hasn't he hurt Meade enough?" she protested. "How can that asshole possibly have the nerve to talk to him, after all the trouble he caused?"

--

With boarded up windows, peeling paint and closed signs nearly ghosted into the stone and brickwork, most of the buildings on the west side of the square existed as mere shadows of their previous selves, like so many others on the surrounding blocks. But, like an oasis in the desert, right in the middle stood a stark exception. LaSalle's Hardware, occupying a large two-story building of as old a vintage as any other in the town, looked as crisp and clean as one would have imagined it upon the structure's completion in 1893, as cited by its ornate Mesker Brothers cornice. Large display windows, flanking the sides of a recessed double-door entrance, acted as well-lit advertisements for the various wares that could be found inside, throwbacks in style and use to a time before the desertion of downtowns for malls and big boxes.

As attractive and nostalgic as the outside appeared, the inside easily trumped it. A long open room with a pressed tin ceiling and massive glass globes illuminating row after row of display shelves filled with every imaginable tool and household item. Two massive brass cash registers dominated the dark-stained oak counter that sat to the right of the entrance, and a wide set of stairs at the back of the room ascended to a second story, where a placard on the wall promised fabrics, notions and toys.

"This is like something out of an old movie," Ryan observed as he and Olivia walked past the counter and into the store, which appeared sans staff or customers.

She grasped his arm with her hand, her warmth prompting a smile from him. "Isn't it something," she agreed. "There's a picture of this same room from about 1928 on the wall over there, and except for the advancements in power tools and appliances, it looks much the same. I see Mrs. LaSalle back stocking shelves. Everyone calls the owner Beau, but his wife is always Mrs. LaSalle, unless you're fifty or older."

The thump of boots on the stairs echoed across the room. "Evening," they heard Beau's voice offer in welcome as he descended. "I bet you're here to pick up that box of stuff for your mother, Olivia. Come on back and I'll get it for you."

They followed him in the direction of his wife, who was hunched over near a counter identified as "Special Orders."

"Betty, dear, we have customers," Beau announced as he neared her.

The older woman's copper-colored hair hung in a heavy bob around her deeply-lined face. "Hello Olivia," Mrs. LaSalle offered in greeting. "And you must be the attractive young man I keep hearing about. I knew your granddaddy, your daddy and your great-granddaddy," Mrs. LaSalle's bright blue eyes twinkled. "They were all good-looking men."

Ryan nodded. "Thank you," he murmured

"You're also the one that wrote that article in the paper that's got everybody in an uproar," she continued. "I don't know that I agree with you completely, but I know Beau's a hundred percent on your side. He even got into an argument at Saturday's summer league baseball game about it."

Beau had vanished through a door behind the counter, but now reappeared carrying a sealed cardboard box. "Stop telling that boy I'm a tough guy," he retorted, a smile on his face. "Here Olivia, this is for you." He handed her the box. "Now, Ryan, you did a great job on the editorial, and, believe it or not, I think you may have actually gotten some of these brick-heads to think. Not necessarily agree, but to think about it."

A nice sentiment, Ryan thought, but he still felt skeptical. "I don't know about that, the hate mail I've gotten far outweighs the love mail," he replied.

The older man smiled and shook his head in a fatherly way. "Don't you see. One piece of mail agreeing with you makes all the difference. A couple of years ago I doubt you would've gotten anything supporting that type of idea. But I think some people realize it may be the only way to save this town."

A feeling of warmth bloomed in Ryan's chest in response to the affirmation. "You're making me feel a little better about it," he offered.

"Glad to do my part," Beau replied, his broad smile exposing nearly every tooth. "If you want a big story for this week, the clown that owns the old high school has filed an action to get us to stop trying to put it through the historic review process."

With the news of the week so far centering on the non-lethal explosion of a meth lab, Ryan felt relief for Beau's suggestion of something with more depth. "If he got his way with this legal action, what would it mean?" Ryan asked.

Beau sighed. "Since this town has such weak planning and zoning laws, he could have it torn down in as little as two weeks," he explained. "We'll know on Wednesday morning what the court has to say."

Great info and no recorder or notepad, Ryan thought to himself. "That should give me time to get it in Friday's paper," he remarked.

The old man nodded. "I think so. This is a story most people in town are on the same side of, to save the old building if it's at all possible. Could you imagine the empty spot this town would have in it without it?"

Olivia slid her arm around Ryan's back and pulled him close to her. "I'd be heartbroken," she said. "I know it's just another empty building, but if the chicken plant goes in and then if Ryan gets renters in his empty buildings, this town might have a chance to live again."

Beau nodded. "Indeed. What are you thinking about doing with your buildings? As I've told you, I have a lot of property here too."

Ryan felt Olivia's arm tighten around him. "I forgot, you don't know," she exclaimed. "Ryan might be able to get contracts set up for people to start businesses in the buildings for low leases, only the money they need to handle renovations, merchandise, insurance and taxes, some of which could come from state and federal historic grants, but the city council would need to declare the old commercial district blighted."

Leaning back against a dusty Old Timer Knives display, Beau mused on the idea. "If it means getting access to state and federal grants, I'd be open to whatever necessary provisions are needed, such as a blighted designation," he consented. "As long as that doesn't make it easier to start tearing stuff down."

Olivia's arm dropped from around Ryan and she stepped toward Beau. "I've been doing some research on the matter and it does not need to change any historic restrictions," she assured him. "As far as Ryan's concerned, he doesn't care about making money off the buildings. He wants to make sure the taxes and upkeep can be paid on them, which would make them a low-cost option for people interested in starting small businesses."

Beau nodded. "This sounds like a great idea. Do you have a proposal put together?"

Ryan shook his head. "No, I haven't," he shot Olivia a questioning look. "I'm only now learning about some of it."

CHAPTER 14

As Wednesday morning passed into afternoon, the bulk of the newspaper's pages sat ready for the printer. But a few holes remained, most notably for the still developing story on the old high school building and then a small place for an article on that night's summer baseball league game.

Thumbing through the page proofs, Ryan could not help but feel pride in the nearly final product, even when considering the largely negative letters to the editor section, which Glo deemed the largest published in two decades. Ryan forced his way through a final read of the country correspondents' columns, one of which provided an almost painful amount of detail on a newly built barn.

Connie stepped into the editor's office, her arrival offering him a break from the tedious articles. "Do you mind if we talk about a personal matter?" she asked, concern marring her normally friendly face.

He motioned for her to sit down. "Of course not."

Tears brimmed in her eyes as she sat. "I'm worried to death about dinner tonight," she cried out.

"I know," he replied, as he also felt uncomfortable about the looming situation "I'm not really sure what to make of it. I wasn't here when that situation happened. but from what you and Olivia have both told me, it was very upsetting for Meade."

The tears trickled down her cheeks as she nodded. "It was. He was never really the same after it happened. I mean, he really loved Justin and then to have those feelings treated the way they were. I don't think the fact Justin later got married and had a child helped either."

Ryan leaned back in his chair. "Meade is a confident, smart guy. Maybe this'll give him an opportunity to bring closure to any pain that came with that situation. He obviously doesn't need this guy."

Her brow, heavily furrowed in thought, added the appearance of an extra decade to her age. "Maybe you're right," she answered with a newfound stoicism. "I need to have a more positive outlook. I'm so worried about protecting my baby, I might be missing the benefit in this." She then sighed and brushed the tears out of her eyes.

Unease lingered in Ryan's gut, but he hoped his theory would prove fact. "I can see it happening, although I can't know for sure."

With a deep breath of relief, Connie got to her feet. "Well. I'm going to follow your lead and have a positive mindset going into it. On a different note, have you heard anything from Beau yet about the court hearing?"

He shook his head. "He said he'd call when the hearing was over and tell me what happened. If the court goes with this guy, that building could be gone in a few weeks or less."

New tears appeared in her eyes. "That'll be a sad day for me and a lot of other people. Generations of people from here went to school in that building."

"If someone really wanted it saved, they could have bought it," he replied.

A heavy frown pulled down her face. "I know," she answered as she shook her head. "I think everyone was expecting someone else, like your grandfather, to secure it. Then time ran out."

Glancing across the office through the front window, he caught sight of the empty row of buildings that filled the opposite side of the street. So many vacancies already crowded the town, perhaps one that big and expensive to renovate crossed a breaking point. "I think it could be modernized into a decent apartment building for people moving into town to work at the plant," he suggested, trying to create positive thought in his own mind as well as hers.

She nodded. "At least then it would have some life in it," she added.

—

As it passed 3:00 p.m., Ryan's anxiety concerning the void on the front page left him pacing the newsroom. He could wait no longer. Barry would need to perform an emergency redesign of the newspaper's news section to get it to the printer in time. But the ringing of the phone cut in before he could give the order.

"I'm sorry for not calling sooner, but the morning items took a lot longer than planned, so they held it until after lunch," Beau offered in apology. "Then the discussion of the school lasted more than two hours, which, frankly, surprised me."

Pressed for time, Ryan felt little patience for what he considered the unimportant details. "What did they decide?"

A pause that hinted at surprise came from Beau's end of the line. "They haven't dismissed it," he responded. "It'll come up for a formal decision in three months, so at least we have breathing room. But, even then, if the owner can prove there's no viable or cost conducive use for the building, he can still get a permit to tear it down."

"But this is good news for now, right?" Ryan asked in clarification.

"Yes, now at least there is a little hope for saving the old girl," Beau explained, which he followed with a quiet laugh. "But, I can tell you, Calvin Woodmont was upset. He yelled until the judge had him escorted out. He said it was his building and he was going to do with it what he pleased."

Ryan looked back at the blur of notes he had been taking, hoping he would remember what they meant once he was off the call. "This will be a great front-page story," he said when Beau had finished relating a few more details of the hearing. "Thanks for your help, I really appreciate it."

After hanging up the phone, Ryan picked up the receiver again and dialed Calvin Woodmont's number, trepidation flooding him as he did so. He did not want to talk to the aggressive and blustery man, but he knew it good journalism to at least try. The phone rang three times before Ryan heard a click. "What the hell do you want?" an angry voice demanded.

"Hello, is this Calvin Woodmont," Ryan politely asked.

He heard exhausted breathing on the other end. "Yes, and who are you?" the man thundered back.

Ryan took a deep breath. "I'm Ryan Shipley with the *Decatur County Times-Gazette* and I'd like to ask you a few questions about the court hearing today."

For the next fifteen minutes, Ryan took notes as the man unleashed his aggravation by swearing and yelling about the injustice of the process. He made himself out as a self-styled savior for White Oak City and the "miserable people" who lived there. In the few instances when the diatribe lulled, Ryan attempted to ask questions, but the man ignored him and instead tried to make it out as some sort of greater political philosophy. The conversation came to a sudden and abrupt end when Ryan asked about next steps, to which Calvin Woodmont declared "none of your business" and hung up the phone.

Glancing down at his notes, he saw maybe eight sentences as printable without having to retract the man's inappropriate language. Using what he had, he pulled together a barebones story, planning to plug in additional specifics and comments from Beau and Calvin Woodmont after the decision.

"Did he say anything about the editorial?" Glo's gruff voice queried. The older man stood in the doorway of the office, looking down on Ryan.

Ryan thought back on the conversation. "He didn't," he answered.

With a slow shuffle, Glo stepped back from the desk. "I'd guess he never saw it," he remarked. "If he had, he would have told you to fuck off the minute he heard who you were."

"I think you're right," Ryan answered, which he followed with an appreciative laugh.

"I know I am," Glo groaned. "I've been doing this longer than you've been alive."

—

"Do I look friendly?" Connie asked as she welcomed Olivia and Ryan inside her front door.

Both the tone and the question seemed uncharacteristic of her, leaving Ryan with an uneasy feeling. "Yes, but you always look friendly," he answered.

"Meade's asked you to be extra nice tonight, hasn't he?" Olivia said.

The stiff smile on Connie's face twisted into a sneer. "That's pretty much it," she admitted. "I think he's afraid I'll shoot Justin and hang him up in the yard like a gutted deer."

The ease with which Connie offered the anecdote goaded Ryan's discomfort. But a few hours earlier she had assured him of her benign approach to the evening, while these wrathful remarks proved she still felt venomous toward the yet-to-arrive guest. Every instinct he had screamed to turn around and leave instead of walking deeper into someone else's domestic drama. Only the sound of Meade's even-keeled voice calling from down the hall calmed his nerves enough that he could keep moving forward.

Hunched over a massive broiled salmon filet, Meade fastidiously arranged garnishes that would doubtlessly be pushed aside as soon as the platter hit the dining room table. And all this zealous attention to detail seemed a sign that despite Meade's reticence about seeing Justin again, he still felt the need to impress him with a meal of relatively sophisticated courses of couscous, gazpacho, and tiramisu for dessert.

"This is a lavish spread," Olivia commented as she brought a freshly baked roll to her nose for a sniff. "I was expecting something more like undercooked TV dinners."

Connie laughed. "That's what it'd be if I was cooking," she responded.

The remarks elicited a disapproving frown from Meade. "Now, now, this isn't just for him, this is for you guys too. Mom's had my cooking, but I've never cooked for you two, so I felt the need to impress."

It seemed like more than the standard amount of self-justification, Ryan thought. "Maybe you're also letting him see what he lost," he pressed.

A slight smile replaced Meade's frown. "May have crossed my mind," he admitted.

Connie patted her son on the back. "That's an idea I can go with. Please tell me he's one of those people who doesn't like fish?"

Embarrassment reddened Meade's face as he shook his head. "He loves fish," he admitted.

"I hope you know what you're doing," Connie cautioned before giving her son a quick hug. "Olivia, come with me and help set the table. We've been ordered to use my grandmother's china and silver tonight. But I'm making sure Justin gets the plate with the chip in it."

The two women left, so Ryan stepped up to the counter as Meade continued working. "Anything I can help with?" he asked, hoping Meade understood he meant it more for his emotional wellbeing than for the meal.

Meade paused for a second before continuing with his preparations. "I've got it pretty under control," he answered. "Just keeping the fish and asparagus warm until Justin gets here."

The tile countertop felt cool against Ryan's back as he leaned on it. "Your mom is worried," he said. "She thinks you're going a bit overboard."

The color bled out of Meade's face. "I know. I agree with her. I am going overboard, and I don't know why."

The last sentence did not feel entirely honest. "You sure you don't know why?" Ryan asked.

After a slight hesitation, a weak smile emerged on Meade's face. "I know why," he admitted. "It's because this little nostalgic part of me is still in love with him. We were best friends for ten years, lovers for two. I was completely devastated when all that shit happened. It destroyed me for a while. If it wasn't for my mom and getting out of here when I did, I don't know what would have happened. I'd be lying if I said suicide hadn't crossed my mind at least once."

Ryan laid his hand on Meade's shoulder, surprised but grateful for the candor. "I can't imagine how tough it was. I've had some heart breaks, but nothing even remotely on the level of what you experienced."

Meade quit fidgeting with the fish and turned around and leaned against the countertop beside Ryan. "This wouldn't be happening if we hadn't run into him the other day," Meade confessed. "I would have gone on in my obliviousness concerning him. I would have kept thinking he was just another insincere asshole. Then we saw him, and he followed me and insisted. Now, here we are, and I've made this nice dinner, creating some subconscious or maybe conscious hope that he'll suddenly be head over heels for me. It doesn't help that he's still so damn good looking. A few years older, but still good looking."

Ryan laughed and shook his head. "I doubt any of my ex-girlfriends would say the same about me."

No good-natured laugh came from Meade in response, as Ryan hoped, instead an exhausted sigh. "I'm glad you guys are here tonight," he said. "I need stability, if I'm going make it through this."

"That's why we're here," Ryan replied. "Want me to open that bottle of chardonnay?"

With the practice of a sommelier, Meade picked up the bottle and inspected it. "Also open the pinot noir," he responded. "Both work with the fish, and I know Mom prefers red, so might as well have it too."

Ryan pulled the corks from both bottles and then poured a gulp of the pinot noir into a glass. He lifted it to his mouth, but the tang barely touched his tongue when the tinkling chime of the doorbell sounded, sending shivers up his spine. He glanced across the table to Meade, whose normally rosy cheeks had paled.

"I guess he's here," Meade muttered.

Olivia's head popped in through the doorway. "Who should answer it?" she asked.

For a moment, Meade only stared, as if confused by the question. "Could you, please," he then answered. "Mom might not do the best job, and I need to finish here." The fidgeting with the fish resumed as Olivia ducked back out of the room.

"Hey buddy, buck up, ok?" Ryan encouraged him. "We're here for you."

Fear simmered in Meade's eyes. "I know," he muttered. "I've always been lucky to have Olivia as a friend, and I'm lucky to have you as one too."

Ryan nodded. "Same for me."

Though muffled by distance and doors, Ryan could hear Olivia's light and cheery greeting at the front of the house, followed by Justin's inaudible response. More inaudible comments followed from Connie.

Meade acted as though immune to the sounds of the interaction in the other room, but the nervous shaking of his hands showed otherwise. "I'm almost done," he said. "Would you take the wine into the dining room and see how things are going with everyone? I'll bring the food out in a few minutes."

Ryan watched Meade for a moment longer but saw nothing else he could add in actions or words, so he grabbed the bottles and passed through the door into the dining room. The situation he stepped into appeared tenser than he expected. Justin anxiously sat in a chair in the corner, lorded over by a standing Olivia and Connie. "Hi Justin, good to see you again," Ryan said in greeting as he butted in between the two women and leaned over to shake his hand.

Relief flashed in the angst-ridden eyes. "Good to see you again," Justin responded in a wavering voice.

Straightening back up, Ryan hooked his arm through Olivia's and stepped her back a few feet. "Meade said dinner is about ready," he announced.

An irritable grimace showed on Connie's face. "We were getting into a good discussion," she commented in a flat tone.

Olivia patted Ryan's arm with a nervous rapidity. "I think that's a topic that can wait for a couple glasses of wine," she nervously interjected.

"It's just life," Connie responded as she shrugged her shoulders. "Justin was going to tell us about his divorce."

Ryan's body went rigid. It's a powerful emotion a mother feels for her children when they are wronged, leading a normally friendly and giving person like Connie to forcefully broach delicate topics.

Justin's hands trembled. "I was saying, we weren't compatible for a variety of reasons."

"I can imagine," Connie shot back.

Justin's shoulders slumped in defeat. "I like the things you're saying in the paper," he remarked to Ryan, a clumsy effort to change the subject.

Ryan forced his friendliest smile. "Anything in particular?"

"The editorial on immigrant workers," Justin replied, nodding his head to an exaggerated degree.

"You're in the minority," Ryan remarked, noting the look of sincerity on the man's face.

"I don't know," Justin continued. "I mean, a lot of people don't like what you said, but you'd be surprised by how many think it could help."

With a deep sigh, Ryan sat down on the sofa to the right of Justin's chair, guiding Olivia to sit beside him. "For me, actions will speak louder than words," he responded. Olivia's warmth bled into his shoulder as she leaned against him, giving him a sense that she shared his relief for the change in topic.

Connie, who had remained steadfast in her domineering stance beside Justin, finally backed off. Receding to beneath the archway that divided the living and dining rooms. "Small towns are fickle," she commented. "They need a lot of proof to make them accept major changes."

The change in subject noticeably calmed Justin, with the trembling in his hands subsiding. "I agree completely, several members of my family ..." he continued in an almost fawning voice, before stopping mid-sentence. His eyes froze, staring past the rest and across the room, where Meade stood beside the dining table, his hands holding a soup tureen and his own eyes frozen in response.

Justin leaped to his feet and bolted toward him. "Let me help you," he insisted as he coerced the bowl out of Meade's hands.

Meade's eyes had a hollowness to them as he handed it to Justin. "Thank you," he muttered in a raspy voice. "I'll be right back." And with a quick step, he vanished back out of the room, with Justin starting to follow. But Connie stepped in front of him, turning him back.

"He's getting the rest of the food," she explained. "Why don't you all sit down, and I'll serve this cold tomato soup."

Though his eyes pleaded with her to let him go, Justin obeyed and started to pull out a chair, which earned him further rebuke. "Why don't you take that one instead," she insisted, her finger wagging at the chair opposite the table from the kitchen door. "Ryan, you sit to Justin's right."

Unwilling to challenge Connie's authority, Ryan nodded and pulled out the designated chair and sat down. Then Olivia, also following direction from Connie, seated herself in the chair on the opposite side of Ryan, leaving three spaces open at the table, though the one on Justin's left held no place setting.

Tense silence filled the next few moments until Meade reappeared, a heavily garnished platter of salmon held in his white-knuckled hands. He paused for a moment, surveying the room, his eyes coming down hard on the unset place next to Justin. With a loud grunt, he offered a frustrated scowl to his mother and hastily dropped the platter on the table before claiming the place setting closest to his high school love.

"Honey, I was going to sit there," Connie complained.

The scowl on Meade's face intensified. "I'm sorry, why don't you sit next to me then," he answered.

The awkward silence returned. "I love salmon," Justin nervously remarked after a moment of quiet staring.

A pained smile appeared on Meade's face. "I remember," he answered in a flat tone.

"Do you remember when we were kids and my dad would take us to Roaring River to fish on the opening day of trout season?" Justin asked

Meade's eyes grew glossy. "Of course, I remember a lot of things from when we were young," he murmured.

—

Justin barely ate a spoonful of his dessert, though he picked at it enough to leave it a mushy, undistinguishable lump. "Meade," he timidly uttered.

Meade's own dessert remained pristine and untouched. "Yes?" he coldly replied.

The table shuddered as Justin's jittery thigh rubbed its leg. "This is the most delicious meal I think I've ever had," he remarked in a shaky voice. "I had no idea you were such a good cook."

Sidestepping a verbal reply, Meade stared into Justin's eyes for a moment before nodding.

"It was very good, thank you for inviting us," Ryan volunteered, hoping to minimize the tension.

"I agree," Olivia echoed. "I know your mom taught you your way around the kitchen. But you appear to have picked up quite a few tips on your own."

A small and grateful smile broke the unease on Meade's face. "You are a bunch of flatterers," he muttered. "I think you're saying it to get as many free meals out of me as you can."

Ryan let out a hearty, and only slightly forced, laugh. "May be true," he admitted. "Though it doesn't mean our thoughts aren't legitimate. But no wonder you don't believe us, you've barely touched it," he added, feeling immediately embarrassed by the obliviousness of his comment.

But Meade took it in stride, not letting on that nerves impacted his appetite. "I've been nibbling on it all day," he offered in justification. "If I don't slow down, I'll be ten pounds heavier by the time I head home."

The table shivered as Justin's jumpy leg thumped up against it. "When are you leaving?" he asked, his voice cracking midway through the question.

"A little over a week," Meade answered.

"Not too long for you, I hope," Connie harshly commented.

A glistening of tears showed in Justin's eyes. "No, no," he protested. "I was hoping you'd be here longer. There's a lot I need to say to you."

Connie's eyes burned as she stared at Justin.

"What do you want to talk about?" Meade asked, seeming to ask it to prevent his mother from doing so.

A fork slipped out of Justin's hand and clattered onto the tablecloth. "I just ... well, lots of things," he responded, unease pouring out of him as drops of sweat trickled down his forehead.

"Give me some idea," Meade demanded.

Justin took a deep breath. "Ok," he softly replied. "I want to talk about how sorry I am I hurt you. That I lied, that I got you bullied, and that I helped beat you up."

Meade's expression seemed distant, though stern. "I see," he calmly responded.

The fork again clattered as Justin fidgeted with it. "For the last ten years I've gotten sick to my stomach whenever I've thought about what happened," he continued.

Meade shifted so he could more directly face Justin. "Me too, but for different reasons," he replied, his expression still stoic, but tears now gathering in his eyes. "You get sick to your stomach because you betrayed me. Because you got me beat up and tormented for being the exact same thing as you. You sold me out to protect yourself. I get sick to my stomach because I loved you, and that wasn't good enough. You destroyed it, to protect yourself."

Unrestrained emotion took hold of Justin, his face flashing red as tears flooded his eyes. "Oh, god," he cried out. "I feel so horrible. For months after it happened I cried myself to sleep. Sometimes, even now I do. You think you're the only one who loved. I loved you, too, so much. I still love you."

Plates rattled as Meade's hand came down hard against the tabletop. "Shut up," he yelled. "How dare you say that to me. If you loved me, why haven't you contacted me in ten years? You could have."

Wet streaks shined on Connie's cheeks, and beneath the table Olivia's grip grew firm around Ryan's hand.

Justin rubbed the back of his hand across the bottom of his nose, wiping away a dribbling of snot. "I was scared," he blurted out. "I was so scared."

The angry, red flush on Meade's face faded. "Yes, you were," he growled. "You made my life a living hell. I hated myself and was so upset by what happened, I even considered suicide."

Justin's face twisted with anguish. "No," he cried, rushing his hands to his eyes to conceal flooding emotions. "If you'd done that, I have no doubt that I would have done the same," he offered in a newly calm voice.

The flush of Meade's face again darkened, but only briefly. "Don't mock me," he warned as he eyed him for sincerity.

Justin sank back into his chair in a childlike way. "I'm not," he countered in little more than a whisper. "You have no idea how badly I wanted to go to you, be with you. I was scared. My parents threatened to take me to a hospital if they found out I'd been doing stuff with you. They said they wouldn't have a faggot for a son. My father, serious or not, threatened to castrate me. Why do you think I got married? I never loved her. The only person I've ever loved is you. Why do you think I'm getting divorced? I couldn't be what she wanted. After a few months, the thought of even touching her was work. I had to force myself to be with her. Why do you think she had an affair? We haven't had sex in a year and a half."

"Tell me," Meade asked in an almost compassionate tone. "Are you gay?"

Nervousness came rushing back as Justin glanced around the table, tears and snot clinging to his face. Then, with a deep breath, he turned back to Meade. "I am," he answered. "You know that, even if I've lied to others." He let out a deep sigh and turned to Ryan. "You can print every word of what I said in your paper, if it helps Meade," he declared.

Ryan leaned back in his chair, his right hand beneath the table still holding Olivia's. "I don't think anyone outside of this room needs to know any of what's being said here," he replied.

Bearing the face of a scolded child, Justin nodded.

Meade leaned forward in Justin's direction. "Why've you stayed here, if you're so tortured?" he asked.

A burst of confidence appeared with the stiffening of Justin's jaw. "Because of my little girl," he responded. "I love her so much. As much as I've always loved you." The last comment triggered tears spilling onto his cheeks. He then stood and pushed his chair back, all while gazing into Meade's eyes. "Is there anything I can do for forgiveness?" he pleaded between labored breaths. "I have to have that. I have to." The breaths melted into sobs. "Please," he begged.

Meade's lips quivered, and his eyes welled as he surrendered to his emotion. Then, he pushed himself up onto his feet and stepped close to Justin, before taking him in a tight embrace. They stood as a starched tableau, holding each other in silence, only the sounds of their affected breathing filling the room. Then, with gentle movement, Meade dropped his arms and took a step back, prompting an anxious whimper from Justin. But this move held no punishment, as he took Justin's tear-streamed face into his hands, leaned in, and kissed him.

—

From her chair at the kitchen table, Olivia craned her neck to peer down the hallway to the front door where Meade and Justin exited after the emotional dinner scene. "How long have they been on the porch?" she asked, her voice hushed.

Stepping away from the soapsuds-filled sink, Connie hustled over to the hall to look herself. "Quite a while. I hope everything's all right," she answered as she stared into the darkness beyond the screen door.

Exhausted by the night's drama, Ryan stepped to the sink to finish the job Connie had abandoned. "Haven't we been involved in this enough for tonight?"

Connie's eyes showed pained offense as she glared at him from across the room. "I don't want Meade to get hurt again," she snapped.

As if purposely defying his remark, Olivia stood and slowly inched down the hallway. "I'm going to sneak down and have a look out the door," she whispered back to them.

Ryan let the dinner plate he held slip loose and sink to the bottom of the dishwater. "Now wait," he protested as he turned around to face them. "I don't think our babysitting is necessary. They're grown men. If there's a problem, they'll either tell us or we'll hear the gunshot and screaming."

Olivia slipped from view without a response.

"I think if they want to be left alone, they should be left alone," Ryan offered in polite protest to Connie, who lingered at the hallway door.

"If it was me, I wouldn't want everyone in the house peering out or listening through a door."

"We aren't being like that at all," Connie countered, a tight-lipped smile on her face. "And, even if we were, after all the trauma Meade went through, I think I deserve to be a little concerned."

While he still preferred to give them their privacy, he realized he did not have the authority in the situation to force his opinion. "I don't entirely agree with these methods," he admitted. "But I'm not the one that watched my son go through that either, so I know I can't completely understand."

Connie stepped near him and slung her arm around his waist. "You're a pretty special guy," she offered.

"You're not going to believe what I saw," Olivia exclaimed as she returned to the kitchen.

"What?" Connie questioned, concern prominent in her tone.

"Nothing bad," Olivia explained. "Just those two sitting on your porch swing making out hot and heavy."

Connie's jaw dropped. "No." She gasped.

The pleased glow on Olivia's face removed any doubt. "They are. Hands all over each other, lips smacking, and I saw more than a little tongue action."

Scarlet embarrassment filled Connie's face. "I can't believe it," she stammered. "After all those years, just like that."

Olivia shrugged her shoulders.

"Meade told me earlier he was still attached to Justin," Ryan explained while drying his wet hands with a dishtowel. "I guess it took a little bit of understanding for them both. But, with Meade leaving in a week, it seems it'll be pretty short-lived."

"I think that might be best," Connie predicted with a hint of lingering animosity. With anxiety etched into her brow, she paced back and forth across the kitchen floor. "How long are they staying out there?" she questioned, her pacing slowing as she spoke.

With a glance back to the front door, Olivia shook her head. "I don't know," she replied. "They still had their clothes on when I looked out.

So, depending on how far they plan on going in that porch swing, it could be a while."

Connie stopped hard in her step, her face turning bright red and her features distorting as she restrained a laugh. "You stop," she scolded the younger woman in a high-pitched voice, the result of her effort to suppress a more amused response. "I wish they'd turned the porch light off. I don't want the neighbors ..." she started, but her thought went unfinished, interrupted by the piercing scream of a siren.

The wailing prompted a confusing burst in Ryan's mind, pulling his eyes to the closest window, as if expecting to see the mushroom of a nuclear blast in the distance. But no such image appeared; he saw only the inky night. "What the hell is that?" he said.

"The city's emergency alarm," Olivia answered as she laid her hand on his arm. "They use it for fires, tornados and the monthly meeting of the volunteer fire department."

An archaic alert system, he thought. "What's it signaling?" he asked.

"The monthly meeting is the last Tuesday of the month, so that's not it," Olivia offered. "And the weather's too calm for a tornado, so there must be a fire."

The screeching continued another thirty seconds before the siren finally went silent, leaving Ryan's ears buzzing and his nerves frayed. "I've never heard anything like that in my life. I was worried we were about to be hit by an asteroid or something," he joked if only to lighten his own mood.

Footsteps pounded down the hallway, announcing Meade and Justin's entrance, walking hand in hand. "Any idea what's on fire?" Meade asked.

Glancing away from them to conceal her maternal concern, Connie shook her head. "Probably a brushfire outside of town," she replied. "There're usually a couple every summer."

The ringing of the wall phone ended any additional speculation.

"Hello," Connie answered once she put the receiver to her ear. A short pause followed. "Hello Ann, what's the matter?" Her face went white as she listened. "No," she gasped. "I'll be right down." And with a shocked stagger, she hung up the phone.

Meade let go of Justin's hand and stepped close to his mother. "What is it Mom?" he asked.

"There's a fire," she answered in an exhale of breath.

Meade nodded. "We figured that, but what's on fire?"

Tears sprouted in her eyes. "The high school," she responded.

"The new one?" Olivia asked.

Connie shook her head. "The old one," she replied before stepping past Meade and Justin on her way to the hallway.

CHAPTER 15

The pervasive glare of red emergency lights bathed the buildings lining the east end of Commercial Street in scarlet. It seemed almost festive, if not for the howl of emergency sirens. Ryan's eyes scanned past those crimson-tinged structures to the epicenter of the evening's unrest. There, at the end of the decaying main strip, stood the once venerable school. Left for years to rot with barely a mention, it had now regained the community's attention, with flames belching out of the charred main entrance and dancing in the windows of the first floor's classrooms. Even from blocks away, the uncontrolled nature of the fire promised foreboding results.

Dim, expect for the ruby glow of the lights outside, the newspaper office rested in an undisturbed evening slumber. Ryan reached for the switch to power the florescent lights that lined the ceiling; but pulled his hand back, content with the ambiance of the moment, and let the illumination blazing through the windows guide him. His grandfather's desk seemed foreign to him in the darkness, but in a beam of rubicund light he spotted the items he needed, a notepad and camera, laid out as if expecting him.

"You're way ahead of me," a raspy voice remarked.

Startled, Ryan swung around to find the slightly hunched shadow of an elderly man. "Glo, did you want to do this?" He stepped toward the older man with the camera and notepad held out.

Glo retreated a few feet, opening enough space for Ryan to pass, and then motioned for him to do so. "This is your paper, that's your responsibility out there," he said.

Ryan neared him. "Are you sure?" He was afraid of overreaching but also excited for the opportunity.

Unrestrained irritation surfaced on the craggy face. "Wait much longer and there won't be anything left standing for a picture," Glo scolded him.

After a quick nod of deference, Ryan dashed across the office and back out onto Commercial Street. At the end of the block, the ravenous fire had lost its contentment with the aged wood of the first floor, funneling up the central tower and nearly reaching the belfry, while simultaneously spreading into the second-floor classrooms. Though not yet fully engulfed like the floor below, an intense display of yellow and orange flickering flame, with a backdrop of wilting light fixtures and blackening walls, played out in the upper story's windows.

Ryan pushed through the swelling crowd of gawkers, who loitered on the lawn of a church across the street from the school. He stopped at the yellow police tapeline and waved his notepad and camera until one of the firefighters motioned for him to cross the line. He paused halfway across the street, which seemed close enough to get the shots he wanted while staying out of the way of the police and firefighters.

The licking flames filled his eyes as he took a deep breath, hoping to stem his own insecurity in covering an event he knew would be dear to many in the town. He snapped a few timid shots at first, but the importance of his role evolved in his mind and launched a rapid photographic assault on the building and the firefighters at work around it, their resources and manpower seemingly overwhelmed by the destruction taking place in front of them.

In the anxious crowd of observers, which itself fell into the focus of his camera's lens, Ryan spotted Olivia, Connie, Justin and Meade huddling together, while numerous other faces he recognized peppered the larger assembly. Many wore pained expressions as they listened to a soundtrack of shattering glass and roaring fire while watching the destruction of a place where many had spent their youth.

As the fire's intensity grew, a deputy sheriff led Ryan out of the street and back in line with the watchers, still crowded along the edge of the church house's lawn. Even from this regressed position, he continued taking pictures, exhaustively chronicling the noteworthy event. And despite yielding earlier, the effort appeared shared, for passing among the onlookers went Glo, notebook in hand, collecting reactions and emotions. Respect swelled in Ryan's chest, nearly bringing tears to his eyes, as he watched the old man. Once a student himself in the now-burning building, Glo focused on his task, not letting his own emotions or sense of loss deter him.

An anxious vibe brought silence to the crowd as the soot-covered firefighters took on a frantic pace in moving themselves and their equipment away from the building, portending for even the last hold-outs the reality of a lost cause. In the eerie silence, all seemed to await the next step in the building's demise, the failure of its weakened structure. "Move back. The tower!" came an echoing cry as the firefighters retreated from the schoolyard and into the street.

Mortar, that for a century bonded the bricks of the building together, crumbled under the stress of compromised infrastructure and brutal heat, showering the front steps with powder and fragments. With the connective strength dissolving, bricks pulled apart from each other, forming a spider's web of cracks from the foundation up to the central tower's roofline, giving the belfry an unsteady swagger.

A waterfall of bricks and mortar tumbled off the sides of the unsteady turret, and a loud cracking emanated from within, followed by the off-kilter clatter of the massive bell. Any lingering chatter among the crowd ceased as 400 pounds of cast iron crashed through the weakened floors beneath it, momentarily coming to rest just inside the main entrance. But then that floor gave way, sending the relic into the building's basement and releasing a geyser of flame and cinder up from the crypt where it landed.

The tower itself, now hopelessly unstable in the aftermath of the bell's plummet, twisted and turned as the flames increasingly ate at it. Then, a final fiery deluge of bricks and boards spilled onto the front steps as the weight of the collapsing belfry pulled the tower back from the front façade and into the burning cavern of the building's interior.

—

"Nothing left to save now," Ryan commented as he joined Connie, Olivia, Meade and Justin on the front steps of the church.

Tears in Connie's eyes sparkled with the fire's bright glow. "All those years I spent in that building," she reflected in a soft voice. "It already seems strange that the space I occupied there, just my one classroom, is no more. It almost feels like watching a loved one die."

Meade slipped his arm around his mother's shoulder and pulled her close. "It'll be all right," he told her. "Just like so many of the people we love, that building wasn't meant to outlive us."

A weak smile of understanding formed on her face.

"Do they know what started it?" Justin asked in a somber tone. "There wasn't any electricity, so that can't be it. Maybe kids causing trouble?"

Ryan turned back to the fire-engulfed building, as loud cracking signaled the collapse of its roofline, with sparks, smoke and flames shooting out of the upper story windows. He shook his head and sighed.

"What do you think happened?" Connie asked, suspicion in her tone.

Though more intuition than fact, Ryan could not help but have a theory. "I won't print it in the paper, but I think Calvin Woodmont's involved," he replied. "I've rarely seen anyone as mad as he was when the city council rejected his request to demolish it. Then, after the court hearing, he sounded even angrier. He comes across as unbalanced and rash. While I don't know if they'll prove it, he'd be my first suspect."

—

An ashy fog lingered in the air as the 4:00 a.m. chime of the courthouse clock sounded in the distance. The fire chief, his face tired and dark from soot, approached the remaining diehards, who huddled on the church steps. "Fire's out, you all should go home and get some rest," he announced.

Behind him, a few firefighters watched the smoldering remains for any sign of resurgence, though the building sat in ruins, little more than a few juts of brick wall, charred pieces of lumber, and twisted metal. A once stately profile and distinguished tower erased from the town's modest skyline.

With the chief's guarded permission, Ryan and Olivia ducked beneath the yellow caution tape and crossed the street to the heat-wilted and soggy schoolyard. A mournful gaze darkened Olivia's expression. "I'm heartbroken," she cried. "I spent four fairly happy years of my life in this building. And think of Connie, who spent thirty-five years teaching in it, and all the people that went or worked there through the years. My mother went here, your father went here, so did your grandfather. Now, it's gone."

His heart heavy with her shared nostalgia, Ryan put his arm around her shoulders. "It's not really gone," he philosophized. "Ok, the building's gone. But think of all the yearbooks, event programs, photos, and other mementos people have that are connected to it. There must be forty yearbooks from this school in my grandfather's house. The entire history of the building is still here, if not the building."

Olivia leaned heavily onto him. "True, but there's something special about having the actual building too."

Ryan's throat felt tight. "You're right," he agreed before taking a hard swallow. "I've only been here a short time, but even I'll notice the absence of this big hulk of a building." The touch of Olivia's fingers against his palm brought dampness to his eyes.

—

The glow of emergency lights and fiery flames that lit up the newspaper office hours earlier had vanished, leaving Commercial Street's sparse collection of streetlamps to fill the void. Thus, the darkened office offered no nostalgia or sense of importance for this moment, so Ryan shed his romantic senses and flicked the light switch on, initiating a hum and green glow from above him.

Olivia curled up on the red couch for a nap, and he settled in to pound out an article that would dominate the front page of the week's edition, at least if an early morning call to the printer, asking him to hold off on printing the version he sent over twelve hours earlier, proved successful.

Using Glo's notes, as well as those he had collected from the fire chief and sheriff, his fingers glided along the keyboard at a rapid rate. The story flowed out of him almost preordained in its composition, typing it out and inserting quotes and comments with an uncommon ease.

By the time dawn's light began infiltrating the office, Ryan felt an almost symbolic relationship between the new day and his completed work.

—

A few early risers clustered near the now-contracted police lines, which no longer closed off the street itself, only restricted access to the school property. Even the emergency crews, which at the fire's apex included ten trucks and cars from neighboring jurisdictions, now numbered only one truck and a handful of firefighters.

Crouching and moving from side to side, Ryan took several shots of the ruins from different angles. He moved as near as he could to the front steps, where someone had pieced together the broken stone block that ten hours earlier had been above the main entrance. He leaned over the yellow tape and focused the camera on the carved lettering that dominated the reconstituted granite slab. It read, "White Oak City High School."

"You should get some breakfast," a familiar voice suggested.

Glo stood a few feet away, a cup of coffee in his hand.

"Not a bad idea," the younger man answered.

The old man's eyes drifted to the inscription on the ruined stone. "Café's open. Order something for yourself and Olivia." he suggested. "She'll be hungry too."

Ryan nodded.

"Good story," Glo added. "Stopped by the office before coming over. Better than I think your granddad could have done."

CHAPTER 16

IN LOS ANGELES, the burning of a vacant school would hardly maintain a day's interest, but in White Oak City, a week later it remained the top topic around town. Of course, the fact that the town's leading news source only showed up once a week did nothing to speed up the conversation.

Like the gossipy locals, Ryan himself remained intrigued by the emerging facts. Within a day the fire marshal ruled it arson, pulling two twisted and warped metal gas cans from the ruins. A day later, thanks to the paranoid taxidermist, security footage detailing the building's demise from the vantage point of the old bank provided a suspect. It revealed a large black SUV barreling down Commercial Street and disappearing around the corner by the old school, followed, fifteen minutes later, by the first flickers of a fire licking out from behind the boarded up the main entrance. Shortly after that, the black SUV retraced its path back down the street and presumably out of town, leaving behind on film a grainy, though recognizable license plate number, one registered to a Calvin Woodmont.

The emotional impact the fire created, along with the discovery of Woodmont's almost certain involvement, enlivened in Ryan a fervor for his newspaper's role in the town. In fact, it even seemed to supplant his previous priority: selling the newspaper.

—

"Think you can break away for a working lunch at your house?" Olivia asked as she stood in the editor's office doorway.

Ryan jerked his head up at the sound of her voice. A stack of county records on the complex recent ownership history of the old school had left him oblivious to her approach. But here she stood before him, her slender and feminine figure framed by the doorway, light bleeding through her airy sundress, and his heart sped up with a surge of giddiness. A feeling of shame also surfaced, for in the last week his focus on the fire had left him to neglect her and the work she was doing to help him with his inheritance.

"That's very doable," he answered, offering her a warm smile as an unspoken apology.

She stepped toward him with swift and graceful movement and laid a soft kiss on his cheek. "Good, because Meade's already there and Connie's picking up lunch," she explained in a tone signaling he had answered correctly.

He gazed up at her in awe and felt grateful that as he focused on the newspaper, she continued to work on helping him save the downtown. "I need to step away from the fire for a while and focus on the presentation," he agreed. "Though, I'm stuck with a bit of an ethical dilemma, as I'm the only one that can cover the council meeting for the paper this week, and it doesn't seem right that I'll be covering my own presentation."

She sat down on the edge of his desk. "Have you asked Glo?" she suggested. "He doesn't typically have plans that would prevent him from doing something like that."

"I haven't told you about that yet," he replied.

The mood in Olivia's eyes turned serious. "What is it?" she asked, her hands balling up in concern.

His chair squeaked as he leaned back in it and sighed. "He came in a couple hours ago and retired. He said I can handle it here on my own, and if I sell, he'd leave anyway."

The sudden slackness of her jaw mirrored Ryan's own shock from earlier in the day. "I can't believe it," she exclaimed. "He's always been here. Now, he's gone?"

Ryan shrugged his shoulders.

"When will he leave? Are you giving him a goodbye party? Though, he'd probably hate that."

"A party won't matter, he's already gone," he answered.

"What do you mean, gone?"

The chair squeaked again, this time as he leaned forward. "He's going to his sister's in Florida for a while. Said he might stay permanently. He said something about staying there until he's brought back in a box. He said his niece, Mark's mother, would watch his house for him."

Olivia stood and started pacing the floor in front of the desk. "How much more change can this town take?" she asked. "He and your grandfather were almost as big of landmarks as the old high school. Now, all three are gone."

—

A sullen glare greeted Ryan as he and Olivia passed Ebetta's desk on their way out. Nearly two weeks had passed since the chicken plant editorial, and the receptionist remained hostile to him and any ideas or suggestions he made in the interim. Even when he gave every member of staff a small raise, she only offered a snide reference to his grandfather's better business judgment, instead of thanking him.

"Ebetta, I'm heading out and I might not be back for the rest of the day, could you let everyone know about Glo?" he asked as he paused by her desk.

She clucked her tongue as she shook her head from side to side. "It's such a sad thing," she offered with notable condescension. "I don't know what we're going to do without him. He was the only one keeping us grounded."

The woman's words made his spine tingle. "Don't worry, everything'll be fine," he retorted. "I'm sure whatever faceless entity I sell to will treat you deservingly."

With a snort of disapproval, she squeezed her eyes shut. "You are a poor substitute for your grandfather," she screeched at him as he and Olivia stepped outside.

The door clicked shut behind them and an exasperated sigh escaped Olivia's lips. "Was that necessary?" she scolded him.

The reprimand felt undeserved. "Did you hear what she said? She deserved every word."

Olivia shook her head. "She means well. She just doesn't necessarily think before saying things. She's conservative and old-fashioned, and I don't think she was trying to insult you so much as she was praising Glo."

—

The sterling silver centerpiece, that normally looked like a floating island on the well-polished mahogany dining table, today appeared like a sinking ship among icebergs of paperwork. A white-collar flood of folders, tabs and sticky notes crowded the table in a disheveled assembly line, which Meade appeared in the act of refining. Ryan took a deep breath as he surveyed the mess. "How're you able to keep track of everything?" he asked, watching Meade dart back and forth from one stack of paperwork to the next.

Without looking up, Meade's nimble fingers slowed for a moment, as he seemed to recollect the construct of his own system. "It's color coded," he responded. "Though it's taken me two hours to feel like I can put together packets that make sense. I've formal proposals and backup information labeled with blue and green tabs, grant forms in yellow, comparisons in red, sample leases and purchase agreements in purple, and contractor estimates for repairs and renovations in orange."

The information burst rolled off Ryan's mind without sticking. "What should I do?" he asked.

Meade paused for a moment, then lifted his eyes off the paperwork and looked at Ryan. "Do you see the documents with pink tabs?"

Scattered among the mess Ryan saw a couple dozen pink tabs. "Yes."

"Gather up those, there should be eight copies of each document, but I think there are four pages that make up each of those individual documents," Meade explained. "Create eight different packets, each with one copy of all four pages, ordered by square footage of the buildings from smallest to largest."

It took a couple of passes, but by the third assembly Ryan felt confident in Meade's system, though it proved more tedious than interesting. And once his first job finished, there came another and another, so when Connie appeared with lunch, an hour later than expected, his brain was numb.

"You told me Glo always treated you well," Ryan remarked as he tidied up a stack of sample leases, his stomach aching for the lunch Connie and Olivia were laying out in the kitchen.

Meade replied with a deep nod. "I've known him my entire life. He's always been a little grouchy, but always nice to me. When I was a kid he'd ask me how I was doing, how school was going and such. I think he felt sorry for me not having a dad at home. Even when the whole gay thing came out, he was one of the few to tell Mom not to worry about it, that I was a good kid and it didn't matter who I loved."

Warmth kindled in Ryan's chest as he listened to Meade tell of the old man's compassion. A confirmation of the observations he also now understood, after setting aside his initial prejudices.

"The night of the fire, before I took Mom home, Glo pulled me aside and told me not to be surprised if he hit the road for a while," Meade confessed.

"You knew and didn't tell me?" Ryan asked.

A rosy flush filled Meade's cheeks. "I was told in confidence, plus I've been so busy since the fire," he offered in defense.

"Now that you mention it, I've hardly seen you since the fire; what've you been up to?"

A sly smile emerged on Meade's face, but before he could utter a word, the kitchen door swung open and Olivia's head popped out. "Lunch is ready," she announced before bobbing back inside.

Finally, Ryan thought as he started toward the awaiting meal. "Meade's going to tell us what he's been up to this week," he mischievously announced as they entered kitchen.

"I'd sure like to hear this," Connie responded. "I've only seen the occasional fleeting glimpses of him."

Meade responded with an uncomfortable smile as he sat down at the kitchen table.

"So, what have you been up to since the 'Justin' night?" Olivia demanded as she handed him a plate.

He shrugged his shoulders. "Been busy with work and stuff," he murmured in response.

Unsatisfied, she leaned toward him. "Busy with work every night for a week?"

"Partially, and Justin," he quietly answered.

Leaning back in her chair, Connie smiled. "Is that why you only slept at the house three nights this last week?" she prodded.

Meade turned to his mother and smirked. "I told you where I was," he countered. "You're just trying to stoke the drama."

"Sounds like someone's getting laid," Olivia teased.

Meade's cheeks glowed pink. "Hey now," Meade protested, eliciting laughter from the others.

"Besides ripping each other's clothes, what else have you been doing together?" Ryan asked, hoping to spare himself the awkwardness of a son talking about sex in front of his mother.

"We took his daughter to Branson one day and went to Eureka Springs one night," Meade offered. "Last night, I even took him to that bar in Springfield."

Connie nodded a cautious approval. "His little girl is adorable."

Meade put his hand on his mother's shoulder. "She's sweet and seems to have a good, though naïve, understanding of our relationship," he explained. "She asked if I was going to live with her dad. The startling thing is that she asked it the second day I knew her. Justin said she doesn't typically take to people as quickly as she has me. But then, nothing about this trip has been typical."

The lines on Connie's face grew deep. "What's next?"

"I wish I knew," he admitted. "I'm playing it by ear. I'm going home in a few days, that's not going to change. I'm happy in Chicago. But I've loved him for so long. I want him in my life. He's agreed to come to Chicago next month for a long weekend. He's never been there, so I'll show him the city."

Olivia looked to Ryan with a soft gaze. "Do you think you could imagine moving back here?" she asked Meade, despite watching Ryan.

The corners of Meade's mouth turned down, then he took a deep breath. "I don't know; it'd be like admitting something, but I don't know what. I thought I'd figured my life out. Then I come here, the place that made me miserable, and it gets turned upside down."

—

Despite being fifteen minutes past the scheduled start time, the city council dais remained unoccupied, leaving only the impatient chatter of a dozen or so residents to fill the room. Five more minutes ticked by, with the restlessness erupting in louder and louder complaints, before the door behind the dais swung open and Beau LaSalle stepped into the room. He took a moment to eye the turnout, before sighing and, in a tone indicating personal annoyance, letting those present know the mayor was running late.

An elderly heckler, unabashedly displeased with the answer, demanded to know why. So, with a roll of his eyes, Beau gave in, explaining that the mayor's wife had accidently backed her car over their neighbor's cat. An anecdote—judging by the mumbles and murmurs around the room—that appeared in character for the woman.

The delay added to Ryan's unease, for each passing minute seemed to embolden his anxiety. He turned to his right, hoping Olivia and Meade might offer relief, but they sat gossiping with each other about a disheveled woman at the back of the room. A woman who, he gathered from their comments, had accidently killed her husband years earlier and subsequently turned into the town's cat lady.

Ryan was hoping to make a discreet appraisal of the woman in question, but instead locked eyes with her. The taste of bile filled his mouth and his stomach pulsed in agitation. Then a door slammed, making his backside leap about a foot above his seat.

The room went silent, and with more waddle than walk, the rotund and red-faced mayor made his way down the center aisle in the direction of the dais, his face twitching in embarrassment. "I'm sorry about being late," he bellowed as he reached his fellow councilmembers, now all emerging from the door behind the dais. "Damn cat. You better bet they were upset. If they didn't want it getting hit, they shouldn't have let it outside."

Expectation of disappointment cut like a bullet through Ryan's chest as he watched the pudgy man nearly trip as he climbed the steps of the council platform. "The plan won't work," Ryan grumbled to Olivia. "This guy's a clown with no tact or foresight. How'd he get elected?"

She sighed and shrugged her shoulders.

A rosy tint still on his cheeks, though the flush on his forehead had abated, the mayor twitched and turned to get comfortable in his chair, which provided him a kingly viewpoint of the meeting's paltry audience. "Where do we start?" he shouted to the city clerk.

Posed with the stiff posture of a schoolmarm, the clerk replied with a scowl before launching into the meeting agenda, while the mayor's head bobbed back and forth like a dashboard amusement.

As the meeting proceeded, Ryan struggled to maintain even a minimal level of interest in the issues discussed. Regardless of the topic, his thoughts dwelled on his own approaching presentation. Even the subject of the old high school, with the town considering the purchase of its lot from the bank that held the mortgage, failed to rouse him. Though his attention was momentarily piqued in response to a couple of pointed comments from the mayor regarding the recent arrest of the old school's alleged arsonist, who unsurprisingly happened to be its defaulted owner.

Finally, after a laborious hour and forty-five minutes, the city council arrived at his presentation. In a raspy smoker's voice, the city clerk announced the proposal as the topic at hand, and Ryan's body flooded with a rush of adrenaline that left his foot nervously tapping against the floor. He stepped up to the speaker's podium while watching the faces of the council members as they perused his materials. Discontent surfaced as the mayor pulled the folder open and inattentively thumbed through the mass of paperwork, his beady eyes barely moving as he stared at the pages. "Mr. Shipley, you sure have provided plenty of reading material," he remarked in a high-pitched squeal.

"I suppose so, but I think you'll find most of it helpful," Ryan explained as he motioned for Olivia and Meade to join him at the podium.

The mayor shook his ruddy face. "You've brought a whole crew with you," he chuckled while making a flippant gesture toward their group.

Self-righteous disgust filled Ryan's head as he questioned the intelligence of the people in the town to put a man like this in charge. "I want you to get as clear a picture of this proposal as possible," he pointedly rebutted.

The crystal blue irises of the mayor's eyes rolled back into his head for a moment. "Let me get this straight," he responded. "You want us to help you sell your buildings. I might not be too bright, but I always thought if you owned it, you sell it."

Ryan felt his face flush as his blood pressure rose. "That's not exactly what we're proposing," he explained in a politer tone than he used for his previous response. "This is a broader project than that. In fact, I'm not necessarily looking at selling the buildings at all, at least not yet. The idea is to offer low rents so interested parties can come in and set up businesses."

The mayor's chair squeaked in protest as the man leaned back in it, disinterest on his face. "How about we give it away to someone to start a chicken plant and hire a bunch of Mexicans," he chided him.

The urge to pick up the podium and launch it across the room at the man taunted Ryan. "We're thinking more along the line of antique shops and specialty stores," he continued gamely, forcing a smile. "The downtown could be beautiful. With the right incentives we could lure a lot of people here to shop for gifts and antiques. We're right off the way to Branson, so it's a great location for a side trip."

The chair squeaked again as the mayor shook his head, his entire body jiggling as he did so. "If it's such a good idea, why're you practically giving the buildings away?" he asked.

A legitimate, if naïve, question, Ryan thought. "We have to get people in here, and inexpensive rent might do it," he replied. "Plus, they'll be required to provide upkeep and renovations to the buildings, something that's next to impossible for me to do myself on the larger ones, like the old hotel. Though, some buildings need little more than a cleaning and a coat of paint."

The mayor now leaned across the top of the council desk, his plump face cradled in his hands, themselves supported on perched elbows. "This is real nice and all, but ..." he started.

"Excuse me mayor, may I say something?" Beau interrupted.

The mayor offered another eye-roll, though his face remained firmly planted in his hands. "Fine," he responded in an annoyed tone.

"I know Ryan, Olivia and Meade have spent a lot of time creating a presentation on this for us, so I'd like to see us give it the attention it deserves," Beau explained.

Another squeak escaped the chair as the mayor collapsed back into it. "I don't see that as necessary," he moaned. "Can't we read all this later and vote on whatever they want us to vote on at the next meeting?"

The hardware store owner shook his head. "I think, for my own information, I'd like the opportunity to hear them explain it and then ask questions about it now," he responded in a firmer, though still reserved voice.

The mayor grumbled and looked around at the other members of the council, who all nodded in agreement. "Fine," he barked. "Go ahead with your presentation; just try not to take too long."

For the first time since arriving that evening, Ryan's anxiety lessened, as there appeared support for the plan from the council, even if not from the mayor. With a rush of confidence, he launched into the presentation. There came a battery of questions from the council, each more probing than the last. Only the mayor remained quiet throughout, though Ryan noticed the flush of his face had faded, hopefully a sign of a decreasing aggression.

Once the presentation concluded, Beau gave the top of the council's dais a firm slap of appreciation. "Spectacular," he offered in praise. "That's the most complete proposal I've seen in my time on the council."

Silence followed, with all eyes shifting to the mayor. "You're asking for a lot of money to help market this," he finally interjected. "We're a small town, with a small budget, so we'll need to think about that."

For the first time during the meeting, there appeared a glimmer of a reasonable man, if still unsophisticated.

CHAPTER 17

Sleep proved fickle. For despite the relief of having the city council presentation behind him, its success inspired in Ryan's overactive mind a whole new round of complications, the most stressful being how to make an exit from the town without derailing those plans. Anxious thoughts roiled in him, leaving him tossing and turning for hours before giving up and stumbling downstairs in the early morning for a glass of milk.

Rest finally came as he curled up on the living room sofa, though apprehension continued to torment him via his dreams. Most vividly, he found himself trapped on the roof of the county courthouse as the buildings around the square collapsed one by one like imploding dominos. Just as the courthouse itself began swaying and crumbling beneath his feet, the doorbell buzzed, jarring him awake.

In the clingy dampness of a sweated-through undershirt, he sat up on the sofa, trying to collect his thoughts and decipher the dream's meaning. The doorbell cut in as it buzzed a second time. Who was bothering him this early in the morning? The clock on the fireplace mantle sat frozen at 2:34, so the true time eluded him. With pained stiffness, he rose to his feet and shuffled to the door, where the shadow of a man showed on the frosted window.

"Good morning," Paul Mason offered in greeting as Ryan pulled the door open.

—

Four stacks of paper sat waiting for him on the dining table when Ryan returned downstairs, having quickly cleaned up and dressed, minus a shower and shave.

"Is Olivia not joining us?" Paul asked as he pulled a fifth stack of documents from his briefcase.

A feeling of jealousy seeped into Ryan's thoughts. "Not today, she's out of town taking care of something," he replied, foggy about what she had told him she was doing. Though he knew it involved one of her professors at the University of Missouri, as she had driven to Columbia to take care of it.

A hint of disappointment showed on Paul's face. "Sorry to miss her," he remarked as he placed the fifth stack of papers beside the other four. "I've brought the sell and lease agreements for the downtown buildings, with provisions for tenant required repairs and upgrades. I've also brought sample sales contracts for the numerous other properties and the newspaper, for which I think we have a serious contender."

Ryan nodded. "Who's interested in the paper?" he asked as he picked up a document specific to the business.

Paul popped open his briefcase and pulled out a business card. "LKM Publishing and Media, Inc.," he read from the card. "They own several smaller papers in the area and are looking to expand. I think it's the best opportunity you'll find."

Despite wanting to feel relief for the opportunity, Ryan instead noticed the churn of anxiety in his gut. "Which properties are these for?" He picked up the second stack of papers.

"This house, three more homes your grandfather owned here in town and the agricultural acreage outside of town," Paul responded. "There's no house on that land, right?"

In his mind, Ryan pictured the rolling green hills, picturesque overlook at the creek, and weathered old farmhouse. "There is," he answered.

"Anyone living in it?" Paul asked.

"I don't think it's habitable," Ryan replied, though he felt a twinge of guilt for saying so.

"Then, we'll say no," Paul clarified.

A sense of melancholy flooded Ryan's thoughts. "Ok," he answered with a slight nod.

Paul pulled a sheet of paper out of his briefcase and jotted down a few notes on it. "I want to make sure I'm getting the info right. Around here, the market can be better for agricultural property with no existing dwellings."

The melancholy intensified. "The house hurts the value?" Ryan asked.

Paul paused in thought. "No, but it could decrease the number of people interested. But, since the house is vacant, and I'm assuming, for all practical purposes, abandoned, we'll treat it like there's no house at all, which is how we will price the property. Let's review the other listings."

Ryan took in a deep breath. Was he ready to reduce his grandfather's legacy to a real estate fire sale? "This is more difficult than I expected," he quietly remarked. "List the houses and farm for sale." A lump of anxiety rose from his chest and settled into his throat as he watched Paul make notations next to the properties on his list.

"And the newspaper?" Paul asked.

Suddenly, Ryan found it hard to breathe, like a panic attack, but not so obvious. "Hold off on an official contract, but get buyers lined up," he responded, though without feeling confident in his reasoning.

Paul's face flushed pink. "I see no point in not having a contract," he argued. "You'll be limiting what I can do for you without it."

It felt like too much at once. "I understand, but not right now," Ryan countered, his hands shaking with anxiety. "Show me serious buyers and we'll go from there."

The response did not ease Paul's visible irritation.

"I'm offering you the contracts for about everything else," Ryan continued in a defensive tone.

The real estate agent shook his head. "The newspaper is the most valuable property," he argued. "It makes it possible for me to spend time on your other properties."

A light throbbing started in Ryan's temples, the promise of an intense headache. "Find out more for this LKM and we'll move forward," he countered.

"Fine," Paul snapped back. "How about the commercial buildings, any second thoughts there?"

Ryan shook his head. "List them all for sale or lease, the lease agreement being the one we worked out. Also, make it so once sixty percent of the buildings are occupied, the remaining can only be sold, not leased."

After jotting down a few more notes, Paul nodded. "Let's go take some pictures and I can get these listings posted."

—

The mid-morning atmosphere of downtown White Oak City felt languid at best, with only fleeting glimpses of human activity. But despite the ghost town ambiance, the golden glaze of the sun across the old façades provided an arresting beauty, making the red of the bricks vividly pop and delivering enough glare to minimize the visual of peeling and faded paint.

At each stop along their tour of Ryan's buildings, Paul enthusiastically snapped away, taking dozens of photos at the most flattering angles, both exterior and interior, at least when decay did not make it counterproductive. For, despite Ryan's grandfather's best efforts, trash, old furniture, and deteriorating ceilings and walls at times made an appealing shot difficult.

As they neared the intersection at the corner of the square, Paul's step livened in the direction of the old bank, which stood as a blinding blaze of alabaster in reflection of the sun against its light gray stone. "I love this building," he said as they reached its towering front doors.

Despite the romantic visage it gave at a distance, up close, with the petrified faces of dozens of animals staring out the massive arched windows, Ryan felt his ambitions for the building and town fade. "My grandmother worked here when it was a bank," he said, while trying to evade the scores of glass eyes leering at him.

Paul smiled in response to the comment and clicked a handful of shots of the exterior. "I bet she knew every customer on a first name basis," he replied. "It looks open for business."

A knot of unease bulged in Ryan's stomach. Despite being one of his few paying renters, he had yet to meet the tenant, a circumstance he would like to attribute to being busy, but he knew better.

Paul reached out and grabbed the bronze door handle, despite Ryan's weak motion for him to wait. Bells jingled as the massive door swung open.

They stepped through a small entry vestibule with a marble floor, then through a set of oak and glass doors and into the main lobby. "Hi, I'm Paul Mason," he announced as he trotted toward an elderly man seated in a shabby wingchair, a copy of the daily newspaper from Springfield in his boney old hands.

Like so many buildings in the town, this one had managed to escape those egregious phases of modernization that so often during the last century replaced style and quality with slick minimalism and mass-produced surfaces. Even with its life as a bank decades past, vintage counters and teller windows remained, the tellers and customers replaced with a frozen zoo, from dozens of birds, including a bald eagle with its wings spread wide, to four-legged animals of all shapes and sizes. Foxes, wolves, badgers and otters, deer and moose heads, and an erect bear with its mouth open in a vicious snarl were included in the collection.

The old man looked up with a grimace on his face. "The real estate agent," he croaked and shoved his hand out into the air before him.

Paul bent down slightly and shook hands with the man. "That's established infamy," he replied with a smile before gesturing for Ryan to come closer. "Do you know Ryan Shipley?"

The old man gave half a nod. "I met him for a minute at his granddaddy's visitation."

Ryan nodded in return, not remembering meeting him.

Paul motioned Ryan even closer. "I'm told you're his best tenant," the real estate agent continued.

A short, dry laugh erupted from the older man. "About the only one," he replied. "Name's Merv."

Ryan offered his own hand for the man to shake, which only happened after a longer than comfortable pause.

"Is this about this half-baked idea to bring new businesses here?" Merv asked.

The comment stung Ryan's pride, but he forced a smile. "I admit it isn't a sure thing. But I don't see how it can hurt to try."

Merv offered an apathetic shrug.

"Merv, we're hoping you'll be a part of the changes," Paul lied through a fake smile.

With a pronounced sigh, Merv laid his newspaper on the arm of the chair. "I appreciate it, but you'll have to do that without me," he answered before lifting a trembling hand for them to see. "Parkinson's."

The admission pulled Ryan's attention away from a menacing bobcat sitting on a nearby windowsill.

Even Paul's forced smile disappeared. "Excuse me?"

Merv cleared his throat, a sign of annoyance. "I have Parkinson's disease," he clarified, again lifting his hand. "It's impossible for me to work anymore, so I'm closing up here in the next month or so."

The sight of the gnarled and unsteady hand left a lump in Ryan's throat. "I'm sorry to hear that," he said, feeling bad about his wish from minutes earlier that the shop would close.

The old man again shrugged his shoulders. "I'm an old man, things like this happen to old men."

"Let me know if there's anything I can do for you," Ryan offered in both obligation and empathy.

A twinkle of appreciation shined in Merv's eyes, as he noted the genuine nature of the offer. "Thank ya, but I'm sure I'll be able to get along as I need to," he answered.

—

Little conversation passed between Ryan and Paul, as the real estate agent coasted his car along the old highway, heading east out of White

Oak City. The excursion through the withered core of the town had left both in dispirited moods. Ryan felt especially doubtful regarding his grand vision for its rebirth. He let his mind drift from the stress of the job at hand and lost himself in the beautiful countryside. A thousand shades of green coated the landscape, from the faintest lime of sun-drenched leaves to the deep hunter and forest greens of shaded enclaves, with spots of yellow and purple popping up here and there as summer blooms. The sound of rubber tires skidding onto gravel jerked him out of his distraction as the car started down the lane leading to the old farmhouse.

"Been a while since anyone lived here," Paul remarked as the car rattled along the bumpy and overgrown drive.

An ache pinged Ryan's heart and brought the faintest of tears to his eyes as the old house became more visible within the canopy of trees that cluttered the overgrown yard. "Some cousins of my grandfather were the last."

The car halted in a clumsy stop, and Paul peered up through the windshield at the weathered home. "We can list the house as being here, it's still fairly straight looking, but we won't include it as a viable structure in the price," he offered as evaluation. "The real value here is all of this land. A couple hundred acres, right?"

The key for the kitchen door rested in Ryan's pocket, but he felt disinclined to share it with Paul. It seemed disloyal, exposing the sacred space to someone seeking only profit.

With serenity on his face, Paul took in the view from atop the red clay bank that overlooked the rushing water. "This is why your family settled here, a close source of fresh water," he surmised.

The fates of the ancestors who lived here long ago ran through Ryan's mind. "I'm sure," he agreed in a trailing voice. "My grandfather's father was born here, before my great-great-grandfather moved the family to town."

A crafty smile broke through Paul's tranquility. "Beautiful spot," he responded almost apathetically. "Should help it sell."

The babbling of the water and song of the birds perched in the groves of trees clumped along the creek banks now sounded more of sorrow than contentment to Ryan. "What type of farming?" he asked.

"Most likely poultry," the real estate agent answered. "Property this large could probably sustain a couple dozen chicken houses."

—

Hiding among the folds of parlor drapes, Ryan watched through the front window as Paul puttered across the yard, taking photo after photo of his grandfather's house. Despite the fact the real estate agent acted only as instructed, Ryan felt increasingly unsure about the actions he'd set in motion.

"This has been a productive day," Paul boasted a few moments later as he stepped into the study, where Ryan had hastily rushed once the real estate agent came back inside. "Here are the last of the contracts, once you sign them, I'll be on my way."

A low buzz started in Ryan's ears, followed by a slight dizziness, which led him to take a seat on the sofa. Closing his eyes for a moment, he took several deep breaths, hoping to calm his unease, but his legs twitched in yearning for him to leap to his feet and run for the door. The sofa shook as Paul landed on it beside him with a hard plop.

"You okay," the real estate agent asked in a voice that sounded more of suspicion than concern.

Ryan opened his eyes and glanced over to Paul, who was fanning out a series of documents on the coffee table. With a few more breaths to reinforce his confidence, Ryan started signing the documents, one by one, as Paul slid them over to him. The paperwork for the buildings downtown came first, followed by contracts for the three rental houses. His pen flowed easily across each, as he found no objection either conscious or subconscious. But that ease of mind ended as Paul placed the next contract in his hand. It felt as if the entire acreage of the property it represented, the old family farm, weighed down on his palm.

"Did I get something wrong on it?" Paul questioned, a sternness in his tone.

Ryan nervously shifted on the sofa. "It's fine," he answered, his anxiety obvious from his labored breathing. "Maybe I'll hold off on the farm. I'm sure I can keep the cattle-grazing lease going on it for now."

Exacerbation sputtered out through Paul's lips. "I was under the impression you wanted to wrap up loose ends as quickly as possible?"

The urge to vomit bubbled up into Ryan's throat. "It might be nice to hold onto a couple pieces of property, in case I want to visit," he muttered.

The color of Paul's face passed from innocuous pink to agitated red. "What do you mean, a couple pieces of property?" he snapped back.

The sweat from Ryan's hands soaked into the document he held. "Maybe the farm, and this house," he replied.

Paul stood and paced with heavy feet back and forth across the floor. "The farm and this house," he repeated. "The two most valuable pieces of real estate you have. You're not having second thoughts about all of this? I would rather clear that up now than later."

Ryan threw a tense glare in the real estate agent's direction, before looking down at the contract in his hand. "You're right," he whimpered. "The farm can go, but I'm holding off on this house until I've finished everything else in town."

The real estate agent snatched up the signed agreement for the farm. "We'll hold off on this house, but everything else is good, right?" he replied as a demand more than an ask.

An uncomfortable rivalry between guilt for being difficult and anger toward the real estate agent's bossy demeanor battled in Ryan's head. "Everything else is fine," he snapped back, unwilling to acknowledge his own fault in the matter.

"Good," Paul nonchalantly commented. "I'll get this in the works. Let me know when to list this house. When are you planning to go back to California?"

The question felt like a dig at Ryan's own procrastination. "I took a three-month leave of absence, and I've got a little more than a month before that ends," he answered.

—

The sky to the west sat on the verge of dusk as Ryan and Olivia stepped off his grandfather's porch, starting the twelve-block walk across town to Connie's house. With Meade heading back to Chicago the next morning, his mother had planned a dinner in his honor. But at this moment, that felt an afterthought to Ryan. A syrupy notion of romance filled his thoughts as he and Olivia held hands and walked quiet residential streets shaded by century-old oaks and perfumed with the scent of gardenias. His senses seemed working against his own fastidiously forced logic because in this evening's air he could not imagine being anywhere other than here.

A warm glow shrouded Connie's house as they neared it, its windows ablaze and the front door open wide in an inviting manner. They climbed the porch steps to find her appreciative smile greeting them.

"Where's the man of the hour?" Olivia asked as they stepped inside.

"Good question," Connie replied. "He called thirty minutes ago and said they were on their way. I haven't seen him all day, and he didn't sleep here last night either."

Ryan responded with a broad smile. "I guess he's trying to get his fill before leaving," he joked, generating an elbow to his side from Olivia.

The older woman shook her head and grumbled. "I'd rather not know if that's the case, and I hope they did more than that."

Feeling too elated to let the conversation take a depressing turn, Ryan continued with his quips. "Who'd want more than that?" he questioned, resulting in an even harder elbow.

Connie rolled her eyes in reply and with a flip of her wrist directed them to follow her to the kitchen. "I don't know that I can forgive Justin for what happened when they were in high school," she admitted.

To which Olivia responded by laying her hand on Connie's back. "Hasn't Meade forgiven him?" she reminded her.

"I suppose, mostly, but he's so sensitive," Connie answered as she pushed the kitchen door open. "He'd forgive anyone."

Stepping into the kitchen, a rush of tempting aromas hit Ryan as the countertop was weighed down with enough food to feed ten times the number of guests.

"Maybe you need to accept his judgment," Olivia suggested as she shot Ryan a look of surprise in response to the outsized feast.

—

The sweet and spicy scent of Connie's molasses barbeque sauce filled the dew-heavy air of the backyard. Ryan had little experience with good barbeque back in Los Angeles, but the alluring smell of this take on the Kansas City-style gave him a growing appetite for it. He flipped the racks of pork ribs on the grill, noticing the tender meat fighting to pull away from the bone, signaling time to take them off.

"I could smell it from the front yard," said a voice behind him.

A shudder ran up Ryan's spine, but turning around he was greeted by Meade's genial face. "I'm sure," Ryan replied as he lifted the slab of ribs up from the grill, before placing it on the serving platter.

"Perfect timing. Hard work's done," Meade offered with a hearty laugh.

"Where's Justin?" Ryan asked, suddenly feeling concerned.

Meade's smile widened. "Out front. He has a surprise for Mom."

Realizing the fragile respite Justin still shared with Connie, Ryan imagined it as a kind gesture. "That's nice," he responded.

Meade's face supported that optimism. "It is," he agreed. "I know what you've heard. But he's not the same person he was in high school. Neither am I."

Ryan offered an approving smile and nod. "I don't think you make many poor decisions in your life," he told him as they carried the food to the kitchen door.

"Not anymore," Meade replied, a jovial bounce in his step. "I got enough lessons from wrong decisions when I was young."

Hearing her son's voice brought a reflexive smile to Connie's face as he and Ryan stepped into the kitchen. "There you are," she exclaimed.

A clump of frosting slid off the end of the spatula she held in her hand, splattering on the counter beside a half-iced cake.

"Here I am," Meade happily rejoined, wearing an expression mirroring his mother's.

"Where's Justin?" she asked, her tone hinting at suspicion.

"Out front," Meade replied, his expression becoming almost conniving. "Go see what he's doing."

For a second, Connie hesitated, but then she gamely put the spatula down and walked down the hall to the front of the house. "Why are you outside?" she called as she emerged onto the porch, with Ryan, Olivia and Meade behind her. "Dinner's about—" she started, before going silent for a moment and then breaking into laughter.

Halfway across the yard stood Justin, a toothy smile on his face as he leaned against a four-foot tall garden gnome with an especially gnarled face.

"What's so funny?" Ryan asked, as Olivia, Meade and Justin joined in on Connie's amusement.

Her face purple from laughing, Olivia pointed to the gnome. "Don't you see it," she responded.

"What's the inside joke?" Ryan questioned, convinced the gnome held a greater meaning.

His cheeks ablaze, Meade gave Ryan a friendly clap on the back. "Mom had one like that, but considerably smaller," he explained. "When we were eight or nine, we were playing tag out here, and Justin broke it, for which Mom became unreasonably upset."

Warmth rose in Ryan's chest as he recognized the metaphoric meaning of the gift. It's his atonement, good faith for the future even, Ryan theorized.

"Something like that," Meade answered before laughing some more.

—

The ruin of half a cake sat on Connie's cake stand, signaling a meal well received, and the clattering of Meade's fork against his plate announced its end. "How about we go out onto the porch and relax," he suggested with a satisfied look.

As if waiting for her cue, Connie jumped to her feet and began to gather the soiled plates and flatware that littered the table. "As long as you're going to help me clear the table first," she remarked to her son.

Meade nodded and joined her in gathering up the debris of the meal. "You got a deal. You three, go get the conversation started while I help Mom." He gave Justin a warm smile.

The humid evening air swaddled Ryan's skin like a damp, warm blanket. He inhaled deeply, allowing the sweet smell of freshly cut grass to linger in his nose as he looked out across the lawn and watched the flickering of fireflies. His chest swelled with sentimentality as intense as the romantic inspiration he felt when he and Olivia had walked here holding hands. He grasped her hand now and led her to the porch swing, which embodied the most ideal aspects of the town's quality of life.

For the first few moments, Ryan silently enjoyed the simplistic beauty of the setting, but a glance to Justin's somber face returned him to other concerns. "What did you two do today, besides buy a giant gnome?" he asked.

The somber look faded, replaced by one hinting of idealism. "We went to Springfield and looked at some historic homes there, and we talked, a lot," Justin replied.

With a push of his foot, Ryan sped up the swing. "Did you take your little girl?"

"Not today, she was at her mother's," Justin replied after a pause.

The soft, smooth skin of Olivia's bare shoulder pressed against Ryan's arm as she leaned on him.

"I love those old houses, you can get one for a pretty good price, though I'm sure they need a lot of work," Olivia commented.

Justin puffed up his chest. "I can handle the work."

Olivia straightened up in the porch swing, pulling away from Ryan. "I didn't know you liked old houses."

A coy smile emerged on Justin's face. "Well enough, and Meade loves them."

With a soft stamp of her foot, Olivia slowed the porch swing down. "I know. He almost cried when the big Victorian by the old high school was torn down."

Justin nodded.

"Any of these houses in Springfield for sale?" Ryan asked, tired of the evasiveness Olivia was using in approaching the question.

"I guess they all were, at least the ones we visited," Justin stammered, his voice quieting with each word.

Olivia leaned forward, her eyes studying Justin's face. "Are you moving to Springfield?" she asked.

In a barely rhythmic manner, Justin nervously tapped his right index finger against the arm of the shellback lawn chair in which he sat. "I'd consider it," he mumbled, avoiding eye contact with either of them.

"Is Meade considering it?" Olivia's eyes were burning into him.

The tapping finger sped up. "You'd need to ask him," Justin replied.

With a gentle push of her foot, Olivia quickened the rocking of the porch swing. "I see," she remarked as her body melted back against Ryan.

Silence hung in the air for a moment but broke as Connie and Meade and their light banter emerged from the front door. Then, catching sight of his friends, Meade's smile morphed into a look of suspicion. "You told them," he groaned.

"They guessed," Justin responded.

Squinting his eyes, Meade scrutinized Olivia and Ryan. "Really?" he questioned them.

A loud stomp of Olivia's feet brought the swing to a jolting stop. "We did," she proudly announced.

Ryan offered a subtle laugh. "We're really quite clever," he added.

"What did they guess?" Connie demanded as she claimed a place standing between them.

Meade shook his head and let out a huff of mild frustration. "Sit down, and I'll tell you," he said.

Connie sat in a weathered wicker chair, her eyes unmoving from her son. "Ok," she prodded.

"This is tentative," Meade took a couple of strides down the length of the porch. "Today, in Springfield, we looked at some houses." Hope brightened Connie's face, while Meade's reddened. "My office seems willing to discuss me relocating to the new office we're considering in Springfield," he continued.

"That's wonderful news," Connie purred and then leaped from her chair to wrap her arms around him.

An embarrassed blush flooded Meade's face as he patted his mother on the back. "Don't get too excited, it's a big if," he warned. "I'm happy in Chicago. I'm going to have to think about this, and it also depends on Justin."

Connie clung to him. "Something'll work out," she insisted.

"It'd mean Justin would likely sell his house here and move to Springfield with me," Meade continued, seemingly uncertain of his mother's reaction.

But despite the strong feelings Connie had displayed about Justin hours earlier, she seemed to almost glow in response to the news. "That's wonderful," she gushed as she reached down to squeeze Justin's hand.

CHAPTER 18

WITH A GRUNT OF EXASPERATION, Ryan flipped over onto his side and reached for his phone, its ringing jarring his sleepy ears. An unfamiliar number showed on the screen. Who calls at 6:30 in the morning? But it had the local area code, and few here knew his personal number. He snorted to clear his nose and swallowed hard to do the same for his throat, then pressed the answer button. "Hello," he muttered.

"Ryan, it's Marvin," the caller replied.

Marvin, Ryan wondered, his mind still sluggish, who's Marvin, but then he remembered "How are you?" he asked, aware of the caller but confused by the time.

"Not good," Marvin answered. "We're in the hospital with Aunt Rosemary."

Ryan's body went tense, jolting him upright in his bed. "What's wrong?" he asked, his breathing now heavy with concern.

"She's old," Marvin soberly answered. "Her body is shutting down, and there isn't really anything that can be done about it."

Ryan stumbled out of the bed, the phone still pressed to his ear, as he searched the floor for the easiest clothes to pull on. "Where are you?" he asked. "I'll be there in a few minutes."

"Mercy Hospital in Springfield," Marvin replied. "She's stable for now, but if you want to see her, hurry."

—

The key turned effortlessly in the lock of the front door of the newspaper office, revealing it as already unlocked. For a second, Ryan stared at the door in a daze. Had someone forgotten to lock it the night before, or had someone arrived more than two hours early? He pushed the door open, triggering the clattering of the cowbell. "Anyone here?" he called out as he walked inside. From the darkness of the back corner, a shadow emerged as a familiar profile.

"I'm here," Connie answered him.

He offered her a weak smile in reply.

"What's wrong?" she asked as she neared him, a cup of coffee in her hand.

His heart quickened. "Aunt Rosemary was taken to the hospital this morning," he replied.

The remaining steps between them quickly disappeared and Connie reached out and rubbed his shoulder in comfort. "I assume it's serious?" she asked.

He glanced down at the floor, avoiding eye contact in hope of subverting tears, and then nodded. "I haven't seen her. I've only talked to Marvin. Her body's shutting down, so I'm heading to Springfield."

In a motherly fashion, Connie slid her arm around his waist and guided him to the front door. "I'll let everyone know, and I'll pray for her," she offered.

A feeling of relief brought a slight ease to his body. "Thank you," he replied. "I appreciate it."

She set her coffee cup on the edge of Ebetta's desk and pulled him into a hug. "Get going, she needs you more than we do."

—

The woman at the hospital's reception desk looked up at Ryan with a sedate smile.

"Rosemary Tagert's room, please," he asked.

Likely an octogenarian, she wore a pin denoting herself as a volunteer. "Friend or family?" she requested in a gentle voice.

"She's my aunt," he replied.

The clicking of the keyboard echoed across the empty waiting room. "Your name?"

"Ryan Shipley," he replied.

More typing. "She arrived this morning, correct?" she asked.

He nodded.

From under the desk came the distinct sound of a printer at work.

"She's in intensive care on the third floor. They'll determine whether you can see her." The woman handed him a visitor badge sticker. "Go down the hallway to your right and use the set of elevators on your left. Take them to the third floor and ICU's to the left."

In less than two minutes, those precise directions delivered him to Marvin and Liddy, sitting together beneath a faded print of Monet's *Water Lilies*.

Her eyes tired from lack of sleep, Liddy greeted Ryan with a warm smile. "Good timing." She stood to give him a hug.

Ryan nodded and accepted her embrace.

Marvin, meanwhile, placed a comforting hand on his shoulder. "She's asking for you," the older man said. "She's very weak, so you won't be able to talk long." He then turned away and stepped up to the nurse sitting inside the window to the left of the ICU entrance. "He's here to see Rosemary Tagert," he said to her.

The nurse nodded and typed into her keyboard. "Let me check with the doctor," she then responded and disappeared.

The three of them stared at the window, waiting for her to reappear, but instead the ICU door opened, and she emerged from behind it. "Are you the nephew she's been asking for?"

—

Heavily swaddled in linens and blankets, Rosemary's frail body appeared already faded of life. Only the steady beep of the heart monitor relayed that she clung to being. Her skin, a pale pink when he had first met her weeks earlier, now looked ashen gray, and her once bright eyes sat sunk deep into her head. He took a deep breath, striving to repress a flow of emotion. "Aunt Rosemary," he muttered as he leaned close to her ear.

At first came no response, he could not even see the movement of her body as she breathed. He glanced back to the heart monitor, still beeping, and then back to her, where her eyelids fluttered for a second before opening. "Hello dear." Her voice was like a whisper of air.

A soft sob escaped him. "Aunt Rosemary, I came to see you," he babbled as a tear trickled down his cheek.

A flinch of pain showed in her eyes as she weakly nodded. "I'm glad."

The touch of a hand on his shoulder pulled his attention back from his aunt and to his right, where the nurse from the ICU window waited with a chair in her hand.

"Her hearing is good, so you don't need to be that close," the nurse told him. "Sit down and talk with her."

He took the chair, setting it as near to his aunt as possible.

In a slow movement, Rosemary shifted her head, so she could see him better, expelling a sigh of exhaustion when the effort finished. "My time has finally come," she offered while reaching her frail left hand out toward him.

With the gentleness he would use with a baby, Ryan took the hand into his own and rested them together on the edge of the bed. "I wish we had more time," he said.

The dullness in her eyes receded for a moment, replaced by the brightness he first saw at his grandfather's visitation. "I've had plenty of time, more than anyone I've known."

He caressed the age-creased hand. "I mean, more for me," he said, his emotions making it difficult to talk.

The dullness returned to her eyes as she lapsed back into her thoughts, but then her grasp tightened on his hand. "Doesn't matter," she responded. "You've gotten to know me, and it makes me happy. Knowing you for this short time has meant so much to me. You're so like both your father and grandfather."

There came a shortness of breath as his cheeks warmed from the tears dribbling down them.

"You've been an angel," he offered.

The brightness reemerged in her eyes. "I hear you're selling some buildings, and the farm," she murmured.

Tears flooded his eyes. He turned away from her gaze, ashamed for her to see him as he admitted his actions, only nodding his confirmation.

The weak hand pulled his closer to her, "You don't need those buildings; I never understood your grandfather buying them," she whispered. "But you're not selling his house."

Still lacking confidence to speak, he again nodded.

"I'm glad," she uttered in the strongest voice she likely had left.

He continued to nod with tears streaming down his face and shame swelling inside of him. "I'm so sorry," he offered in apology, his voice cracking. "I should have told you. I should have talked to you about it."

She reached her right hand out and laid it on top of his, which gently cupped her left. "They're yours, your grandfather gave them to you," she stated in understanding. "Do what's right for you."

The cooling of the dampness on his cheeks gave him a shiver. "It's hard to make the right decisions sometimes," he said.

A weak, though appreciative laugh, broke through her pale lips. "I know, but the right decisions are usually the most obvious, we avoid them because we don't know how to make them fit with how we view ourselves." Her voice grew weaker with each word. Her face then grew dim as her body eased back and her eyes closed.

Again, Ryan felt a hand on his shoulder.

"Mrs. Tagert needs to get some rest," the nurse said in a quiet voice.

Glancing up at her kind face, Ryan imagined she dealt with situations like this often, and he appreciated her demeanor. "Of course," he replied as he stood. Then he paused, looking down at his aunt, her mind again receded inside her dying body. "Thank you," he whispered as he leaned close to her ear. "Thank you for being good to me. I love you." Then he kissed her on the cheek.

—

"How is she?" Liddy asked once Ryan returned to the waiting room.

His shoulders dropped in exhaustion and he let out a disheartened sigh. "I can't imagine she has much longer left."

A nod of agreement came from Marvin. "It's inevitable."

The sorrow in Liddy's eyes bled away, replaced by a hard stare. "It's that bitch Ebetta's fault," she sternly proclaimed as she stood up.

Her bluntness shocked Ryan. "What do you mean?" he asked.

Marvin shook his head. "Liddy, that's not fair," he pushed back.

Rolling her eyes to her husband's scolding, Liddy turned toward Ryan. "It's true," she stated. "Yesterday, Ebetta called and told her about you selling the newspaper and your property. Then this happens this morning. Don't tell me it isn't related."

Tears gathered in Ryan's eyes as he thought about his actions. "I should have told Aunt Rosemary before I signed the papers," he said in reflection.

Marvin laid a reassuring hand on his shoulder. "This isn't your fault."

"It's Ebetta's," Liddy cried and shook her head. "I've never liked that nosy woman, always in everyone's business. She took it too far this time. She doesn't even need to work but felt slighted about you selling the newspaper."

Envisioning Ebetta's smug face welled up anger in Ryan's gut. "Aunt Rosemary didn't mention selling the newspaper. She just talked about the house, which I'm not selling."

"Aunt Rosemary doesn't care about the newspaper or those other buildings, she urged your grandfather to get rid of them," Marvin offered.

Liddy sat back down in one of the waiting room chairs. "That's right, but your house and that farm, well, those she does care about."

A thought popped into Ryan's mind, bringing him a wide smile. "That's not all she cares about," he said.

"Oh?" said Liddy.

Ryan sat down in the chair beside her. "She cares about me, about me making the right choices for myself," he explained.

No one spoke for a moment, then Marvin took the seat on the other side of his wife. "What is your right choice?" he asked.

Ryan leaned back and thought. "I don't know yet, but I almost do."

—

Ryan's chest jutted out in front of him as he took in a deep breath. He closed his eyes and cleared his mind before pushing the door open, triggering the clanging of the old cowbell. The office seemed unnaturally quiet, as if the normal work buzz came to a halt when he stepped inside.

"We weren't expecting you back until later," Connie remarked as she stepped out from behind her desk to give him a hug.

The rest of the staff, while not being as familiar as Connie, approached him, expressions of curiosity and concern on their faces. It made him uneasy, like an animal on display, his emotions and behaviors under scrutiny. They silently looked back and forth between each other, evaluating who should speak first.

"How is she?" Connie finally asked, breaking the awkward silence.

Ryan grimaced at the thought of his frail aunt in her hospital bed. "Not well," he admitted. "She doesn't have much time."

More silence followed, then Mandy stepped up beside him. "I'm sorry, Ryan." She laid her hand on his arm. "She was one of the first people I met when I moved here. I've never known anyone sweeter."

The rest nodded their heads.

"Did they say why?" Connie asked.

"Nothing specific, her body's just shutting down," he replied.

Another brief silence was broken by the one voice Ryan preferred to avoid. "I talked to her yesterday, sounded fine then."

With an angry jerk, Ryan turned to face Ebetta. "I know you did. You told her all about how I'm selling everything, including this newspaper and all the buildings and property I own."

A defensive scowl appeared on Ebetta's face. "How dare you!"

For the first time he could recall, Ryan seriously considered slapping a woman. "All the stress that conversation must have caused could well be responsible for her sudden downturn."

Ebetta's jaw dropped and she cut into him with piercing eyes. "You're blaming me?" she screeched, her voice louder with each word.

He shook his head. "How unfair of me," he said in a condescending tone.

Her face red with anger, Ebetta's clenched fists trembled at her sides. "You're blaming me. You're saying it's my fault," she shrieked. "I won't take this. It's your fault. You come here with your big city ideas and attitude and think everyone should go along with them. I won't allow you to blame me. Blame yourself for coming in here and selling off everything she loves so it can be bulldozed or turned into some queer paradise."

Connie gasped, and the rest of the staff shuffled their feet uncomfortably as they watched the exchange.

But Ryan stopped his attack, privately pleased with the display of the unpleasantness of Ebetta's character. "There are only two places I'm selling she cares about. My grandfather's house, which isn't for sale, and the farm, which is but I'm considering pulling it off the market. Everything else she is fine with me selling. I think the first thing to be sold will be your desk." As soon as he spoke the last comment, he knew he had gone too far.

Ebetta's right hand came down with a loud slap against the top of her desk, which Ryan imagined as a surrogate for his face. "Shove it up your ass," she screamed. "I quit. I wouldn't spend another ten minutes in a room with the likes of you." Her face blazing with anger, she grabbed up everything on the desk she could and stuffed it in her purse.

"I'll know not to expect you at the service," he snapped at her.

"That's entirely too much," Connie chided him.

Though his anger still throbbed, filling his face with a heated flush, Ryan agreed with her. "I apologize for the last statement, it was inappropriate and uncalled for," he offered as he walked toward Ebetta's desk.

Her eyes burned into him. "It's just the type of thing someone like you would say," she snapped before yanking her purse, overflowing with personal items and office supplies, up on her shoulder and trotting toward the door. She paused before stepping outside and looked back at him. "You aren't half the man your grandfather was," she hissed. "And your father was a bum just like you."

Ryan said nothing more, letting it end with the slamming door. A pleased smile came to his face, while behind him, the entire staff remained standing, waiting for a response. "Sorry about that," he muttered, forcing the smile off his face. "I should have handled it more professionally than I did."

—

The text on the monitor blurred as Ryan's mind refused to focus, for at any moment the phone could ring with news. He pulled his fingers back from the keyboard, where they had drifted above the letters, unwilling to type. But they would not land in his lap or come to rest on the desktop; instead they pulled at the album of family photos his grandfather had kept on the shelf beside the desk. Through its pages his journeying began, a time traveler or historic voyeur, visiting people and times he never knew. Even for those few individuals whom he did know, he recognized only the ghosts of their past selves, frozen in another place.

One image struck him. Marked as Rosemary's high school graduation photo, it dated to some seventy-five years prior and depicted a young, spunky woman on the verge of discovering life. With dark hair cut into a bob and sparkling eyes, the cheery face showed no understanding of the long life of experiences promised to it. The phone rang, at first a faint buzzing in the recesses of his mind, then he blinked, no longer focused on the image in the album but on the waiting call.

He shut the cover, placed the album back on the shelf, and leaned back in his chair, almost afraid to answer. With an uneasy breath in his lungs, he picked up the receiver and put it to his ear. "Hello."

"It's Marvin. I tried calling your cell phone, but you didn't answer."

The image of his cell phone sitting on the seat of his grandfather's car flashed in Ryan's mind. "How is she?" he asked, already assuming the answer.

A pause followed. "She's gone. Ten minutes ago," Marvin replied.

The world around him softened as tears glazed his eyes. "Were you able to talk to her any more?" Ryan asked.

"She went to sleep when you left and stayed that way until the end, as peaceful as we could hope. I'll let you go, but Liddy and I'll stop by your house this evening."

Ryan placed the receiver back on its cradle and closed his eyes, letting his mind flood with emotion and warm tears dribble down his cheeks.

—

Had the church felt this cold the day of his grandfather's funeral? Ryan recalled feeling numb and bewildered that day, all the new people and being pulled this way and that, but memory of an icy temperature escaped him. Today, with his aunt at rest in the rose-colored casket a few feet away, the chill in the air gave him a notable shiver, despite being layered in a long sleeve dress shirt and suit jacket.

In the four days since her death, he had again found himself on the receiving end of condolences, most from those knowing her for decades, compared to his few weeks. But despite the brevity of their acquaintance, the small, frail woman's impact on him had been significant.

The casket sat closed at Rosemary's request, with a large spray of white roses atop it and framed photographs of her and her family on an adjacent table. Among those images, he spotted her and her late husband, her with his grandfather and father, her with Marvin and Liddy, and even one of them together, taken but a few weeks earlier. Tears spilled from his eyes upon seeing it, as he felt unworthy of the honor.

With a wry smile on his face, the now-familiar Methodist pastor announced the service would be pleasant and short, as Rosemary had requested. He spoke of her personal philosophy of life, and how it mirrored that of Jesus, and offered a prayer, before stepping aside so Marvin could recite her obituary and offer a brief remembrance. The only excess came with a heartfelt rendition of the hymn "In the Garden," sung by a misty-eyed Hazel Loutrou.

—

The sun rested high in a clear sapphire sky as Ryan walked alongside Olivia among the monuments of granite and marble. The small tent raised above Rosemary's grave sat a few rows away from the resting spot of his grandfather, where grass proved slow to return in the peak of summer's heat.

Dozens of mourners crowded around them, and again they listened as the preacher offered words of solace and salvation, ending with another prayer and inviting those there to return to the church's fellowship hall for lunch.

More condolences followed as Ryan and Olivia passed through the crowd on their way back to her car, words meant to evoke comfort, but instead summoning in him sadness and guilt. The thought of lunch at the church among the mourners left his hands trembling with anxiety. "Can we do something else?" he asked once they made it to the car.

—

An intense chill vibrated through Ryan's body as he slipped his bare foot into the ice-cold water. The rushing creek, lapping at his calves, drew his mind away from both the afternoon heat and the lingering sorrow of his aunt's death. He savored the pastoral scene, the red clay ledge lurching out above the water and the lush groves of trees piled up on the creek's edge. He held tight to Olivia's hand as his head swam with nostalgic thoughts, he leaned over and left a whisper of a kiss on her lips. "Thank you," he told her.

She smiled and leaned against him. "You're welcome. I've always loved this spot."

A breath of nature-sweetened air filled his lungs, and, with a playful smile, he let go of her hand and began unbuttoning his shirt. The warmth of the sun embraced his bare shoulders as he pulled the shirt off, and then tossed it on the gravel bank.

A bashful coloring rose in Olivia's face as she watched the performance. "What're you doing?" she asked in a voice more playful than serious.

With a wink of his eye, he unbuttoned and then unzipped his slacks. "I'm going swimming," he cheerfully replied as he pulled them off, leaving on only a pair of boxer briefs.

She broke into a girlish giggle. "What if someone comes down here?" she warned him, still smiling.

Hopping from one leg to the other, he pulled his underwear off. "They're going get a good show," he declared, now naked with the water running between his knees.

"You're going to sunburn that little guy," she playfully warned him.

He smiled. "Ain't that little," he proclaimed, before diving into the deep blue pool beneath the red clay ledge, splashing her in the process.

"You ass," she yelled at him and stepped back out of the water, looking down at the wet dappling on her dress.

Bobbing up and down like a child's bath toy, he smiled at her. "I thought you liked my ass," he taunted. "You're wet. Better take your clothes off so they can dry."

A defeated, though affectionate sigh escaped her. "I see what your plan is," she said.

Despite the cold chill of the creek water, Ryan felt only warmth when he looked at her. "I don't have a clue what you're talking about," he impishly countered. "It's hot, so I got in the water. You should join me."

Olivia paced back and forth, dropping a piece of clothing on every pass, only offering the occasional silent glance in his direction.

"Hurry," he teased her.

"Look away, and I will," she proposed in surrender, a serious expression on her face.

With the pout of a punished schoolboy, Ryan stuck out his lower lip. "But watching is the best part," he whined.

She scowled at him and shook her head. "If you want me to come in, turn around," she demanded.

Though still sporting his sour look, he begrudgingly turned. "Fine," he conceded. "But hurry up." The creek itself then caught his attention, the contours and flora that defined the rough, natural edges of the living waterway, moving and transforming with each proceeding year, as it had done for eons. "Ready yet?" he called, his thoughts receding from nature and returning to more lusty pursuits.

"No," she responded in warning.

He splashed water behind his back in her direction. "Should I trust you?" he joked. "Are you throwing my clothes in the creek and taking off in the car." She laughed in response, but not from behind him, instead it seemed to hang over him. "Don't take that as an idea," he warned her.

"Don't turn around yet," she warned him again, her voice, like the laugh preceding it, from somewhere other than he expected.

The creek and its undiminished views returned to his mind, as not a single human improvement visibly existed either upstream or down. What would poultry houses mean for that? he wondered. "Ready?" he called out. No response. "Are you ready?" he repeated, feeling slight apprehension. Still, he heard no response. "I'm turning around," he announced, feeling the silence gave him the right. But as he did so, a pink blur of nakedness came plunging into the water from atop the red ledge, dousing him with a massive splash.

A second later, Olivia's smiling face burst up through the surface. "You're right," she cried through blue lips. "This does feel good, but it's also cold."

He shook his head and laughed. "I deserved that."

"Damn right," she agreed as she swam toward him. "Give me a kiss."

CHAPTER 19

WITH A SWEEP OF HIS HAND, a groggy Ryan sent his ringing phone tumbling off the nightstand and onto the floor. He groaned and pulled his body to the edge of the bed, from where he blindly groped along the floor. His grasp hit a shoe and then a sock before his fingers finally stumbled upon the phone. A memory a week and a half earlier, the morning Rosemary went to the hospital, flashed in his mind. He shook the negative thought out of his head.

"I've got great news," the chipper voice of his real estate agent, Paul, offered in greeting.

What constituted good news? Ryan wondered to himself. "What?" he mumbled.

"Confirmed interest from the potential buyer for the newspaper," the real estate agent happily answered, ignoring his client's early morning apathy. "They own several weeklies in Kentucky, Tennessee, Arkansas and Missouri, including three within a hundred miles of you."

Unease raged in Ryan's gut as the real estate agent continued with more details. Even though this offer should be the light at the end of his tunnel, the last few weeks left him doubting his intentions.

Awkward silence stepped into the conversation as Paul finished talking and waited for a response. "What do you think?" the real estate agent prodded after a long pause.

The question forced Ryan out of his silent introspection. "Are they coming here?" he asked.

"Yes, next Friday," Paul responded, obviously unconcerned about Ryan's schedule.

The phone felt heavy, like a brick, in Ryan's tense grip. "I suppose that'll work," he replied.

"Late morning," Paul continued.

A gagging sensation tickled at Ryan's throat. "Ok," he agreed, forcing back his physical reaction.

The clicking of fingers on a keyboard carried through the phone line. "Great," Paul exclaimed, still sounding gleeful. "I'm making progress on some of the other properties too, but we'll talk about that later."

Disorientation clouded Ryan's mind for a moment after he hung up the phone. The longer he stayed, choices that originally seemed simple grew increasingly complex. And now, on the verge of a concrete conclusion, he increasingly felt like a traitor to his grandfather, Rosemary and the town. But he held little confidence in his ability to handle the responsibilities left him or even being happy trying. He liked Los Angeles and usually felt happy there. Could he settle in White Oak City, possibly the rest of his life? Why would anyone choose to stay in a dried-up shell of a town?

He climbed out of bed and made his way to the kitchen where, with a light jerk, he pulled open the refrigerator door, causing the bulky appliance and its contents to rattle. It sat on an uneven floor. Damn old house, who'd want to live in some archaic old place like this? He poured a glass of orange juice but left it untouched on the counter as he drifted out of the kitchen and into his grandfather's study.

He wandered through the room, examining the artifacts and keepsakes that cluttered it. The history and nostalgia it encapsulated overwhelmed him, leaving him to collapse on the sofa, his eyes transfixed on the painting of the ocean above the fireplace. The soft grays and greens of the waves melted together in his mind, while his serious questions faded into abstraction, at least until a faint strain of music began, along with a vibration against his leg.

He pulled his ringing phone out of his pocket and looked at the screen. Olivia—the first good news of the day. "Are you at home?" she asked in response to his good morning. "I called the office, but they said you hadn't arrived yet."

The clock on the mantel, which he had wound the day before, showed 9:30. "I had no idea it was this late," he replied, realizing he had sat on the sofa and stared at the painting for an hour or more.

She paused, which seemed like implied concern. "Alarm not go off?" she asked.

It had, when he was in the kitchen, he remembered. "It did, but my mind fell on other things."

Another pause.

"Like how to get all your stuff out here from Los Angeles?" she offered in a playful manner.

The first twinge of a headache pulsed behind his right eye. "No," he countered. "What are you doing today?"

"Taking my mom's dog to the vet in Springfield. I should have already left."

Queasiness fired up from his stomach in a burst of heartburn. "I wanted to take you to lunch," he replied, hoping to garner enough guilt to get her to change her plans.

"Not going to work today. I'm going to lunch with a friend after the vet," she answered, not playing into his manipulative effort. "If you don't have dinner plans, we can go to Springfield. It is a Friday."

A sharp pang ached in his stomach. He did not want to wait that long to talk to her, but it seemed the only option. "That works," he conceded.

—

Only the quiet hum of technology punctured the silence of the office, with the high school staff still in school and empty desks marking the permanent absences of Ebetta and Glo.

"Good morning," Connie greeted him with a warm smile. "Wondered when you were going to show. Olivia called looking for you. Did she get ahold of you?"

With but a slight nod, Ryan answered the question.

"You ok?" Connie pressed, concern in her voice.

He paused as he contemplated what answer to give. "Just a headache," he replied, only a partial lie.

Her purse came flying up onto her desk. "I have some ibuprofen," she offered as she began digging into her bag.

He shook his head and kept walking. More greetings followed from Barry, Jerry and Mandy, to which he replied with a series of nods, before stepping into the editor's office and closing the door behind him.

The day proceeded with a war of contradicting emotions taking place in his head. But they provided no clear resolutions, as with every battle the victor idea canceled out the one from immediately before it.

The day wasted away around him, and as 4:30 approached, Connie knocked on the door, forcing him out of his stupor. "Go home for the day," she suggested.

"I don't mind staying," he replied, feeling guilty for completing so little.

She shook her head. "Go home," she repeated in a firmer voice. "You have something on your mind. Plus, I think everyone else would like an early day too. I'll stay and watch the phones for the last thirty minutes."

The exhaustion that had gnawed at him all day erupted in a loud yawn. "I guess so, if you don't mind," he agreed, to which she responded with a relieved smile.

—

Still troubled by the choices he would soon have to make, Ryan slouched back in the front porch glider, allowing its tranquility to fade his worries as much possible.

"Enjoying the evening air?" Olivia asked as she trod up onto the porch steps.

He nodded, and with a twitch of his foot slowed the glider's motion. "I am," he answered with a welcoming smile. "Wanna join?"

The glider gave a shuddering pause as she dropped down into it beside him. "How was your day?" she queried.

A tense whistle of air escaped from between his clenched teeth. "All right. I was kind of distracted."

She nodded. "I heard."

He shifted his body to better see her. "You've been talking to Connie?"

She nodded again. "She's worried about you. Is it something to do with selling the newspaper?"

His body went rigid, stiffening his legs and bringing the glider to a stop. Was he that transparent? "Why do you think that?" he asked.

"It's what Connie thought," she replied with a shrug.

Pushing down slightly with his right foot, he returned the glider to motion. "How would she know that?"

She shook her head. "She just assumed that's what's most likely to be bothering you," she explained. "She's not a fool. She knows your plans, and she knows you're conflicted about it."

—

"What about you?" Ryan questioned Olivia as they sat together at the bar. In front of him rested drink number three, or at least the third since they'd finished dinner.

"What about me?"

With a cock of his head to the right, his eyes bored into her. "You don't want to stay in White Oak City," he pushed.

Sadness emerged from her like watching stars blink out. "It's not that," she replied in a restrained voice. "I'm a researcher. I research patterns among people on all aspects of their lives, and there's only so much of that I can do in White Oak City. When you're career oriented, it's hard to stay in a place like White Oak. You're forced to give up something. For now, for me, that's White Oak City."

An upsetting answer for an unfair question, he thought as he downed the rest of his three-quarters full drink. "Telecommuting, isn't that possible?" he asked, now using a politer tone.

She sat her wine glass on the edge of the bar and then gently clasped his arm with both her hands. "Maybe one day, but I'm new at this. I must put in my time at a university or research facility. Maybe, once I prove myself, I can do it from a distance, but for now I've got to go to them."

Disappointment clouded Ryan's mind. He knew that if she stayed in White Oak, his decision would lean toward it as well.

—

The following days slipped away with Ryan sorting through his grandfather's life, trinkets and artifacts and mountains of paperwork, photos and histories covering generations of the family's ingrained relationship with the town. His family heritage unveiled to him, offering pride of pedigree and a feeling of inadequacy for any attempt to step into the roles of his forbearers.

On Sunday night came a call from his mother, informing him of her arrival in less than a week. For two months he had delayed her visit, but his tactics no longer worked, prompting her to make plans and wait until afterward to tell him.

Monday and Tuesday came and went with him maintaining a friendly and positive attitude with the newspaper staff. But by Wednesday, unease grew as the visit from the potential buyers lingered two days away, and the time arrived for him to make his second pitch to the city council.

The council's agenda included a proposed vote on a preliminary revitalization plan for the blocks around the square, but questions remained concerning the council's level of commitment to the idea. For, despite Olivia working together with the city planner to remove as many objections as possible, rumors around town signified that resistance remained, either to the proposal or to him personally.

He sensed this as well, noting a subtle animosity toward him and his "liberal" ideas, and he knew Ebetta took an active role in campaigning against his plan. Not because she disagreed with it but because hurting him seemed a more important goal. She appeared especially active in a whisper campaign focused on killing the proposed tax code exemption without which he could not afford to offer low enough rents to attract businesses. He also needed the city council's support for adding the business district to the National Register of Historic Places, as its placement on that list would help buildings qualify for preservation grants and tax credits.

With these concerns weighing on him, he huddled behind the closed door of the editor's office for most of the day, working on his presentation. By 3:30 his mind felt numb, as if he had used every ounce of imagination and ingenuity in it, all in hope of charming the council enough to support the plan. Feeling unable to type another coherent word, he took a deep breath and looked up from the computer screen, spotting across the office a smiling Olivia chatting with Connie. Her confident pose inspired in him a needed boost of courage, so he took three more deep breaths, bringing his anxiety under control, and stepped out into the newsroom.

At first, the staff offered only an apathetic awareness of his presence, but as he continued to move among them, their eyes drifted up to him, displaying expressions from curiosity to concern. "All the articles this week are really good, we're going to have a great paper," he muttered, his face warm with flush. "But that's not what I need to tell you all," he added in a somber voice. "We're having some visitors on Friday." He felt cold, despite his body's hot flush.

A hand slipped up into the air. "Who's visiting?" Barry asked and then quickly pulled his hand down.

"I don't remember their names, but they own a lot of weekly newspapers like this one," Ryan answered while avoiding eye contact.

Another hand rose, like in a grade school exercise. "Why are they coming?" Mandy asked with sternness in her voice.

A loud chortle cut off Ryan's hesitant start. "It's obvious," Jerry interrupted. "They're thinking of buying this paper. Isn't that right?"

Barry's jaw dropped as he looked up at Ryan. "I thought you'd decided you were going to stay," he said.

Ryan shook his head. "I never said that. It's true I feel closer to White Oak and this paper and everyone than I imagined I would when I first arrived for my grandfather's funeral. But my home is in Los Angeles."

Silence followed, with a tossing of uneasy glances back and forth, while Connie held fast to Olivia's arm, pained expressions marring both their faces.

"What happens to us, our jobs?" Mandy asked.

Nervously shifting his balance from one foot to the other, Ryan turned to face her, almost tripping in doing so. "I would encourage them to keep you all," he answered. "You're a great team, they'd be stupid not to."

Jerry leaned back in his chair, which creaked in its archaic oaken frame. "Let's be realistic," he countered. "Lots of papers around here have been bought up by companies like this. First thing they do is get rid of the graphic designers, downsize the advertising staff and move most of that work to a regional office."

"That's half of us," Barry protested. "That'd be me, Mark, Casey and Mary Beth. I mean, Mark and Casey'll go to college soon, but Mary Beth and I need our jobs."

Ryan felt a growing dampness on his forehead and upper lip. "We don't know what would happen here, and I might not sell to this company," he countered, hoping to keep the group calm.

Jerry shook his head in response. "Even if you don't sell it to them, you'll sell to somebody, and they'll probably do the exact same thing."

Ryan took three more deep breaths. "I never said I was going to sell," he said.

—

A rush of fresh summer scents greeted Ryan as he stepped outside, offering a slight ease to the turmoil he carried away from his disastrous announcement of a few moments earlier. Olivia, a hand's grasp away, kept silent as they made their way down Commercial Street, and then up the hill to his grandfather's house, intuiting his need for both company and quiet contemplation.

Her hand finally brushed against his as they crossed the front yard. Above them, the breeze rustled the leaves of the old oak tree. "I don't necessarily think you should sell the newspaper, but it is your right to do so," she remarked as they paused a few feet from the porch steps. "The staff needs to respect that, even if they don't like it."

A hollow sigh rattled up from Ryan's lungs. "If I knew I was doing the right thing, I'd agree," he replied. "But I don't know that I am doing the right thing."

She rewarded him for his admission with a light kiss on the cheek. "What about the council meeting, is that the right thing?" she asked.

A sweet scent of wild roses helped calm his senses. "That is the right thing," he answered. "I wish there was some way to make it an even better deal. I'd give away every building I own, if I thought it would help the town."

The warmth of her body enveloped him in her embrace. "You're excited about that, but not selling the newspaper," she summarized. "Why?"

The crisp white visage of his grandfather's house glowed in the late afternoon sun. "I'm afraid I'll screw it up," he answered.

—

Ruddy-faced, as always, the mayor flashed a broad smile as he leafed through the binder that laid out Ryan's proposal. But even with that positive cue, worry persisted in Ryan's mind that the council remained unconvinced or might even strike it down for personal reasons. He knew at least a couple of its members socialized with the acid-tongued Ebetta.

"I want to thank Mr. Shipley for being so accommodating to the suggestions myself and the other members of the council have made in the last couple of weeks in response to his original presentation," the mayor began. "I like the advisory panel you suggest putting together to decide on what types of businesses would qualify for low rents in your program, and the guidelines you've already outlined. I hope you mean to fulfill it."

Standing behind the speaker's podium, Ryan nodded.

The mayor opened his mouth to continue, but the tapping of a finger against a microphone cut him off.

With a somber look on his face, Beau LaSalle cleared his voice. Previously, the hardware store owner ranked among Ryan's biggest supporters, but he also counted Ebetta as a close friend. "I'm pleased as well," Beau agreed. "It bodes well for the future of this town to put intelligent, well-reasoned forethought into selecting tenants, especially considering the help we may offer them."

With that, debate erupted as all five members of the council launched into questions of various worth. Their verbal assessments and opinions showed they believed it held varying levels of value, with only one dismissing it outright. And as he listened to it play out, a giddiness of success began to swell inside of Ryan.

Nearly thirty minutes of questions, debate and a few snide remarks passed by the time the mayor, appearing weary of the continuing discussion, cut his fellow council members off and asked for a motion on the property tax issue. Ryan's eyes darted back and forth between their faces, trying to discern his allies. The first member voted no, tossing his stomach for a loop. He failed, he thought to himself. Then the mayor called on the next member, who answered with a yes. He felt a jolt of reinvigoration, though his anxiety remained. The third said no, a second denial.

His mind raced as sweat coalesced along his hairline. Now for Beau and the mayor, if either voted against it, it died. If it died, with no reservation, he would sell the newspaper. Beau voted in favor. It now rested in the hands of the mayor. Olivia had spent the last several weeks promoting the local leader as a fair man, if a bit backward. But Ryan feared a grudge remained concerning the editorial on the chicken plant.

The obese politician relished the role of tiebreaker, leaned back in his chair and glancing at the members on both sides of him. He then leaned forward so that his lips touched his microphone. "I vote in favor," he announced in a booming voice. "It passes. Congratulations Mr. Shipley."

Elation engulfed Ryan, leaving him with the sensation of floating on air. His actions created success. And while more work needed to be done to get tenants in the buildings, the plan could move forward.

—

"A bit sluggish this morning," Connie remarked as Ryan stepped inside the office, nearly thirty minutes late. "Up late celebrating your good news from the council meeting?"

The dryness in his mouth felt as though it would crack apart if he uttered a word. He offered only a slight smile as he passed her desk.

The staff watched as he crossed the room, their typing falling awkwardly out of rhythm as he passed each person, greetings restrained to shallow nods. But as he neared the quiet, protected sanctuary of the editor's office, Jerry's voice brought him to a stop. "I'm working on the story about the city council vote last night," he announced. "I suppose it's the lead on the front page."

The comment felt like it came with an underlying bite. "I'm not sure," Ryan remarked, his voice coming out as a harsh whisper.

A displeased smirk showed on Jerry's face. "Biggest news this week, not that we typically have much big news," he countered. "We'll put a disclaimer in that you are *currently* the editor and publisher of this newspaper, at least as far as I know. I've inserted some quotes from you in it, so you can look at them and change as you want."

Desperate to curtail the discussion, Ryan shrugged his shoulders in de facto agreement and then stepped inside the editor's office, closing the door behind him.

His chair let out a rusty squeak as he collapsed into it. A hopelessly broken-down relic, it retained enough comfort and from its vantage point gave him a commanding view of the newsroom and front office. Sitting there and looking out, he could not help but think the office a timeless place, especially with the morning sunlight streaming through the front windows, its reflection glimmering on the glass of the framed photographs that graced the cracked plaster walls.

Would selling it be the end of this Americana-drenched setting? Would a new owner shutter this dusty, yet beloved old space and move a condensed office out to one of the bland strip mall office on West Commercial Street? He shook his head and planted his elbows on top of the desk, unknowns bubbling in his mind and leaving him on the verge of weeping.

A dull ache pulsed behind his right eye, the precursor to a headache, if he did nothing to ease it. The desk phone began ringing, a loud old-fashioned ring that paired well with its archaic black rotary dial.

"Hello," Ryan answered as he put the receiver to his ear.

Paul Mason greeted him from the other end, sending a wave of anxiety through his body. "Just confirming I'm coming with the potential buyers tomorrow."

The dull throb blossomed into its full headache potential as Ryan nodded in understanding before remembering he needed to provide a verbal answer on the phone. "I've got it," he offered after an awkward pause. "We can have lunch at the diner, since it's right across the square."

"That's fine, I don't think either of them are picky," Paul responded in a tone that hinted of condescension.

The phone's bell gave a weak ding as Ryan dropped the receiver back into place.

—

Ryan wandered into the empty office, thankful for its 8:30 a.m. solitude, allowing him a few moments to privately prepare for the day to come. He still did not know what to expect of either himself or the staff when the potential buyers arrived. Even Olivia's calming presence in bed beside him through the night had done little to calm him, as sleep proved evasive while his mind raced with concerns.

Darkened computer screens and empty chairs created isolation, like an omen foretelling the future sacking of most of the staff. He took a deep breath and surveyed the room, making note of all the sights within it, and his eyes lingering longest on the door that led to the upstairs apartment.

The stairs creaked and groaned as he ascended. To sell the newspaper and its building would mean sorting through the relics left behind, as it did not seem right to let strangers sift through his great-grandparents' belongings.

The front door loudly clattered below as he reached the top step, signaling another presence in the building. But he pushed the interruption out of his mind and stepped into the large front room that looked down upon Commercial Street. From the large center window, he found an almost enchanting view, with the gentle sepia tones of the morning light washing across the buildings on the opposite side of the street.

The stairs creaked and cracked as someone followed his trail. "Morning Ryan," Connie's voice offered in greeting from the doorway.

"Good morning," Ryan answered without glancing back, though he listened as her footsteps approached.

"I hope you're not allergic to dust," she remarked, now standing out a few feet from him.

He turned toward her, a grim smile on his face. "Suppose there's anything up here worth keeping?" he asked.

"Don't know," she replied as she gave the dust covered boxes and old furniture a quick glance. "When are our guests arriving?"

He wished he could hit a pause button and delay the visit for a few more weeks, but it would only delay and not prevent a decision. "Around ten," he answered.

She nodded. "You're early then."

A deep breath filled his lungs with the room's musty air. "Woke up and couldn't get back to sleep," he replied.

Her arm slipped around him and pulled him against her in a hug. "It's all right," she offered.

"What's all right?" he shot back, trying to stem a sudden pulsing of emotion in his chest.

"Whatever choice you make." She gave him a motherly pat.

The mustiness seemed less oppressive now, as if his senses had dulled to it. "Go back to Los Angeles?" he suggested.

She shrugged. "If that's the right one."

The knot in his stomach shifted to his right side.

"I'm going downstairs to get the office properly opened." She turned away.

With a drag in his step, he followed her downstairs, slunk into the editor's office and closed the door.

An uncommon quiet kept hold of the newsroom throughout the early morning, despite the presence of nearly the entire staff, which normally meant a constant buzz of gossip and banter. Was the silence the manifestation of their own tension and stress, or did his concerns create a hypersensitivity to their actions?

Unable to focus, a stack of copy in need of editing sat untouched on the desk as he buried himself in the *Kansas City Star's* website, perusing even the most inconsequential stories and features. Then, midway through a story on the building of a new high school in the city, he heard the clatter of the cowbell. His stomach seized inside him, and he kept blankly focused on the computer screen right until Connie opened the door of his office. "Your appointment has arrived," she announced, an empathetic look on her face.

He nodded. "I'll walk up with you," he replied, feeling his hands tremble with apprehension.

Eyes burned into him as he crossed the newsroom. Everyone stared, not even pretending not too.

He stopped at the chair rail divider, letting Connie pass through its gate before him. He offered Paul a polite nod. Two men waited with the real estate agent, one older, with a heavily-lined face and thinning gray hair, while the other, unmistakably a relative, appeared about twenty years younger with a stocky build and dull eyes. All three brandished broad grins, forcing Ryan to reflectively extend his own insincere smile.

"Ryan, good to see you," Paul offered in greeting, extending his hand to him. Ryan nodded and shook Paul's hand. The real estate agent then turned toward the two men he brought. "I want you to meet Sy Bladenship and his son Matt," he offered in introduction.

"Good to meet you," Sy replied as they shook. Matt followed with a similar greeting.

Ryan held the gate open and motioned for the visitors to follow him.

With a waver in his voice, Ryan introduced the three men to each member of the staff. He noted that while both Sy and Matt acted polite and interacted well with everyone, a subtle disinterest bled through. Was it a sign of an operation that dictates standards, stripping away local traditions? Or, perhaps, he was simply overthinking the situation. But, regardless, Ryan kept his jittery hands buried deep in his pockets.

After fifteen minutes of meeting and chatting with the staff, Paul more than Ryan, corralled the four of them into the editor's office and closed the door.

"I'm glad you're able to see the operation first hand," Ryan offered, forcing a smile.

Sy nodded. "We always check out the merchandise first," he replied, his discolored teeth a hue reminiscent of buttered corn.

The word "merchandise" made it sound like little more than buying a new car.

"Do you have questions for me?" Ryan asked, trying to ignore his unease.

The number of wrinkles in Sy's forehead doubled as the man thought. "We've seen the books, they look fair, though I see opportunities for increasing revenue," he explained. "Is there any possibility for another paper to swoop in and get the county and city announcements and notice contracts?"

His office chair squeaked as Ryan leaned back in it. Yes, a simple business deal, no interest in the integrity and quality his grandfather and great-grandfather instilled into the newspaper. "We're the only county-wide newspaper," he replied, still forcing a smile. "The two others within the county only circulate within their towns, and each have readerships of less than 1,500. We're at 13,500, so I think those are secure."

Sy nodded. Matt blankly smiled.

The room felt stifling with the door closed and the four of them stuffed inside. Sweat beaded along Ryan's hairline. What about the newspaper's legacy? he wondered, did they care about it? "My grandfather was committed to the county and this newspaper," he explained, hoping to inspire interest in the business's heritage.

Another nod came from Sy, something between condescending and passive. "Glad to hear it, should make our approach to managing newspapers easier to integrate," the older man predicted. "We typically have a different approach to management than most independent newspapers, but financially we're more successful and our readers are generally happy with the results."

"I suppose some of our methods are a bit old-fashioned compared to what you do at most of your papers," Ryan remarked, realizing his overtures to legacy seemed lost on the men. "We still have several country correspondents for instance."

A hearty laugh filled the room as Sy's ample frame teetered back and forth in his chair. "I like country correspondents, especially when they do it for free," he responded.

Guilt, for not paying the correspondents, felt like a hard jab in Ryan's side. "They get a free subscription, and a tin of cookies at Christmas," he admitted.

The yellow teeth again flashed as Sy smiled. "Good policy," he declared.

—

Walking down Commercial Street toward the diner for lunch, Ryan pointed out to Sy and Matt the buildings he owned and shared the basics of the redevelopment plan. Sy had prompted the discussion, signaling that Paul had shared the plans with them in advance of the visit.

"That's a lot of empty commercial space," Sy remarked as he eyed the old bank building.

Uneasiness turned in Ryan's gut. "My grandfather kept most of them in fairly good repair," he explained, hoping to counter the negativity in Sy's comments. "They all have decent roofs and several of them even have upgraded electrical and plumbing. Not all of them, but enough to help attract initial investors and build momentum, I think."

Sy's slouched composure expressed doubt as he squinted his eyes in the midday sun. "It helps that this is the county seat," he conceded. "If it wasn't, I'd say your best bet would be to call in the wrecking crew and have them taken down. Even with that said, you still might consider that with the old hotel. Those structures are pretty impractical, and I don't know that you'll find a good use for it."

In a close second to the old bank, the hotel stood as the most grandiose and ornate structure Ryan had inherited. Was it worthless? His face flushed red as he thought through the man's remark. "Could be retail on the first floor and maybe apartments on the second and third," Ryan replied, hoping to inspire confidence in the old building.

Giving no verbal response to the contrary, Sy only offered a shrug that seemed there only for placating Ryan's ambitions.

A deep breath helped Ryan keep his emotions below the surface and flushed the conversation's irritations from his mind. "Let's have lunch," he said, eager to change the topic.

Sy nodded. "Sure, but what's with the newly cleared lot at the end of the street?" he asked, pointing in the direction of the recent fire. "Is it new construction?"

A chill ran up Ryan's spine. "That's where the old high school was," he answered.

"Torn down?" Sy questioned.

Still peeved at the man's comment about the hotel, Ryan held back, determined to share only the basic facts. "Burned," he answered.

"When did that happen?" Sy questioned, eagerness in his voice.

Ryan remained quiet and Paul's face turned sour as silent seconds passed. "A month ago," the real estate agent interjected. "Arson. The owner wanted to tear it down, but the city council said it was a historic structure. There was a court hearing in the city's favor, and that night it went up in flames. Isn't that right Ryan?"

Amused laughter escaped Sy. "Did the owner torch it himself?" he queried while waving his hands in delight.

Paul's sour look progressed to a scowl as Ryan continued his silent protest. "Yeah," he answered, trying to make up for his client's mute behavior. "He's in jail now."

Sy's large hand excitedly grasped Ryan's shoulder. "I bet a scandal like that sold some papers," he bellowed.

—

The lunchtime hum paused as Ryan entered the diner with his group of strangers. Inquiring faces stared at them as if watching animals at the zoo, at least until the waitress, with a knowing look on her face, sat them at a table in the middle of the room, offering the least amount of privacy possible.

"What's with the building?" Sy thundered, his voice nearly making the silverware clatter.

The tips of Ryan's fingers tingled. "It's a package deal," he quietly replied, hiding his jittery hands beneath the table. "Business and building go together."

A loud creak sounded as Sy adjusted in his chair. "I see why you'd want that," he stated. "You already own too many old buildings in this town, so don't blame you for wanting to shed one. But I prefer to rent."

A dull throbbing pain emerged in Ryan's right temple, which when combined with his tingling, jittery hands likely qualified him as a nervous wreck. "Why?" he asked in return.

Nodding his head, Sy appeared to have finished his personal assessment of Ryan. "It helps control the bottom line," the older man replied. "It means I'm not responsible for maintenance and other issues, so focus remains on the newspaper. This works for us. It's fine to own the building, if you only own one publication, but the more you own, the more of a hassle it becomes."

Despite the desire to challenge Sy's logic, Ryan held back, as the old man likely told the truth. But his ideal still involved selling the building with the paper.

By the time they finished eating, only uneasy chatter remained between them. Then, after an uncomfortable lull in the already weak conversation, Sy leaned over and whispered into Paul's ear. To which the real estate agent responded by nodding.

"Ryan, if you might head back to the office, Sy and Matt would like to discuss what they've seen today," Paul suggested.

The room around them sat full of eavesdroppers, people likely to know more about Ryan's business than he would in a few moments. But asking them to take their conversation elsewhere seemed pointless. He obligingly stood and offered a brief nod to both Sy and Matt. But Paul remained in his chair. "Are you coming?" Ryan asked the real estate agent, suddenly wary of the situation.

Paul shook his head. "No, I'm going to hang back to answer questions they might have," he replied with a shallow smile.

—

"I hope you had a good discussion," Ryan remarked when, nearly two hours later, Sy, Matt and Paul finally returned to the newspaper office.

A genuine, if also cunning, smile showed on Sy's face. "We did," he responded, his teeth looking even yellower now than a few hours earlier.

Too much coffee and cigarettes, Ryan thought to himself. "Excellent," he exclaimed. "Bring me up to speed."

Then, as if rehearsed, Paul pulled a document out of his briefcase and spread its pages across Ryan's desk. "I am happy to say that Sy has made an offer for the newspaper," the real estate agent announced, a self-satisfying grin on his face.

For a brief second, it felt as if Ryan's entire body stopped working; heart, lungs, everything seized. But just as quickly, the shock faded. "You didn't need much time, did you?" he responded, almost meaning to sound rude.

The smile on Sy's face widened. "We'd seen your books and were already siding with an offer. But it's necessary to check out things in person," he replied.

Paul nodded with overexcited agreement. "There are a few specifics," he commented as he picked up one of the pages. "This is only for the business itself, all existing contracts, equipment and office supplies; it is not for the building. But they've agreed in this contract to rent this space from you for at least the next five years at a rate that is ten percent more than the current rate for a similar space here in White Oak City. They feel this will help with your concerns about selling the business without the building. And, if we're successful in getting the other buildings in town rented or sold, it could well drive up the value of this building in five years, which would be beneficial to you, if you decide to sell it at that time."

Ryan leaned back in his chair, Paul's new loyalties appearing confirmed. But despite his frustration, he managed a sedate look while nodding in understanding. "What are you thinking about for the employees here?" he asked.

Sy motioned with his hand for Paul to stop talking so he could answer. "Most will stay in the same positions and obviously we'll need to find a new editor, possibly someone already here, or maybe not, whatever ends up being the best fit," the man replied.

An ache in Ryan's gut belied a feeling of mistrust. "When you've purchased other newspapers, have you typically reduced the size of the staff?" he probed.

The smile on Sy's face seemed less sincere now. "Depends on the existing business model," he answered.

Again, Ryan nodded. "What are your thoughts on the business model here?" he continued questioning.

Sy's frown exposed his growing discomfort. "It's fine for what you needed," he responded. "Obviously, based on my experience, I always see room for improvement. But I'm not expecting significant realignment."

Ryan offered another smile and stiff nod, despite the fact he suspected the old man of already mentally slicing and dicing the staff.

Paul pushed the purchase contract across the desk to Ryan. "Oh, the price," the real estate agent exclaimed. "I'm very pleased with the offer they're extending."

Ryan gave in and picked up the papers, scanning through laborious legalese until he came to the meat, which outlined a $325,000 bid for the entire business, minus any outstanding debts, of which none existed.

The yellowed teeth of Sy's grin gave off a dull gleam. "What do you think of that number?" the old man proudly boasted.

Ryan forced a smile. "It definitely gives me something to think about," he answered, as it did exceed his expectations, especially knowing his grandfather only cleared about $65,000 in profit and pay the previous year.

"You won't get better," Sy proclaimed, a scowl on his face.

"It sounds more than fair," Ryan responded, still faking a smile. "This is happening very quickly. I want to be able to think about it, would that be ok?"

A vermillion flush filled Sy's cheeks and forehead, giving even more emphasis to his discolored teeth. "Wait a minute," he irritably spouted. "I thought you wanted to sell."

A spasm at the base of Ryan's spine sent a spike of pain up his back. Was it unreasonable to want some time to think about the offer? He glanced at Paul, his mouth hardened into a firm line, the color of his lips fading into the palest of pinks. "I want to be upfront. I've never officially listed the business for sale. I told Paul I was thinking about it and he said he'd see about locating possible buyers, which is when he told me about you. I'm not saying no, but I want to think about it."

The intense red of Sy's face slightly receded, but his agitation remained visible. "I hadn't realized there's not a contract for selling the business," he remarked while giving the real estate agent a displeased glare. "I'm a reasonable man, so that offer's still good. I think this paper'd be a good fit for our company and I'm sure you'd be much happier back in Los Angeles, enjoying the benefits a city offers, especially compared to this one-horse town."

Ryan let his body ease back into his chair. The tension in the room felt at a more palatable level, though he could not help feeling insulted by the man's last comment.

"Would a week from next Tuesday give you enough time to think it over?" Sy suggested.

The weight on Ryan's stomach lightened slightly. "That's plenty of time," he replied.

The older man's hand reached over and engulfed Ryan's in a forceful handshake. "Good," Sy declared, gripping a bit too hard and long.

The action then repeated, though in a more subdued manner, with Matt. Then the father and son stomped out into the newsroom. "We'll talk in a week and a half," Sy called back in a newly genial tone. "Let us know if you have any questions." He then turned to Paul and tersely stated, "We'll be in the car."

Paul waited for Sy and Matt to exit the building before he stepped back into the editor's office with Ryan and closed the door. "What was that? I thought we had an understanding," the real estate agent began.

Anger flooded Ryan's thoughts. "You wait," he shot back. "You said you'd help locate some potential buyers, but we never signed a contract."

Paul's lips went white. "It was an understanding," he hissed.

A sliver of guilt cooled Ryan's anger as he recognized his own indecisiveness. "There still is," he responded. "I may very well accept this offer. It's a good offer."

Paul offered a curt nod. "It is. You'll not get better, so I'd suggest you take it," he pushed back.

The aggressive behavior only incensed Ryan's stubborn side. "I'll take that into advisement," he responded with a snide smile.

With a frustrated huff, Paul spun on his heels and reopened the door. "I'll talk to you next week," he remarked as he stepped into the newsroom.

"Sounds good, and you know, had you told me you were acting as Sy's broker as well as mine, some of this could have been cleared up," Ryan charged as he followed him.

The newspaper staff watched with wide eyes and mouths agape.

"I have lots of clients, residential, commercial and business," Paul offered in defense. "And it'll mean you only have to pay one commission out of the profits."

Ryan shrugged his shoulders. "I suppose, but it makes one wonder which clients are getting the better treatment," he remarked.

"I make sure all of my clients get the best deal possible. I don't compromise one for another," he countered, his cheeks now crimson. "Let's not forget, I'm the only real estate agent who would touch you. I know how many turn downs you got before I said yes, and I've bent over backwards to appease your silly idea to save the relics you had dumped on you in this town. Before you pass judgment on me, remember everything I've done."

CHAPTER 20

THE DISTINCTIVE FEATHERED HAIRSTYLE fit better in the 1970s than the twenty-first century, but for Ryan it was a timeless symbol of love. His mother first discovered it in high school, and while it hadn't been a constant in all the years since, and had grown noticeably shorter since her high school senior photo, it did make frequent appearances. This morning, as its unmistakable silhouette appeared in the open door of the *Decatur County Times-Gazette*, he felt a welcome rush of comfort.

He held back for a moment, watching as Connie and Kate greeted each other, as if life-long friends. Expressive hands flew into the air and girlish laughter penetrated the still sullen atmosphere, making him grateful for her arrival.

"Mom, I'm so happy to see you," he exclaimed as he hurried toward her, his arms extended for a hug.

Subtle tears rested in Kate's eyes as she embraced him. "I'm happy to see you too," she warmly replied and kissed him on the cheek.

A blush filled his face, like a teenager reacting to over affection. "How was your trip? I could have picked you up at the airport," he prattled.

"Everything was fine," she replied, followed by a quiet laugh. "I forgot how pretty it is here."

The comment struck him as disingenuous, so he cocked his head to one side. "The empty storefronts, crumbling bricks and flaking paint," he countered.

She placed her right hand against her cheek, a playful pose that easily skimmed two decades from her sixty-plus years of life. "You sound like your father," she scolded. "He was also afraid of admitting how much he loved it here."

A sigh of regret, though regret of what he did not know, escaped him. He hooked his arm through hers and guided her back into the newsroom, introducing her to the members of the staff as they passed them. And despite the emotionally charged events of the last few days, nothing but politeness and friendliness greeted her, each person offering up kind words, even about him.

Once the last introduction had been made, Ryan and Kate stood silent for a moment, standing together in the middle of the room.

"It hasn't changed in twenty-five years," she remarked as her eyes drifted around the room, soaking up everything from the framed photographs cluttering the walls to cracks in the plaster that probably predated her son's birth.

He offered a nod of understanding and then led her back to the reception area. "Do you mind if Olivia has dinner with us tonight?" he asked, cautious that she might want him to herself.

"Not at all, at least not if you invite Connie as well, so I have someone to talk to," she replied.

—

The soft mechanical whine of the porch glider and the murmur of subdued conversation drifted in through the screen door. Olivia had arrived early while Ryan was dressing upstairs, preempting his rehearsed introduction of her to his mother.

"We're out here," Kate called to him, likely having heard him coming down the stairs.

The screen door swung open with a hint of a squeak, the type a minor douse of WD-40 would eliminate. Every sound suddenly seemed amplified.

The two women smiled at him as they sat together on the glider, which swayed back and forth. "I see you've met," he remarked before leaning down and offering Olivia a kiss on the cheek, too embarrassed to kiss her on the lips with his mother present.

The evening's air held warmth without humidity, while his grandmother's flowers offered a scent of delicate perfumes as lightning bugs twinkled across the lawn.

The lightning bugs had amazed him when he first arrived, but their number had diminished as the summer dragged on, a cycle ending. "You should have seen it a few weeks ago, Mom," he said. "There were thousands of little glittering lights out there. It was magical."

Kate watched her son with an approving smile. "It is a special place," she replied. "All you have to do to see them again, is stay until next year."

He leaned back against a porch post and shook his head as the two women continued rocking in the glider. "I wondered when I was going to start hearing your opinion on my dilemma," he responded.

Despite his bait, Kate did not bite, instead she sighed and lightly pushed her foot to keep the glider moving. "Where are you taking us for dinner?" she asked after a quiet moment.

The reflection of headlights on the azalea bushes across the street signaled a car coming up the hill, hopefully Connie's. "Springfield, for someplace a little nicer than what we have here in White Oak," he answered.

Kate shook her head. "I'm sure the restaurants in White Oak are just fine," she chided him.

"It's not that," he countered, ashamed of his snobbish remark. "There are just more options there."

—

With her third glass of wine in her hand, Connie leaned back in her chair and gave Ryan a curious look before turning her attention to his mother. "Kate, is White Oak City like you remember it?" she asked.

Kate then also glanced at her son before turning toward Connie. "Still full of charm, wonderful old buildings, and big trees hanging over the streets and offering the houses soothing green canopies. But it's not nearly as lively as I remember it. So many closed shops, and the emptiness where the old high school stood."

Silence lingered for a moment. "Even a place as resistant to change as White Oak City must change, and almost because of that resistance, when change happens, it's often not for the best," Connie philosophized.

Kate took a sip of wine. "Do you think Ryan and Olivia's plan for the old buildings will work?" she asked.

Connie opened her mouth to respond, but paused for a moment in thought before continuing. "I hope so. It's the only chance White Oak City has. Having the commercial district on the National Register of Historic Places and offering a break on property and sales taxes really might encourage people to start or move businesses here. Those old buildings would be great for antique shops, craft shops, little restaurants, and more. It's a very intact downtown. There are lots of towns that have old buildings, but I can't think of one that is as original as ours."

Beneath the table, Olivia's hand gently squeezed Ryan's knee, and glancing at her face he caught a glimpse of pride.

"It's a brilliant idea," Olivia interjected. "And if it fails no one will be able to fault Ryan for not doing everything he could to save the character of White Oak City."

The edges of Ryan's mouth dropped as his mother nodded in agreement. "You're in a rather special position," she said to him.

The pleasant evening suddenly felt less so. "Do we have to ruin dinner by getting this bandwagon going right now?" he asked, scowling at his mother.

She offered a sympathetic shake of her head. "Of course not. But there's a decision you'll have to make."

He nodded, hoping it was enough to end the conversation. Olivia again squeezed his knee.

"Kate, I know you're retired, but what do you do to keep occupied?" Olivia asked.

Kate's eyes brightened. "A lot of volunteer work at a local hospice and for a couple charities," she replied. "I also paint a little—watercolors. I collect antique glassware and I like to cook."

"It sounds like you keep busy," Olivia observed.

"It occupies me, though if I lived out here I'd probably open a little shop selling vintage glassware," she said with a smile.

—

Exhausted from their night, Kate collapsed onto the living room sofa as Ryan slipped into the kitchen to make them tea before bed. The evening had proved more emotionally trying than he expected, but he was still glad for his mother's visit. Returning to the living room, a cup of tea in each hand, he found her curled up at one end of the sofa, leafing through the pages of an old photo album. "Anything interesting?" he asked as he sat her cup on the table in front of her.

Tears floated in her eyes as she glanced up at him. "So much," she replied in a misty tone as he sat beside her. "And all carefully labeled, so you know who everyone is and when they were taken."

Staid faces in faded browns gazed back at them from the album's brittle pages. "Someone knew them all," he said.

She nodded. "Rosemary would have known most of them."

On a right-hand page, two familiar yet distant faces caught Ryan's eye—his grandfather as a young man standing beside Rosemary, who while not young, substantially preceded the nonagenarian he knew. He laid his finger on the photo, bringing his mother's attention to it. "It's interesting how close together they died," he muttered.

"Your grandfather was a shock, but Rosemary was old," she replied.

"She was a fine lady," he said.

Laying her hand on his, Kate looked to her son, her eyes still glistening. "Your dad thought so too. He said she couldn't have children, so she treated everyone else's like they belonged to her. What did she want, for you to stay or move?"

The face of his kindly aunt sitting beside him in the church pew emerged in his mind as he sipped his tea. "She thought it should be my choice but made no secret about how much good she thought I could do here," he answered.

Kate turned to the next page of the album. "She said that specifically?"

He nodded.

"Have others said that as well?" she pressed.

A Rolodex of faces flipped through his mind. "A few, in actions if not words," he responded, not wanting to reveal the full degree of pressure he felt.

"A few," she repeated.

An understatement, he thought as he nodded. "Aunt Rosemary, Connie, the mayor, some others," he conceded.

She closed the album and laid it on the coffee table, and then picked up her teacup and leaned back into the sofa. "They've laid an awful lot of responsibility on you," she said.

"It's frightening how much faith they've put into someone who showed up for his grandfather's funeral," he replied in a sharp voice.

With a soothing stroke, she rubbed his shoulder. "People in this town have a lot of faith."

"As in God?"

She shook her head. "No. Sometimes, especially in small towns where everyone is so reliant on their community, people put a lot of faith in their neighbors, friends, and even an occasional person who shows up out of nowhere. Maybe it's a person who brings a fresh perspective. Some resent it because they don't like change. But a lot of people here understand there has to be change or the things they love the most about this community will be lost."

A lukewarm swallow of tea passed across his tongue. He sat his empty cup down and let his body ease back into the cushions of the sofa. "Like the buildings downtown being torn down?" he asked, though he knew better.

She shook her head. "The buildings are the outward manifestation of what they would be losing."

"What are they losing that they're trying to save, or at least want me to help them save?" he asked.

"Community spirit, pride in their hometown, the ability to retain something of this place for their children and grandchildren."

All insights that aligned with the quiet work of preservation the late Dean Shipley had performed through the years.

"I haven't heard anyone here give that type of analysis on what they would lose if I left," he responded, though he could not deny its truth.

"I don't know that they recognize it as such," she said.

A nervous twitching caused his fingers to flutter. "How can I stay here and risk failure? It'd be humiliating, and it wouldn't make a difference to this town," he countered. "The program for getting tenants in the buildings is a long-shot anyway, bound to—"

With a wave of her hand, she interrupted him. "I've discovered your problem."

"What do you mean?" he replied, ready to curb his mother's armchair psychology. "I've told you my problem. I don't want to stay, but everyone here wants me to."

Despite the abrasiveness of her son's tone, she smiled. "Maybe, but you don't want to go back to Los Angeles either. The charm of this place has grown on you. Having people count on you gives you a sense of place. You appreciate the history and prominent role your ancestors have had in this town."

He slowly shook his head. "Why would I stay where failure and not living up to my late grandfather's legacy is all I can look forward to?"

"You know that's not necessarily true," she countered.

Unease ached in his stomach. "How can I succeed?" he shot back at her.

"You may not, but everyone here'll know you tried to make it work, if you stay."

For more than two months she had avoided delivering pronouncements to him, but less than twelve hours in town and already she had made a full assessment of the situation. "This is ridiculous," he insisted. "I'm selling the newspaper and leaving here as soon as possible."

Her eyes stung him with their sharpness. "How about this house, you better sell it too?"

His ears warmed as blood rushed to his head. "What do you know about that?" he yelled.

"You decided not to put it up for sale," she calmly answered.

He rose from the sofa and walked across the room to the front window. "This house is too ..." he started, freezing before finishing.

"Too what?"

Emotion would erupt from him if he told her the truth, and he could not bear breaking down in tears right now. "I'm still here, I need a place to stay," he answered, skirting the truth.

"What about the farm, do you want to sell it?" she asked.

Couldn't these questions stop, at least for the night? "No, I don't," he replied. He wanted to yell at her, but she held no fault in his frustration. She asked honest questions representing uncertainties he needed to face.

"Why not?"

Tears bubbled up in his eyes. "The last ones that lived there, his cousins," he began. What could he say about them? He never knew them, and all he did know came from what remained in the old farmhouse.

Silence hung in the room for a moment, until his mother began humming. "What about them?" she muttered as she continued her song.

He took a deep breath, hoping to dampen the pressure that trickled to every inch of his body. "They lived there their entire lives, taking care of it, taking care of the house and the farm where their ancestors started. They had one son, and he died, but they kept living there, day in and day out. Their stuff is still out there. I wondered why my grandfather didn't clean it all out and rent the place or tear it down."

The sound of bare feet against hardwood announced his mother's approach. "For the same reason you don't want to leave," she answered. "He was afraid if he changed it, those cousins would in some way cease to exist as the people they had been in life. They would become only names on a headstone in the cemetery or scribbling on the back of a photograph. Without a child to carry on their memory, they could fade from history, so he created a shrine to them. He preserved, in some manner, their home, the home they preserved for him, the home where his grandfather was born, where his family first blossomed when they settled here."

Ryan reflected on her reasoning. "How does that relate to me?" he asked.

Gently pulling on his hand, she turned him from the window to face her. "Because if you leave here, you're afraid it'll continue to fade into nothing. People'll still live here, It's the county seat, but that sense of community and sense of pride that makes it special could turn into something else, something less welcoming and friendly. It's almost inevitable if someone doesn't try to save it. Your grandfather tried. That's why he bought all those buildings, because even if he didn't have the energy to put the work into it, he hoped someday an opportunity would appear that could make something out of this town again. People here know that, and they think you're the right one with the right ideas."

The speech moved him. He felt it in his heart. But there remained so much doubt. "What if I fail?" he protested again.

She leaned against her son and hugged him. "They'll love you even more for trying."

"What about my career and my future?" he pushed, resorting to his second most popular reason for not staying.

She stepped back a few feet, as if her argument stood and he needed to decipher the other uncertainties. "What type of career and future do you want?" she asked him before turning and heading toward the stairs.

"One where I don't fail an entire town," he retorted. "If I was failing myself at some point, that might be bearable, but not to fail an entire town. That'd be humiliating."

CHAPTER 21

HIS EYES BURST OPEN in alarm as his sweat-bathed body twisted and twitched in spasms. A loud gasp escaped Ryan as he struggled to catch his breath, his mind racing.

The nightmare, though emotionally fresh, became instantly vague in detail. Despite an intensity savage enough to rip him from his slumber, particulars fled his mind before he could give them concrete form, leaving only uncomfortable shadows. He wanted to scream out for his mother, as if a child. But she had returned to Los Angeles the previous day.

Agitation shivered through his body, so he laid back against his pillow, the cool dampness of his sheets adding to his unease. He took three deep breaths, and focused on positive thoughts, pushing the negative feelings from his mind. His body eased with his success in muting the lingering darkness of the dream, but other negative thoughts emerged, namely his need to decide on the sale of the newspaper. Why had he stayed here so long? He should have hired someone to run the business and returned home. But instead he had stayed and got attached.

It was Saturday, he reminded himself, his clammy body shivering despite the warmth of the room, and he was alone. He had asked Olivia the day before to stay the night with him, but she needed to get up early to drive to St. Louis for a job interview. If she left, why should he stay? His affection for her had clouded his thoughts all summer long, despite her persistence that she would leave soon herself. And although he had known her only a few months, he knew it was disingenuous to deny he loved her.

He pulled himself up out of the bed, hopeful that he could leave his night terrors behind him, and stumbled down the stairs into the kitchen.

The heavy molasses of the brown sugar he piled on top of his oatmeal soaked into his tongue. Its dark sweetness offered his first pleasure of the day. He sunk his spoon into the bowl for another bite, but the ringing of his cell phone interrupted.

"Hello," he mumbled as a greeting.

"How are you," Olivia asked in a chipper return.

How honest should he be? "I'm good," he lied.

She did not counter, so he must have sounded better than he felt.

"I'm glad. Want to drive to Springfield and have dinner tonight?"

A smile spread across his face, though a verbal answer did not follow.

"Do you?" she asked again, concern in her voice following his awkward silence.

A flush of embarrassment warmed his cheeks. "Of course," he replied, glad she could not see his goofy demeanor.

"I'll be at your place around six," she told him.

—

"You haven't asked me about St. Louis," Olivia said as they waited for their drinks to arrive.

Ryan's stomach churned with unease. Their drive to Springfield had played out awkwardly, in that both avoided the two most immediate topics: the sale of the newspaper and St. Louis. "I figured you'd tell me, if it was important," he replied.

Her hand slipped around his and squeezed. "It is," she responded in a serious tone.

A shudder ran up his spine as he nodded. "I figured."

Using her free hand, she accepted her glass of white wine from the server and brought it directly to her lips for a drink. "I've been offered a job," she explained once she finally set the glass on the table.

Pain throbbed in his chest, a feeling akin to his heart preparing to explode. "That's great." He forced a smile.

"It's at a research and evaluation firm," she continued.

A weight built up on his gut. "A four-hour drive, isn't it?"

She stared at him for a moment, and then nodded. "It could be worse, though with the schedule they've proposed, I'll be lucky to make it home once every six months."

The buzzing of a thousand wasps suddenly filled his ears. He took a deep breath and looked down at the table, where a brass ring kept the white linen napkin neatly rolled around his silverware. "Did you accept?" he asked, his mind dazed.

The frown on her face exposed her displeasure with him. "I'll let them know Monday," she responded.

He nodded. "Is it what you want to do?" he said, without meeting her eyes.

She gently patted his hand. "Yes," she answered.

A tingling sensation ran up the sides of his face, and his eyes blurred. "You should take it." He took a deep breath.

"I am," she said.

—

The car stopped with a halting jerk, shaking Ryan awake. Raising his head, the glare of the porch light blinded him. "I'm sorry, I fell asleep," he groggily apologized.

Dried tear streaks had marred Olivia's makeup. "It's all right," she replied before reaching over and taking hold of his hand.

"I'm sorry I haven't been more supportive," he said, without looking at her.

A quiet sob escaped her lips. "You have a lot on your mind," she muttered.

Whether because of the evening's alcohol or the emotion evoked by her teary face, he wanted to share his feelings. "It's more than that …" he started.

Shaking her head, she waved her free hand at him, warning him to stop. "We're in a tough spot, you and I."

He nodded, and they continued to sit in the car, neither speaking, both seeming to consider how to move forward.

"We've only known each other a few months, and I have to do what's best for me," she finally said. "You understand, don't you?"

The rejection hurt, but he also felt the sting of a double standard. "Why don't people understand the same about me?" he tersely asked.

A smile, the first since they had sat down at dinner, appeared on her face. "There's a lot more expectation on you, than me," she replied.

—

The dull throb of a hangover headache crowded Ryan's brain. He had drunk a quarter bottle of whiskey after Olivia dropped him off the night before. Whiskey that in turn gifted him with a variety of aches and nausea for the morning. The thought of breakfast crossed his mind, but by the time he reached the bottom of the stairs, the queasy churning of his stomach dissuaded him. On the small table beside the front door, he spotted Pearl S. Buck's *The Good Earth,* which he had discovered in his grandfather's bookcase the week prior. He grabbed the book and stepped outside onto the sun-drenched porch, wearing only a pair of tattered athletic shorts.

The dew-dappled metal of the glider felt cool against his bare skin, and the swing brought comfort as he got it to slowly rocking. He opened the book and let his eyes fall on the words. At first, he read in an unfocused way, but the throbbing in his head began to subside, his attention tightened, and the words translated their story.

Ten pages along, a sensation against his leg interrupted his thoughts, though his mind, still dull from the night before, struggled to place the source. He laid his hand against his thigh and felt the vibrating of his phone. He shifted slightly and sunk his hand into his pocket to pull out the device, which showed Marvin Tagert's name.

"Hi Marvin, what can I do for you?" he asked.

A genial greeting, followed by an invitation to come to Rosemary's house for mementos and keepsakes came in response.

While the thought of sifting through his aunt's belongings held no appeal, a feeling of responsibility countered. It represented a necessary part of family and surviving, and Ryan appreciated Marvin sharing the process with him, even if he derived no enjoyment from it. Someday, he imagined, it would be an event he would replicate for his mother, and possibly others in his life. And again, someday, someone would go through his own belongings in such a way.

—

Ryan stepped inside the door of Rosemary's house for the first time since her death, and possibly the last time. Glancing around, all appeared normal, but the atmosphere itself felt altered, as if her absence of but a few weeks allowed the warmth to drain out. And he noticed a disheartening silence, that of something missing, some subtle, always-present murmur gone.

Drifting into the living room, the fate of the home became more obvious, with half-packed boxes cluttering the floor and a dishevelment of the rest, as if every item had been picked up and inspected, then replaced slightly askew. On the wall he spotted the source of the eerie silence, the antique wall clock unwound, its pendulum and weights hanging limp in the case. It had been a gift from her husband, purchased when they were on a trip to London for their fortieth wedding anniversary.

He stared at his reflection in the gold and porcelain face, until rustling sounds from down the hallway pulled his attention from the stilled timepiece. Carefully, he made his way through a maze of displaced furniture and boxes that crowded the hall and came to a stop in the doorway of his aunt's bedroom, where he found Marvin and Liddy sitting on the bed, sorting through a battered old shoebox.

"Ryan, I'm glad you could come." Marvin stood to shake hands with him.

Ryan nodded and met the older man's grasp. Much like the rest of the house, this room existed as a preserved shrine to the 1960s.

The shoebox still in her right hand, Liddy followed her husband in standing and offered Ryan her arms in a comforting hug. A simple show of affection, but one he only realized he needed upon receiving it.

"There are several things here from your side of the family, so we want to make sure you get them, if you want," she explained as she let go of him, and then motioned for him to follow her to the dresser.

The dresser top was cluttered with old beauty supplies and small haphazard piles of jewelry, except at one end, which was cleared off apart from a piece of black felt with three rings and a pocket watch laid out on it in a reverential manner. "These are the pieces I think you'll be interested in," she said.

An anxious rush sent Ryan's heart beating fast as he bent down to inspect them. "Who's are they?" he asked.

Liddy picked up the pocket watch and handed it to him. "This belonged to your great-great-grandfather, and the opal ring to your great-great-grandmother." She placed the two thin, plain gold bands in her palm and held them out to him. "These were their wedding rings."

The pocket watch weighed heavy in his hand, though he felt it more perception than actuality. He laid it back on the felt and took the two wedding bands from her. "They're small and plain," he replied.

Liddy nodded. "They were poor when they got married, I imagine it's all they could afford."

Feeling the smooth cool gold of the rings inspired a feeling of pride, an intimate link to his ancestry. "You don't want them?" he asked, feeling guilty about claiming such sentimental items.

Marvin smiled and shook his head. "It's your side of the family, not mine."

Another treasure needing protection, Ryan thought as he nodded in understanding. He held the rings up to the light of the window, letting the sun glint off their contours. "How old are they?"

Liddy stepped forward and appraised them with her eyes. "A hundred and ten years or so, their marriage date should be in the genealogy your grandfather put together, so that'll give you more exact information."

Ryan placed the two rings back on the felt, then rested his index finger on the slighter larger and his middle finger on the smaller. "Would it be improper for someone to use them, if they got married?" he asked.

"There wouldn't be anything at all wrong with that," Liddy answered, followed by a look of dawning surprise. "Have you asked Olivia?"

An absurd question, Ryan immediately thought. But the night before remained fuzzy in his mind, forcing him to take a moment to recall whether he had. "No, I meant it generally," he responded, confident he had not gone that far the evening prior.

"Oh, ok, not that we would have a problem with that," Liddy said. "Let me put these in a jewelry bag for you. There are some other family pieces for you and a lot of photographs too. And let us know if there's anything else you want. Marvin and I have already taken the items we're keeping."

Ryan glanced around at the kitschy cream-colored bedroom furniture that had survived pristine for decades under his aunt's meticulous care, a vintage set unblemished though dated. "What happens to the rest?" he asked as his eyes rested on an avocado green crackle-glass lamp.

"Vonnie might take some of the furniture, the rest will be sold at an estate sale," said Marvin.

"It won't all be boxed up and stacked in a building somewhere?" Ryan inquired, recalling the boxes and furniture stored in the upstairs of the newspaper office.

"No, there's been enough of that in the family," Marvin answered.

—

The final act in the transition from Rosemary's home to real estate listing arrived in the late afternoon when a moving truck and three hulking men appeared in the driveway. With the claimed items weeded out, Marvin directed the men to those possessions that sat unwanted, at least by Rosemary's small group of heirs. Ryan, with melancholy engulfing him, leaned back against the wall and watched as the rooms thinned of their furnishings, until nothing remained but empty walls and echoes.

Ryan had only claimed a few items, the family jewelry, some historic photos and papers, and a few pieces of furniture and glassware that Marvin told him belonged to various ancestors. Items largely unneeded but carrying enough family connection to warrant protection from being shuffled off and sold to strangers.

Once the rumble of the moving truck, carrying off the last physical remnants of Rosemary's life, faded from their ears, Ryan and Marvin took a final walk through the house, a nostalgic review before it slipped from kinship's hold.

"Vonnie's coming tomorrow to clean it before the real estate agent starts showing it," Marvin remarked as they stood in a now vacuous living room, their exit tour completed. "She's out of work with both your grandfather and Aunt Rosemary gone. But she was remembered in the will, an equivalent of five year's salary. I think she'll be able to survive."

Ryan nodded as he watched Marvin lift the antique wall clock off its nail, and cradle it in his arms. A bequest to the county historical society.

"I never imagined a place I know so well could seem so foreign," Marvin said as his eyes surveyed the empty room.

—

The humidity felt like a damp sponge against Ryan's skin as he stepped out of his aunt's house onto the porch. In the distance the sky darkened, the promise of a summer shower. His shoulders gave way into an exhausted slump and he shuffled across the yard to his grandfather's car, shortness of breath greeting him upon reaching it. Unease burdened his thoughts, forcing him to glance back at the house. Even on the outside it now seemed almost unfamiliar, the curtains and shades snuggly cinched, eroding its hospitality.

Sadness welled inside him, dampening his eyes and forcing him into retreat. The car door popped open, offering refuge from a draining day, but the sound of footsteps stopped him before he could fully escape into it.

"Thank you for helping." Marvin extended his hand toward Ryan.

Ryan offered his own hand in response. "Glad to," he replied, and then abruptly dropped into the driver's seat, anxious to put the day behind him.

"There is one more thing." Marvin held out a white envelope.

Ryan looked at the envelope for a second before pulling the car door shut, accepting the offering through the open window. "What's this?"

A smile bloomed on Marvin's face. "It's from Aunt Rosemary. In her will, she asked that I give it to you after we closed out her house."

The envelope, though as warm as the steamy air, sent a chill through Ryan's hand. "What's in it?"

Marvin's smile grew wider. "Open it."

The sealed envelope had Ryan's name scrawled in ink across the front, written in his late aunt's shaky hand. He slipped his index finger under the flap and pulled, ripping it open and exposing a folded paper, which he pulled out, along with a check fastened to it with a paperclip.

The letter outlined a bequest of money for him, though for a use. She wished for him to restore the old hotel, preferably as a bed and breakfast, but as office space if he thought that idea best. Sixty-five years earlier she had spent the first night of her marriage in the hotel and wanted it saved. He pulled the check free and gasped at the $750,000 amount. "That's a lot of money," he cried out.

The smile on Marvin's face abated to mere contentment. "That's how much, plus about $100,000, your grandfather told her it would cost to restore and modernize it," he explained.

The value of the hotel, as is, equaled less than $30,000 according to the real estate agent. Why would she leave him $750,000 to restore a building only worth $30,000? She must have been senile when she wrote it. Who would leave an incredible amount of money for an ordinary old building? A beautiful, ordinary redbrick building with hand-carved stonework, leaded-glass windows, and a row of stone finials along the roofline. "What if I sell it?" he asked.

"Then the humane society in Springfield will be happy for the donation," Marvin suggested with a dour expression.

The check felt heavy in Ryan's hand. "Lots of dogs and cats could use the money," he reflected.

Marvin nodded. "As could that old building on Commercial Street."

—

Crowded with Monday's lunchtime patrons, Ryan felt a slight frustration toward Olivia for choosing the diner for lunch. He wished for somewhere with more privacy. But she had dictated more than suggested this choice, and he felt no need to contradict. His patty melt, usually a favorite guilty pleasure, rested greasy and unappealing on his plate as unease instead filling his stomach. "I've been thinking about your job offer," he muttered as he pushed a French fry around his plate with his finger.

She tilted her head slightly away from him. "How so?" she asked.

"What do you get by moving to St. Louis?"

"It's not about St. Louis, it's about me finding my place in the world," she answered, her voice soft and empathetic. Their voices and even their movements quieted, until she reached across the table and laid her hand on top of his. "Ryan, do you really think I haven't fallen in love with you too?"

The admission surprised him. "Really?" he stammered out.

"Of course," she murmured as tears twinkled in her eyes.

He clasped her hand tightly with both of his. "Why didn't you tell me?"

With her free hand, she brushed tears out of her eyes. "Because I'm not a fool," she answered.

The comment stung. "What do you mean?"

She pulled her hand from his grasp. "Despite loving you, I won't compromise myself."

The air bled from his lungs, though an idea sparked in his mind. "I can compromise," he exclaimed.

Silence.

"I know, and I appreciate that," she whispered in response.

He grabbed hold of her hand again. "Come to California," he pleaded.

"What?" she gasped.

A rush of confidence filled him, and he straightened up in his chair. "Forget all of this, come to California with me."

"What are you saying?" She frowned.

He leaned across the table toward her. "There are jobs for you there," he continued.

Her face darkened. "I'm not sure what to say," she responded in a hollow tone. Again, she removed his hands from her own, then stood and without waiting for him walked across the dining room, stopping at a window that looked out across the town square.

Was he supposed to follow her? "Is it that tough of a question?" he asked loud enough for everyone in the restaurant to hear.

She turned toward him, though not directly facing him. "Not really," she responded.

"We can leave together," he said.

A murmur rippled across the patrons and a rose flush filled Olivia's cheeks.

"Goddamn you," she loudly proclaimed. "I'm not that selfish."

Embarrassment burned Ryan's skin as he sunk low in his chair. "What do you mean?"

In three long strides, she again stood beside the table. "I say I have a career and you say, 'you can have me and a career, all it'll cost is your hometown,'" she seethed back at him.

The trembling in his upper lip begged him to cry, but he took a hard swallow and choked out, "I didn't say that."

The sound of her foot tapping on the floor beside him droned in his ears. "Yes, you did, you just don't realize it."

"It's not what I meant. I love you," he professed, fully exposing his feelings.

For a few seconds, she stood still, staring into his eyes. Then, with a graceful bow, she leaned down and kissed him on the cheek. "I know, and I love you," she acknowledged before straightening back into a stoic stance.

"Come with me," he pleaded. "Work in Los Angeles. We can be together."

Her hand gently flowed across his cheek. "You'd be turning your back on White Oak."

It remained about the town. "I might anyway," he protested.

Tears dribbled out of her eyes. "At least this way, it won't be entirely my fault," she said.

"I want you with me," he whined, unconcerned about the watchers around them.

Faint tears streaked from her eyes. "Ryan, please let me find myself," she implored him.

He shook his head. "I found myself with you," he declared.

Her lips quivered, as if to respond in a rash way, but she paused and gazed back out the window and across the square. "You found yourself here, in this little town that can't even offer me a job," she countered.

"I don't want to stay," he barked back. "Why should I?"

Her eyes narrowed. "You're supposed to," she snapped. "Life isn't easy, neither are the choices. I can't stay here as much as I would love to because I wouldn't fulfill myself. But I think if you stay, you will fulfill yourself."

This was not what he wanted. "The only fulfillment I've had here is with you," he responded.

The blush of her cheeks darkened to crimson. "That's a lie, and you know it," she retorted.

CHAPTER 22

THE MORNING HAD LARGELY PASSED by the time Ryan finally stepped outside the house, with the sun high in the clear blue sky. The world offered a cheerful day, ideal for relieving tension; except for him, as each step he took brought increased anxiety.

The screen door slammed behind him, and a soft fluttering flash prompted him to look back. A white envelope lay on the porch in front of the door, knocked loose by his exit. He bent down to give it a closer look, reading his name written on it in his mother's hand.

Unsealed, he unfolded the envelope's flap and pulled a sheet of paper out. The two paragraphs offered nothing of real depth, with the first relaying that she remained in California, having instructed Connie to leave the note for him to find this morning. The second expressed her love for him and assured him that whatever choice he made would be the right one. It added to his anxiety, though he still felt glad in receiving it.

Reaching Commercial Street, he cocked his head in the direction of the vacant lot at the end of the road. The image of the old school appeared in his mind, despite its absence for several weeks. For as neglected as it stood, it held its own as one of the four grand cornerstones of the old business district, together with the courthouse, the bank building, and the shuttered hotel. The enraged actions of one man had erased it from the landscape of the town, and Ryan knew it would not take much to repeat that event. For in as little as a few weeks, he could likely have every building he owned leveled into parking lots. The thought dredged up guilt in his gut, especially when thinking of the $750,000 Rosemary had left him to restore the old hotel.

Nearing the newspaper office, his breathing became shallow. Through the front window he spotted Connie at her desk with a smile on her face as she talked on the phone. She saw him and offered a friendly wave. He replied with a tense smile and picked up his speed, passing by the office instead of going inside. A blur of two blocks went by before he finally paused in front of the old hotel, its large first story windows covered with plywood, the doors secured with heavy locks.

What type of business could thrive here? Months earlier, when Connie first took him inside, he basked with amazement at the old building. The mahogany front desk still looming large in the lobby, and all the other furnishings and fixtures, though tattered with age, remaining in place.

Decades earlier, when the railroad operated passenger service to the town, the old place must have buzzed with life. And he imagined that in 1916, when Decatur County's last public hanging took place in the center of the town square, people watched it from their guestroom windows.

—

"How are you feeling?" Connie asked as Ryan stepped inside the door.

For a moment he offered no response, despite anxiously loitering near her desk. "A little nervous," he finally answered. Eerie silence filled the newsroom, despite the entire staff being present, prompting him to continue to linger near the safety of Connie's desk.

"Do you need anything?" she asked, concern in her eyes.

A sigh escaped him. "It's all me from this point," he acknowledged.

She nodded and returned to her work.

He inched into the newsroom as if in a daze, offering a few nearly inaudible hellos and trying to ignore the probing stares, then rushed into the safety of the editor's office.

The door creaked as he pulled it shut behind him, hiding from judgment. He closed his eyes and leaned against the wall, taking deep breaths to calm his nerves. Slightly more at ease, he reopened his eyes and made his way to his chair, finding as he did so an envelope—the second this morning—perched on his keyboard. He ripped open the flap and pulled out the paper.

Ryan,

I'm sorry I've hurt you. But this is the way things are. I love you, and, if circumstances were different, I would marry you. The time's not right for either of us. I hope you stay in touch. The decision you make will be the right one for you.

Olivia

Nausea flooded his stomach and chest. He had hoped for a change of heart, but this dashed that fantasy. At least her motives and decisions stayed consistent and honest, unlike his own. He slipped the letter back into the envelope and tucked it into a desk drawer.

The computer chimed as he tapped the power button. He collapsed back into the chair. Whether emotional exhaustion or residual hangover, every inch of his body felt drained. A second chime announced a new email. He clicked the icon, and nine new messages appeared, all from Paul Mason. He closed his eyes, a weak effort to calm the headache bubbling in the front of his skull, but even that was futile, as the phone's abrasive ring interrupted.

Connie's extension glowered at him from the display. "Hi Connie, what is it?" he asked.

An awkward pause followed. "You have a call. The real estate agent," she replied.

He closed his eyes and took three deep breaths; a calming exercise his high school guidance counselor had taught him after his father died, when he developed trouble concentrating in school. "Hi Paul," he offered in a falsely cheerful greeting once he heard the phone line click.

"We caught you," the real estate agent commented in a voice more snide than sincere. "Sy and Matt Bladenship are on the line, so let's get down to business."

No more putting off the decision. "Right now?" Ryan asked.

A disingenuous laugh came in response. "Of course," Paul remarked as more demand than question.

Every excuse to avoid the conversation suddenly bled out of Ryan's mind. "Now's fine," he croaked in reply.

A few cryptic comments passed between Sy and Paul, again leaving Ryan to question the loyalties of the real estate agent.

"How's Saturday for getting together and formalizing the paperwork?" Paul asked.

Was it over, had Ryan agreed to sell? He didn't recall saying anything, but had his brain taken over and subconsciously done it for him?

Sy's voice cut in. "That's fine, but aren't we forgetting something?"

Silence.

"What's that?" Paul asked.

An irritated grumble. "Ryan hasn't said he's selling," Sy pointedly observed. "At least not to me, maybe you, which is fine, but I want to make sure we're all kosher here."

Paul let out a nervous laugh. "Nothing wrong with a little formality," he answered in a wavering voice, followed by another stretch of silence. "Ryan, don't keep us waiting, are we good to go?"

Ryan closed his eyes, took three breaths and pulled the receiver to his mouth.

CHAPTER 23

"Take that to the front parlor," Kate barked at Ryan as she pointed to a large box sitting on the kitchen countertop. "And don't drop it," she added, before darting out of the back door.

The last six hours had exhausted his patience regarding his mother's demanding moving day orchestration.

He lifted the box off the glossy marble countertop. It felt light, but by the way it balanced in his arms he could tell it held several loose items, all layered across the bottom. A mischievous idea popped into his mind, to give the box a hard shaking, but he thought better of tempting his mother's ire. Though, despite his self-control, a smile appeared on his face as he considered himself clever for the destructive impulse while he carefully carried it to the "parlor," as she insisted on calling the front room.

Did she intend it as archaic or ostentatious? he wondered. He glanced around the space, the first time it had held any furniture in ten months. Gone were the grimy dustcovers and cracked plaster, the faded green floral wallpaper stripped away and a pleasant robin egg blue paint replacing it. But all the Victorian millwork and features remained, though cleaned up, repaired and painted a fresh matte white.

"Almost done, boys," Kate announced as she marched through the house to the foot of the stairs. Her right index finger launched up and out, like an arrow about to be shot into the second floor. Two burly men followed, hoisting a queen mattress up to hip height before beginning the upward trudge.

"There's no way I'll have my kitchen together by dinnertime tonight," she remarked to Ryan as she joined him in the parlor. "Do you mind if I come to your house and make something for the both of us?"

He shook his head. His house, he thought to himself, after having shared it with her for the last six months.

She smiled as she appraised the room.

The smell of mold and decay lingered no longer, a welcome contrast to a year earlier when he first stepped inside the old farmhouse, then unoccupied for some thirty years. It now seemed as if that derelict era never existed, the stately frame structure restored beyond even its former glory, with a modern kitchen holding all the accoutrements of the twenty-first century without sacrificing any nineteenth century charm.

When the first contractor had come to give a bid, nearly a year earlier, and unapologetically recommended tearing down most of the interior walls to give it an "open concept," Kate fired him on the spot, despite having not even hired him. She would not be responsible for gutting the past out of this house, she declared. Even the solemn bedroom upstairs, which belonged to someone else's long-dead son, she treated sympathetically, retaining the furniture and much of his personal belongings, though gently transforming it from shrine to guest room.

"Are you good here?" Ryan asked her, eager to leave before the unboxing started, as he knew he would not put anything in the right place. Upstairs, the mattress loudly flopped onto the box spring in the new master bedroom, one of the few indulgences she allowed in the renovation: combining the smallest bedroom with the largest to create an en suite.

She did not answer, but instead began to float around the room, a space bathed in the sun's glow as it streamed through stained glass. A lifetime spent in suburbs, and now she would retire among gently rolling hills and the sounds of livestock and nature. She had caught him off guard when she told him—insisted really—that she would live in the old farmhouse while he stayed in his grandfather's house in town. Hearing the declaration created an unexpected urge in him at the time, that he should live in the country. But he couldn't deny her, and he did enjoy his five-minute commute of walking down the hill to work every day.

The movers stomped back down the stairs, tightened and strengthened in the renovation, and he and his mother led them through the house and even waved as their truck rumbled off down the newly grated and graveled driveway.

"I give you a day before the cicadas and owls and cows mooing drive you back into White Oak, begging to stay with me," he kidded her.

A warm breeze ruffled his hair and grazed his nose, introducing him to the pleasing, yet unfamiliar, scent of cut fescue.

"You're only saying that because you'll be lonely without me," she countered with a smile.

He laughed, though he knew a little truth existed in the comment. His entire life had changed when he decided to keep the newspaper and live in Missouri. And even though the last year had been a whirlwind, restoring the farmhouse and hotel, and giving the newspaper office some much-needed upgrades, at times a feeling of isolation from the rest of the town, and even the world, surfaced in his mind. It happened less often than he had feared, but it still occurred.

He walked across the driveway to his car and climbed in, looking out the open window at his mom, the freshly painted white farmhouse standing proudly behind her.

Should he have sold? he wondered to himself. If he had, would he ever have experienced the pride he felt now as he looked at this house and saw it alive again, alive because of him? Or the hotel, once verging on ruin, now nearly restored, with a restaurant on the first level and a dozen modest and clean rooms almost ready for letting? Every day he walked around the town nodding and smiling and greeting all he met, and they the same to him. He feigned modesty as compliments came regarding the improvements to the town or something printed in the paper, while inwardly basking in the warmth of his accomplishments.

The car started without complaint and he steered it down the fresh lane toward the highway, a dust cloud following. No need to look in the review mirror, as his inheritance no longer taunted him as something to fear or lose.

ACKNOWLEDGEMENTS

I would like to express my special thanks to some of those who have been a part of the journey in the writing and publishing of this work. To my husband Caio Giffoni Billington, who has been my number one cheerleader in getting it published; to Ben Sevier, who years ago endured my nonstop chatter when I first started writing it; to Katheryn Johnson, who provided a first critical read and gave me vital feedback; to Chad Stebbins, my college advisor and the one who introduced me to the term "chicken dinner news" in my first journalism class; to Alana King, who oversaw the development edit and acquisitions read for this novel at Vine Leaves Press; as well as so many others who have encouraged me along the way. I'd also like to mention my use of the public domain hymn "Softly and Tenderly" and acknowledge its composer and writer Will L. Thompson (1847-1909), for its gentle tune was a common presence in the small country church I attended as a child and still reminds me of so many of those from that time that are now gone, especially my great grandmother, who spent forty years playing the piano in that little church.

the USA
rmation can be obtained
sting.com
40124
V00016B/228